The Road to Avalon

Guinevere
Book Six

Fil Reid

ARE YOU SIGNED UP FOR DRAGONBLADE'S BLOG?

You'll get the latest news and information on exclusive giveaways, exclusive excerpts, coming releases, sales, free books, cover reveals and more.

Check out our complete list of authors, too!

No spam, no junk. That's a promise!

Sign Up Here

www.dragonbladepublishing.com

Dearest Reader;

Thank you for your support of a small press. At Dragonblade Publishing, we strive to bring you the highest quality Historical Romance from some of the best authors in the business. Without your support, there is no 'us', so we sincerely hope you adore these stories and find some new favorite authors along the way.

Happy Reading!

CEO, Dragonblade Publishing

Additional Dragonblade books by
Author Fil Reid

Guinevere Series
The Dragon Ring (Book 1)
The Bear's Heart (Book 2)
The Sword (Book 3)
Warrior Queen (Book 4)
The Quest for Excalibur (Book 5)
The Road to Avalon (Book 6)

Dedication

To my daughter, Laura, who at first couldn't bring herself to read a book her mother had written because it had a sex scene in it, and now can't put them down.

Chapter One

IT'S LATE SPRING, and in the little wood behind the house the bluebells are already out in a thick azure carpet, their scent wafting down to me where I sit on the patio outside my open kitchen door. When I walked up there before breakfast this morning, with the dog running between the trees after squirrels, the little yellow stars of celandine and the white of wood anemones dotted the blue, but I can't see that from here.

Swallows dart in and out of their nests under the eaves, swooping down to take inflight drinks of water from the trough in the paddock, and doves preen themselves and puff out their chests on the slate apex of the roof. Where the purple moorland comes creeping down the mountain, bright with golden gorse, a warbler calls and I think I hear a chiffchaff. Today, there are none of the usual raucous cries of gulls, blown inland from the nearby coast.

I glance up at the sky. Will it rain? With the mountain peaks clear of mist, and scarcely a cloud to be seen, it seems to promise a dry day, but you never can be sure with Welsh weather. Not to be relied upon. If I hang out the washing, I'll have to be prepared to run and fetch it in again later.

But I'm too lazy to do my chores. The dog, Cabal, a shaggy wolfhound, sleeps by my feet on the sun-warmed flagstones, his ears twitching from time to time as though he's dreaming. We have a suntrap here, and I'm as content as he is. I stretch out my jean-clad legs and take a sip of my coffee. Black and strong, the way I like it in the mornings.

And I remember.

WE SHOULD NEVER have taken Amhar with us to the Council of Kings at Viroconium. But when the messenger arrived bearing King Caninus's invitation for Arthur to attend, Amhar happened to be with us in the Great Hall at Din Cadan. If he hadn't been, would any of what followed have happened?

"Do I get to go this time?" Amhar asked, his voice edged with a defiance that was borderline rude. "Or is eighteen still too young? I remember you took Llacheu with you when he was younger than I am."

Last time we'd gone, he'd pestered me to ask his father to let him come, but Arthur had been adamant. Fifteen was too young. Amhar would have to stay behind with Cei and learn from him how he coped with ruling Din Cadan, because one day he'd be doing it by himself. Amhar had so badly concealed his fury, Arthur had grown angry and ended up shouting at him.

I sighed. Why was Amhar always so surly? Probably because he was a teenager with a much older brother who seemed to do nothing wrong, and whom he unsuccessfully strove to emulate. The years of jealousy that had come creeping up to taint their relationship had gradually eroded the admiration Amhar had once had for Llacheu. A jealousy his brother, who'd never been jealous in his life, seemed quite unaware of.

Arthur shrugged. "Why not? Perhaps you'll find the proceedings at the Council more worthy of your attention than you do the problems of our people here at Din Cadan." He managed to sound as surly as Amhar, matching his scowl and going one up on it. He'd always been good at scowling, and Amhar had inherited it. He grunted. "I'll leave Din Cadan in Llacheu's capable hands."

Four years ago, my stepson had finally married Ariana, the daughter of Anwyll, one of Arthur's bravest warriors. Almost, but not quite, on the tip of a sword. She'd been pregnant at the time of their marriage, but had lost the baby a month later, and since then had been pregnant three more times, losing each baby after only three or four months. She'd made it to five months this time and we all hoped she'd be able to hang onto the baby long enough for it to have a chance to live.

With that sorted, the next day we left for the Council of Kings.

VIROCONIUM STANDS IN a curve of the Sabrina River close to the border between England and Wales. Not far off, the huge hill of the Wrekin rises from comparatively flat land, where, before the Romans came, the local British chieftain lived in a hillfort not unlike Din Cadan. To the west lie the mountains of Wales.

By Roman road in the mild weather of late spring, and not hurrying our horses, it took us nearly a week to cover the hundred and sixty miles from our home in Dumnonia. With Custennin a much more trustworthy ally than his father had been, we took only enough men to make certain no brigands would find us a tempting target.

And Amhar, of course. Poor boy, he'd never even been as far as Caer Baddan, our nearest large town. If you could dignify it with that title in its state of ever-increasing decay. Not that I wanted him going there.

Viroconium was a different basket of eels. The late afternoon sunshine bestowed on its towering walls a fake brilliance – until you got up close and saw the patches where the plaster had fallen away, and the stone and brickwork showed through. But nevertheless, compared with any other city or town in Britain, this was the jewel of the bunch.

Much about Viroconium, including its place as a trading hub, harked back to the days of the legions, when Britain had been a thriving colony. As though here, in this little corner of a barbarian world, Rome still maintained her tenuous hold.

The wide, Roman road we traveled had been busy for quite a while with wagons going to and from the city. People on foot jumped quickly out of our way, shooing before them pigs or sheep or cattle which had splattered the causeway with their droppings in an uncalled-for show of generosity. A man driving a wagonload of thatching reeds pulled by a pair of bullocks shouted at everyone to get out of his way, and three girls walked barefoot carrying baskets of spring flowers.

Amhar and I rode side-by-side, tucked in behind Merlin, Cei and Arthur at the front of our column of horsemen. I remember how his face had lost the surly expression he'd had plastered onto it for at least the last eight years and how suddenly he was my little boy again. A faint flush colored his pale cheeks, his mouth hung slightly open in wonder and his eyes grew wider with every sight.

One of the flower girls sidled up to offer him a posy. "For your lady love," she said, with an exaggerated wink for a handsome young man, her hand on his for a moment too long to be by chance.

He took the posy of cowslips and violets with a blush that rose from his neck to his ears, and tucked it awkwardly into his sword belt. The girl flashed him a wide, seductive smile, and, with a shake of her dark curls, danced away after her friends.

"It's big, isn't it?" I said, pretending I hadn't noticed his discomfort.

He grinned, the blush subsiding. "That's a bit of an underestimation. I thought Caer Baddan was big, but this…" He shook his head. "D'you think even *Rome* can compare with this city?"

I shrugged. Rome was a place neither of us were ever likely to see.

The road split into two at the double-arched gateway, people coming out through one arch and in through the other. On the far side, we found ourselves in the familiar, narrow streets of the city, every thoroughfare bustling with people going about their business. The buildings crowding on either side had achieved a patchwork appearance thanks to the deterioration of their once-tiled roofs. Now, thatch dominated, and some of the houses had either fallen down or been demolished. In their places stood lean-to animal sheds, workshops, vegetable gardens and pig sties, cheek-by-jowl with the houses of the wealthy and the tenements of the poor.

People crowded the narrow, raised walkways to either side of the streets. Women bustled in and out of awning-shaded shopfronts with their daily purchases, and men leaned on counters in open-fronted bars or ate street food on corners. Grubby children ran this way and that, spurning the walkways and steppingstones, the most daring snatching any food left unattended for a second. And dogs, pigs, chickens, geese and even the odd cow wandered here and there, adding their contribution to the general stench of animal droppings, woodsmoke, cooking food and garbage rotting in the gutters.

I doubted Rome could beat Viroconium for the sheer vitality of its seething streets.

"It stinks," Amhar remarked, forced closer to me by the crowds. "But oh, doesn't it smell good." His eyes sparkled with excitement.

Not quite how I'd have described it. Yes, almost everywhere in Dark Age Britain had a far more pungent smell about it than my old world in the twenty-first century, but breezy Din Cadan, on top of its high hill, had become the measure by which I gauged all other places. And I'd never have described Viroconium's town stink as good.

"You'll get used to it," I said, waving away a girl trying to catch my eye with a tray of pies. "I tolerate it for the week of the Council, but I'm always glad to leave it behind." I had more than a few bad memories of Viroconium that he didn't need to know about.

Amhar's incredulous look said he couldn't believe I didn't like it here, so I smiled and shrugged. "That needn't stop you enjoying it, though."

We turned down a quieter side-road, leaving behind some of the noise and stink, but not the alehouses. On the corner of every insula, the building block of Roman town planners, sat a tavern. As the day drew to a close, these bulged with men slaking their thirst before returning home to their wives.

Amhar's eyes went hungrily, or should that have been thirstily, to every tavern we passed.

At the Domus Alba, where we usually stayed, a familiar face greeted us in the courtyard: Karstyn, once the chief cook for the house and now promoted to housekeeper and equipped with a generous ring of hefty keys that dangled importantly from the girdle of her gown, clanking as she moved.

"Milady Guinevere!" Her doughy face creased in a smile. "And Milord the King." He was very much an afterthought, but as she'd known him since he was a boy, she could get away with that.

I didn't stand on ceremony either and hugged her squishy body tight, planting a kiss on a cheek that had grown drier and wrinklier since the last time I'd seen her.

Arthur elbowed me aside with cheerful good humor and hugged her as well. "I hope you've been baking honey cakes for me. I'm ravenous."

Her cheeks flushed with color, and she gave him the kind of coquettish smile most women brought out for him. "When were you ever not? I have indeed, Milord."

Amhar cleared his throat.

I caught his arm and, pulling him forward, introduced him. "Twenty years ago, I helped Karstyn deliver your cousin Medraut – while your father and his brother quarreled over who was going to be king after your grandfather." I smiled, mainly because with the passage of time, that frightening experience now felt as though it had happened to someone else. Well, I *had* been someone else back then. "You know that old story."

Karstyn's critical gaze ran over Amhar, as though assessing him. Then she humphed and pursed her lips, her eyes fixed on his.

I narrowed my eyes, suddenly wary.

Had she weighed our son up and found him wanting? And if so, why was I, his mother, who should have been biased in his favor, so aware that she might have done so? A mother was supposed to see no wrong in her children, yet I'd never felt like that, and especially not about Amhar. Perhaps I was as bad at parenting as Arthur.

"Which is my room?" Amhar asked, his tone abrupt. He turned away from Karstyn as though she merited no further interest, but the excitement had gone from his face as though he felt her disapproval.

I'd brought Amhar up to be more polite than this with servants, but alas, none of us had been able to teach him common sense.

Karstyn's gaze sharpened. "This way, young lord."

THE FIRST INTIMATION we had that things weren't going as planned came that night, when Amhar didn't join us for the sumptuous welcome feast Karstyn had prepared, consisting mainly of Arthur's favorite foods.

"Have you seen my son?" Arthur asked Merlin the moment he arrived to join us in the spacious dining room.

Merlin, as unchanged as ever and even managing nowadays to look a bit younger than Arthur and me, which is annoying, shook his head. No doubt he had other more important things on his mind here in Viroconium. This was where the daughter he never saw lived with her mother, Morgana. "Not since we arrived. I knocked on his door and looked inside on my way here, but the room was empty."

The same question went to Cei, Bedwyr and Gwalchmei in succession, as they appeared, smart in their clean clothes.

"I think I saw him heading toward the kitchen a while back," Gwalchmei said. "Probably hungry. Boys that age always are."

The frown on Arthur's face deepened, and an uneasy feeling settled in my stomach. More than likely he'd gone straight out to explore the city, but as a country boy, that could be dangerous. If only we'd brought his older half-brother, Llacheu, who could have shown him around and kept an eye on him. Although Amhar probably wouldn't have liked that.

"We'll eat without him," Arthur snapped and pulled out his seat at the head of the table. "He can go hungry for all I care."

We settled ourselves for the first course of oysters, me with one eye on the open door onto the courtyard and no appetite. Amhar did not arrive.

Servants came to clear our plates, and Arthur crooked a finger at the oldest of them. With a worried look on his lined face, the man made a low, almost obsequious bow. "Milord?"

Arthur cleared his throat. "Can you go to the kitchens and see if my son is there, please. *He* may have decided he wants to eat in the kitchens, but *I* want him here." He paused. "If he's there, you can tell him that."

"Milord." The man bowed again and hurried off on his mission as other servants brought more food to the table.

Karstyn arrived a few minutes later, red in the face and puffing slightly. "He were in the kitchen earlier," she said, having made a hasty bow to all of us. "He said as he were hungry after his long journey. One o' the girls, she found him some bread and meat and a beaker o' fine cider." She paused, a frown wrinkling her brow. "I din't think to ask him if he were goin' back to his room." She smoothed her skirts down with floury hands, her face clouded with concern.

Cei snorted. "He'll have gone out on the town already," he

said, voicing my own suspicions. "I don't know why you're worrying, Arthur. He's a young man, and young men need to sow their oats. He's barely had the chance at Din Cadan. I wouldn't worry. He'll be back when he's exhausted. Or drunk." He paused. "Or both."

Arthur huffed. "It's not where he's gone that bothers me," he said, a little stiffly. "It's the fact that he doesn't have the manners to beg leave of his mother and me and has left us wondering where he's got to."

Did he have the same uneasy feelings about this city as I did? Enough bad things had happened here for us to have the right to be wary. And Amhar, however he saw himself, was an innocent abroad. There'd be women who might give him diseases, cutpurses out to rob him, and new friends who'd have no care that he was heir to a kingdom. Or maybe if he told them who he was, they'd wish him harm just for being his father's son. No doubt that spiteful witch, his Aunt Morgana, had people on the streets who'd let her know our son was out and about on his own. I knew all too well what tricks she might get up to.

Arthur heaved a sigh. "Thank you, Karstyn. Should he appear in the kitchen again tonight, could you send a message, please. Meanwhile, we'll enjoy this perfect meal you've prepared."

Karstyn departed, and the meal went on, but for me the food remained tasteless and unappetizing as I brooded on the feeling of disquiet that had settled over me. Something was waiting to happen, but I didn't know what.

Even then, I might have been able to prevent it if I'd had the wit.

Chapter Two

I DIDN'T SEE Amhar return. After the meal and a cheerful song from Gwalchmei, and with darkness already descended, we all wove our way back to our various rooms.

Arthur closed the door behind us with a bang that set the oil lamps flickering, and stomped over to the bed. "Little shit," he said, not beating about the bush. "Who does he think he is? This is our first night here, and he's buggered off somewhere on his own."

I kicked off my sandals and undid the wide leather belt that cinched my waist. "He's just being young." If only I'd known then what Amhar's "being young" would lead to. I laid my belt on the table, unlike Arthur, who'd just tossed his onto the floor. Too many years of people picking up after him.

He pulled his tunic over his head and that joined his belt, and his boots skidded across the mosaic floor as they came off. "It's not the going out and enjoying himself I object to." He pulled off his undershirt, the lamplight flickering over his well-muscled chest. "It's the not having the good manners to tell us what he's doing. On our first night here." He shook his head as he stood up and unfastened his braccae. "He can go out every night he's here for all I care, so long as he tells us."

He sounded just like any father from my old world, demanding of his teenager to let him know where they were going. Things never change.

Naked, he strode across to the table and began brushing his teeth with angry vigor over the bowl of water a servant had left. "I thought we'd brought him up to show respect," he spluttered and spat the residue into the slops bucket beside the table. Straightening, he eyed me up and down. "Are you taking that dress off, or do I have to do it for you?"

I scowled at him. "That's not the most romantic proposition I've ever had," I said, picking up my own toothbrush. "Talking to a girl like that could get a man a thick ear."

He sat down on the bed and watched in silence as I brushed my teeth and washed my face. Still with my back to him, I slid my sleeveless gown, which was secured by clasps, slowly off my shoulders to let it pool at my feet, revealing my lack of underwear.

He whistled.

I refrained from telling him that nice girls don't like wolf whistles. Instead, I turned around and met his gaze, which could best be described as smoldering. With a smile, I moved closer, and he got to his feet.

I glanced down. "I see you're anticipating something."

He caught me around the waist and pulled me to him, our bodies pressed together. "And it's not a thick ear."

I chuckled. "I could still give you one if you like…"

For answer, he bent his head, his hungry mouth finding mine.

I buried my hands in his thick hair and my body melted into his. How easy it was to forget everything when in his arms, with his mouth on mine, his body pressed against me.

His hands left trails of fire across my skin. Nineteen years of married life hadn't dimmed any part of our attraction for one another, and now my body ached for his with a desperation that had to be sated.

He pushed me down onto the bed, and, laughing, I pulled him with me. Amhar was, unwisely, completely forgotten.

➤➤➤◄◄◄

I AWOKE WELL after first light to find Arthur's side of the bed empty.

I lay for a few moments in the strange bedroom that had once been Euddolen's and Ummidia's, with the sunlight dancing with dust motes as it poured in through the high, unshuttered windows and spot lit the faded mosaic of Orpheus that decorated the floor. An unwelcome image of those two, long-dead people and their tragic teenage daughters pushed its way into my head. To banish them, I shoved the covers back and scrambled out of bed with a little too much haste.

With no sign of a maid, I dressed myself in a plain, calf-length blue tunic, cinched the waist with my favorite belt and headed into our outer chamber.

Still no Arthur. The doors stood invitingly open onto the sunlit courtyard, and the tinkling sound of running water carried on the morning air. Not for the first time, I wished I had some way of telling the time. What was it? Some nameless hour later than early morning, but not yet mid-morning, either. By the rumbling of my stomach, breakfast time, for sure.

But no breakfast in sight. Common sense took me to the kitchen.

Karstyn, hands on ample hips, was supervising the preparation of bread and cakes, a task being carried out by half a dozen young girls in floury aprons, who promptly seized the opportunity to cease work and gaze at me with their mouths hanging open. Karstyn clapped her hands at them, and, with a scurry, they all returned to work, heads down, but most with one eye still on me.

"Command suits you well," I said. "Is there something for breakfast?"

Karstyn rounded on the nearest girl. "Cinnia, what've you done wi' the Queen's breakfast tray? Where've you left it, you lazy girl?"

What Karstyn lacked in height she more than made up for in intimidating width. The girl, a small, mousey thing of no more than thirteen or fourteen, with a pertly turned-up nose and a dimple in her chin, gaped up at her superior out of wide, frightened eyes. "Oh, mu'm, I did take it, but she were still in bed. I did peek in her door, but she were sleepin' still, so I brung it back here. Mu'm." She used the word 'mu'm' as a term of respect, not through any blood tie, but this was lost on Karstyn, who no doubt saw poor Cinnia's failure to carry out her orders as a reflection on her own organizational skills.

"You foolish girl," Karstyn snapped, clapping her pudgy hands again. "You should'a left it for Milady. An' you *don't* go peekin' through doors at kings and queens. Not in their bedchamber nor nowhere. I've a mind to send you back to your mother for bein' so silly. An' no doubt she'll give you a beatin' for losin' such a respected placing."

By now I'd spotted the offending tray dumped on a table at the side of the room, so I held up my hand to stop this tirade. "Don't worry, Karstyn. I'll have it now, out in the courtyard beside the fountain. Nothing could be nicer." I fixed the trembling Cinnia with a firm gaze. "You go and get it and bring it out to me. I shall enjoy eating outside this morning… in the sunshine."

With a furtive glance at Karstyn, who she perhaps suspected might deal her a blow in passing, Cinnia edged over to the tray and picked it up. With her following, I led the way into the courtyard and across to the fountain, past beds of sweet-smelling roses and lavender bushes that badly needed weeding.

The lily-filled square pool had a wide edging of flat stone at the right height for seating, so I sat down. Cinnia, eyes cast down the better to study her sandaled feet, set the tray of bread rolls, butter, honey and figs, beside me. Then, hands fiddling with the hem of her floury apron, she began to edge away.

I called her back. "Don't go. I have a fancy for some company while I eat."

With great reluctance, and a few shifty glances back at the

kitchen door, she hovered two paces from me, shifting her weight from one foot to the other. Did she think I intended to berate her as well?

"Sit down, Cinnia," I said, indicating the space on the wall on the far side of the tray.

With even more reluctance, she perched herself on the very edge, looking as though she might leap up and flee at any moment, like a wary bird.

"No need to be afraid," I said, as I spread butter onto one of the rolls. "I won't bite." I added honey. "You're new here since last time I visited. You're just learning the rules, I should think."

She nodded, still fiddling with her apron. The nails of her reddened fingers were bitten to the quick.

What a pretty little thing she was, with that elfin face, when she wasn't looking so frightened. "Well, if Karstyn asks you to bring my breakfast tray to my room in the morning again – which I'm sure she will – just give a little knock on my bedroom door and call out to let me know you're there, so I can come out and eat it." I smiled again, intent on setting her at ease. "Sometimes I'm not so good at getting up in the mornings."

She managed a return smile, her face lighting up. "If she do let me after today."

I chuckled. "I shall tell her I'd prefer to have you bring it, then. How's that?"

She nodded, her gaze going to where the fish swimming in the pool had seen us and come nosing their little round sucker mouths out of the water searching for food. I handed her one of the rolls. "Here, break it up small and give it to the fish. A bit at a time."

She looked down at the roll, which was no doubt of far better quality than any bread she'd ever eaten herself. With a shrug of resignation at the apparent waste, she broke a small piece off for the fish. They fell on it like a shoal of piranhas in the Amazon jungle, and her laughter rose like music over the splash of the fountain. My heart warmed at the sound.

Movement by the doors from the atrium caught my eye. Amhar came striding into the courtyard, his cloak folded over one arm. He spotted me and headed my way. "Mother." Again, he wasn't looking so discontented, his smile giving him a hint of the handsome charm his father and older brother possessed in liberal quantities.

Cinnia peeped up at him, her gray eyes wide with a mixture of fear and admiration, as Amhar's appreciative gaze slid over her. Color sprang to her pale cheeks.

I stood up. "Run along, Cinnia. I'll be sure and speak with Karstyn about tomorrow." I held out my arms to my son. "And where have you been? You might have left a message." I didn't need to warn him of his father's ire. He lived in a perpetual state of disapproval where Arthur was concerned.

He gave me a hug and grinned, with something of his old enthusiasm. "I couldn't stay stuck in here last night, Mother. Not with the city beckoning me." He waved a hand in the general direction of the exterior of the house. "And what a night! I've not slept at all."

Chuckling to himself, he sat down in Cinnia's vacated seat and took one of my rolls, breaking it open and slathering on butter. "I'm starving. Karstyn fed me before I went out, and we found a tavern that did the most delicious pies. Bran said it was cat in them, or rat. I didn't believe him. But that was *hours* ago." His strong white teeth bit into the bread. "Delicious, but not enough. I'll go back to the kitchen in a moment." He chuckled again, eyes alight with mischief. "And perhaps I'll see that sweet little flower who was with you just now, if I'm lucky."

"She's too young for you," I said, keeping my tone light. Nothing like being forbidden to do something to inspire a boy to do it.

I poured him a beaker of milk. "Drink this. It helps with the alcohol." He certainly had the appearance of someone who'd drunk a lot but not yet reached the hungover stage.

He gulped down the milk and held the beaker out for more.

"Although best consumed before you go out rather than after," I said, refilling it. "To line your stomach."

He finished the roll and wiped his milky mouth on his sleeve. "That would spoil all the fun – I *wanted* to get drunk. To live. To do what I want with no one to stop me." He laughed. "And I want to do it every night we're here. In fact, after last night, I'm not sure I want to come home."

Inside, I quailed at the thought of what his father might say to that, but I stayed silent. Best if one of us had a decent relationship with our son, and he was heading for twenty and still wet behind the ears in most senses. He *needed* this more than Arthur would ever understand.

Amhar picked up a dried fig. "And you'll never guess who I met. In one of the first taverns I went into. I spent the entire night with him and his friends. He knows all the best places to go. The best taverns, the best gaming dens, the best of everything." He raised his eyes expectantly, wanting me to guess, as he chewed on the fig.

A little voice inside my head whispered caution. "I can't guess," I said. "You'll have to tell me."

He beamed in delight. "Medraut, of course. He's here with King Clinoch of Alt Clut and his party, for the Council. He was with Clinoch's youngest son, Cinbelin. They're great friends, and now I'm friends with them as well, and with all their group. Great fellows to spend the night with enjoying what the city has to offer."

My stomach lurched. Not Medraut. Not after all this time. I had to fight to control my expression. As a boy desperate to be a man, he'd left Din Cadan seven years ago to further his career as a warrior and had not been back since. If I had to admit it, I'd secretly been hoping he'd met some unspecified and faraway fate and that we'd never have to see him again.

But here he was, still going strong, and in what seemed to be a position of influence over a prince from a distant court. The bad penny that keeps on turning up even after you throw it away with all your strength.

Arthur had dispatched him to help with the refortification of Dinas Brent, one of our small coastal forts, but he'd remained there only three years. His commander, Morfran of Linnuis, had been forced to send him packing to join his mother, Morgawse, in the port of Caer Legeion.

I'd found it difficult winkling the reason for this out of Arthur, but I'd managed it in the end. As a lusty fifteen-year-old, and with all the major work on rebuilding the fortress completed, Medraut had taken to visiting the village and farms that clustered around the foot of Dinas Brent's high hill. He'd not been the only one, of course, but he *had* been the only one to bring trouble to the gates of the fortress.

"It's only to be expected he'd want a bit of female company," Arthur said, for some reason inclined to excuse his behavior. "Boys need to become men in more than one way." Funny that he didn't seem to think the same thing about his own son, now.

I held my tongue at that, convinced the sort of man Medraut wanted to become was not the sort I'd like.

The problem was that he hadn't just gone to the tavern, where he and his friends could meet up with women who were willing to lie with a young warrior for a few drinks. No, he cast his net wider, and it snared the pretty young daughter of the village baker, so successfully that she fell pregnant.

"It happens," Arthur said, with a wry smile, as he recounted the story. "How d'you think I got Llacheu? I wasn't much older than Medraut, you know."

When she couldn't hide her growing belly any longer, the girl's irate father and brother came storming up the hill demanding Medraut should make an honest woman of her. She was a girl expected to make a good marriage to a man of similar standing to her father. He thought he'd snared a warrior for her.

Medraut didn't kill them, but it was a near thing. They'd had to be carried back down the hill on boards. The girl miscarried her child, possibly from shock, and she and the baby died.

Arthur's source of information about all this was a rambling message from Morfran, explaining why he'd had to send Medraut off to his mother in Caer Legeion, and asking Arthur's belated consent. As the villagers were up in arms to the point of wanting to send a lynching party up the hill and not caring which warrior they caught, Arthur sent them a flock of sheep in payment for their loss, which Morfran informed us had served to mollify their hurt feelings.

But that was four years ago now, and we'd had no news of Medraut since. In my baser moments, I'd indulged in hoping he'd either gone to sea with his father and drowned, or set off to seek his fortune in Gaul or beyond.

And now here he was, back again.

"Medraut?" I managed, my breath catching in my throat and making me hoarse. "He's here? In Viroconium?"

Amhar nodded, ladling the honey into his mouth with the spoon. "Mmmmm. This is the best sort of honey." His tongue darted out to lick his sticky lips. "I said so, didn't I? He's been here a good few days already. The house he's staying in isn't too far from here." He dipped the spoon in the honey again. "I'll have to go to the kitchens, I think. I wonder if they have bacon. I could eat a whole flitch."

He stood, brushing the last crumbs of bread from a tunic front bespattered with wine stains. "I'll talk to you later, Mother. When I've caught up with some sleep."

I watched him walk away across the paved courtyard, my mind in a turmoil. In the nearly twenty years I'd been living as Arthur's queen, the knowledge I had from my old life had never stopped burning a hole in my heart. I'd counted through the twelve major battles the ninth century monk, Nennius, had attributed to Arthur in his *Historia Brittonum*, and every one of them had turned out to be based on fact. Something Arthurian scholars would have been amazed to hear.

Seven years ago, on the Wiltshire Downs, I'd watched the final one, Badon, unfold. A rousing victory for the British, with

Arthur supported by two unlikely allies: Cerdic of Caer Guinnt-guic and Cadwy of Powys. Both kings with Saxon blood in their veins, and both men Arthur had good reason to hate. But they'd rallied to the cause of saving Britain, and it had worked. The Saxon leaders, Aelle and Octha, had agreed to a treaty limiting their settlement to the east, and peace had reigned since then. Only minor, still-to-be-expected disputes, and a few small incursions in the west from the Irish, had marred the tranquility of Britain.

But none of that had made the looming threat of Arthur's last battle any less frightening. Camlann, a battle over whose location many later academics would wrangle. A battle mentioned here and there in places like the Black Book of Carmarthen, the Welsh Annals and Geoffrey of Monmouth's pseudo history of Britain. If Nennius's twelve were real, surely Camlann must be as well? And if that were so, then Medraut seemed destined to lead the opposing side. Not of raiding Saxons or Irish, but of men of Britain, in a revolt against their own High King.

I swallowed my fears, no longer hungry.

Chapter Three

ARTHUR DIDN'T RETURN to the Domus Alba until nightfall, and with him he brought Medraut and a stocky, red-headed teenager with galloping acne and a face like a potato. Cinbelin, youngest son of King Clinoch of Alt Clut, that godforsaken kingdom lying northwest of the Wall, once ruled by King Caw.

After defeating Caw and storming his nearly impregnable stronghold at Dun Breattann, with an air for the dramatic, Arthur had bowled the rather-the-worse-for-wear head of his son Heuil to him across his flag-stoned hall. To ensure a lasting peace, he'd taken Caw's youngest and favorite son hostage. Gildas, now a monk at the abbey on Ynys Witrin, showed no desire to return to the unforgiving north of Britain. And with his father dead, nothing now existed to draw him back.

Merlin and I were sitting by the fountain, as the shadows of evening crept across the courtyard and delicious smells wafted from the kitchen. Amhar had not yet shown his nose outside his bedroom, so last night must have taken a lot of sleeping off. Medraut and Cinbelin had gone on to the dining room, and Merlin and I were waiting while Arthur changed his tunic.

"You'll have to explain how Cinbelin's father came to be king in words of one syllable, in case I put my foot in it at dinner," I said to my friend, as he sat trailing the fingers of one lean hand in the cool water. He'd dressed splendidly for dinner in a deep-red tunic, and his long hair hung in a braid down his back. I flicked water at the fish, and they darted away. "When I last saw him, Caw had so many sons I'd like to know why one of them didn't inherit the throne. What happened to them all?"

He chuckled as a bold fish returned to nibble on his fingers. "How does it ever happen in the north? By feud, by deposing a king you don't like." He glanced up. "By murder."

"Now I'm intrigued."

He grinned. "You're right about how many sons Caw had. But he wasn't a peaceable man, and sons often die in battle. And when there are *that* many, fathers and jealous brothers can perceive them as a threat." He raised his hand from the water. "You know yourself how even between just two brothers there can be endless trouble."

Very true. Arthur and Cadwy had hated one another, and now Amhar and Llacheu had managed to fall out. Or rather, Amhar had taken against his brother. Although that was a slow burning thing rather than a sudden quarrel.

"Did Caw's sons all die?" I asked.

Merlin shrugged. "A few, I'd guess. Some went to be monks or priests. A good way of getting rid of the excess. But Caw had daughters as well, and one of them married a grandson of Ceredig Wledig, who'd ruled Alt Clut a long time back before Caw snatched the kingdom from his line. It was only reasonable for Ceredig's heir to want back what had been stolen."

Dynastic wars. Not unexpected.

"So, Clinoch is that heir?"

Merlin chuckled. "Not quite. But he had no trouble stepping over his uncle's body to regain the throne he saw as his. He probably had something to do with his uncle's… early departure."

I frowned. "I suppose it was his by right, really."

He shrugged again. "Perhaps. He made sure of it by marrying another of Caw's many daughters. She'll be Cinbelin's mother. A man who rules can never be certain his son will follow him, nor claim to have followed his father in true line of succession. Too many rivals for a crown, and too tenuous a hold on it by any king." He shook his head. "But what would you say gives one man license to rule over another? What makes a king different from the lowliest of servants? Why should one man claim the right to rule and decree another must obey? Enough men to question that, and kingship is lost."

Goodness, he was sounding very modern in his thinking.

Under the shade of the colonnaded walkway, the door from our rooms swung open before I could compose a reply, and Arthur emerged, looking very splendid in a tunic and braccae so deep a blue as to be almost navy. The hint of a red undershirt showed at his throat and cuffs – an innovation I'd introduced having grown fed up with always having to wear creamy white shirts that turned gray once they'd been washed a few times. The flash of bright color suited his dark good looks.

He spotted us and strode over, and my heart performed the customary flip it made every time I laid eyes on him. He was smiling, and the smile transformed his normally serious face, making him more attractive than ever. I couldn't help but think about the night to come.

I got up and he kissed me on the cheek, one arm going around my waist. "We'd better not keep our guests waiting any longer. Come along."

I glanced toward Amhar's still closed door. "What about Amhar?"

A frown creased Arthur's brow. "What about him? If he can't be ready on time, then he'll have to go hungry or eat in the kitchen with the servants again." He steered me toward the dining room, and Merlin got up and followed.

I couldn't help my curiosity about how Medraut would have turned out. The last time I'd seen him, he'd been a tall and sturdy boy of not yet thirteen but already with the promise of manhood about him. Would he resemble Theodoric, his Goth father, a little more than he had before? Or would he be more like his petite mother? Probably the former.

I was right.

Theodoric, like Arthur's half brother, Cei, was a giant of a man by fifth-century standards. Both stood over six feet tall, with wide shoulders and bodies to match, but whereas Cei was a redhead, Theodoric, being a Goth from Gaul, possessed the golden hair and ruddy coloring of a Saxon.

He hadn't passed this on to his only known son, but he had passed on his build. When we entered the dining room, Medraut was standing by the wooden sideboard where the servants had stood the tall earthenware jars containing the decanted wine, filling a goblet for himself and his friend. Probably refilling. Both of them had the ruddy-faced look of young men who'd started drinking before they'd even got here.

I stared. As tall as his father and nearly as broad, he made Arthur look quite slight, which he wasn't, and would have dwarfed slender Amhar. If he'd been here. My nephew's thick dark hair, that had once reminded me so much of my husband's, had been cut short and clung close to his head in a thick fleece of almost black curls. Verging-on-bushy dark brows overshadowed slightly too small and close-together eyes. His fleshy lips gave him an unnerving resemblance to his uncle Cadwy, but unlike Cadwy's son, Custennin, whose features they enhanced, they gave Medraut an oily, wet-lipped look that I didn't like.

But then, I *was* heavily biased.

The other young man only reached Medraut's burly shoulders and wasn't even as tall as me, but his barrel-chested body matched Medraut's in width and musculature. Prince Cinbelin. The hint of Pictish blood that was the legacy of many young men from north of the Wall showed itself in his broad, high-cheekboned face and thick scattering of freckles.

"Aunt Gwen," Medraut exclaimed, abandoning his goblet of wine and hurrying across the mosaic floor to meet me. "How lovely to see you again." His voice had deepened and was probably the most attractive thing about him. He caught my hands in his. "May I kiss you in greeting?" And before I could say no, which was my first inclination, he planted a wet kiss on my cheek.

I resisted the strong urge to wipe my cheek clean and snatch back my hands from his warm and sweaty ones. "Medraut, what a surprise." I couldn't find it in me to say it was a nice surprise.

Gwalchmei, Cei and Bedwyr arrived at that moment. Luckily for me, Medraut had to greet them as well, and I was able to reclaim my hands and surreptitiously wipe the feel of his kiss off my skin, whilst suppressing a shudder.

Introductions to Prince Cinbelin, who seemed an affable and not very bright young man, although that might have been due to his obvious inebriation, went on all round. He, at least, didn't want to kiss my cheek or hang onto my hands.

A servant filled goblets for everyone, and we took our seats at the long table. One seat stood empty, of course. But not for long. As the servants brought in the first course, the door from the courtyard banged open. Amhar almost catapulted into the room with a definite case of bed-hair and a disheveled look to his clothing that betrayed the fact he'd been sleeping all day in the clothes he'd gone out in last night, wine stains and all.

"Medraut!" he exclaimed. "One of the servants came and told me you were here." He then remembered himself, reddened, and bowed to everyone, clearly thinking one would do for us to share. "I'm sorry, Father, Mother. I was asleep, but I came as soon as I could." He flopped down into the empty seat, which happened to be beside mine and opposite Medraut's. "I could eat a horse."

Arthur shot him the sort of glance that threatened he'd deal with him later. "Let us hope that's not what Karstyn has planned for us this evening."

For once Amhar didn't seem to notice his father's sarcasm. He grinned across the table at his older cousin, more cheerful than he'd been in a long time. "How is it you're here? I didn't think to see you before tonight."

Medraut smiled widely, revealing large white teeth, a little overcrowded on his bottom jaw. "I met your father today in the palace, and he invited Cinbelin and me for dinner. Such an honor to dine at the table of the High King."

Was that a sarcastic undertone I detected, or was I just being hyper-critical?

As the servants continued serving the first course, oysters again, out of the corner of my eye, I spotted Arthur and Merlin exchanging glances. Cei, who was seated beside Cinbelin, had engaged the tipsy but cheerful young prince in conversation, but Bedwyr and Gwalchmei were watching Medraut and Amhar just as I was. I doubted either of them had forgotten his autocratic and bullying ways as a boy at Din Cadan. However, it looked as though Amhar had.

In between tipping oysters down his throat with lip-smacking greed, Medraut chatted to Amhar, and I listened.

"Cinbelin and I were in the palace today with his father. He was to meet with King Caninus, and he wanted to take Cinbelin as well, so *I* got to come. Such an honor. Cinbelin and I are like this." He crossed his fingers. "We're closer than brothers."

A hint of jealousy flashed across Amhar's face, swiftly controlled. The thought that Medraut was deliberately trying to instill this emotion occurred to me only to be quickly dismissed. What did he have to gain from doing that?

Medraut downed another oyster. "And who should we meet there but my uncle." He inclined his head toward Arthur. "I was never more pleased to see someone in my life. And of course..." He leaned forward across the table, arching his brows. "It did my credibility with Cinbelin no end of good to see my uncle embrace me like a lost son."

This time Amhar wasn't the only one to give him a hard look. But Medraut was of the sort for whom hard looks meant nothing. Hide of a rhino, that one.

He threw his head back and laughed. He had a loud, raucous laugh, almost a roar, that made everyone turn their heads to look at him. No doubt he'd intended that. "You should have seen the faces on my friends who were there attending their kings. They all thought *they* were the most important of the young warriors.

They soon saw I was, not them."

Hmmm. I doubted this would go down well with Amhar, but he seemed to have himself under control, although the light of excitement had gone from his eyes.

He managed a laugh himself. "Wait until they see *me* with him then," he said, with false bravado, and laughed again, but his laugh sounded brittle and fake.

I kept an eye and ear open for Medraut, watching for any sign of his old bullying ways returning, but he was the picture of jovial politeness with everyone. He chatted with whoever gained his attention, showing more subservience than that initial speech would have led me to expect, and seemed to want to include Amhar in his circle, constantly talking about *us* and *we*. So much so that after a bit, a wide smile spread across Amhar's face to replace that initial hint of jealousy.

I couldn't help but worry that he seemed to be fast reverting to his old state of hero worship for his older, stronger cousin. I chastised myself for jumping to a too hasty judgement of Medraut, and then again for not believing my gut instinct. Everything I knew about my nephew pointed to him being just what I feared. A threat to both Arthur and Amhar.

Amhar had always been an easily led boy, and I'd been glad when Arthur had removed Medraut from his circle of friends. I might have to do something decisive now, though, to make sure this relationship didn't pick up where it had left off seven years before. Although if Medraut had firmly tied himself to Cinbelin, and thus to Alt Clut, maybe I didn't have to worry quite so much. Fool that I was.

After a bit, I found Medraut watching me out of eyes that for a moment could have been called calculating, before he veiled them and smiled cheerily at me. If he was to be my enemy, which I feared he was, then I needed to get to know him better.

I smiled in return, but something told me he wasn't fooled and already knew I didn't like him. Maybe that had been why he'd so deliberately greeted me with a kiss. I metaphorically girded up my loins for battle. "Tell me, Medraut, what have you been up to since you left Din Cadan."

He set down the leg of chicken he'd been gnawing and wiped his greasy fingers on a cloth. "I've been here and there, doing a variety of things, some more fun than others. I imagine you know the story of how I left Dinas Brent?" He raised his heavy brows, a challenging look in his eyes. A *sleazy* look that had me disguising the shiver I felt.

I nodded. "I did hear that, yes."

He grinned, fingering a gold coin hanging on a chain about his neck. He must have seen my eyes go to it because he held it up. "A gold aureus from one of the old emperors. My father gave it to me. We looted a ship in the Middle Sea, and this was part of the booty." He turned it to show me where someone had drilled a hole for the chain. "Do you like it?"

I shrugged. "The gold coin of a long dead emperor and nothing more." I touched the ring on my finger, considering how that had come to me from another such man. An emperor of Rome, but one who'd married a British princess. "You sailed with your father, then?"

He nodded. "Far and wide. I liked the life at sea. After I left Dinas Brent, I went to my mother's house in Caer Legeion." A frown lowered his brows. "I soon found out I couldn't stay there with her, though. She thought I was the child she'd left behind at Din Cadan and treated me so. When my father returned with his fleet, I asked him to take me with him, and he did. She kicked up such a fuss." The frown lifted and a smile of pure pleasure flitted across his face. But whether it was from the memory of his sea voyage or how he'd upset his mother, I couldn't tell.

Maybe he was just a boy who'd needed the guiding hand of his father all along. Theodoric had never been a hands-on parent even in the loosest terms, and sailing with him might have been the making of his son. Hopefully, parental guidance hadn't come too late. Then I remembered it was Theodoric we were talking about, with his penchant for brothels and bawdy houses. Still, maybe any father was better than no father.

"Where did you sail to?" I asked, more than curious to hear how the two of them had got on.

He grinned, suddenly more boyish. "All over. My father took me to Hibernia, to Armorica and Belgica, and south to Aquitania and Hispania. And one time, we sailed between the Pillars of Hercules and into the Middle Sea, where we did a bit of trade and a bit of pirating." He chuckled, most probably about the pirating. "In Mauretania I saw men as dark as this old oak table, and wonders you'd never believe. The world is a wondrous place." His infectious enthusiasm went part way to breaking down the barricade I'd erected. Until I remembered who he was.

"What took you to the cold seas of Alt Clut then?" I asked, angry at myself for being almost taken in. "That's a long way from the heat of Mauretania."

"We sailed north along the west coast of Britain and stayed at Dun Breattann a while. We'd carried some slaves back from the Middle Sea and heard there was a good market for *exotics* north of the Wall. My father sold them to Cinbelin's father – women, mostly, of course." His eyes glittered. "Those women have some *fancy* tricks."

I didn't think I wanted to know about their tricks. Whatever they were, he was talking about North African girls enslaved for sex, and that left a nasty taste in my mouth, made worse by the knowledge that I could do nothing to help them. "I take it your father left you there. What made you decide to stay?"

His face clouded for a moment, then swiftly brightened, as changeable as a stormy day at home. "We agreed to a parting of our ways. He was all for patrolling up and down the Hibernian Sea, and I'd had my fill of that. I liked sailing with him, but part of the enjoyment was the exotic ports." He sniggered. "Not many of them along either side of the Hibernian Sea in winter."

He was probably right about that.

"And anyway, I'd made friends with Cinbelin, and he wanted me to stay. Like I said – we're like *brothers*." His eyes slid sideways to where Amhar was talking to Bedwyr, perhaps hoping my son might be half listening.

I schooled my face to impassivity. Was there more to this than met the eye? He was a young man who'd already severely wounded or killed two men over an impregnated girl, and more than likely something along those lines might have caused him to fall out with a father well known for his womanizing. Rivalry over a girl, perhaps? The old lion bested by the young one and not happy about it?

I steeled myself. "And now you're here in Viroconium, what do you intend to do?"

He returned a guileless stare that was most likely anything but. "Do? Why, I intend to return to Din Cadan with you. Amhar has invited me. And Cinbelin, who has two older brothers, has permission from his father to accompany me." He smiled, a sly, calculating smile. "I've a wish to meet Archfedd and Reaghan again – and see for myself how they've turned out now they're women grown. We're both looking forward to it."

I didn't like the way he said that one bit.

Chapter Four

AMHAR WENT OUT every night we remained in Viroconium, returning early each morning and sleeping for most of the day. Much like a teenager in the world I'd left behind. For a young man who'd grown up in a hillfort, he was taking to the thrills of city living like a duck to water. Encouraged, of course, by Medraut.

Arthur made no more fatherly attempts to curtail our son's excesses. "He's a man grown, and at least he's told us where he's going. It's not for me to prevent him sowing his oats," he declared, when I broached the subject on the fourth day Amhar, with pouches under his eyes, had come staggering back as we were eating our breakfast in the courtyard.

"But he's not used to this sort of life," I said, annoyed at his response. "He's not a city boy, like you were." What I really wanted to say was that he shouldn't be out with Medraut every night, but I held my tongue on that one. For now. I'd learned it was best not to push Arthur in the direction I wanted him to take, or he'd dig his heels in.

Arthur laughed. "Is that how you see me?"

He'd been brought up in his father's palace at Viroconium until, at the age of fifteen, his father had dispatched him to rule Dumnonia. Probably if he hadn't left then, Cadwy would have found a way for his younger brother to have had a handy, and fatal, accident. He'd tried enough times since.

I frowned, not sure this made Arthur a city boy in quite the same class as Medraut and his friends. "Not really, I suppose," I conceded. "But you *are* someone who spent at least part of his youth in a city." I raised my eyebrows. "I'm assuming you weren't out gaming and drinking... and chasing women... when you were under fifteen."

He laughed again. "I liked girls, of course, but back then my friends and I admired them from afar. We were more interested in hunting and having adventures than we were in girls and gambling." He shook his head. "But Amhar has nearly four years on the boy I was then, and he's a man with a man's needs. We have to let him spread his wings. And he's not on his own. He's with Medraut."

I pressed my lips together, bracing myself. "That's as may be, but I'm not happy with him learning to spread his wings in that young man's company. He isn't a good influence."

Arthur sighed and rubbed his stubbly chin. "Medraut's just having fun while he has the chance. Before life gets in his way. At least Amhar isn't moaning as much as he usually does." He paused, looking reflective and a touch surprised. "Not at all, in fact."

I shook the last few crumbs of bread into the fishpond as a servant took our empty breakfast tray. The doves on the tiled rooftop rose in a flutter of wings, disturbed by a prowling ginger cat edging along the ridge toward them.

"Well, don't you think that's a bit odd in itself?" I said, unable to accurately pinpoint the cause of the unease I felt. I had to admit Arthur was right about one thing, though. Amhar was indeed only doing what young men had always done and always would do – running riot in a city and discovering the heady pleasures of bachelor life.

Arthur caught my hand. "You're fussing over nothing. Relax a bit. Enjoy our son learning to have fun. It's what he wants to do. I'm pleased he's made so many new friends. Let's hope being with young men his own age, who are all warriors or kings' sons from other kingdoms, will encourage him in the right direction. They could be a good example." He kissed me on the forehead. "Stop worrying. Or you'll be caught frowning when the wind changes and then you'll be stuck like that."

So spoke the expert on childrearing.

I collared Merlin after Arthur departed to yet another meeting, this time with a different set of kings. Britain consisted of so many small kingdoms it was hard to get them all seated at the enormous round table in the hall. And all of them wanted a semi-private audience before the Council began with the High King and Caninus, who acted a bit like a company secretary.

Merlin was setting out his chess set on a sturdy board beside the fountain. This was a game I'd taught him, after persuading one of our better craftsmen to fashion two sets – one from creamy-white bone and a dark set from bog oak. The tactical side of the game appealed to Merlin's cunning brain, and he carried his chess set wherever he went.

I sat on the edge of the fountain and waited as he finished arranging the board, giving me the white set. Without glancing up at him, I moved the King's Pawn two spaces forward and he counteracted by moving his own King's Pawn out to face mine. I thought for a moment then moved my King's Knight out to its left, and he retaliated with his Queen's Knight. Only we called them "Warriors" not Knights.

The hot sun beat down on the back of my neck. "I don't like Amhar going out every night with Medraut and his friends," I said, trying to keep my tone neutral, as I considered my next move. Yes, the King's Bishop could come out of hiding and move to face Merlin's Warrior.

Merlin kept his eyes on the board. "I don't either." His hand hovered for a moment, then descended on his own King's Bishop, sliding him out to stand between his Warrior and my Bishop.

I studied the pieces, but my mind was elsewhere. "And I don't want Medraut coming back to Din Cadan with us." I moved my Queen's Bishop's Pawn forward to stand behind my Queen's

Bishop, hoping that was a good move. I didn't often beat Merlin nowadays, and being distracted like this was a clear path to defeat.

Merlin brought out his King's Warrior and raised his eyes to look at me. "What would you like me to do?"

I moved my Queen's Pawn forward two squares. "I don't know what you *can* do. I wish we'd never brought Amhar. If I'd thought for a minute Medraut would be here, I'd never have let him come. Whatever Arthur said, I'd have put my foot down." Though what good that would have done against the two men in my life, I couldn't say.

The doves on the roof fluttered down into the courtyard as a servant came out and scattered corn for them. Merlin took my piece with his Pawn.

I moved a white Pawn forward to threaten his Warrior.

Merlin didn't hesitate but jumped his threatened Warrior forward to safety in the spot three places in front of my King. Unlike me, he never seemed to have to think about the moves he made. "You could try talking to Amhar – reasoning with him."

I snorted, and moved my Bishop to threaten his Warrior, preventing him from moving his King's Pawn forward to consolidate his center. "Chance'd be a fine thing that he'd listen to me." I paused. "*You* could try talking to him. He might listen to you. Suggest that maybe Medraut isn't the right friend for him."

"Are you deliberately trying to distract me?" Merlin asked, moving his Warrior forward to directly threaten my Queen.

I moved my King one square and took his Warrior. "Maybe."

He pounced and took my Queen's Bishop's Pawn with his black Pawn and smiled. "Do you really think he'd listen to me? Check, by the way – with my Bishop."

So it was. I'd walked into that one.

I sighed. "Probably not. But you at least know how important it is that Medraut doesn't end up doing what we think he might do. And having him come to Din Cadan with us, as a friend of Amhar's, is *not* a good thing." I studied the board again, considering how to get out of check for a long minute. Hah – there. I moved my King to the square in front of his Warrior's Pawn, so he could lurk.

His sneaky little black Pawn took one of my front-line Pawns in front of my Queen's Warrior and threatened both my Queen's Rook and my Queen's Bishop. Drat him. If I wasn't careful, he'd have a second Queen. Merlin really was too good at this game. I should have known better than to teach it to someone who had the Sight and could probably guess what moves I was going to make even before I thought of them.

I took his Pawn with my Bishop, as that was the only possible move to make.

"If he's at Din Cadan," Merlin said, his hand hovering over the board again as though in indecision, as if *that* ever happened, "then at least we can keep a good eye on him. There's that, at least. Better than having him elsewhere plotting unrest." He glanced up and gave me a cheeky grin as he moved his Warrior to take the space in front of his King. "And it may never happen. The stories you know could still all be wrong."

I took my time over my next move, enjoying the warmth of the spring sun. Swallows darted into the eaves of the building with nesting materials in their beaks, ready to reoccupy last year's accommodation. Maybe I needed to be a bit more aggressive, and not just over this chess game. I moved my Warrior forward to threaten Merlin's front-line Pawn. "I hope you're right, but I can't help fearing that everything's falling into place for what we fear will happen."

He promptly moved his Warrior forward and took my Bishop, exactly as though he'd been expecting me to do that. Of course he had. My strategy hadn't worked.

Now what? I took the Pawn, anyway, putting my Warrior right beside his King and threatening his Queen and the Rook still in place on the corner square. Only the King threatened me, but I couldn't take him.

He grinned in obvious delight and castled, so now his Rook

was right beside me and it was my turn to be under threat. "There is one thing you haven't considered," he said, sounding a tiny bit smug. "That you don't know how far in the future your Camlann might be. Arthur's comparatively young, yet, and Medraut's younger still, so it could be many years off."

"And you haven't considered this," I said, taking his Queen with a flourish.

He chuckled, and moved his Bishop forward to sit beside my King. "Check."

What? How had I not seen that coming? If I took his Bishop, I'd be in the direct firing line of his Rook, so I retreated the King one space.

He cleared his throat and moved his dead Queen's Pawn forward one space, and now my King was in direct line of the Bishop he had hiding on the back row. "Check."

I moved my brave Pawn forward to stand in the way. "I can only hope you're right, or I might have to consider lacing Medraut's food with poison." Did I mean that? Maybe.

Oh no. He ignored my poison comment and moved his Warrior to threaten the King. "Check." I was beginning to feel besieged, and not just on the chessboard.

But a King, even though he can only move one square, can still take another piece, so I moved the king forward to beside the Warrior, mentally crossing my fingers.

Now under threat himself, Merlin moved his Warrior back. "Bit drastic. Poison, that is."

I took his Warrior with mine and humphed. "Not really. I'd do anything to keep Arthur safe. Anything." Half of me was wishing I'd done something to harm Medraut when he was born, but back then Camlann had seemed an eternity away, and I hadn't even decided I was staying in the Dark Ages. How swiftly the years had passed.

He took my Warrior with his freed-up Bishop. "Check. I believe you would."

I stared at the board, the sound of someone sweeping under

the colonnade suddenly loud. How to get out of this. Only two squares I could move the King to. I moved him forward one, closer to his enemy. Was this where Arthur was headed with Amhar's invitation to Medraut?

Merlin brought his Rook forward to sit beside my King, but that also put him between me and the Bishop. I moved back a square, definitely on the retreat now and about to lose.

Merlin brought his Pawn forward so my King was attacked on both sides.

I took my King back another square, retreating into the corner in front of the useless Rook and his unused Pawn. Down came the Bishop, and I was caught. Merlin grinned at me. "Checkmate."

Was that what would happen to Arthur? Was he like my white King? Would he be driven into a corner he couldn't escape from by Medraut, and would Camlann be as unavoidable as this checkmate? I shivered at the thought.

Chapter Five

T HE DAY AFTER my conversation with Merlin, Arthur went off to the Council of Kings. Having been to the Council enough times in the past and had my fill of standing for hours on end listening to the kings drone on, I remained in the Domus Alba. Arthur, who was taking most of his men, insisted on Amhar accompanying him. "One day, *you'll* be the king leading your people to the Council," he said when Amhar complained. "None of us can tell how long we have left in this world. I need to be sure you're well prepared for kingship. You're a man now with a man's obligations."

A little shiver of foreboding trickled down my spine at his words, and I wished them unsaid with all my heart. Behind my back, I made the sign against the evil eye, although how efficacious it was at fending off bad luck remained a moot point.

Amhar, who'd been planning on another day in bed after a night probably spent in debauchery, got himself ready to go with barely concealed reluctance and bleary, bloodshot eyes.

"Medraut will be going," Cei pointed out. "And so will Cinbelin. You're a king's heir and need to see what it's all about, much more than they do. And more importantly, you need to be seen by the other kings at your father's side."

Merlin confined himself to shooting Amhar a piercing look before turning away, no doubt thinking more about Medraut than about Amhar, just as I was. The idea that Medraut might be preparing himself for kingship sent another shiver down my spine.

Over my dead body. Hopefully not literally.

The Council could go on for hours, although, as many of the needed agreements had been made in the preceding days, most of what they'd be covering should be straightforward. As usual, not every king had turned up, but Arthur had assured me they had a sufficient number to go ahead and make decisions.

No doubt the hall would be packed with nosy townspeople wanting to listen to what was said. Especially if it concerned them, which it often did. They'd have come for the pure spectacle, as well. To see most of the kings of Britain gathered in one place, and all out to impress one another with their robes, their entourages, and their speeches. You can have enough of spectacle, though.

I had something else planned for my morning: a ride out and a gallop to blow the cobwebs of city life away, across the inviting flat lands outside the city walls. As soon as everyone had departed for the Council Hall and a blessed silence had fallen over the Domus Alba, I changed into my riding clothes and hurried down to the stables.

In the freshly swept stableyard, a grizzled, potbellied old groom stood holding my new horse, Enfys, along with a horse for himself. After I'd lost Alezan at the ripe old age of twenty-five at the start of last winter, Arthur had found Enfys for me. She'd made a worthy replacement.

The discontented look on the groom's weather-beaten face betrayed how fed up he was with having to escort me for a ride when he could have been asleep in the hayloft all day with no one to disturb him. Even his bow was sulky, but I ignored that.

With an airy word of thanks and a deliberate, cheery smile, I took Enfys's reins, checked her girth and mounted, my heart fluttering with excitement at the prospect of getting out of the city at last. The groom, being portly, scrambled aboard using the stone mounting block, and I gave him a moment to settle into the saddle.

Then, as the gates stood open, I led the way into the street. He kicked his garron, a beast as portly and unenthusiastic as its rider, into a shambling trot to catch up.

An abnormal quiet reigned in the narrow streets. Most of the inhabitants must have gathered in the forum outside the hall, the early birds jammed inside, which would be horrible in this warm weather. Glad of not having to stand for hours in stuffy heat, I touched Enfys with my heels, and she broke into a joyful, springy trot. Not the most comfortable of paces for my stirrup-less groom, but he'd have to put up with it.

As we approached the massive east gates, a clatter of hooves to my left heralded the approach of another rider in a hurry. I frowned as annoyance washed over me. Medraut, who should have been with his friend Cinbelin, almost exploded out of a side street. He was struggling to keep an over-excited and sweat-drenched, showy black cob under control while trying to maintain a nonchalant grin. For whose benefit? Not mine. Bad riding of a badly trained horse was never going to impress me.

I sighed. So much for him having gone with King Clinoch and his mate Cinbelin to the council. But what was he doing here?

He forced the snorting cob in by my side, wrenching on what looked like a far too severe bit, and made me as flamboyant a bow as he could, considering he was on an almost out of control horse. "Milady the Queen, well met." He sounded breathless from the struggle.

As I was thinking the exact opposite, I refrained from answering.

He waved his hand at my groom. "You may go back to the Domus Alba. I shall be accompanying my aunt on her ride. Off you go. She'll be quite safe with me."

I twisted in my saddle, opening my mouth to tell the groom not to go, but I was too late. He'd already taken the opportunity to go home to put his feet up and had turned his horse to trot back down the street as though that were much preferable to being my escort. If I shouted to him, I'd probably just look stupid. Instead, I pressed my lips together in a tight line of irritation. How dare Medraut assume I'd want him as my escort. But I had no intention of foregoing my longed-for ride because of him.

I'd have to put up with his unwanted company.

We passed through the open gates and rode in silence for a couple of minutes as our horses negotiated the cluster of shops and houses that hugged the road frontage outside the city walls. His ongoing battle with his horse to keep it in a walk continued. Wherever he'd got it, it would never make a warhorse. But then, a young man like him probably only wanted it for show.

As we emerged onto the farmland, the fields spread out before us, green with cereal crops pushing up through the rich, river-valley soil. His cob a little more under control, he turned to me with a smile on his face that almost, but not quite, rendered it pleasant. "I thought you might take the chance to ride out while the Council was in progress. Amhar told me you weren't going last night." He laughed. "Or was that this morning? I forget."

The cob tossed its head, spraying us both with gobbets of thick foam from its bit. "So, I decided I wouldn't go either, but would watch out for you and join you for a ride." His horse pranced sideways and the hefty kick he gave it with his opposite leg sent it cannoning back into Enfys, sandwiching my leg against his. Far too close for comfort.

Well, he was nothing if not daring and upfront. I unfolded my lips. "That was very kind of you, but I can assure you I would have been quite happy with my groom for company." I paused, wondering how I could get rid of him. "I don't plan on a long ride, anyway. Perhaps just around the walls to the south then back again. Enough to let my horse stretch her legs."

He grinned. Ostensibly he appeared friendly and relaxed, but I couldn't shift the sensation that something more lurked beneath his pseudo-amicable exterior. That this was a young man with an agenda.

"Come, Aunt," he said with a chuckle. "Don't tell me you

don't like to gallop any longer. You have a new young horse, I see. Is she as fast as old Alezan? She's very pretty." He looked me in the eye with a touch of insolence. "Much as you are."

What? Was he *flirting* with me? Indignation bubbled up. "Medraut," I said, as frostily as I could. "I don't doubt you think your attentions are flattering, but let me assure you that they are not. If anything, I would prefer to ride alone and have a time for private reflection. I came out for some peace and quiet, not to have to converse with anyone." *And especially not you.* But I kept that one inside my head.

He laughed out loud. "You haven't changed a bit, have you? You're just as outspoken as I remember you from my boyhood." He gestured around us at the small square fields and the narrow tracks running between them. "You never know, there might be *brigands* lurking." But he was mocking me now.

I heaved a sigh, resigning myself to him spoiling the ride I'd been looking forward to. "Very well," I said, keeping my tone curt to discourage any more attempts at flirting. "You may ride to the river and back with me, and that's all. Then I shall be returning to the Domus Alba." *And you won't be getting an invite.*

He beamed at me as though I'd just bestowed a great honor on him, which only served to irritate me further. *Little shit.* Only not so little now. In an effort to get away from him, and hoping his horse would play up, I touched my legs to Enfys's sides, and she sprang into a lively canter. But he had his horse in check through brute force, and together we cantered our horses toward where the river curved south in a wide silver ribbon edged with willows.

After five days of inactivity, Enfys wanted to have her head and gallop and was nearly as hard to control as Medraut's fiery cob. I had a hard job holding her back. Medraut was in the same situation, as his black cob tugged at the bit and tossed its head, its nostrils flaring red. But we reached the riverbank in one piece and pulled our horses to a walk, steam rising and flies gathering to swarm around their heads.

For five minutes we followed the river downstream, letting the horses have a breather, until we reached where a sizeable flat-bottomed boat bobbed beside a rickety wooden jetty and a dilapidated house. Probably a crossing place, as a matching jetty, with no attendant house, protruded into the water on the far bank. A goat grazed on a tether in a small orchard, and the ripe smell of pigs hung in the air.

Far enough for me. I swung Enfys around and headed back toward the city gates, letting her trot, ignoring the problem Medraut was still having with controlling his own mount. Glad of it, in fact. Spitefully so.

However, his trouble proved short-lived. He brought the cob up so close to Enfys that his left knee kept nudging mine, hot and invasive and making my skin crawl. If she'd been Alezan, she'd have soon sorted that cob out, but she wasn't. Pushing her over with my right leg didn't help, either, because Medraut and his horse followed, and I didn't seem able to get away from the burning contact that was making me want to slap him bloody hard.

Why didn't I just tell him to bugger off? I wanted to, that was certain, but something held me back. Maybe it was the desire to find out what he was after, because it seemed evident to me that he *was* after something. I just needed to work out what.

With his horse mostly under control, he talked about the birds overhead, the crops, his horse, hunting – the things any young man his age would talk about. None of this seemed to require any contribution from me. But behind it all lurked something else – some purpose I couldn't fathom. After another short canter, we slowed to a walk to cool off our horses before we arrived back at the gates. And that was when he put out his hand and grabbed mine.

I recoiled in shock, and tried to snatch my hand back, but he held on so tight it hurt, staring down at the ring on my finger. Enfys and the cob halted, and now I pulled with more force, and he let go. I glowered at him, my heart hammering.

Unfazed by my open anger, he grinned, looking more than ever like his dead uncle, Cadwy. Goodness, did he grin a lot, showing the large white teeth he'd inherited from his father. A sight too much grinning to be genuine. I was reminded of the line from Hamlet – "one may smile and smile and be a villain." How very apt those words felt right now.

"I just wanted to see it again," he said. "I'd quite forgotten what it looked like. The ring of the Ring Maiden herself. The woman who made my uncle what he is today."

I tucked my hand away under my arm, not wanting his eyes on it. "The ring did nothing," I snapped. "It's just a story. Your uncle has forged his own fate. I've had nothing to do with it."

He laughed, and this time I heard the spite in it. "Everyone knows that the man who holds the Ring Maiden is destined to be the greatest king ever born." His thick lips curved in a smile that was almost a sneer, and my blood boiled with impotent rage I failed to hide.

Why hadn't I seen all his smiles were the same? Only skin deep. That beneath his cheery exterior lurked the same bully he'd been as a boy. A leopard can't change its spots. "That's rubbish," I snapped.

He snorted. "But he does have everything, doesn't he?" His horse curvetted under his too tight grip on its reins. "He has you, the Ring Maiden, that bloody sword of destiny, and on top of that, he has the sword of Macsen Wledig – Excalibur."

At a loss for words, I dug my heels a little too hard into Enfys's sides and she sprang forward into a canter. I had to rapidly gather my too-long reins and didn't look back over my shoulder to see if he was following. At the gates, I pulled her to a walk. A few people on foot were passing in and out, but not many. As I joined them, I finally twisted in the saddle to find out where he was.

He was standing where I'd left him, staring after me. Not for the first time that morning, a shiver ran down my spine, and I urged Enfys into a trot in my hurry to escape his line of sight, nearly knocking over a woman with two buckets of milk suspended from a wooden yoke. The milk slopped over the road, and she shouted with indignation, but I was through the gates by then and not listening.

Chapter Six

FOR THE THREE days following the Council, more meetings
had to be held, and Arthur remained busy every day, leaving
me to my own devices. I didn't try another ride, afraid of
repeating that disturbing encounter with Medraut, but remained
within the comparative security of the Domus Alba's walls. So,
with nothing else to do, I contented myself with making notes on
the thin strips of wood I always carried with me, and picking
Merlin's brain about what had gone on at the council and the
other meetings.

Amhar begrudgingly accompanied his father, Cei and Merlin
to several of these meetings, looking bleary-eyed and hungover
from his nights on the town with his new friends. Arthur, who'd
been known to get drunk himself from time to time, showed him
no mercy. As far as he was concerned, if Amhar wanted to be out
all night, he'd have to put up with performing his required duties
during the day as well. He could sleep when he could find the
time. Or not at all, as the case might be.

On the fourth day, we set off for home, somewhat increased
in number and in bright sunshine. Not only had Medraut and
Cinbelin joined us, but a dozen others, all young men of
Medraut's following, had decided the invite extended to them.
Two were the Princes Bran and Cyngal of Ebrauc. Who knew
how they'd persuaded their grandfather, King Garbaniawn, to let
them come.

As our column followed the dusty road south, I deliberately steered clear of Medraut, keeping my gaze averted whenever I could, in case he'd decided I was his new best friend. But to my relief, he chose to ride at the rear with his followers, in a noisy group that now included Amhar. However, I couldn't expect to avoid him without at least one person noticing, and that, of course, was Merlin.

We'd reached the last leg of our journey before he took the opportunity to speak to me about it. Bringing his horse up beside mine, he edged me away from where Arthur and Cei were discussing a possible hunting expedition.

The path stretched wide and green before us, braiding between huge oaks and beeches bright with their new growth of leaves, and our whole party had spread out. At the back, the young men had broken into a drinking song, their carefree voices rising toward the swaying branches. More than a little ribald, if anyone took the trouble to listen to the words.

"Why have you been avoiding Medraut like he has the sweating sickness?" Merlin asked, always one to come straight to the point.

I glanced across at Arthur, but he was still deep in conversation with Cei. "There's something about him I don't trust," I said. "On the outside, he seems as though he's matured into a nice young man, but he's let his guard slip once or twice with me, and I don't like what I've seen. All this cheery camaraderie is a veneer."

Merlin regarded me thoughtfully. "You may well be right on that. I'm not blind. He has the feel of a man playing a part, and with a purpose he's keeping hidden. But that's not why you're avoiding him, is it?"

I shook my head, bitter gall rising in my throat, and ignored his last sentence. "Well, we know what that purpose is, don't we?"

Merlin nodded. *"If* the stories are true."

There we were again. It all came back to this every time. Did

I really know what the future held for all of us, or were the stories from my time just the product of some fevered, late-medieval imagination – someone embellishing the story with their own twist? The fact that I had no way of telling was enough to drive me mad. Maybe it already had.

I couldn't help my backward glance toward where the object of my disquiet rode beside Amhar, a position he'd held throughout our journey, as though Amhar were his new best friend. Did I just dislike him because of the stories, or was he truly as black as I wanted to paint him? "I suppose at least we'll have the chance to keep an eye on him," I muttered.

"That doesn't answer my question," Merlin said.

I chewed my lip for a few seconds to gain time and gather my thoughts. If I told Merlin how Medraut had behaved to me, he might feel it his duty to tell Arthur, and that might lead to enmity between them which in turn might set them firmly on the road to Camlann. But I still wasn't certain Medraut had done anything that warranted this deep feeling of suspicion.

"It's nothing," I said, taking the plunge. "On the day of the Council I went out for a ride. Medraut was lying in wait as though he knew I'd be going that way. Before I could stop him, he told my groom to go back." I frowned. "He didn't really *do* anything. But… he made me feel… uncomfortable… and dirty. He seemed fascinated with my ring. And he said I was pretty…"

Merlin smiled, a small, tight smile. "He wasn't lying."

I shook my head. "It was the *way* he said it. It gave me the creeps. He rode his horse so close to mine his knee kept touching my leg. It… it was horrible. Like I was being defiled. Touched by something wicked."

The smile vanished. "I thought I was the one with the Sight."

"It wasn't anything like that. It was just the feeling he gave me. When I got home, all I wanted to do was take a bath and wash that feeling off, but it wouldn't go." I met his gaze. "It was the way he looked at me – as though he could see right through my clothes. As though he *knew* what I looked like naked. Ugh –

that's made me shiver all over again. Can we not talk about this? I'll need another bath." I managed a small chuckle.

Merlin gave me a long, hard look.

EVENING WAS RAPIDLY falling when we at last wound our way up the cobbled road to Din Cadan. A gladness to be back home swept over me, and, having handed Enfys's reins to a groom, I hurried up the hill to the Hall.

I found Archfedd inside, helping Coventina and Reaghan organize our servants for a homecoming feast. Heads turned as I entered, and work ground to a halt. Even the boy in charge of the hearth stopped turning the spit.

For a moment no one moved, then Archfedd ran down the hall and threw herself into my arms with the sort of enthusiasm I'd have expected had I been gone several months instead of a few weeks.

"Mami!" She'd never quite abandoned what she'd called me as a small child.

I enfolded her in my arms, breathing in the scent of the lavender on her clothes and the sweet freshness of our hilltop home in her hair. So different from the stink of the city that had managed to linger in my nostrils for most of our journey home.

She wriggled free and planted a kiss on each of my cheeks. "You've been gone too long. I've missed you. We all have." She waved an airy hand at the spit boy, who'd remembered his duties and was turning the carcass of the deer again. "We've venison for dinner." The smell of the cooking meat filled the air, mixed with the other heady scents of home – dusty reeds, dogs, stale food and acrid smoke. A mix I'd come to love.

I held her at arm's length, taking in my beautiful daughter as if I'd never seen her before. At fifteen she was almost a woman grown, and had swapped the gangly chubbiness of childhood for the gentle curves of femininity. Her long hair, as bright a chestnut as mine, hung down her back in a single thick braid, and wispy tendrils curled about her oval face. She'd inherited my hazel eyes along with my hair, and had her father's long straight nose. Above a pointed chin, a full-lipped mouth smiled to reveal nearly perfect teeth.

"I swear you've grown more beautiful in my absence," I said, unable to wipe the grin from my face. "And Reaghan, too. Come here and kiss your aunt."

Reaghan, a good year older than Archfedd, wiped her hands on the apron she was wearing and hurried over. She resembled her mother, Coventina, a little too much to ever be classified as pretty, but nevertheless she'd turned into a striking young woman. Her bright auburn hair framed a pale, freckled face, and her eyes were a wide and luminous blue, like Cei's. Some young man was going to drown in them one day.

She kissed me on the cheek, and I turned to her mother, my best friend. I was about to hold my arms out to her when the doors of the Hall banged open again behind me.

Expecting it to be Arthur, I spun around, and so did everyone else.

It wasn't.

Medraut stood on the threshold, gazing around himself... an acquisitive, even possessive look on his face, almost as though he owned what he surveyed, or intended to. Maybe I was the only one who saw that, though. Resentment rose in me, and by my side my fists balled. Had he abandoned everyone else at the stables to get here first? Ahead of Arthur?

We couldn't help but become the audience he so clearly wanted for his return. He set his hands on his hips, feet apart as though on the deck of one of his father's ships, and surveyed each one of us in turn, his eyes appraising and sharp. As a king would survey his people. And like fools, we stood there mute, letting him do it, too surprised to protest.

It didn't take him long. After a moment he stepped further

into the Hall, and the doors banged shut behind him.

None of us said a word. Probably I should have introduced him, but the thought that he might go unrecognized didn't occur to me.

"Well," he said, letting that one word hang in the air. "These little beauties must be my cousins. Now, which one is which? Reaghan was the redhead, if I recall, so *this...*" he paused as his attention fixed on my daughter. "*This* must be Archfedd." He paused again, giving her a second look up and down, just the way he'd looked at me on our ride. Every nerve in my body wanted to leap down the Hall and knock him down. With a large club.

Archfedd fidgeted under his intense gaze, color rising to her cheeks. He had an unnervingly hard stare that made its subject want to flinch and run away.

Coventina found her voice first. "Is that little Medraut come back to us?" She bustled forward, stepping neatly between him and Archfedd, as always with a hitch to her gait caused by the nerve damage she'd sustained at Reaghan's birth. "Welcome home, my boy. Welcome home." She gave him a hug, and, after a moment's pause, he hugged her in return, his predatory gaze fixed on Archfedd over her shoulder.

Coventina released him and took a step back to study him through narrowed eyes. Archfedd took the opportunity to edge closer to me, which wasn't like her at all. Her hand slipped into mine as though she felt she needed my support. I squeezed it.

"Goodness me," Coventina said to Medraut, a wide smile on her homely face. "Who'd've thought you'd have grown so *big*. You're like your father in that, indeed you are. You might have the Pendragon coloring, but I see Theodoric *and* your grandfather in you, my lad."

Medraut's face softened into what might well have been a genuine smile, but whether it was at the thought of being likened to his father or grandfather, was anybody's guess. "It's lovely to see you too, Coventina," he said, not at all sincerely, or was that just me thinking the worst? "And wonderful to be back here after so long. It feels as though I've come home." Okay, maybe that last bit *was* sincere. Worryingly.

From outside came the sound of voices. Before we had the chance to say any more, the doors opened yet again, and this time it *was* Arthur, an arm around Llacheu's shoulders and accompanied by Cei, and Merlin, with Amhar trailing behind them. The other young men of Medraut's faction must have been attending to their horses, thank goodness. I'd had more than enough of wild young men.

Archfedd relinquished her hold on my hand and ran to her father, who released his hold on Llacheu, spun her off her feet and twirled her around. "You've grown prettier in my absence, my Chick," he said, echoing my words. He set her down and she hugged Amhar, who hugged her back with enthusiasm. However he felt about Llacheu, he loved his little sister.

"I see you're well on with your preparations for the feast," Arthur said to Coventina. "I think we all need to wash the dust of the road off before we eat. How long do we have?"

Coventina caught his hands and planted a kiss on each cheek. "An hour at most, Little Brother."

Cei turned to Medraut. "Better come with me." He put a guiding hand on that young man's back to steer him toward the doors. "I'll sort out where you and your friends are to sleep. We've some spaces in our barracks, I should think. And Amhar, you can show him where to go."

At the door, Medraut paused and looked back, but not at me with my coveted dragon ring. No, he had eyes only for my pretty daughter.

Chapter Seven

A S LATE SPRING turned into early summer, Medraut and his friends slipped easily, too easily maybe, into the routine of the fortress. They trained with Arthur's men, hunted with Boden's hounds, and as far as I could tell without too much nosing, partook of such carnal pleasures as were available within the fortress walls or in the village at the foot of the hill. And Amhar was all the time in the thick of their activities, basking in being his cousin's new favorite, even above Prince Cinbelin.

I kept a wary eye on their activities, but the fortress was large, and it wasn't an easy task. They'd been accommodated in a couple of the long barracks houses in the northeastern corner, close to the training ground as were most of the other young warriors. The older ones, mainly married with wives and families to care for, had houses scattered all over the hilltop, with small gardens crammed between them where they grew vegetables and herbs and kept a pig or two.

Arthur seemed happy with the new recruits to his army, and was more often than not to be found down on the training ground sparring with them, or working with the young horses being schooled as remounts. A lot of work went into turning green colts into the efficient killing machines of war; as good, Arthur swore, as having an extra warrior on your side.

One afternoon, a few days after midsummer's day, he and I walked down the hill to the village to check the hay. The headman had come up the day before to let us know of its readiness for cutting, and Arthur wanted to see for himself.

I cherished these moments when he felt like mine alone. We sneaked away early, before any offers to accompany us could be made by Cei or Archfedd, or, perish the thought, the ever-present Medraut, who always seemed ready to poke his nose in where it wasn't wanted.

We left by the north gates, walking carefully down the stony track with the sun strong even this early in the morning. Due to its steep incline, this track was used far less than the main one. Nevertheless, we encountered a couple of sun-bronzed, bare-armed farmworkers using it as a shortcut up to the fortress, a man and a stripling boy.

They saw us coming and moved politely into the bushes growing at the side of the track to let us pass, tugging their forelocks in respect at Arthur and bobbing clumsy bows to me. "Milord. Milady." They carried scythes over their shoulders.

"Dingad, Rhun," Arthur, who knew all the villagers by name, said with a grin, eyeing the scythes. "What's taking you up the hill?"

Dingad, the elder, a man with a thick thatch of pepper and salt hair, tugged his generous forelock a second time. "Gotta get our scythes ready for the hay, Milord. Both o' these need a bit o' work. I did break the blade o' this un on a stone."

Rhun ran his hand along the rusty looking blade of the one he carried. "And mine ain't seen no work for a number o' years. She do need fettlin'. 'Tis my first year cuttin', Milord. An' I doan want to be told I ain't done it proper."

Arthur gave the boy a slap on the shoulder. "Then off you both go and get it done. I'll have mine out for a fettling when I get back from inspecting the crop."

Dingad and Rhun, grinning widely at their king's reaction, shouldered their scythes again and continued up the hill. If Arthur had reigned in my old world, newspapers would have said he had "the common touch."

I linked my arm through Arthur's as we approached the cluster of thatched village buildings and the little wattle and daub church. Men were hoeing the vegetable patches between the houses, and even this early, women had brought their looms out into the sun, their hands darting back and forth as they created cloth. I'd tried my hand at that at Conventina's suggestion, my skill at sewing being so poor, but alas, I'd discovered myself to be equally bad at weaving. She'd heaved a sigh of resignation, but I'd been glad – I had better things to do with my time.

"We'll walk down to the water meadows and see how the grass is coming along down there," Arthur said, returning the bow of the village baker, a red-faced, rotund man who looked far more jovial than he really was, and so fat he must regularly eat half his produce. By contrast, his skinny little wife, sitting outside their house nursing the newest addition to their family, had the look of someone who only got the crumbs.

The dusty track led us between the houses and out into the fields, where already the fat seedheads on the wheat and barley were taking on the faint blush of golden ripeness. Stone and earth banks topped with spiky hawthorn bushes protected the corn from agile and greedy sheep, and willow hurdles blocked the narrow gateways.

"We should get a good harvest this autumn," Arthur said, leaning over a wall to survey the crop. "With this much grain, we should be able to keep more livestock over the winter. And if the hay crop's as good…" He grinned, suddenly boyish. "I'll race you to the stream."

"You'll have to give me a head start," I said, too late. He was already off, loping along the narrow track toward where the willows marked the little river's course.

I bolted after him, helter-skelter, feet pounding, my thick braid bouncing on my back, all queenship stripped away with no one around to see me.

Arthur let me pass him. He hid it well, but I knew he had. Ahead, the line of willows drew closer, and I threw myself down onto the grassy riverbank under their drooping shade, gasping for breath but laughing. Somehow, I'd left behind my many worries inside the fortress gates.

He flopped down onto the grass beside me, panting hard.

I lay back, gazing up at the sky where it peeked between the swaying branches. I'd picked a spot with a knobbly root, of course. When did I ever not? But the feel and scent of the solid earthy ground, the brush of the gentle breeze on my hot cheeks, the music of the rippling stream and the call of small hedge birds lulled my thoughts.

Arthur leaned over me, blocking the light and my view of the cascading leaves, his face serious. "I could lie here beside you forever."

The idea that we could just up and run away and leave Dumnonia to Amhar erupted inside my heart and head. Yes. We could avoid Camlann by leaving, by running away and just being us, forever. The thought only lasted a moment. No. How wrong that would be to abandon our people. We weren't just anybody and couldn't please ourselves. We were a king and queen, and out there, on the hill and below it, and all across Dumnonia, were our people. We owed it to them to stay until the bitter end.

"What is it?" he asked. "Why the long face?"

I dredged up a smile and put my hand up to caress his cheek – freshly shaved that morning. "Nothing. Just someone walking over my grave." I rubbed my thumb across his skin and let my fingers slide into his hair. "I, too, wish we could lie here in peace forever."

He bent and his lips brushed mine in a featherlight kiss. "The world would never let us."

Much the same as I'd concluded for myself, but I wanted to hang onto this moment, to never let it go.

My fingers tightened in his hair. "Love me," I whispered. "Here, in the sun, away from the fortress. When there's just us. No one to drag you away from me. No demands on your time."

He kissed me again, more deeply this time. "I'm supposed to

be looking at the hay…"

I slid my hand up under his shirt, letting my fingers trail across his skin. "I don't care. Today is ours. Love me, Arthur."

He did.

Let it always be like this.

THE NEXT DAY the haymaking began. Arthur organized our men to take their scythes down the hill to work with the villagers. We'd been able to do this for a number of years, now, with the peace Arthur had brokered with the Saxons in the east still continuing, and every year we'd cut more hay than the one before. Along with more wheat and barley for bread and beer, this meant more animals could over-winter, which meant more youngstock in the spring, and more food for everyone. And of course, better fed, bigger horses.

Archfedd, who still slept with Maia in the little room beside ours that had been hers since childhood, came bouncing into our room first thing in the morning, eyes bright with excitement, to find Arthur already gone and me hurrying to dress. "Aren't you ready yet? Maia has made the picnic and Reaghan's already outside waiting with Seren." She waved a hand in the air. "And the sun's shining down on us like God's smiling on our work."

I fastened my ankle boots. Like Archfedd, I'd dressed in a simple short-sleeved tunic that only came halfway down my calves, and had girdled it with a plain leather belt – the same outfit as yesterday, which made me smile at the memory of what I'd got up to in it. No need to dress up for haymaking, even if you were a queen, and cool clothes were the order of the day.

I straightened and smiled. How pretty my daughter was. Arthur always said she took after me, but I'd quite forgotten what I looked like after so long without a decent mirror. I could see him clearly stamped in her, though – with her straight nose and loose-limbed walk, not to mention her dogged determination and outspokenness. Although perhaps he would have said they both came from me.

"I'm done," I said and stood up. "Let's be off then." I picked up the bread and cold bacon Maia must have left me, and followed her out through her bedroom into the sunshine. Maia and Reaghan were waiting with little Seren, the pony who'd served Llacheu and then both my children well. Now well into her twenties, her pretty dapples had long gone, and her snowy white coat was flecked with those little brown patches of hair that so closely resembled freckles but had to be called fleabites. Her back sagged a little with age, but all she'd be expected to carry in her two panniers today would be our food and drink.

"The men've already gone," Reaghan said, hopping from one foot to the other. "We'll be late if we don't get a move on." She patted one of the panniers. "Mother made us mutton pies for our midday meal." Coventina wouldn't be coming, as it was now too far for her to walk. Old age, which she stood with stoicism, seemed to be galloping up on her.

With Maia leading Seren, we took the road to the north gates and ambled down the steep track toward the village. The already hot sun beat down on our backs, making me wonder if we should have worn our straw hats. Before us, the plain stretched away toward the line of complicit willows that marked the stream, and beyond that to the distant hump of the Tor at Ynys Witrin. Shreds of mist still clung to that hill like drapes of chiffon, despite the heat of the morning.

The courses of such drainage ditches as the local farmers had cut stained the landscape with the bright green of their lush grass, and in between them, the small square fields of our farms crowded together, marking the higher ground. The pale green of the hayfields stood ready for our men's scythes; the nearest ones dotted with the tiny figures of men. And the fields of wheat, barley and oats rippled in the breeze like a gold-tinted green sea.

Other women from the fortress, some with their children on their hips or tagging behind, had joined us, heading to help their menfolk. The ant-like figures working in the hayfields grew larger. Soon we were walking along the narrow paths between the stone and earth walls, all bedecked with the blue of cornflowers, the red of campion and white of stitchwort, the aroma of the leafy wild garlic strong. These walls served only to keep out any wandering livestock rather than to delineate one man's field from another's.

The hay was already falling in fat swathes to the rhythmical swing of the men's scythes, and the music of voices joined in song rose toward the blue sky, where larks circled, joining their bubbling cries to the men's melody.

I never tired of the turn of the seasons in my chosen world. Despite the warfare and the battles, what really governed life was nature: the tilling of the soil in spring; the sowing of the seed; the haymaking with everyone lending a hand; early autumn's harvesting; the bounty of the hedgerows; the birth of calves and lambs; the birth of children. With everything bound together, the whole thing worked like some machine of many cogs, contributing to a life of harmony broken only by the threat of danger from outside.

Our warriors worked stripped to the waist alongside the farmers, their voices uplifted in the songs of the earth, backs bronzing in the sun, sweat beading on their foreheads. Good, honest toil, a million miles from riding into battle.

We women didn't have much to do this first day, but tomorrow we'd be forking over the rows of cut hay and fluffing them up so they could dry while the men cut more of it. If we didn't make the hay ourselves, no one else would. Unlike in my old world, we couldn't just go and buy it somewhere else. A single warhorse can eat a ton of hay over a winter, and we had a lot of horses.

We found Arthur and Merlin laboring in a field on the far side of the village with a dozen of our men, Llacheu and Cei amongst them. Having removed Seren's panniers, we tethered her where she could graze and sat down on the grass to watch our men at work, a not unpleasant chore. None of them carried any extra weight – the life they led didn't encourage that. Muscles rippled beneath sun-kissed skin, and although many of them were now over forty, they still moved with the ease of young men, accustomed to daily hard work.

We'd brought jars of cider, and after a while Arthur called a halt and the men all came to sit with us and the other wives. They smelled of sunshine and sweat and cut grass, a heady mix that always warmed my heart. The urge to lure Arthur back to the riverbank of yesterday was great.

The cider jar did the rounds. I'd spread a couple of thick blankets, and when he'd drunk his fill, Arthur flopped back onto mine, squinting up into the sky where a buzzard wheeled on a thermal. "I could be happy being a farmer," he mused. "The rhythm of the seasons, the providing for my family, the new life springing every year."

An echo of yesterday. Maybe he'd been thinking the same thing as me.

I lay down beside him, finding his hand. "A day like today makes me feel like that as well." I kept my voice low – the next remark just for him. "A day like yesterday."

For just an instant in time, again, we were ordinary people and not a king and his queen. The warmth drenched my body, and I let my eyes close, floating on an idea of just him and me and no worries ever again, just as I'd done the day before, wanting to capture that feeling and bottle it so I could take it out whenever I needed to relive it.

"A rider coming," Llacheu, who'd been leaning against the wall, called out.

Arthur sat bolt upright, and so did I, snatched from my reverie. A rider always meant news of some kind and not always good.

A hundred yards off, a man on a bay horse was threading his way between the fields, heading toward the road up to the fortress, his gaze fixed on the summit and ignoring what he must have taken for laboring peasants.

"Give him a shout," Arthur said, confident the message must be for him.

Cei, who had a voice worthy of a town crier, lumbered to his feet and heaved a breath in. "Hoy! Over here, messenger boy. The king's here, not up there."

Heads turned in every field and the rider swung his horse in our direction. Arthur and I got to our feet, and we all watched the rider's approach.

Six paces from us, he halted his horse and dismounted. It being summer, his cloak was rolled on the back of his saddle, and the young rider wore only a light tunic and braccae, but nevertheless, the heat had flushed his cheeks, and moisture beaded his downy upper lip. Sweat drenched his spent horse and foamed on its chest and neck. The warm smell of it carried on the breeze.

The messenger bowed to Arthur, showing admirable lack of surprise to be addressing a half-dressed farm laborer on the edge of a hayfield as his lord. "Milord King," he began as he rose from his bow. "I bring you news of the death of a fellow king."

Almost unnoticed, the men in the nearest fields had drawn closer out of a natural curiosity about what news the young man had brought. A murmur of comment now rippled through them, and they edged closer still. Work appeared to have stopped in every field. They must all, like me, have been wondering which king had died.

"Who?" Arthur asked.

Sitting cross-legged on our other blanket, Merlin, who'd been talking to Archfedd, stared at the messenger expectantly.

The young man straightened his back. "My liege lord, King March of Caer Dore in Cornubia, has breathed his last. I'm here to ask you, as the High King, to attend his funeral rites."

Old King March, who'd been white-haired but not bowed by age the first time I'd laid eyes on him nearly twenty years ago. The man who'd married Essylt of Linnuis, even though she'd been in love with his son, Drustans. For a moment I was back in Caer Lind Colun, capital of Linnuis, with Essylt sobbing to me that it was Drustans she loved and not his father whom she'd never met. But she'd been betrothed, and her father had dispatched her south to marry the old king, while I'd kept Drustans away from her. I'd longed to help, but my hands had been tied by Dark Age protocol.

Someone pushed their way to the front of the now sizeable crowd around us. Drustans himself. Now in his early thirties and still unmarried, his handsome face blazed with light, and his whole body quivered with unconcealed excitement. No sadness for a dead father in him. Instead, he must be thinking that at last Essylt could be his.

So why did I have such a bad feeling in my stomach?

Chapter Eight

THE DEATH OF a fellow king didn't always require Arthur's attendance at the funeral rites, but March had been a neighbor, and with his kingdom being out along the southwestern toe of Britain there'd likely be no other kings attending. Arthur declared it his duty to go.

With the summer heat, speed would be of the essence. The messenger was provided with a fresh horse and, after refreshment, packed off on his return journey to let Caer Dore know we would be hot on his heels.

Back at the fortress we prepared to leave, the haymaking forgotten.

"We won't need to take a large force with us," Arthur said as he sloshed cold water over his suntanned torso in our chamber. "Cei will come to pay his respects, as Lord of Din Tagel. And I'll take Merlin, too. Llacheu can remain in command here and organize the men I leave behind to continue with the haymaking. It's important we don't miss this window of good weather."

I pulled off my simple dress and joined him in his ablutions. "I'll come too. Essylt will need some feminine support."

He brushed wet hair out of his eyes. "Yes. As my queen, you'll need to come. We should both honor March with our presence."

While I finished washing, he began rummaging in his clothes chest and flinging clothes at his saddlebags where they lay on the bed. "Better take my crown."

Which meant I'd better take mine too. I hurriedly found the braccae and tunic I used for riding and wriggled into them, then joined Arthur in packing. My version was much tidier than his.

A knock rattled the door into the Hall.

"Enter," Arthur called, without looking up.

I'd expected it to be Merlin or Cei, but it wasn't. Drustans stood there, everything about him bright with expectation. My wary heart did a little flip of fear. There were things I knew about Drustans I'd never told anyone, not even Merlin, who knew about his and Essylt's short-lived love affair. Right now, the sense of dread wasn't far away as I stared into his excited eyes. The stern, humorless young man of recent years had vanished, and the romantic boy stood before me in his stead, almost quivering with longing.

Despite his excitement, he managed to remember to make a quick bow. "Milord. I shall accompany you to claim my throne," he declared, chin raised, almost in defiance. "I am a king, now."

So he was, but that thought didn't still my nagging fears. Back in my old world, my father had taken me, as a child, to see this young man's rocky tombstone, clearly marked even then with the carved inscription in ancient capitals – DRUSTANS HIC IACET CUNOMORI FILIUS. *Here lies Tristan, son of Cunomorus.* His father's nickname – hound of the sea. No mention of Drustans ever having been a king. Although what that meant, I had no idea. Probably nothing good.

Arthur stepped away from our bed, a matching light of excitement burning in his eyes. "You are indeed, my Lord of Caer Dore." He made a sweeping bow. "But I shall be sorry to lose you to your kingdom. You've served me well as a warrior and you'll be missed."

Drustans made a poor job at suppressing his grin. "And every moment has been an honor and a privilege. But now I must claim my throne and serve my own people. I only hope I can be as good a king as you, my Lord Arthur." Unspoken, but hanging in the air nevertheless, were the words "and claim my bride." Not that Arthur knew anything about their previous liaison. Knowing the punishment for adultery, I'd never breathed a word of what had gone on between those two lovesick teenagers. All Arthur knew was that Drustans had loved her purely from afar. Merlin's reaction when I told him what I'd caught them doing had been bad enough.

I pushed away my misgivings and fastened the straps on our saddlebags. Shouldering mine, I handed Arthur his. "Here. Let's be on our way."

Archfedd was already in the stables waiting beside her saddled horse.

"What're *you* doing here?" Arthur asked as he shouldered his way along his own horse's side to put her bridle on. "This isn't a social outing."

Archfedd shot me a look. "I know, but I'd like to come and pay my respects. Drustans has always been kind to me, and it *is* his father."

What was going on here? I'd never noticed him pay any attention to Archfedd, not even now she'd grown so pretty. He didn't have eyes for any of the girls, as far as I knew, even though many had thrown themselves at him. I'd long suspected he still carried his love for Essylt in his heart, which by the look on his face earlier, he did.

"You should stay," Arthur said, his voice sharp. "We have to ride fast and hard to get there in time. And there's no need for you to attend."

Archfedd shifted her weight, a frown furrowing her brow. "But I'd *like* to come." Her eyes slid sideways to meet mine, pleading, perhaps willing me to understand. I didn't, but the feeling this was important to her hit me.

"Let her come," I said to Arthur. "She isn't needed with the haymaking. We're leaving enough men to bring in a goodly amount." I paused, searching for a reason he'd accept. "She's a king's daughter and yet she's never been further than Ynys

Witrin. She deserves to see something of Britain."

Arthur was doing up the throatlash on his bridle. He peered over his horse's head at us. "You women," he muttered. "Ganging up on me again. All right, you can have your way, and she can come. But I don't want her being a nuisance."

Archfedd's shoulders rose in a sigh of... what? Relief? Why was it so important for her to come? Perhaps I was looking at it the wrong way around and the important thing was not to be left behind.

Not an hour after we'd returned from the hayfields, we were riding down the cobbled road from the southwest gates with forty warriors, leaving the ever-trustworthy Llacheu in command of the fortress in our absence. The journey to Caer Dore was something over a hundred miles, and whereas the messenger could have completed that in not much more than half a day, using the changes of horses we had stationed along the route, we would be taking longer. And in that time, with this heat, March's corpse would be getting steadily riper. No time to waste.

A horse walks at about four miles per hour, trots at six or seven, and canters at up to twelve, but can't do that top speed for hour after hour carrying the weight of an armed warrior. And armed we were, despite the comparative peace – only a fool would assume himself safe on the roads of Britain even now.

Three days would be needed to reach Caer Dore, most of it following the old Roman roads, but the last part over the rougher, countryside tracks of wild Cornubia. Plenty of time for me to wheedle out of Archfedd the reason for her request to come with us.

The summer weather held, a blessing in one way as we didn't get wet, but in another a problem as we sweated profusely in our heavy mail shirts. We camped in the open, under the stars, which Archfedd found a huge adventure, and set out early in the mornings with the dew still fresh on the grass.

On the last stage of our journey, as we rode across the high granite uplands of what would one day be known as Bodmin

Moor, I finally persuaded her to open up to me.

In the distance wild ponies and cattle grazed, with here and there a few sheep, small and brown rather than the fat white land-maggots of the twenty-first century. The chirruping song of a wheatear carried on the breeze, and overhead a merlin falcon called to his mate, his kek-kek-kek loud and insistent.

"It's so beautiful everywhere," Archfedd said, bending her head back so she could squint up into the powder-blue sky in an effort to spot the falcon. "Look. That's like the bird Merlin has on his shield."

"That's because it is," I said. "I imagine that's why he chose it as his sigil."

"Clever of him," she said. "Could I have a sigil, do you think?" She tapped her plain white shield where it hung from one of her saddle horns, something she knew well how to use. "You've got your dragon ring on your shield, and I'd like to have something on mine."

I smiled. "When you marry you could have the sigil of your husband." If he was clearsighted enough to allow her the freedom to carry arms.

She frowned. "What if I don't want to marry?"

Ah. At her age many girls were already mothers, but I'd not wanted that for her, and Arthur didn't seem to have noticed she'd got so grownup. Or maybe he, too, didn't want to lose her to some distant king or prince's court.

"Well," I said, trying to sound decisive. "Then a sigil for you is something we need to ask your father about. But maybe have some ideas ready of what you'd like on your shield when you ask him." I chuckled. "Or he'll have a suggestion of his own that you won't like."

She chuckled back. "I'd like a dove. A white dove. I was talking with Llawfrodedd about it, and he said whenever he sees one, it reminds him of me."

I smiled to myself. He was the one who'd taught her to fight, and with whom she still practiced, and in return she'd taught him to read and to speak properly. From the scrawny boy who'd come to us asking to become a warrior, he'd turned into the sort of young man I could trust with my daughter.

We rode on, disturbing a herd of deer, who bounded away across the heather, white rumps bouncing like small targets.

"Why was it you didn't want to stay behind at Din Cadan?" I asked, after a while.

She glanced sideways at me out of wary eyes.

I was right – something lay behind this.

"You can tell me," I said, pushing Enfys closer so I could lower my voice. "We don't need to tell your father if it's something private."

She looked me in the eyes, her own narrowed and speculative. Maybe she was weighing up what to say. "I didn't want to stay there without you."

I blinked in surprise. "Why not? You've done that before. And you would've had Maia to keep you company at nights and Coventina and Reaghan during the day."

She gave a little sigh. "I know all that. But I didn't want to stay where Medraut was. Is." She bit her lip. "I don't like him."

"Oh." As I didn't either, this came as no surprise. "But you'd hardly have seen him. Would it really have mattered?"

She regarded me from troubled eyes.

I waited, my breath catching in my throat with the suspicion that there was more to this than met the eye. "Why don't you like him?"

She shrugged her slender shoulders. "I can't rightly say. He's polite to me, pleasant, offers to help if I'm carrying something, keeps asking if I'd like to ride out with him. But there's something about him that... frightens me. Something under his skin, deep in his heart, inside his head. Something nasty."

Her grandmother and aunt had the Sight, as did Merlin. Did she? Or was this merely women's intuition?

"Easy to avoid him, though," I said, trying to keep my voice light, but knowing in my heart that in a place the size of Din

Cadan, this wasn't true.

She shook her head. "That's just it. It's not. It's like he's waiting for me around every corner, dropping into step beside me, trying to make me talk to him." She shuddered. "And when he looks at me it feels as though he sees me naked."

Just as he'd done to me in Viroconium. I struggled to suppress the shiver that threatened to rack me, berating myself for not having noticed his attentions or her discomfort, recalling the way he'd looked at her on his arrival. Did he pose a threat she'd instinctively recognized when I hadn't? Was that why she'd been so anxious to come with us?

"Do you want me to speak to your father about this? Get him to tell Medraut to keep away from you?"

Indecision filled her eyes. "No. I don't think so. He hasn't *done* anything to me. He's never once tried to even touch my hand. I don't think the way he looks at me is enough for me to ask father to be angry with him." She paused. "Others of the warriors do that to me as well… sometimes. And I know they do it to other girls." She gave a little mirthless laugh. "I suppose it's something most young men do. But it doesn't mean we girls like it."

Like men the world over in any era. Women, especially pretty ones, were to be ogled, lusted after, competed for. Disgust rose in me. I'd experienced it myself enough times and laughed it off, but now it had happened to my fifteen-year-old daughter, all I felt was horrified shock.

Oh, how she was growing up. Perhaps she did need to be married and settled, with a protective husband and a child on the way that would deter the attentions of other suitors. But she could never avoid the attention her looks would bring.

"Is there any young man you really like?" I asked, having severe difficulty keeping my voice level.

A blush colored her cheeks, making her prettier than ever. "Maybe."

I smiled. "Can you tell me his name?"

More blushing. Her hands came up to cover her face, letting her reins hang loose, hooked over one of the horns on her saddle. "Llawfrodedd," she muttered, peeking at me between her fingers.

Aha. A romance that had been simmering since childhood. Even though he had a good six years on Archfedd, she'd begun a friendship with him that had endured into adulthood. Should I be surprised she'd come to admire him in a different way now?

She lowered her hands, her cheeks rosy.

I smiled and reached out to take her hand in mine. "And a fine young man he is for you to have chosen. Does he feel the same way about you?"

She picked up the buckle end of her reins again in her free hand. "I don't know. I haven't… we haven't spoken of it." She licked her lips. "I *think* we're just friends still. I don't know how to tell him I have… feelings… for him."

I squeezed her hand and released it so she could gather in her looping reins. "Don't rush things. He'll realize you feel like that if you give him time. And I'll wager he feels the same about you."

She gave me a sideways peek. "Don't tell Father, will you?"

"I won't if you don't want me to," I said, my eyes on Arthur's back where he rode ahead of us, chatting to Merlin and Cei. And most likely I wouldn't tell him about Medraut, either, as she'd given me nothing concrete to say. Boys and young men tend to follow girls around, and what had Medraut done that any other young warrior wouldn't have? Nothing. All we had to go on were our feelings.

Chapter Nine

THE FORTRESS OF Caer Dore sat on a high ridge of land overlooking the valley of the River Fowi. Much less impressive than Din Cadan, its two deep ditches and earth ramparts enclosed barely an acre. However, an impressive stone-faced defensive wall, revetted with huge timbers, topped the inner bank. Outside, a sprawling agricultural settlement meandered downhill toward the distant sea, and fields stretched east into the river valley and west toward the inlet of a hidden bay.

We'd crossed the river a good way upstream and arrived at the fortress by a ridgeway track from the north, the spread of what would one day be Cornwall laid out before us. Evening was fast drawing on, and out in the fields the hay lay forked up to dry, the sweet smell carrying on the still air. Just as at home. With Britain's uncertain climate, the chance of a week without rain to get the hay dried and safely stacked was never to be missed, not even for a dead king.

Drustans hustled his horse to the front of our column of warriors, edging her in between Arthur and me, his face flushed with eagerness and excitement. I didn't need Merlin's Sight to guess he must be thinking of Essylt, and cold fingers of unease tightened around my heart.

"How does it feel to be coming home at last?" I asked, pushing away those thoughts.

He beamed. No love lost here for a father who'd married the

girl he loved, even though it had been unknowingly done. "It's the only thing I've ever wanted," he said, the happiness in his voice palpable. "I've longed for this day for nearly twenty years. Well, for nineteen, I suppose. I never thought it would finally arrive." He leaned closer and lowered his voice. "And I know in my heart she's been waiting for me just as I've waited for her."

He'd claimed the kingship to Arthur, but did it perhaps mean little to him? Was Essylt the thing he wanted from this? I could read the hunger for her in his every lovesick word and from the almost manic expression on his face. A shiver ran down my spine. The nineteen years his beloved had been married to his aged father were sure to stretch like a chasm between them – nineteen years in which the pretty, excitable girl he remembered could have changed immeasurably. Did he expect her to be the same girl who'd taken him to her bed with such passionate abandon in her father's palace at Caer Lind Colun?

We passed between the village's clustered buildings, what road there was twisting and turning around pigpens, barns and newly thatched hayricks sitting on their thick mat of insulating bracken. Chickens scuttled, squawking, out of our way, and from his position on the ridge of one of the thatched roofs, a lone cockerel crowed.

Most of the people would be inside their houses by now, after a long day in the fields. Here and there a curious face appeared in a doorway, watching us in suspicion as we rode by, but showing no fear. They must have known we'd come for the funeral.

On the far side of the village, the outer fortifications of Caer Dore rose up high and grassy. We passed through the narrow gap in the banks and a set of substantial towers came into view, sheltering inside the outer embankment, the gates themselves standing wide open.

The two guards on duty stamped the butts of their spears on the bare ground with a thud. Probably, they wouldn't recognize Drustans as their returning king. After all, he'd left as a boy nearly twenty years ago and now was returning as one of the High

King's mightiest warriors.

He gazed around, eyes wide with wonder, and once again it struck me how returning home had slid the years from him and remade him as the innocent boy I'd first met. Perhaps Caer Dore seemed smaller to him than before, something that so often happens on return to a childhood home.

The inner ramparts enclosed only the royal buildings: a hall, small by Din Cadan's standards, separate kitchens, storage barns, stables and a few barracks houses for the king's warriors, all clustered tightly around the central cobbled courtyard into which we rode.

So, this was where protocol had forced me to let old King Manogan send his daughter. This was the home in which poor, beautiful, lively Essylt had spent more than half her life, married to a cantankerous old man. I felt an overwhelming surge of gladness for everything I had at Din Cadan. How hard must it have been to come here after being brought up at the enormous court in Caer Lind Colun, and to swap her handsome, virile young lover for an old man.

We halted our horses in front of the hall, which had a thatched porch halfway down one side to shelter the single, closed door. Arthur swung down from the saddle and the rest of us followed suit. For a moment we stood in silence, the awkward feeling of having intruded where we were not wanted, strong. Then the door of the hall opened, and a woman stepped out.

Essylt had left the softness of girlhood far behind. Gone was the slender, sweet-faced girl who'd helped herself to my breakfast the first time I met her. In her place stood a mature woman with a face hardened by time and circumstance, and a waist thickened by childbearing. She wore a plain, dark brown gown that did nothing to enhance her pale skin and lovely auburn hair, which she'd scraped back from her face and fixed in a single tight braid that hung to below her waist.

From the shadows behind her stepped a young man.

I couldn't help but stare.

Superficially, he resembled Drustans as a boy, being tall and slender, with a mass of dark chestnut curls about his solemn face, but Essylt's genes were in there too, and those of his father, March, showed in his hooked nose. For this had to be his and Essylt's son.

Arthur stepped up to Essylt and held out his hands. "My Lady the Queen. We're here to witness the laying to rest of your husband, as requested."

She looked up at him out of cold, blank eyes devoid of all emotion. Then, after a moment's hesitation, she took his hands. "My Lord the High King. I am honored. As is my son." Yes, this was the voice of the Essylt I remembered. She glanced at the young man beside her. "Seleu, step forward and present yourself." Gone was the irrepressible joy, the laughter, and the childlike innocence. Had March knocked all that out of her? Nineteen years must have felt like a life sentence.

The young man took a step forward. "My Lord." He made a deep bow to Arthur, who returned a slightly lesser one.

Essylt's gaze moved to take me in, but no sign of recognition touched her cold eyes. "My Lady the Queen. You are most welcome." Had she perhaps never forgotten the part I'd played in keeping her lover from her in the days before her father had dispatched her south to wed her betrothed? Until now, it hadn't occurred to me that she might feel resentment.

From behind me came the sound of someone catching their breath. I glanced over my shoulder. Drustans, who'd hung back as we approached his old home, now stood half-hidden behind Cei and Merlin, one hand covering his mouth, as though he couldn't believe his eyes. Wise of him to hang back and not crowd her. She was a queen in mourning, after all, and surely no declaration of undying love would be welcome.

For a moment, Essylt's gaze fixed on Drustans' face, but she gave nothing away. Then it returned to her son, and her face softened. "This is my oldest son, Seleu." She touched the boy's shoulder with a hint of pride. "My husband's *heir*." The last word came out like a challenge, but perhaps I was the only one who saw her eyes dart back to Drustans for the tiniest moment.

I twisted to look at him. His face had blanched, and his chest heaved as though he fought for breath, but he didn't move. His hand had dropped from his mouth and now both fists had clenched. Had his father bypassed him and named his half-brother king? Could you even do that? But this was the Dark Ages, so most likely yes. Drustans hadn't seen his father anywhere but at the Council of Kings in nineteen years. He wouldn't have been at the forefront of the old man's mind when he lay dying. No wonder the old man had chosen the son, already old enough to rule, of his young second wife.

Arthur was doing a good job at not looking shocked. Showing admirable equanimity, he clasped forearms with the new young king, who must have been barely seventeen, as though nothing had just happened, and he didn't have the man who'd thought the throne was his standing behind him with the horses. "My congratulations to you, King Seleu," he said. "And my sympathy for the death of your father."

"You are most welcome here, my lord," the boy said, his voice deep and pleasant, reminding me even more of Drustans at the same age. A lump rose in my throat for what had been lost here. If only this boy were the child of Essylt and Drustans, here to honor the man who should have been his grandfather, not his father.

Essylt touched her son's arm. "Our guests will need to prepare themselves for our evening meal. I have had rooms readied." She snapped her fingers.

From nowhere, servants arrived to take our horses, and others to escort us to what I'd taken to be nothing but simple barracks houses. Instead, the first one at least turned out to be reasonable guest accommodation. I tried to see where Drustans went but failed, as Arthur and I were shepherded to the best room Caer Dore had to offer.

As soon as the servant had gone and we were alone, I turned

to Arthur. "He's made that boy his heir?" My words came out with more than usual vehemence. "Instead of Drustans. Can he even do that?"

Arthur threw his saddlebags on the large, fur-covered bed. "It's within his rights to have done so."

I added my saddlebags to his. "Drustans thought he was to be king. You know he did. Is it right his father should have chosen a stripling *boy* to rule instead of a man grown?" My indignation for the slight given to our warrior kept on rising. "Is it even wise? What experience can a boy like that have?"

Arthur shrugged. "Don't forget. Drustans hasn't been home to remind his father of his existence in nearly twenty years. At every Council of Kings, he's steered well clear of him. Can you blame March for preferring the boy he's seen every day of his life? The boy who was there at his deathbed." He gave me a wry smile. "The boy he's seen grow to be a man."

I sat down with a thump. "And Essylt. She's not the same girl I remember." I couldn't keep the disappointment out of my voice.

He nodded, sitting beside me. "The years will do that. People don't remain the same, no matter how much you want them to. No one is unchanged by the life they lead." He shook his head. "And don't forget who she's been married to. A man famous for having not a speck of joy in him."

True.

I swallowed. "Do you think she'll remember Drustans? He thinks she will, I'm certain. It's like he's been living for the moment when he could become king and come and claim her."

He frowned. "I took the opportunity to speak with him on our journey. He's lost none of his impetuosity. I warned him that before he speaks to her, we need to get the funeral done, and reminded him that she's a queen in mourning for her husband. I hope he's possessed of enough common sense to follow my advice."

I pursed my lips. "When has he ever taken anyone's advice?"

That made him laugh. "In that, he's just like you. When was

the last time you even *asked* for my advice?"

I gave him a playful punch on the shoulder. "Nonsense. I do so all the time."

THE FUNERAL WAS to take place the next day. They'd waited long enough in the summer heat and an ever-increasing aroma of decay hung about the storage barn where the king had been laid in state, generously wafting its way across the fortress. Apparently Essylt had refused point blank to have his body laid out in her chamber. Not that I blamed her. Wise move.

We ate that night in the hall. The small top table was taken by Essylt, with her son on her right, then Arthur beside him, then me, accompanied by Archfedd, on the end. Our warriors ate with the Caer Dore warriors at the two long trestle tables set to either side of the smoldering hearth fire. Drustans did not appear.

Surely Essylt had expected him to accompany us and I hadn't been wrong when I'd thought she recognized him outside. But maybe she didn't feel the way she had as a girl. Maybe their few days together were just a forgotten incident in her life, filed away as over and done with.

But she'd picked him out amongst our men. Surely that meant something. A part of me longed for their story to have a happy ending, even though I feared it wouldn't.

She made no mention of him at dinner. Not that I got any chance to speak to her as the two kings took up the center of the table and we queens were consigned to either end. But out of curiosity, I watched her as closely as I could.

I did manage to eavesdrop on Arthur's conversation with Seleu though.

"I'll be doing the funeral oration," that young man informed Arthur. "As my father's heir, it's my place to do that." He had a slight pomposity about him that in one so young was amusing.

Did he *know* his older half-brother had accompanied us? Had he seen him in the crowd when his mother had? I did catch him scanning the faces in the hall from time to time – perhaps searching for a face that might seem familiar.

Arthur was silent a moment, as though considering this statement. "Where are you burying him?" he asked at last, steering clear of asking the boy why the oldest son wasn't performing this important task.

"Nowhere," Seleu said. "We have a funeral pyre prepared beyond the village. This was what he wanted. It's the way his own father was sent on to the next world. My mother has agreed we should fulfill his wishes."

Arthur nodded. "Best to do that." A certain superstition clung on that if you didn't carry out the wishes of the dead to the letter, they'd be back to haunt you with their protests. He took a swig of his wine. "You have brothers and sisters, I gather."

The young man nodded. "I do. Two brothers and a sister. My brothers are young now but will one day be amongst my warriors, and my sister will be in need of a husband shortly. She is fourteen and ready for marriage."

At fourteen? Not in my opinion she wasn't, but there'd be nothing I could do about this. Girls married at that age every day, and this poor princess would be the same if her pompous older brother had his way. I wasn't sure I liked young Seleu.

He drew in his bottom lip, his gaze moving past me to Arch-fedd, sitting quietly on the end of the high table sipping her wine. "And I myself will have need of a wife," he said, with deliberate emphasis. "Your daughter has caught my eye."

Bloody cheek. Pompous wasn't a good enough adjective for him. *Jumped up, arrogant, self-important little shit.*

Arthur, who'd imbibed more than his fair share of the not-so-good wine, laughed. "And she'll be needing a husband soon."

My eyes widened in shock.

If Arthur hadn't drunk so much, it might have occurred to him to consider what Caer Dore had done to Essylt and decide he didn't want it to happen to Archfedd. But instead, he clapped Seleu on the back and said, "Sensible young man."

Over my dead body would she end up living here.

Chapter Ten

AT LEAST THE funeral itself went to plan. The next morning, six sturdy warriors, with their noses blocked with twists of rag, and posies of lavender around their necks, carried the bier on which King March lay in all his stinky glory to the pyre that had been prepared for him. The rest of the funeral procession followed at a discreet distance, and took up positions upwind of the corpse.

All our forty warriors attended, as well as Essylt's men, and a crowd of local inhabitants who wisely hung back out of sniffing range. Nowhere did I spot Drustans.

After prayers from the local priest, and a speech as pompous as I'd expected from young Seleu, he lit the brushwood at the base of the pyre with a ceremonial torch. Then we all stood well back while March crisped and sizzled on his way to meet his maker.

With flames leaping and thick black smoke billowing upward, our solemn procession, led by Seleu and Arthur, headed back toward the fortress under the hot midsummer sky. A feast in celebration of the passing of the old king had been prepared in the great hall, and the new young king was to be crowned without any further ado.

As High King, it fell to Arthur to officiate over Seleu's coronation and declare him king. And this was to be done before the feast could even begin. The smell of roasting meat – a little too similar to the stench from the funeral pyre for my liking – met us at the doors as we all processed inside the torchlit hall. Once again, Arthur, Archfedd and I were to sit at the high table, but before the funeral feast could begin, the throne had been carried forward to stand on its own where all could see.

Drustans had once told me the story of the throne of Caer Dore. Many years ago, the bole of an enormous tree trunk had washed up on a nearby beach during a storm, a gift from the sea god, the people believed. Wherever it had come from, a craftsman had carved it into a throne, cleverly incorporating each knot and curve into its shape, and a clear memory of its origins clung to it.

Every king of Caer Dore had been crowned on it, stretching back long before living memory to a time even before the arrival of the legions, who'd never really had a hold on this part of Cornubia. Drustans had confided how he liked to sit in it as a small child, when his father had his back turned, and pretend he was king.

When he'd recounted this story, a lump had formed in my throat, and now, looking at that throne, it formed again. I couldn't get the picture out of my head of Drustans' tall memorial stone, shifted from its original position to stand beside the road into Fowey. When I'd stood beside it myself, long ago in a world almost forgotten, I'd wondered at the only thing remaining to mark a long-dead young man's life, never imagining he would one day be my friend. Had been my friend. Who knew which tense to use?

Essylt positioned herself to one side of the throne, her two younger sons, boys of less than ten, and her daughter, a girl as pretty as she'd once been, huddled a few steps behind her with a maid. Arthur took his place on the other side, gripping the gold circlet crown of Caer Dore in his hands. Archfedd and I stood side-by-side a few feet away. Ringside seats.

If only we'd known.

Seleu had paused at the doors to allow us to arrange ourselves, and now he walked in stately splendor up the aisle between the pushed-back tables and close-packed ranks of his watching people, past the fire and the roasting carcass of a young ox and up to the throne. He held his head high, a look of regal nobility on his young face, a small smile curving his lips. No, he wasn't as like Drustans as I'd thought. Something adhered to him that I didn't like. Some ruthlessness. Something of his dead father, perhaps. He'd probably make a better king than his brother, though, just for its possession.

He stopped in front of the throne, and for a moment his speculative gaze took in Archfedd before he looked forward again.

I took her hand as color rose to her cheeks and a slight frown furrowed her brow. Perhaps she had some inkling of his interest in her, although there'd been no time for Arthur to talk to her about him. I gave her hand a comforting squeeze.

Seleu's gaze left her, and he swung around to face the crowd who'd jammed themselves inside his hall. Their muttering died to nothing as their attention fixed on him, their new young king. Tall, handsome, full of youthful vigor and a stark change from the wizened old man they'd just immolated.

Seleu paused again, taking the sea of faces in with a sweeping stare, before lowering himself onto the throne and setting his hands on the arms, gripping the knobbly wood. Everything about him seemed to glow with nobility, from his shoulder-length chestnut curls to a face that could have been carved from marble in Renaissance Italy. On the fingers of his left hand, gold rings glinted, and around his neck hung the heavy links of a gold chain. His father's, no doubt.

Arthur took a step forward with the crown held up before him.

And at the same time, Drustans shouldered his way out of the crowd into the center of the aisle to stand with his feet planted squarely in the rushes and his hands bunched in fists by his sides.

"Stop," he ordered, his voice cutting through the silence.

For a moment nothing happened, then the crowd erupted with angry shouts, but as they were partly made up of our own men, not all the shouts were in protest about the interruption. Drustans held a popular place with his fellows.

He didn't move, and neither did Seleu, whose face had darkened, probably in both anger and surprise.

Arthur swung his right arm out toward me, and I had to grab the crown to prevent it dropping to the floor. He stepped in front of the throne, holding his arms up for silence. It took a while, but eventually he had it. Behind him Seleu sat in stony silence, his cold gaze fixed on Drustans.

Our men had shoved their way to the front of the crowd on either side of Drustans. Faces grim, they held back the people of Caer Dore who'd come to see their new king crowned, and who, by the angry looks on their faces, felt affronted at this interruption. A protection probably required. How many of these people even knew who Drustans was?

Arthur lowered his arms and nodded to Drustans. "Say your piece."

A hiss of discord resonated around the hall from the largely Cornubian crowd.

Drustans looked past Arthur at Essylt. "Do you not know me?" His voice held pleading, desperation even, and anguish.

Her cold gaze met his as Archfedd's hand tightened on mine. "What's going on?" my daughter whispered.

I shook my head and put a finger to my lips.

Essylt, elegant in a dove-gray gown girdled with a dark belt, her light cloak still about her shoulders, took a small step forward to stand beside Seleu, squaring her jaw as though to meet a fight. "Drustans. Of course I know you."

This time the hiss was one of recognition as the older people present finally realized their lost prince had returned. But after nineteen years, did those who remembered him still care for him?

Drustans' Adam's apple bobbed. How hard this must be for him. "I am come for you, Essylt," he said, his voice deepening as he gained confidence. "I am come to claim my throne... and my bride."

Essylt's eyes widened, and her right hand shot out to clutch her son's shoulder, her fingers digging into his flesh, perhaps to force him to stay seated. He'd turned to look up at her, and I couldn't quite see his expression from where I stood. No king, young and uncrowned or not, would accept another's attempt to claim their throne.

"I am *not* your bride," Essylt said, enunciating every word clearly. "And this is not *your throne.*"

Drustans didn't take his eyes from her, the pain written across his face for all to see in letters a mile high. He shifted his weight, clearly nonplused by her reaction, and the crowd pressed in against our restraining warriors as though they'd like to take a hand in this. He cleared his throat. "I am my father's oldest son. This is *my* kingdom..." He paused, swallowed, and tried again, his voice cracking. "And *you* are the woman I have loved since boyhood."

I glanced at Arthur, but he remained silent. Not his place to interfere, not even as High King.

"You presume too much," Essylt said, her tone emotionless. "Caer Dore is not yours to come back to after so long away. You cannot claim it as though it were your right." But tension quivered through her body, and the hand not holding her angry son in place had fisted by her side.

Her own warriors and the ordinary village folk hung on her every word, the tension zinging around the hall rafters. She was their queen, wife of their dead king. And this? Could this man be the boy some of them remembered? And why was he trying to claim her as his wife? A muttering arose. I didn't need to possess Merlin's Sight to read the thoughts passing through their minds as they stared in angry confusion from Drustans to Essylt and back again.

Even our own men knew nothing of Drustans' illicit liaison with his father's betrothed.

Drustans took a step closer, his hand on the hilt of his sword, emotions flashing across his handsome face: disappointment, puzzlement, shock. "As king, I shall make this boy of yours my heir," he said, seizing perhaps upon the only thing he could offer. Did he feel hatred for Seleu as the son Essylt had given his father – perhaps been forced to give? When she'd left Caer Lind Colun, perhaps he'd hoped she was with child, and that the son she'd give his father would really have been his. She hadn't been.

Seleu at last shook his mother's hand from his shoulder and rose to his feet, stepping to stand beside Arthur and face his brother. He looked him up and down out of eyes as cold and calculating as his father's. "Who is this man?" He glanced at Arthur. "Someone tell me."

Pulling Archfedd with me, I edged forward in order to see better. She came willingly, her mouth still hanging open in shock.

Drustans' hand tightened on the hilt of his sword, the knuckles whitening. He stared his brother in the eye. "Has no one told you? Did my father *never* mention me?" His voice filled with scarce concealed hurt. "Did *your mother* never tell you who I was and what I meant to her?"

Like she would have done with March around.

Seleu's gaze slid to his mother's face for a moment, incomprehension in his eyes. "Who *is* he, Mother? How does he claim to be my father's son?"

Understandable that Essylt had never mentioned Drustans once she'd arrived here. She must have had to shut away that part of her life and never think of it again, or her life with March would have been intolerable. Perhaps it had been intolerable anyway. Perhaps she'd hated him. But remembering her lusty young lover and what she'd lost would not have made her life any easier.

But why had March himself never told his younger son about Drustans? Maybe he'd been so angry at his oldest son joining Arthur's army that he'd written him out of his life. A proud, autocratic and bad-tempered old man, an old man with a new wife and new sons. No wonder he'd forgotten his firstborn when the time came to choose a successor. The boy who'd never left him, of course.

Essylt licked her lips, her eyes hostile still. "Before your father married me, he had another wife, and by her he had another son." She paused, never taking her eyes from Drustans' face. "This man is that son."

Seleu's eyes narrowed as he glared at Drustans with no shred of brotherly love. "And he is back now, this *prodigal*, thinking to steal what my father meant for me?" His hand also went to the hilt of his sword. "Interrupting my rightful coronation."

Damn it. Why were they all fully armed at a funeral?

"The coronation you have stolen from me," Drustans snapped, eyes dark with fury.

Seleu already had his sword half out of its sheath as Essylt caught his arm above the elbow. "No," she hissed, loud in the laden silence of the hall. "*You* are the king, and this would-be usurper will not succeed. He's not wanted here."

Drustans staggered back a step as though she'd slapped him. "Essylt." His voice cracked again. "I'm here because of our *love*. I'm here to make you mine, that we may rule together... *be* together. As I've yearned for throughout these long years." His hand went to his head. "As I've dreamed of every day since we parted."

Essylt's eyes flashed with anger, her calm exterior falling away. "I am *no* man's," she spat. "*You* let my father send me away from Caer Lind Colun to be the bride of an old man you *knew* was hard and cold. And you did *nothing*. You left me here for nigh on *twenty years*. You knew what he was, and yet you lived your life and left me here – with *him*."

Seleu's eyes widened at his mother's words.

Drustans took a step closer. "I could do nothing else," he pleaded. "You were betrothed to my father when we parted in your father's palace. What would you have had me do? Seize you and run away? Where to and to what life? You would have been unhappy as a poor man's wife."

Her knuckles whitened where she had hold of her son's arm. "And you think I was happy here? Married to... that *monster*."

Archfedd stared at me wide-eyed with shock. Her sheltered upbringing had done nothing to prepare her for this first foray into the society of another kingdom. Essylt's other three children had shrunk back into the shadows, also wide-eyed, their maid's mouth hanging open.

That Seleu had made no move to contradict his mother seemed significant. Whatever kind of a monster March had been, I'd have laid odds on his children having experienced it for themselves.

Drustans held out his hands to Essylt, palms uppermost in supplication. "I'm here now, aren't I? I've come to claim you, Essylt. To make you mine. Just as we always wanted."

"Not *my* always," she retorted, spit bubbling at the corner of her mouth and making her look mad. Maybe she was. "I've had enough of being used like a chattel. I'll *never* belong to any man again." She spat on the floor between them. "You come here thinking you can pick up where you left off, that I'll still be the little Essylt you remember. Fool. Fool of a boy, because that's *all* you are." She released her son's arm and his sword slid back into its sheath.

Phew.

Arthur took a step away from them, his eyes alert and wary, closer to me and Archfedd, maybe thinking we might need protecting.

Drustans reached for Essylt. "This is *my* kingdom, Essylt. And you are my one true love. I refuse to walk away from either."

Seleu, face contorted with anger, stepped between Drustans and his mother. "You are wrong. This is *my* kingdom you are in, given to me by my father as he lay dying. I am king here and my word is law." He paused. "My mother has spoken. She does not want you. No man will take my father's place. And today is my coronation as king of Caer Dore."

Drustans reached for Essylt again, but she shied away from him. He groaned. "No. Whatever he's done to you, my love, I will undo. I love you, Essylt. I've carried my love for you through all these years." He slapped his hand against his chest. "Here in my heart. You will remember. You *will*."

Seleu shoved Drustans, his hand on his shoulder. "She will not. She cannot. She doesn't want you. Leave my mother alone."

Arthur shot a glance at where Cei and Merlin stood in the body of the hall and jerked his head. Drustans needed removing so this coronation could continue.

He was too late. We all were.

"Get out of my way," Drustans grunted, shoving Seleu hard in retaliation. "She will remember. I know she will."

A collective gasp rose from the audience. Touching a king in aggression was strictly forbidden.

The younger man staggered against his mother who, uttering a little cry, almost fell.

Drustans, trying to push past his half brother, reached for her a third time, and she cried out in alarm. Voices rose in the body of the hall. Angry voices. The people surged against the barrier our warriors had made, straining to do what, I had no idea.

Seleu's hand went to his sword again, but Drustans was quicker. His blade flashed with reflected torchlight as it arced through the air towards Seleu. Merlin and Cei dashed forward at the same time as Arthur.

But Essylt was quicker than all of them. Whatever it was that Drustans intended, she stopped it, a she-wolf defending her cub. Her dagger took her one-time lover in the chest, sliding up to the hilt between his ribs with the power of her blow.

The sword dropped from Drustans' suddenly slack fingers to clatter on the flagstones, and his eyes flew wide in a look of utter shock. His hands scrabbled for a moment at the hilt of the dagger, his imploring eyes gazing into Essylt's, inches from his face, as seconds stretched to an eternity.

Silence fell, as though a collective breath were being held, only the sound of forty swords sliding out of their scabbards breaking it.

Cei and Merlin caught Drustans as he fell backwards, his eyes rolling up into his head, and lowered him to the ground. Dropping to his knees, Cei cradled Drustans' head and shoulders in his lap.

Our men held the crowd of Cornubian warriors and villagers back at sword point.

Archfedd's hand gripped mine and her free hand went to her mouth, but her startled cry remained just an indrawn breath.

Essylt stood transfixed, staring at the smears of blood on her hand, then down at the man lying on the rush-covered flagstones of her hall with her dagger in his chest. "I-I've killed you." Her words came out as a whisper. "Oh God, I've killed you." Her horrified eyes fixed on Drustans' white face.

She fell to the floor beside him. "I didn't mean to." One hand went to her heart. "I thought you were going to hurt my son." Her breath caught. "I didn't mean to."

A little blood seeped out to darken Drustans' fine green tunic, but the dagger was forming a plug. If we were to pull it out, he'd bleed out in a bare minute. His freshly shaven face had gone parchment pale, and his lips were turning blue.

I let go of Archfedd's hand and joined Essylt in the rushes beside him, catching his hand in mine. "Drustans," I called. "Stay with us." A feeble request. This was a dying man before me. Nothing could save him now.

Essylt took his other hand and held it tight, despair emanating from her in waves. "My love." Tears ran down her cheeks. "My own true love. What have I done? What have I done?"

A bit late to discover she really loved him after all.

Drustans coughed, and blood trickled from the corner of his mouth. His eyes focused on her face. "Essylt, my love." He had no strength, and the words were like a faint breath of wind.

"I didn't mean to," she moaned again in some sort of mantra. "I didn't mean to. I thought you were going to hurt my boy. I had to protect him." Her voice broke. "He's my son."

Seleu loomed over her, angry and righteous. "He *was* going to, Mother. He wanted to kill me. You did the right thing."

Her other children still huddled in the shadows with their nursemaid. Out of the corner of my eye, I spotted Archfedd going to them, ushering them away from the tragic scene unfolding here. Sensible girl.

Drustans licked his lips. "Essylt," he whispered. "I would that he could have been *our* son." He paused, fighting for breath. "I wish our lives could have been different... I wish I'd taken you and run... Even if we'd had to live as poor farmers..." His eyes closed as he struggled to get the words out. His hand clutched hers, and as his eyes opened, I saw the desperation in them. "Tell me you still love me. Let me die with that knowledge in my heart."

With a sob, she bent forward and kissed him on his bloody lips. "I love you, my heart. I have loved you since the day we met, and I will *always* love you. I didn't dare to dream that one day we might be together again. But we shall be. I promise."

His eyes closed. His breath rattled out of his chest. His head slipped sideways, limp and lifeless.

No one moved. I released my hold on Drustans' limp hand. He'd gone. The happy boy, the passionate lover, the brave warrior – all gone. Wiped away in a moment's folly, by the hand of the woman he loved. No Shakespearean play could have been more tragic.

Essylt's lips pressed together in a firm line. She set both hands on the hilt of the dagger and drew it out. It came with a rush of blood. For a moment she held it before her face, staring at it with wild, devasted eyes.

I should have seen it coming.

She was too quick for us. None of us foresaw her reaction, and only Cei and I were close enough to have prevented it. Before either of us could stop her, and probably before she had time to consider what she was doing, she plunged the dagger into her own chest just beneath her ribs, driving it upwards toward her heart.

"I'm coming, my love," she cried, as the knife slid home. "Wait for me."

"No!" I launched myself at her across Drustans' body, but there was nothing I could do. With a gasp, she fell forward across the chest of her one-time lover.

"Mother!" Seleu cried, but he was already far too late.

Chapter Eleven

T HE EVENTS OF the coronation rather put a damper on our visit. With his mother lying dead in front of him, Seleu grabbed the crown from my hands and jammed it onto his head. "There, *I'm* the bloody king now," he cried, as though a dead mother and brother didn't matter so long as he got what he wanted. How very like his father.

Our men held the angry crowd back at sword point, but with the king they'd expected at last successfully crowned, even if it was by his own hand, their anger subsided. Very few would have had memories of Drustans as a boy, but they all must have known Seleu, and the feeling buzzing amongst them was one of general relief that their lives had not been upset by internecine strife. The ordinary people do not like disturbance.

But now we had two more bodies to sort out.

"My mother will join my father on his pyre," Seleu declared, his tone imperious. Impossible, as that was now ashes. They'd have to build another.

I kept my mouth shut, in case I came out with something I'd regret later. But my insides bubbled at the injustice of what I'd just witnessed, and the cold acceptance of it by Essylt's son.

"She wanted to be with Drustans," I protested to Arthur, some time later after the bodies had been removed and everyone had dispersed. We'd retreated to our chamber, while Gwalchmei and Merlin attended to Drustans' body, and I'd revealed the true story of their love to my husband. As nothing could hurt them now, I didn't see that keeping their secret mattered any longer. "She should be with him in death, at least. With the man she longed to be with in life but never could be."

Arthur scowled at me, brimming with indignation that I'd known this for nineteen years and never told him. Typically taking it as an insult and making it all about him. Men.

Archfedd had followed us inside and listened to the story. "I agree with Mami," she said. "It's such a romantic story even though they're both dead. He must have loved her all his life. And she loved him, despite wanting to protect her own son. Nothing should part them now."

Arthur shook his head, still angry and sticking to protocol. "It's not for us to say what happens to Essylt's body. She was Seleu's mother, the Queen of Caer Dore. He will decide."

"That's so unfair," Archfedd said. "You're the High King, Father. Can't you intervene?"

Arthur shook his head again. "No. Seleu is king here, and I refuse to interfere. But if you want my opinion, then I'll give it. Essylt will be lucky to get any funeral rites at all, as she's a suicide."

Of course. This was a time when suicides were buried at crossroads with a stake through their hearts. What would Seleu's priest have to say about this?

A lot. He flatly refused to give Essylt any kind of service, even under threat of being beheaded. Maybe he guessed a boy Seleu's age didn't have the guts to carry out his threat. Although if I'd been him, I'd not have been so confident.

Drustans was a different basket of eels. He'd not died by his own hand, and the priest was more than willing to give *him* a decent burial. This time Seleu was the problem.

"I refuse to have him buried here," he snapped, probably still smarting from being outbluffed by his priest. "He brought about my mother's death."

Not quite true. But the priest had final say over the graveyard around his tiny, wattle church, and it lay far enough away from the fortress for a burial there to be considered inoffensive. Or at any rate, not so offensive as burying him closer would have been.

"I want his grave marked," I said to Arthur, as the next day we stood watching his shrouded corpse being lowered into the gaping hole of his grave, the warriors who'd been his friends solemn faced beside us.

He nodded, slightly less angry with me now. "I'll have the mason in the village prepare a stone."

Archfedd squeezed my hand, tears trickling down her cheeks. "He was always kind to me. He deserves some memorial to remind others who he was. No one should be forgotten."

I nodded. "He never will be. And I have the words for the stone. Here lies Drustans, son of Marcus Cunomorus."

HIC IACET DRUSTANS CUNOMORI FILIUS – the words I'd read so long ago in a future that had become my distant past. Words I'd had no way of knowing I'd chosen myself to mark the grave of a man blighted in love. A man whose memorial would last forever. The only known grave marker of any of Arthur's warriors.

WE SET OFF on the long road home two days later, with no more mention of any kind of betrothal between Seleu and Archfedd. She remained blissfully ignorant of the hand fate could have played her, and I wisely didn't bring up the subject with Arthur. Hopefully, he'd seen the error of his ways when sober, and after the fiasco at the coronation. I didn't even ask him if Seleu had brought it up again and had to be rebuffed. Best not to know.

It was a party incongruously lighthearted with the relief of leaving Caer Dore and its grisly memories that set out northward on a fine summer morning. But we were not going straight home. We would be visiting Cei and Arthur's mother, the Lady

Eigr, in her stronghold of Din Tagel.

Lucky me.

Strictly speaking, it wasn't hers, but Cei's. However, as he chose to spend his time with his brother at Din Cadan, she ruled in his absence. He visited her a couple of times a year, ostensibly to check up on her stewardship and visit some of the local mines and farms, although he'd told me in confidence that she was a better steward than he could ever have been a ruler.

Since that time when Arthur, after the death of his father, had visited her for the first time since his childhood, he'd been back with Cei only a couple of times. He always made out it was against his will, although I suspected that might have been untrue. I'd never accompanied him after that first visit, and been happy not to.

This visit was Cei's idea. "I haven't seen my mother since last autumn," he reasoned, as we three rode side by side following a narrow sheep track across the windy moor. "She's not getting any younger, and I can't help feeling it's time I took more of an interest in what goes on there."

Arthur, who had never forgiven his mother for abandoning him as a child, only grunted.

"And as we're so close, it seems only sensible to visit." Cei grinned across at Archfedd. "And I'm sure she'll be pleased to meet one of her granddaughters." He winked. "I've told her all about you and Reaghan. Amhar too."

"And I'd like to meet *her*," Archfedd said, with a small frown. "I just wish Amhar had come too. I'm sure my Lady Grandmother would be more pleased to see him than me." She chuckled. "He *is* Father's heir, after all."

I frowned at the natural assumption she'd made that her brother would hold more importance in her grandmother's eyes than she did. "She'll be pleased to see you. I'm certain."

No such thing as girl power in the Dark Ages. Well, not much of it, anyway. I'd made sure Archfedd hadn't grown up educated only to be a wife. She could read and write in fluent Latin and fight as well as any boy her age. She'd have made a better queen than Amhar would a king. But all of that might be swept away unnoticed when she married. No husband was going to like a wife cleverer than him, nor one who could best him in a sword fight.

I heaved a sigh of resignation. I could fight against the way women were treated forever, but I'd never win. Gone were the days of Boudicca leading her people into battle. And even she had been someone's wife before she'd become a war leader.

The twenty-odd miles between Caer Dore and Din Tagel's rocky promontory on the north coast of Cornubia took all day to negotiate. The tracks we had to use mostly linked farms and hamlets, and weren't meant for navigating long distances. They skirted lowland boggy areas, twisted through forests and around the higher ground, and often were too rock strewn and uneven to take at more than a walk without risk of a horse breaking a leg.

Eventually, Archfedd stood in her stirrups and pointed ahead of us. "What's that? Look, there where the land dips. Look at the horizon. The land's just sort of stopped." Her voice rose in excitement.

Of course. She'd never seen the sea up close. It had been barely visible from Caer Dore and we'd not had time to go and take a better look.

As we rode down the rocky defile toward the gates of Din Tagel, and the wide expanse of the ocean opened up in front of her, Archfedd's eyes grew rounder and rounder.

She bubbled with questions. "What's that smell? And that noise? This is the sea? Where Medraut's father has his ships? It's so huge! Where does it go? To the edge of the world?"

Her enthusiasm proved infectious, and the mood of depression that had settled on me the nearer we came to Eigr's lair lifted a little as I tried to answer her questions. "You can smell the seaweed on the beach, and the sea has a special smell all of its own. The noise is the waves breaking on the pebbly beach and against the cliffs. And Theodoric's ships are a long way off, not on this bit of sea – it's around the edge of our whole island. You've seen my maps. And there *is* no edge of the world – it's a globe, like an apple, and we're on one tiny bit of it."

This last she scoffed at, and I didn't press. Let her cope with trying to appreciate our coastline up close for the first time in her life.

The fortress of Din Tagel clung to a rocky promontory that jutted into the sea above towering cliffs. Waves crashed incessantly at its feet, and all the defense the inhabitants needed was a single curtain wall running across the narrow neck of land. The cliffs provided the rest. Down below the fortress, a tiny harbor sheltered a shingle beach, where sometimes tradesmen from far away beached their small merchant ships to unload their cargo. Other, larger vessels, had to dock at high tide against the precarious rocky landing stage on the island's northeastern side. Right now, both beach and landing stage lay empty.

Guards flung open the stout gates, and we rode through to the long, low stable block where it hunched, stuck to the headland like a limpet on a rock, as though it feared the fierce prevailing wind might prise it off and blow it away.

Cei surveyed the building with a critical eye. "That thatch is in need of patching," he said. "The winter storms have damaged it. I'll have to speak with my mother about that."

Eigr. Not a woman with whom I was particularly keen to renew my acquaintance. We hadn't parted as enemies, but neither had we as friends. People who'd agreed to tolerate one another, perhaps. And then, there'd been her scrying glass... No wonder I'd not been back.

Darkness had fallen by the time we'd dealt with our horses. Was Arthur as reluctant to approach Eigr's hall, perched halfway up the rocky slope, as I was?

Beyond the looming bulk of the headland, the sea spread out, luminous and pale, white-capped and never still. Impossible to see if the hall also needed attention on its roof. Cei pushed open the door, and we passed inside – him, Arthur, me, Archfedd and

Merlin. The rest of our men had gone to the barracks to find beds for the night.

A fire smoldered in the central hearth, the smell of smoke and bitter soot strong, and around it a pile of sleepy hounds raised their heads to look at us. Not much good as guard dogs, they lowered their heads again as though we didn't interest them. Maybe they knew Cei's scent.

An old woman was stirring a cauldron that sat in the hot embers, and the savory aroma of cooking meat and onions mingled with the smell of dogs and smoke and dusty reeds. She straightened up with difficulty and made an awkward bow, her face lined with the pain of rheumaticky joints. "Milord Cei, Milord Arthur. I'll tell yer mother yer here." She hobbled to the door into Eigr's chamber and disappeared through it.

We waited. Cei went to the cauldron and lifted the spoon to sniff the contents. My stomach, having long forgotten our midday meal of bread and cheese, rumbled as he tasted the stew.

He grinned. "Good stuff and plenty of it."

The door of Eigr's chamber opened. A woman emerged and stopped on the threshold, staring at us, her eyes, once the blue of the summer sky but faded now, moving to each of us in turn. Tall, and thinner than I remembered, she leaned her weight heavily on a gnarled stick, the hand that held it equally as gnarled.

Time and the life she must lead here at Din Tagel had eroded the beauty of the woman I'd first met when I was expecting Amhar. Her thick white hair had thinned, but still hung in a neat braid down her back, and her skin had sunken inward, clinging to the bones of her face and making a skull of her features. Her pale blue gown, which must have been made for her before the flesh had fallen from her bones, hung loose about her frame.

"Cei." Her voice had lost none of its strength, though. "Arthur." Her age-thinned lips pulled back in a smile. At least she still had all her teeth. The ones I could see, at any rate.

Cei stepped forward and took her hands in his. "Mother." He kissed her on either sunken cheek then put his arms around her, hugging her to him. She almost disappeared inside his embrace.

Arthur glanced at me, and I gave him an encouraging nod. He stepped forward.

Cei released his mother and she turned to her younger son, those faded blue eyes wary.

"Mother," Arthur said, bending to kiss her cheeks. He didn't hug her like his more impetuous brother. Had he ever? I wanted to tell him to put all his lingering resentment behind him and take her in his arms. That she was the only mother he'd ever have, and he couldn't know how long she had left. That this might be the last opportunity he had to do this. That I wished I'd been more aware of my own mother's impending death. I didn't.

Eigr turned to me. "Guinevere."

My turn to pay my respects. The skin of her cheeks was dry and papery under my lips, the scent of lavender on her gown and in her hair strong. "My Lady Eigr."

Her gaze travelled past me as I took a step back. "And who is this?" she asked, eyes fixed on Archfedd as my daughter made an elegant bow. I'd taught her to curtsey, something no one else was likely to be doing for another thousand years, but she couldn't do that when dressed in boys' clothes.

"My daughter," Arthur said. "Princess Archfedd."

What was that look Eigr gave her, so knowing and crafty? A little shiver of apprehension tickled the hairs on my body upright. Did Eigr know something I didn't?

Chapter Twelve

NO WAY WOULD I allow Arthur to usurp his mother's chamber, with her so frail and old. Her seneschal, a practically bald old man of much the same vintage as his mistress, managed to produce perfectly adequate accommodation for us in some of the houses nearest the hall. However, Eigr took a strong fancy to Archfedd. "My granddaughter will have a bed in my chamber," she declared, her voice autocratic and a touch querulous. That of an old woman unused to being crossed. "I wish to become better acquainted with the child."

Despite my misgivings, on the spur of the moment I couldn't think of a way to deny Eigr this. I had to let Archfedd follow the old lady into her chamber. Our daughter cast an imploring, nervous glance over her shoulder as she went, but all I could do was give her an encouraging smile, even though I couldn't think of a single good thing that might come of this. I didn't trust Eigr one bit.

"Dinner," the wispy-haired seneschal informed us, "will be served in one hour, Milord." With an unsteady, wrinkled hand, he turned over the hourglass timer on the table in our room to set it ticking off the minutes and reversed out of the room, bowing as he went.

A timid girl had brought a bowl of water to wash in, but testing the temperature with my hand proved it to be tepid, at best.

"Water's nearly cold," I told Arthur, who'd lain back on our bed with his hands behind his head and was watching me out of speculative eyes. I could guess what he was thinking. Men. Did they ever think of anything else? Probably not.

He grinned. "Best to hurry, then, before it gets any colder."

Ignoring his suggestively raised eyebrows, I stripped down to my undershirt. Under his close scrutiny, I made the most of the water then daubed on some of the perfume he'd obtained for me via this very port. Visiting his mother seemed to merit its use.

I unfastened my hair tie and loosened my hair, sending it cascading down my back in a heavy veil of chestnut. Where was my comb?

Arthur pushed himself upright. "Come and sit here, and I'll do your hair for you." He had my comb in his hand.

I sat on the bed beside him and for a few minutes let him comb my hair, enjoying a sensation I'd loved since childhood and that still reminded me of my long dead mother. However, Arthur's version of hair combing involved a fair bit of him running his fingers through it as well, and those fingers were wont to stray elsewhere. "Is that a gray hair I see before me?" he asked at last, with a chuckle.

"What?" I pulled as much of my hair as I could round to get a look, and he burst out laughing.

"Fooled you. Not a gray hair on your head. Yet…"

I gave him a playful slap. "Let me look at *your* hair then. Hmmm. I swear I see a hint of gray appearing in your beard."

He dropped my comb and rubbed his stubbly chin. "Damn it. I'll have to shave more often."

I pulled his hands down and leaned in for a kiss. "Don't worry. I'll still love you when you're old and gray, and as a matter of fact, I think a few gray hairs on a man make him look distinguished." I resolutely pushed away the nagging thought that he might never get to be old and gray.

For a moment we were preoccupied as the kiss deepened and I felt that familiar stirring of desire. Did we have time before dinner? As we parted, we both glanced toward the hourglass and then chuckled in unison.

"Are you thinking what I'm thinking?" he asked, a wicked glint in his eye.

Desire growing, I nodded. "Most likely." My hands went to his belt. "Let's get you out of these clothes."

Difficult to undress a man you're kissing, but I managed. As soon as he was naked, I pulled my shirt off and we fell back onto the bed together, my hair tumbling about us. It was going to need combing again. He rolled me onto my back and leaned over, eyes burning with the same desire rising in me. I reached up and buried my fingers in his hair, pulling him closer still. "I want you, Arthur Pendragon," I growled. "Now."

He grinned. "Your wish is my desire."

OUR PINK FACES and slightly disheveled hair might well have given us away when we arrived in the great hall for the evening meal. Cei gave Arthur an elaborate wink and a thumbs up, which I could have done without, and Merlin raised his eyebrows, but neither passed comment.

Eigr came in after us, taking small, stiff steps and leaning on her staff with one hand, and on a solemn-faced Archfedd with the other. Her servants had prepared three tables, one down each side, and the top table across the head of the hall, and banked up the fire, taking the heat to furnace level. "I'll have my grand-daughter beside me," Eigr said, hobbling to her seat, which was really Cei's throne. "And my boys."

Her boys. I didn't like the way she'd said that. Arthur wasn't hers, and, as far as I was concerned, Cei wasn't either. Despite the truce she and I had come to nineteen years ago, an uneasy feeling persisted in my heart, of not entirely trusting this woman. I caught her sharp gaze on me. In all probability she felt the same way toward me, the woman she claimed to have seen in a vision, drenched in blood. After nineteen years in the Dark Ages, I was a bit more inclined to believe in visions than I used to be.

Arthur pulled some more seats out of the shadowy corners of the hall. The fact that the only seat behind the table was the throne Eigr had lowered herself into implied she usually must sit there alone, presiding over her son's hall. We took our places, with our men and Merlin at the other two tables, and servants brought the food.

The meal was strained, to say the least. Cei, ever good natured, did his best to jolly proceedings along, but his mother was never going to be the warmest of hosts. Archfedd sat stiffly at her grandmother's left side, picking at her food and clearly not at ease. She answered the few questions that came her way with polite economy and kept her head down. As Cei had taken the place on his mother's right, and I was on the end next to Arthur, no opportunity arose for me to speak to Archfedd and reassure her.

I was very glad when the time to rise arrived.

Archfedd shot me a beseeching look, but all I could do was widen my eyes and shrug. She'd have to go with the old lady and humor her. If I had my way, we wouldn't be here for long.

Once Eigr and Archfedd had departed, the atmosphere relaxed.

"Some flagons of that good cider my mother has in her storehouse," Cei called to the servants hovering in the shadows. "And quick about it."

They hurried to do his bidding.

Arthur strode down the hall and threw open the double doors. "And let's get some fresh air in our lungs." The night rushed in on a salty sea wind, the torches guttered, and the flames on the hearth fire leapt in the draught, but the searing temperature dropped by several degrees in an instant.

The scurrying servants returned with the cider, and everyone left the hot, smoky fug of the hall to sit outside in the cool twilight. Perched on the platform by the hall doors, or on rocks like the gulls roosting on the cliffs below, we gazed out across the pale expanse of the endless ocean. In the velvet darkness of the sky, a billion pinpricks of light shone, and the sea shimmered with their reflected light as though sprinkled with stardust.

Horn cups filled with cider like magic, men emptied them and came back for more, and Gwalchmei fetched his lyre and strummed a plaintive melody. The sweet notes rose through the night air, and my heart soared with them. I pushed away the memories of Drustans and Essylt, those tragic lovers, and the fears I had for Archfedd with her grandmother.

Men laughed and joked, or joined in with songs, with every-thing about the evening much more convivial than the meal had been. It felt as though our men had let out a collective sigh of relief once Eigr had retired, as though they thought her as much a witch as her daughter, Morgana.

I sat on the edge of the raised platform with Arthur's arm draped around my shoulders. The ever-present sea wind, redolent of salt and seaweed, cooled the sweat on my hot body. If it weren't for Eigr's disturbing presence, I could have sat there forever.

⇥⟫⟫⟫⟪⟪⟪⟻

CEI HAD WORK to do while we were at Din Tagel. Normally, Arthur would have accompanied him, but, wary of Eigr, on that first day I asked him to stay with me. His indulgent smile, that I could have smacked off his face but didn't, told me he knew exactly why I'd suddenly become so clingy. Instead of him riding out to visit the local farms and tin mines, the latter a staple part of Din Tagel's economy, Arthur and I took the opportunity to act like tourists. Not that he'd have been familiar with the concept.

Hand-in-hand, we walked up over the windy headland and, at its furthest point, stopped to stare out across a changeable sea that could one moment be gray and white topped, and another the blue of aquamarine. A stiff westerly snatched at our cloaks and hair as we gazed into the distance – a distance only I knew ended in the Americas, an idea too foreign to share. Something Arthur didn't need to know.

We settled on the tufty grass between high banks of purple heather that sheltered us from the warm wind, and lay in each other's arms, squinting up at the white clouds racing across the powder-blue sky overhead. A chough landed on a rock near us and sat preening himself in the sun, and the never-ending raucous cries of gulls filled the air.

"I love it here," Arthur said, his voice dreamy. "Cei's lucky to have it. There's something about the sea. It's at times like this I understand why Theodoric loves it so much. More than his own wife, perhaps." He turned his head and smiled at me. "I sometimes wish I had another life. A life without constant fighting. A life just with you."

Oh, if only that could come true.

I shuffled closer and touched my lips to his in a feather-light kiss. "I quite often wish the same." I sighed. "To be without all the worries and responsibilities for other people. For you never to be in danger again, and me never to have to worry about you being killed in battle." I couldn't say this without the fear, never far away, returning to remind me of what lay ahead of us.

He rolled onto his side, eyes fixed on mine. "Make love to me." His hand ran down my body and hitched at the hem of the gown I was wearing, his fingers on my bare leg. "Here, under the endless sky, on the edge of the world."

I cupped his cheek. "I love you so much."

We made love in that grassy nook, our bodies entangled in passion, with the sun warming our skin. Afterwards, we lay naked together in the quiet hollow, as though nothing else mattered in the world. If only we could have stayed there.

Chapter Thirteen

O N OUR SECOND day in Din Tagel, I was sitting above the cliffs, perched on a slab of stone someone had set up as a low bench and staring out to sea, when Merlin came upon me. I'd been throwing crusts of stale bread scrounged from the kitchen up into the air for the gulls to swoop and catch, delighting in their skill.

He sat on the stone next to me and watched for a while until I ran out of bread and the gulls gave up. They'd have a long wait before they'd be able to dive-bomb tourists to steal their chips in my old world.

"Did you know?" he asked.

Taken by surprise, my eyes widened. "Did I know what?"

"About Drustans?"

"Ah." I bit my bottom lip. "I understand."

"Well?" he persisted. "Did you?"

I heaved a sigh. "I had an inkling."

The westerly wind blowing in off the sea tugged at his loose hair. I'd never known him to have it cut short as other warriors did from time to time. He brushed it out of his eyes. "What does *that* mean?"

"That I didn't think he'd ever become king."

He frowned. "Can you explain?"

I told him about the memorial stone in Fowey, and what it said.

His eyes narrowed as he nodded. "Those words you chose. You seem to have a habit of creating history."

I bristled. "Isn't that what you brought me here for?"

"You're right. I suppose I shouldn't complain when you do."

We sat in silence for a while, not looking at one another and listening to the pounding of the waves.

"Do you think it was inevitable?" I asked, at last. "That we couldn't have done anything to prevent it?"

He turned to look at me. "I don't know. Perhaps. Maybe even if you'd known how and why he wouldn't become king, none of us could have prevented his death. Nor Essylt's." He shook his head. "Maybe no matter how we rail against fate, there's nothing we can do to change the path it has mapped out for us."

That wasn't like him.

I swallowed. "Do you think I can do nothing, then, to prevent Camlann from happening?"

Was that compassion in his eyes? Had he seen it galloping up on us as well? He shrugged. "I don't know. But maybe if we can't avert it, we can change things by how we treat it." He paused. "How we react – how we let it affect us." He waved a hand around expansively, encompassing the view. "How it changes our world."

"That's not enough for me." I shook my head in determination. "I want to stop it happening." I paused. "But the trouble is, I don't know if it even will. Or, if it *is* going to, how it will happen, or even where Camlann is. I thought it might have been at a fort on the Wall – Camboglanna – but it wasn't. Or it might still be if we have to go back up there."

I paused again, marshalling my thoughts. "For me, it's just a story I've known all my life, but it's from a book, and for all I know, it might not be what fate has in store for any of us. All my fears might come to nothing. Or they might not. And even if I'm right, how can I stop something when I don't even know what the signs are that it's approaching? Might I even *make* it happen by my actions? Am I an integral part of what the future will unroll?

Am I damned if I act *and* damned if I don't?"

He sighed. "I think you might be."

THE NEXT DAY, Cei and his mother settled down to spend a few hours going over the trading accounts she kept. While Arthur and Merlin rode out to visit one of Cei's tin mines, Archfedd and I scrambled down the narrow path to the shingle beach below the headland so she could paddle in the sea.

From the valley above, a little stream cascaded over the towering cliffs in a waterfall. And under the headland, where the low tide had exposed some patchy sand, and the smell of the seaweed was strong, the dark maw of a large cave gaped in open invitation.

I'd stood on this beach in a past life, with my father, and now I stood on it with the granddaughter he'd never see. He'd taken me into the cave, and I'd stared around with childish wonder, believing him when he'd said it was "Merlin's Cave." Later on, I'd found out local legend called it that, not just my father. Now, though, I knew it had nothing to do with my friend.

"Look," Archfedd cried, scrambling, in feet bare from paddling, over the tumbled rocks and round pebbles thrown up by the sea. "Look, you can walk right through it. Come on, Mami."

I followed her through a long tunnel, carved out by thousands of years of tides, that passed right through the headland. The walls shone and dripped with running water, and from the far end came the thunderous crash of waves. We emerged onto a far rockier, but a little more sheltered, beach than the first, beneath cliffs too steep to climb.

I sat on a boulder made smooth by wave action. "The tide's still going out. We'll be safe here a while."

Archfedd bent over, examining the rock pools. "Why *does* the sea come in and out the way it does? Grandmother told me how, when it's right in up to the cliffs, the smaller trading ships can beach themselves. They let the sea recede, unpack their goods and take on the tin ingots. Then their boats refloat when the sea comes up again. I'd like to see that."

I pushed a few strands of loose hair out of my eyes, squinting against the intensity of the sunlight. Had it ever been this bright in my old world? "I believe it's the influence of the moon that causes tides."

She snorted. "That's silly. It's so *small*, and some nights it's barely there at all." She laughed at the impossibility of so tiny a thing having power over the sea, and, losing interest, wandered away. I leaned back against the warm rocks and closed my eyes, content to doze in the sun. The ever-present gulls, backs bent like scimitars against the wind, called to each other, and the waves thundered on the shore, retreating with a sucking sound.

I'm back on the other beach with my father: him dressed in his customary tweed suit, bow tie and brogues; me and my twin brother, Artie, in more appropriate summer garments of shorts and t-shirts. "Some thought this site was only a religious one, populated by Celtic monks," my father proclaims, pointing up toward the out-of-sight remains of the thirteenth-century stone castle. "And some foolishly thought those stone ruins up there were Arthurian." He snorts with derision. "It came as a surprise to many when evidence proved that Tintagel must have been the stronghold of a powerful Arthurian era warlord."

Cei, and before him, his father, Gorlois.

Archfedd sat down beside me with a thump, disturbing my dreams.

I opened my eyes.

The wind had loosened strands of her sun-bleached hair and made a tangle of it, and her face was flushed from the wind. She leaned back as I was, eyes narrowed against the brightness.

We sat in silence for a while, just a mother and daughter, like any mother and daughter from my old world, catching a few rays on a beach. A world and life she'd never know.

Archfedd broke the silence. "Has Grandmother ever shown you her scrying glass?"

My eyes, that had fallen shut again, jerked open, all sleepiness banished. Wide open. "Her scrying glass?" For a moment I couldn't gather my wits to find an answer.

She nodded without looking at me, her gaze fixed on the far horizon.

What to say? I struggled with the urge to lie, not wanting to think of what I'd seen in it. "A long time ago."

Archfedd drew her bottom lip under her top teeth, as though thinking. Maybe she felt as reticent as I did. "She showed it to me yesterday."

Instinct warned me not to make a big thing of this. "She did?"

She nodded. "In that little round hut of hers." She paused. "It's… claustrophobic."

Where she'd taken me that time, offering me what she thought was a reward for me sharing my knowledge of Arabic numerals and teaching her how better to manage her accounting. I'd stepped all unwarily into something I hadn't liked, unable to break free. I glanced sideways at Archfedd, but she still stared straight ahead. Impossible to tell what she had or hadn't seen, nor how she felt about it.

"I know it," I said.

A cormorant settled on a pillar of rock on the headland, preening his dark feathers, and the sea pinks hanging over the cliff's edge danced in the breeze.

Her tongue darted around her lips. "Did you *see* anything when she showed you the glass?" She was trying to sound casual, but the tension in her voice crackled.

I was back in that little hut again, the stifling darkness all around me as I peered into the black mirror of Eigr's scrying glass on the tabletop, seeing more than just the opaque surface – more than I wanted to see.

I hadn't been able to tear my eyes away. Nor close them. Before me had lain a blood-stained battlefield littered with broken banners. Dead horses and a river that ran red with spilled blood. And overhead the setting sun had stained the sky to match, drenching the world in crimson. A world where Arthur lay as if dead, eyes closed, his waxy face a mask of blood.

How could I ever have forgotten what I saw?

"No," I said. "I saw nothing."

We sat in silence for some minutes as clouds obscured the sun and a chill descended. A chill that sent a shiver to my bones, despite the heat of my rocky seat.

The urge to ask my daughter what she'd seen increased, but the fear she might have been privy to the same scene I'd witnessed sealed my lips. Better left unsaid.

At last, she broke the silence, her hand sneaking to take hold of mine. "She showed me the glass. Her grandmother's glass, she said. She told me you'd looked into it and seen something. She wanted me to look, as well. She said I might have inherited her Sight. She wanted to know if I had."

"I saw nothing," I repeated. "Nothing but my fanciful imagining. There's no truth to be found in a scrying glass."

She turned to look at me out of anguished eyes. What had she seen to make her look like this?

"Mother. Mami. I looked into her glass, and I saw things I didn't understand. Don't understand."

I bit my lip.

"She said you could explain them to me."

Oh, how I wished myself anywhere but here. How I wished we'd left Archfedd with her brothers at Din Cadan and that she'd never had to meet her grandmother with her witchy tricks – the tricks she'd passed on to Morgana. Tricks she seemed to think Archfedd, also, might possess.

I couldn't help it, though. "What did you see?" I asked.

Heat rose to Archfedd's cheeks, coloring them pinker than the wind had done. "I – I saw myself." She paused. "On a *throne*." She sounded incredulous.

Not without reason. I stared. Of all the things I'd feared she'd say, this had not been one of them. "On a *throne?*"

She nodded. "With a crown on my head." She swallowed. "Mami, it was *your* crown."

For a moment the world spun around me, and if I hadn't been seated already, I might have fallen. My daughter – a queen. Why not? Not unexpected that the daughter of the High King would make a good match. But in *my* crown? Something different altogether. If she were wearing that, then where was I in her vision?

Schooling my face to hide my fear, I squeezed her hand. "And were you old?" I asked, clutching at straws.

She shook her head. "No. I looked just as I look right now. Young. No different to the girl I see in my copper mirror every morning."

What did this mean? A million possibilities tumbled inside my head, but on the outside, I fought a battle to hide the terror washing over me. If Archfedd sat on a throne in my crown, then was it *my* throne, as well? Her father's throne? And where were her brothers?

I forced a laugh. "Just your fanciful imagination," I said, with careful determination. "Every girl likes to see themselves raised up. And you have reason to expect that more than most – for one day soon, when you marry, you'll likely be a queen yourself."

Her smooth brow furrowed. "But why in *your* crown, Mami? Why was I wearing your crown?"

I drew a steadying breath. "Because you've seen no other crown but that one, of course. So in your imagination you placed it on your own head. What could be simpler than that?" I squeezed her hand again. "Your grandmother is an old lady who likes to frighten people. She thinks she has powers above those of other women, but she doesn't. Put an impressionable girl in a dark room with a black mirror and a candle and she'll see anything. Her imagination puts it inside her head." I forced a smile. "Of *course* you saw something in the mirror – I'd have been surprised if you hadn't."

Her troubled eyes cleared. "Yes. You're right. It was just a trick of my imagination. I won't let her do that with me again."

I had the distinct impression I hadn't really convinced her.

WE RODE HOME the next day, leaving Eigr to her solitary clifftop existence.

"I need to visit her more often than I do," Cei said, twisting in his saddle to stare back down the hill toward the fortress gates. Eigr wasn't waiting there to wave us off, of course, but I couldn't miss the wistfulness in his voice. Nor the worry. No doubt existed in my mind that Cei loved his mother.

"She does seem old, all of a sudden," Arthur said with unusual insight for him.

Merlin nodded. "It comes to all men."

Not him, though. When I'd first met him, he'd appeared to be a few years older than Cei and Arthur, but now, if anything, he seemed younger. Whatever magic he had, he must have somehow harnessed it to hang onto his youth. Good for him. If I possessed his powers, I'd have done the same. No one really wants to grow old. Only now I thought about it, I *did*. I longed for Arthur and me to grow old together. Very old. Centenarians if possible. I didn't care if we became frail and doddery, nor if we lost our teeth and hair.

I just wanted Arthur to live long enough to be old.

We took our time on our journey, sleeping out under the stars or staying overnight at small ramshackle villas, the inhabitants still clinging doggedly to the ways of their Roman forebears, at small farms or in the ghost-ridden ruins of old buildings. The weather held, and by the time we reached Din Cadan, all the fields around our hill stood cleared of the hay crop.

Hayricks thatched against the weather stood beside every barn and dotted the fields, fenced off from the sheep and cattle now grazing the stubble and manuring the ground. Inside the fortress walls, sweet-smelling ricks dotted every spare corner. Unwise to have them all in one place, in case of fire. Spread out like this, if one burnt, the others would be safe, and our animals wouldn't go short of winter fodder.

Glad to be home, we left our horses in the stables and walked up the road to the Great Hall, my heart leaping at the thought of seeing my son and stepson again.

Chapter Fourteen

ARTHUR EMBRACED A serious-faced Llacheu in the Great Hall. "Come through to our chamber and tell me how it goes," he said, throwing an arm around his son's broad shoulders. "I bring sad news about Drustans, but that will have to wait. I need to know how you've managed in my absence."

I followed them through the door into our chamber, and we all sat at our small round table. Maia brought a flagon of wine and filled three goblets. "Shall I fetch bread and cheese and cold meat?" she asked, hovering just behind Arthur's chair.

He shook his head. "You may go. We have business to discuss."

I nodded to her. "Go to Archfedd. She's tired and will want hot water to wash in."

Maia scuttled away, the look on her face telling me she felt miffed at being excluded. As my maid, she'd been privy to many private discussions, and, as far as I could tell, never spread gossip.

Arthur waited for her to close the door between our chamber and the one she shared with Archfedd, then turned back to Llacheu. "What's wrong?"

Llacheu's lips came together in a downturned grimace of resignation. "How did you know?"

The smallest of smiles flitted across Arthur's face. "I can read you like a book."

Well, not quite true. Being able to tell what our children were thinking had never been his strongpoint, but if he wanted to think he could, I wasn't about to argue.

Llacheu managed a brief smile back. "Nothing I can put a finger on. Everything's run smoothly. We brought the hay in, as you'll have seen. A plentiful crop. I've sent out patrols daily, same as you do. The south coast remains peaceful. The corn is ripening well, and we should have a good harvest before long. No big disputes between any of the men…" His voice trailed off, and he gazed down at where his hands lay clasped on the table.

"Sounds good," Arthur said, but his brow had furrowed. It didn't need anyone with the Sight to tell Llacheu wasn't happy about something.

"How is Ariana?" I butted in, determined to lighten the mood.

Llacheu's face lit up. "Still pregnant." He grinned. "Donella told her to stay in bed. I've been making her put her feet up and do nothing. Donella says that's the best way to keep this baby. I berate my servants every day and tell them to make sure she does nothing at all. Tulac is in charge, and he's like an old mother hen with her." Tulac was the body slave Llacheu had grown up with.

Ariana must be nearly six months gone by now, which was further through than she'd ever got before. Surely, this time she'd be able to get a baby to the stage where if she went into early labor, it had a chance to live. If she'd been born fifteen hundred years from now, a doctor would have put a stitch in her cervix to hold the baby in place, but here there was nothing anyone could do apart from telling her to rest.

Arthur clapped his son on the back. "You'll make me a grand-father yet, mark my words." His proud grin vanished as he reverted back to Llacheu's problem. "If nothing bad has happened, and Ariana's still in one piece, what's bothering you? Any idiot can see you're not happy."

Llacheu sighed, his shoulders drooping. "I can't put a finger on it," he said, rubbing a grubby hand across his brow. "But the atmosphere here has changed. The fortress has felt different with you away." He paused. "And it hasn't been a change for the good."

My ears pricked.

Arthur frowned. "Can you be more specific?"

The impression that Llacheu didn't want to tell us was strong, and my own apprehension rose, the little hairs on my arms and back prickling upright.

Llacheu shrugged. "I always thought I got on well with Amhar," he began, speaking slowly as though measuring his words. "He's been a bit odd with me a few times over the years, but this time... I don't know. It's like he hates me."

He shook his head, looking up at his father with pleading eyes. "He's your heir, Father, yet you put *me* in charge when you go away. Every time." He hesitated. "I think... no, I'm sure, that if you were to give Amhar more responsibility, he might... feel better about himself. Perhaps regard me in a different light." He grimaced. "I might be your son, but I'm not your legal heir. *He* is. I don't want to tell you how to treat him. It's not my business. But I feel he resents me being always left in charge. Not him."

I fixed my gaze on Arthur. His face had gone very still. I had a nasty feeling his reaction to Llacheu's words might not be what was needed here. Tact was not his middle name.

"Has he been causing trouble?" Arthur asked, his voice flat and emotionless. Not a good sign.

Llacheu shook his head again. "No. Not really. Like I said, I can't put my finger on it." He clasped and unclasped his hands as though resigning himself to having to be honest. "He and Medraut whisper with their friends when I walk past. Their eyes follow me. At the evening meal in the Hall, when I'm in your place on the high table, they have their heads together, laughing. It's me they're mocking. Me they have something against. More and more of the younger warriors have been joining in."

If I hadn't known better, I'd have thought this the behavior of stupid little boys at school, ganging up on another they perceived as different. But if it included Medraut, it had to be taken seriously. What was he up to, undermining Llacheu like this? Encouraging Amhar, who'd long been jealous of his older brother, to do the same. That Medraut lay behind all this seemed obvious to me. How I wished he'd not come back with us after the Council of Kings. How I wished we'd not taken Amhar there and laid him in the path of his manipulative cousin.

Arthur gave a snort of laughter. "They're boys," he said. "And you're a man grown and a warrior of standing. You should rise above their foolishness." He slapped Llacheu on the back again. "And you're no less my son than Amhar is. It's I who will choose my heir, and if it suits me, I can choose any man, baseborn or not, to follow me. Amhar would be wise to think on that."

Thank goodness Amhar wasn't present to hear *that* incendiary speech.

Llacheu's earnest eyes met his father's. "I have no wish to be king after you, Father. I'm content to serve whoever rules here at Din Cadan with my sword. To serve my brother when he's king – long in the future, I hope. But Amhar behaves as though he sees me as his rival, when I'm not."

Arthur smiled. "I only wish Amhar could be as content as you."

So did I.

But we didn't get any further with this conversation because, just then, the door of our chamber burst open and Cei catapulted into the room, his face a mixture of shock and fury. "Arthur," he shouted, even though he was right in front of us. "Reaghan's gone."

We all stared at him for a long few seconds.

"Ah," Llacheu said, shifting in his seat as though embarrassed. "I'd forgotten about that."

"What d'you mean?" I asked, my eyes darting between my furious brother-in-law and my stepson. "Where's she gone?"

Llacheu swallowed. "Coventina gave her permission. I couldn't really stop them – her. What was I supposed to do? Lock her up when her mother had said she could go?"

Cei loomed over him. "Did you not think that *I* wouldn't give *my* permission for such a thing? That this was not what I had planned for my daughter?"

Llacheu remained seated. Maybe he suspected that if he got to his feet Cei might deck him. His uncle certainly had his hammy hands clenched into enormous fists.

Arthur did stand up, and put a restraining hand on Cei's arm. "You haven't told us *where* she's gone yet."

Cei spluttered as though he could barely get the words out. "She's gone to Ynys Witrin." His breath was coming in heaving breaths as though he'd been running. "She's gone to be a... *religious.*" He said the last word with so much venom anyone would have thought she'd gone to sell sex on the streets of Caer Baddan.

"Is-is that so bad?" I ventured. Not what I'd want for Archfedd, but this was an era of strong religious beliefs, so if Cei's daughter had decided the life of a nun was for her, who were we to object? Not that I'd ever noticed her having a strong religious bent before. That she should suddenly decide she had one puzzled me a bit.

The door opened and Coventina limped in.

"Well," Arthur said with a hint of exasperation. "That's almost all of us. Now we just need Medraut and Amhar, and the whole family'll be here giving their opinions."

Cei swung round on his wife. "Why did you let her go?"

Coventina sank into Arthur's vacated chair and put her head in her hands. "I couldn't stop her. She told me she had a vocation. A calling. I couldn't stand in her way. What would you have had me do?"

For answer Cei just growled.

Arthur frowned. "Wait a minute. We've only been gone three weeks. How does a girl come by a religious vocation in so short a time? Answer me that, someone?"

Cei nodded. "He's right. What's been going on?"

A silence fell.

At last, Coventina raised her head from her hands. "She's been riding over to Ynys Witrin," she whispered. "With Medraut and Amhar."

Everyone stared at her.

"Why?" Cei asked after a moment, his voice laden with menace. "Why has she been riding with them? Who let her do that? A girl with two men. Was she unescorted?" It didn't matter that they were her cousins. A young unmarried girl shouldn't be alone with a man – still worse with two of them.

Llacheu eyed his aunt. "I didn't know she was until it was too late."

Of course. Archfedd had told me how Medraut had pestered her to ride out with him. With her gone, had he turned his attentions to Reaghan? What was going on here? The suspicion that Medraut had some hidden purpose nudged at me. He wasn't a young man who did anything without a good reason. But why encourage Reaghan to a religious life? How did that suit him? I refused to consider that he just wanted to be friends with his younger cousins – there had to be an ulterior motive behind his actions.

And for some reason Amhar had involved himself in this, as well.

Coventina bit her lip. "He's such a polite young man," she whispered. "And he's her cousin. As is Amhar. He asked me if he could take her riding and I – I said yes. I didn't find out they'd been going as far as Ynys Witrin until it was too late."

Arthur's frown deepened. "But what were they doing on the holy island? The monks at the abbey wouldn't have let Reaghan in. They don't take in female religious devotees. They're all male."

Tears trickled down Coventina's cheeks. "You're right. They don't. But there's a little chapel there that a woman called Brigid set up. She was an Irish woman, fled from the wilderness that's her homeland. She came here a few years ago and settled on Ynys Witrin, but I think she's gone, now. They call her chapel Bec

Eriu. It's there that Reaghan's gone."

"Then I'll go and fetch her back," Cei stormed. "No daughter of mine is wasting her life in a chapel when she could be married and giving me grandsons."

Coventina shook her head. "She won't come. She's set her heart on this. I did try to dissuade her, I promise you, but she has it in her head that she has a calling. That she's meant to live the life of a religious, like Brigid did."

"She'll do as she's told," Cei snapped.

Arthur rubbed his chin and shook his head. "Do you really want to charge over there and drag her back kicking and screaming?"

Cei nodded. "Yes, I do. She's my daughter and she has to do as I say."

"What do you think that will do to her?" For once Arthur was showing insight into how our children thought, although if this were Archfedd he'd already be on his way to snatch her back. Easier to be sensible about someone else's child.

Cei paced across the room to the door, spun, and paced back. "She'll be angry."

Arthur caught his arm. "Yes. She will. But if you leave her, let her have her way, I'd wager she'll be home in a week or two, or at the latest when winter sets in and she's cold and hungry in her chapel. Let her come to her senses by herself."

How surprising that Arthur should have wise words on parenting for his brother, considering the endless mistakes he made with Amhar.

I put my pennyworth in. "That's good advice. Let her come back when she's ready. We all know Reaghan, and she's not a girl who can do without her creature comforts. As soon as it gets cold over there, she'll be back."

Cei looked at Coventina, who gave him a nod and wiped her hand across her eyes.

He heaved a deep sigh. "Against my better judgement, I'll follow your advice."

Chapter Fifteen

I SOON WORKED out that Llacheu was right in his assessment of Medraut and Amhar and how the atmosphere of the fortress had subtly changed in our absence. As he said, it was hard to pinpoint exactly what the change was, but I noticed straightaway that beneath the daily life of the fortress ran a strange undercurrent of dissatisfaction, the tendrils of which appeared to lead back to those two young men.

That evening in the Hall the sense of there being factions amongst the men seemed evident. A glance at Arthur, who was frowning down the hall toward the lower tables, told me that he, too, had noticed. Whereas before, only the very youngest had sat together at the lowest tables, now, it seemed, almost all the younger warriors had joined them instead of mingling amongst their elders.

The sense of trouble brewing strengthened.

I liked to take a walk around the perimeter of the wall-walk every morning if the weather was fine, and sometimes even if it was bad and I had to wrap my cloak around me to keep out the rain. Occasionally, Arthur joined me, but more often than not I had to make do with Merlin for company, Arthur being usually too busy either dispensing justice in the Hall or down on the training grounds with his men.

The morning after our return, I left Arthur holding court and met Merlin outside. We strolled between the houses together, heading for the ramparts, the summer sun beating down on us, even though the hour was early. The song of larks riding the thermals high above us carried on the light breeze.

The fortress women had begun their morning's work at dawn, as usual, and now were hanging out washing, beating rugs, and sweeping doorsteps clean. From the forge came the sound of hammering, the smoke from Goff's furnace mingling with the scent of baking bread and the farmyard odor of middens, pigsties and stables.

Children, in this weather turfed out of their homes with a heel of bread at first light, galloped down the narrow passageways between the buildings, chasing dogs or scrawny chickens and screeching with delight, or played elaborate games on patches of grass, their laughter echoing across the plateau. When Din Cadan teemed with life like this, the specter of war seemed far away.

We climbed to the top of the grass-covered ramparts by a set of wooden steps to stand looking out over the flat plain toward far-off Ynys Witrin and the distant hump of the Tor. I'd done this so many times now but had never yet tired of the view. The rich farmlands and green pastures surrounding our hilltop stronghold eventually gave way to the dark shadow of forest in full leaf. Beyond that, but invisible from here, lay the boundless marshes that stretched as far as the coast at Dinas Brent. All of it peaceful and quiet in the warm summer sunshine.

I linked arms with Merlin and steered him toward the training grounds, curious to see the young warriors at work, and hoping Medraut and Amhar would be among them.

"I hear Reaghan's gone to be a religious," Merlin said as we walked.

I nodded. "Arthur thinks she'll be back when the weather changes."

He chuckled. "He may well be correct. I don't see her wearing sack cloth and sandals in winter, nor enjoying a pallet bed with a straw-stuffed mattress and one thin blanket."

Down in the vegetable patches some of the women and older

girls were on their knees weeding the cabbages and carrots, turnips and beet, radishes, onions and garlic. These grew in the small fields, with the gardens around each house dedicated for the most part to herbs, both for cooking and healing. Every woman kept her own supply of medicines with which to dose her family.

We walked a bit further, and, in the village below, the church bell rang out. Just a small thing, tinny and harsh, that hung by the door of the little thatched building, calling to those who wanted to come to worship. Something not everyone did – the old gods of pre-Christian times still managed to keep their hold amongst the country people.

Merlin smiled. "Time someone gave them a better bell."

"A louder one, maybe. Then all those who avoid attending will hear it better and be unable to say they missed its call. Maybe I'll get Arthur to have one made."

"The villagers wouldn't thank you for that."

I nodded. "I do know that. I wouldn't really do it. Let them worship their old gods in their own houses if they want to. I don't want to interfere in what they believe."

"Neither do I."

I stopped and leaned on the crenellations, staring toward the tiny dots in the distance that were a herd of horses with foals at foot out on the grazing lands beyond the cultivations. "I suppose with that argument, we should let Reaghan have the freedom of what she believes as well."

He leaned beside me, but looked inward toward the distant practice grounds where groups of warriors were engaged in sword fighting, archery, spear throwing and wrestling. "You're probably right."

Why was he always so non-committal? The fact that he never seemed prepared to give a straight answer could be so irritating.

"It's odd, though, isn't it?" I said, controlling my annoyance and without looking at him. "Odd that it came upon her so suddenly – this compunction to be a religious."

Overhead a buzzard mewed, plaintive as a cat.

"I believe people *can* feel the calling like that. Out of the blue."

I got the impression he was being evasive. Well, he was evasive more often than he was straight, so nothing new there. "Within three weeks? Less than three weeks, as she's already gone. I can't quite get my head around that."

A puzzled frown creased his brow, so I reworded my sentence. "I mean, I don't quite believe it could have happened that quickly."

"Not much we can do about it, though. Arthur has it right. Let her work out for herself that she shouldn't be there." He squinted up at the buzzard. "She'll be back with her parents by the time we've had the first frost of autumn. Chilly in those hermitages, and that's all that chapel will be. They're not designed to offer the comforts of home to devotees." He grinned. "It's common knowledge that religiouses of both sexes like to feel they're suffering for their faith. They don't think they can be devoted enough if they're warm and cozy, with full bellies and decent clothes."

I turned away from the view and caught his arm again. "Let's go and watch the men at practice. I've a yen to see what Amhar and Medraut are up to."

His eyebrows rose, but he let himself be guided along the wall-walk in the direction I wanted.

The practice ground stretched along the eastern side of the fortress, butting up against the rampart and providing enough space for horses to be trained as well as men. The wall-walk provided a perfect viewing platform.

No horses here today. The men had divided into their normal smaller groups, with the youngest boys being taught by Llawfrodedd, Archfedd's friend. Although only in his early twenties himself, he had a way about him of kindness and patience that suited him to teaching – perhaps something to do with the deprivation he'd known in his early life, and his appreciation of what he had now.

He'd matured from the scrawny boy who'd first arrived in Din Cadan seven years ago into a tall and powerfully built warrior. With his broad, flat face and over-large nose, he'd never be handsome in a classical way, but nevertheless the attractiveness of his spirit shone from his cheerful countenance, and I could see why Archfedd had her eye on him. The boys he taught looked up to him as they did no other.

Archfedd could do no better than marry a man as well-loved as this one. I didn't care that he wasn't a prince with a pedigree traceable back to Cunedda. With him, instinct told me, she'd have a man who'd value her above all else.

"You like him, don't you?" Merlin said. "For Archfedd."

I nodded. "I'll need to speak to Arthur about a match. She's told me she likes him, and I suspect he likes her back. And as he's the one who taught her, he's not a man to interfere in her longing to be a warrior."

Merlin nodded. "And she'd remain here. A prince from another kingdom would marry her for her status alone, and take her away." He smiled. "I know you don't want to lose her."

When I'd first met Merlin, he'd have thought a princess obliged to marry where her father willed. His long association with me had mellowed his outlook. Almost, but not quite, he'd learned to value women as his equal. Well, women other than me. He knew better than to try telling *me* what to do.

Medraut and Amhar were in a large group of young men much the same age as them, practicing with wooden swords. This wasn't because they feared hurting one another, which they didn't – more that the weight of the swords built muscles in their fighting arms, making their regular weapons seem light and easy by comparison. Personal experience had taught me how tiring sword fighting could be.

I scanned the other groups for Arthur but didn't spot him. Maybe too many supplicants had arrived at the Hall to air their grievances to their king, and he didn't have the time to join his men this morning. But there was Llacheu, with his bow, at target practice with some of his friends. Their laughter carried to me, along with the twang of their bows and the soft thud of arrows sinking into the tightly packed straw of the targets.

Closer to where I stood, Medraut and Amhar's companions had gone into a huddle with them, heads together as though a team discussing strategy before a football or rugby match. I lowered myself to sit on the edge of the wall-walk with my legs dangling, the morning sun warming my back, and Merlin settled beside me.

"I don't like the look of that," Merlin said, jerking his head toward Medraut's group.

Amhar emerged from the huddle, a belligerent look on his face, and the other young warriors fell back in a group behind him that looked too much like an audience for my liking. An air of expectancy hung in the air about them, of salacious anticipation, as though they knew what was coming.

Medraut stepped forward and clapped Amhar on the back in a theatrical show of bonhomie, and a smug smile flashed across his face as he glanced back at his watching friends. Cinbelin gave him a thumbs up, and Bran and Cyngal of Ebrauc jostled one another, grinning. Amhar set off toward the archers.

Something was going on here. I sat up straighter, curious to see why Amhar was marching off alone and with such apparent determination. Beside me, Merlin did the same.

To find Llacheu, that was why.

Amhar, his wooden sword still in his hand, strode up to where his brother was organizing the archery target practice well out of the way of the other groups of warriors, and tapped him on the shoulder. Bullish bravado emanated from him in waves. His fellows followed him at a wary distance, like spectators waiting for something big to happen.

Llacheu turned around, and his face broke into a smile. I was too far away to hear what Amhar said to him, but the smile vanished and Llacheu shook his head.

Visible even from here, Amhar's body bristled with anger at

his brother's response. He raised his left hand and poked Llacheu on the shoulder so hard his brother took a step back, thrown off balance by the blow.

A few calls of encouragement rang from the ranks of Amhar's friends, if you could have called them that.

Llacheu frowned, said a few words to Amhar, and turned back to his own companions, who'd all been standing around with their bows pointing at the ground.

Amhar raised his wooden sword, swung it, and landed it with a crack on Llacheu's right arm above the elbow. A crack so loud many heads turned. Some of them must have been close enough to have overheard what had passed between them.

Llacheu spun around, and now his face contorted with anger. In the sudden heavy silence, his raised voice carried to me on the breeze. "What the hell did you do that for?" His companions drew closer. One or two of them held bows with arrows still knocked. All training ceased as the rest of the men on the practice grounds realized something was going on and downed weapons to come and see.

Amhar stood his ground, feet braced, the wooden sword raised in front of him. In the expectant silence, I heard his every word. "You don't walk away from me like that," he snarled. "I'm my father's heir, and if I challenge you to fight, then you're obliged to do as I say."

Uh oh.

He sounded like the spoiled child he was. But that didn't make this any less dangerous.

I grabbed Merlin's arm. "Stop them, can't you?"

Llacheu rubbed his arm, flexing the fingers, and the anger left his face. "Don't be so silly," he said, his voice cold and measured, but with more than a hint of an adult addressing a child. "Go back to your friends and ask one of them to fight you. I'm busy at target practice." A murmur of agreement rose from his companions.

Not good.

I made to get up, but Merlin's fingers closed around my wrist. "No. Leave them to it. They only have wooden swords. The worst either of them can get is a sore head. This has been coming for a while, now. Best to get it over with. Hopefully once they've battered one another they can go back to being their old selves."

I let him pull me down again, my lips compressed in a thin line.

Amhar turned toward his friends, a sneer on his face, but I could see that it was to Medraut he was looking. "He's scared to meet me face to face," he jeered, the anger in his voice barely hidden. "I've challenged him, but he refuses to fight."

One of Llacheu's friends, maybe Seisyll, leaned in close and said something with a laugh, and Llacheu nodded.

Amhar spun around again, probably driven by what he'd see as mockery. "Fight me, you coward. Fight me for my inheritance. I know it's what you want. If you win, it's yours. That's what you've always wanted, isn't it?" The words shot out of him in bullets of venom.

Llacheu set his hands on his hips. "I don't want your inheritance, Little Brother. I never have. And I don't want to fight you." His gaze settled on Medraut, standing at the center of Amhar's so-called friends. "Nor any of you."

Perhaps he wasn't including Medraut in that, though.

Medraut, keeping his gaze fixed on Llacheu, leaned in to Amhar and said something into his ear, and Amhar gave the smallest of nods. Then, his face bright red, Amhar pointed his wooden weapon at his brother's chest. "You're no man," he spat. "If Ariana were mine, she'd have a child at her breast by now. She keeps losing them because of *you*. Maybe she'd rather have another man. Maybe I'll offer her *my* services."

Medraut's eyes flashed with unmistakable malice, swiftly veiled.

Oh no.

Llacheu's calm face dissolved in fury. Seisyll made a grab for his arm, but Llacheu shook him off. "I'll show you who's a man, you little shit," he growled. "Give me a sword." He held out his hand as though expecting one to magically appear. It almost did. Someone thrust a wooden weapon into his grip. A good thing that was all they'd been practicing with.

"Fight. Fight. Fight," chanted Medraut's cronies, spreading out to form a circle, eyes alight with bloodlust. The other warriors, who'd been standing listening to the exchange, hurried forward to get a better view. For an instant, I had a good view of Medraut's face, flushed with triumph, as though this was exactly what he'd wanted. As though, perish the thought, he'd engineered this showdown between the brothers – by feeding the flame of Amhar's jealousy and telling him Llacheu wanted his place as heir.

Ignoring their audience, Llacheu and Amhar circled one another, their feet shuffling in the dirt. Only Amhar had a shield, and from the look on Llacheu's face, he was going to need it.

"Amhar's got no chance," I said to Merlin, who still had my wrist tightly in his grasp. "Llacheu will best him in no time." I'd never been the sort of mother to think my children perfect, and besides which, it felt like *two* of my children were in opposition here.

Height-wise, they were well matched, with Llacheu the heavier by a little thanks to the muscular development of increased maturity. But how alike were their manes of dark hair, their dark eyes and their loose-limbed bodies that made their wary shuffle almost a dance.

However, Llacheu possessed something Amhar didn't – patience. His face redder than ever, Amhar charged in with a flurry of blows that his brother parried with ease, the wooden blades thudding together again and again, every time Amhar doing all the work with the heavy weapon. Llacheu didn't bother to attack, but waited, playing the game of defense, letting Amhar tire, and tire he did.

The fight didn't last long. As soon as Llacheu saw Amhar's sword arm begin to flag, he switched to the attack, and in a moment had knocked the sword from his brother's hands with a blow that must have stung. It flew across the dusty grass and landed by Medraut's feet. He glanced down at it then across at Amhar, the faintest hint of a triumphant smile on his lips. Had he *wanted* Amhar to lose? In front of everyone?

"Told you they'd be fine," Merlin said, sounding satisfied, as Amhar shook his right hand as though it hurt.

Llacheu turned away from his brother and took a step toward his watching friends.

The expression of humiliated fury on Amhar's face warned me of what was coming next even before it happened. My hand shot to my mouth to stifle a cry as Amhar launched himself at his brother's retreating back.

"You bastard," he shouted, as the two of them crashed to the ground. The watching crowd closed in, shutting off our view and drowning out the grunts of their scuffle with shouts of encouragement coming from both sides. Young men always like a fist fight.

Wrenching my hand free from Merlin's grip, I slid down the grassy rampart onto the training ground and ran toward the crowd. I had to shove my way between the press of hot bodies of the excited, cheering warriors. "Let me through," I shouted, pulling at them. "Let me through."

As they realized who was hammering on their backs, they parted before me, and within a minute, I was at the front of the crowd. My boys were rolling in the dirt, locked together and trying to hit one another but not really getting any decent blows in as they were so close. To be honest, it was more of a playground tussle than anything else.

Merlin appeared beside me, an unholy glint in his eyes as though he might be enjoying this spectacle. He was a man, after all. "Stop them," I shouted above the encouraging cheers of the crowd.

"How?" Merlin yelled back, as Amhar managed to get his hands round Llacheu's throat. "What d'you think *I* can do?"

"Stop!" roared a voice like a foghorn.

Total silence fell in an instant. The warriors, young and old, retreated back several paces, as though trying to distance themselves from any responsibility. Amhar and Llacheu froze.

On the far side of the crowd stood Cei, his hands on his hips and his face flushed with anger. "*What* is going on here?"

Amhar and Llacheu struggled to their feet. Amhar had a bloody nose, and his hair was full of dirt. Llacheu winced as his hand went to his split lower lip, blood from it running down his chin. Both of them had the makings of black eyes.

"To the Hall," Cei ordered. "Now."

Chapter Sixteen

MY COFFEE HAS gone cold. I wipe the tears that have formed in the corners of my eyes away with my fingers. How long ago this was, yet only yesterday. If I close my eyes, I see my son standing before me now, an unhappy, discontented shade of a lost life, and this the turning point, the pivot on which all the events that followed turned.

Hindsight can be a gift, but a little knowledge can be a curse, and I had both, back then, and used neither, fool that I was. And as for Merlin… what use was he when I needed him most?

I get up and go into the kitchen, but Cabal stays outside, sleeping in the sun. I fill the kettle and set it on the hob to boil. A hot cup of coffee and my dreams of a life long gone await.

THE CROWD OF watching warriors parted, albeit a little reluctantly, and Merlin and I followed Cei as he escorted Amhar and Llacheu up the slope to the Hall. A few of Medraut's cronies made to come too, but Cei rounded angrily on them. "Get back to your training. This instant." I'd never seen him so furious before.

I glanced over my shoulder at Medraut, who'd remained standing with his friends as though he guessed he'd be repulsed if he tried to accompany Amhar. But the sly look on his face told me he longed to see how this would unfold. I fixed him with a cold stare, before hurrying after Merlin.

A cluster of villagers waited outside the Hall in the hot sun, one of them with a fat goose tucked under his arm, most likely queueing to go inside and put their disputes and problems before the king. When they saw the looks on our faces, they shuffled out of the way in haste, the goose honking its displeasure loudly.

Cei gave the two young combatants a shove through the open doors into the cool, dimly lit interior. Amhar stumbled on the threshold, and Cei gave them both another shove. As I followed them inside, my eyes went to the far end, where Arthur sat in stately splendor on his throne.

The spare and balding man who'd been standing, floppy straw hat squeezed in his hands, in front of the throne, peered over his shoulder at the commotion, eyes widening in shock. That one look had him hastily stepping aside into the gloom by the side wall.

"Keep going," Cei spat, as Amhar hesitated beside the cold hearth.

Llacheu had no such reticence about him and stepped up to take the supplicant's place, the fancy tassels on his boots shaking as he walked. He executed as neat a bow as he could, in the circumstances. Amhar joined him, keeping a good six feet away, his bow a little sketchier and his shoulders hunched in what looked like surly defiance.

I slid down the side of the Hall with Merlin behind me, and moved to take the seat beside Arthur's throne, where I often joined him in judgement. I wanted a ringside seat for this. Merlin melted into his usual unobtrusive place in the shadows behind the throne.

"What is this?" Arthur asked, his gaze traveling over his two sons, taking in their disheveled, dirty appearance and blossoming bruises.

"I found them fighting," Cei said. "Not in practice but in

aggression. And not with swords but rolling on the ground like wild animals. I put a stop to it before it went any further."

Llacheu, his hands clasped behind his back, stood up a little straighter. "I'm sorry, Father." Unsurprisingly, his voice held shame and contrition; he'd not wanted this and had avoided it until Amhar had gone out of his way to provoke him. Part of me wanted to tell Arthur that, but another part held my tongue silent. Twenty years had taught me that in a situation like this, a father ruled, and a mother had little say. At least, not in public.

And this *was* in public because those waiting villagers had come creeping in through the open doors to stand staring up the Hall, open-mouthed and agog.

Arthur's gaze went to Amhar's rebellious face. Not a shred of shame or contrition marred his ruddy features. His bottom lip stuck out, much as it had done when he'd been a sulky child, and his dark brows had formed a frown worthy of his father. Arthur waited.

The silence stretched out.

His patience paid off at last.

Amhar shot a look of pure hatred at his brother. "I'm not sorry," he hissed. "He deserved it."

Llacheu's eyes flew wide open. "What? What did I do?"

Cei stepped between them as they bristled at one another.

"You heard me," Amhar snarled. "You think you're so wonderful. You think you're Father's favorite. Well, you're not. *I* am. *I'm* his heir."

"Be quiet," Arthur snapped. His hands had tensed on the arms of his throne, the knuckles whitening. His gaze went from one angry face to the other. "Who started this?"

"He did," Amhar spat. "He wants my place as your heir. He's trying to undermine me with the younger warriors."

Llacheu gave a snort. "I am *not*. He's gone mad. And if you want to know how it started, he came marching over and challenged me to fight." He threw me a pleading glance. "Ask Gwen. She saw."

"Don't call my mother Gwen," Amhar snarled. "She's your queen, not your friend."

What on earth had got into him? I held up my hand. "Llacheu has always called me by my name," I said, and would have kept going, only Arthur waved me to silence.

"You, Amhar," he said, his voice level and measured, "have been my heir since your birth. Although it *is* within my power as king to choose any man I wish to follow me, be he nobly born or poor."

Amhar glared back at him out of eyes that might well have been mad. What had Medraut been whispering in his ear? Or maybe I was just paranoid and wanting to blame the handiest person.

Arthur glared right back. "Do you think I'm going to choose a foolish boy so full of jealousies he can't control himself? Would I want a man like that to govern my people after I'm gone? Would he make a wise king, good in judgement and strong in battle? Do you really think so?"

Uh oh.

Llacheu's eyes filled with concern. "Father, he didn't mean this. It was the heat of the moment, I'm sure. His words were spoken in haste and not considered."

Of course, Llacheu, the understanding older brother, who'd always known he couldn't be the heir and had never wanted it, wouldn't want the boy he'd loved since they were children dispossessed. If only Amhar could see this.

Amhar shot him a look of unconcealed venom. "I don't need *you* to defend me."

Arthur tapped his fingers on the arm of his throne. A bad sign. He fixed his gaze back on Amhar. "You accuse me of having a favorite. I do not. You are both my sons, and I love you equally."

"That's not true," Amhar spat, his left leg twitching as though he wanted to stamp it as he'd been wont to do as a child, and his lower lip starting to wobble. "Every time you're away, it's *him* you turn to. It's him who's left in charge here. You say you want me to learn the ways of governing this kingdom, but you never give me the chance. It's him you favor. Him you love. Not me. Not me, your trueborn son."

His voice wavered as he said the last few words and he clamped his teeth over his bottom lip, perhaps to still the shake. Was he remembering that time long ago when he'd almost voiced the fear, from a vile rumor put about amongst the boys, that he wasn't his father's son? When he'd been on the verge of repeating what his so-called friends had taunted him with? Did he still, deep in his heart, think that lie might be true?

I glanced back at Merlin, but he stood unmoving in the shadows, face impassive.

Arthur drew in a breath. "Listen to me, boy, when I speak. I do *not* have a favorite and never have. Llacheu is older than you by seven years, and as such he has more experience than you do." He glanced at Llacheu. "That is the only reason I leave the governing of Din Cadan and Dumnonia to him when I'm away. I didn't leave him in charge when he was your age. It does *not* mean that I intend him to be king after me, as you seem to think."

He rose to his feet. "But if you carry on like this, giving in to your petty jealousies so easily, then that is something I may well consider." He glowered at Amhar. "Apologize for the trouble you have caused."

Amhar's face blanched under the dirt, but he still knew better than to refuse his father. Thank goodness. "I'm sorry, Father." The words forced their way between his teeth, and he kept his gaze averted from Llacheu.

Arthur nodded to Cei. "I have more worthy causes to hear this morning than those of foolish boys. They can go."

Llacheu bowed to his father, but Amhar spun on the spot and stalked out of the Hall without a backward glance.

This was far from over.

A FRANTIC HAMMERING on the door of our bedchamber dragged me roughly from my sleep and into sudden alert wakefulness, cold sweat springing out on my skin. Arthur, as quickly awake as I was, rolled over in bed and slid out from beneath the covers. He padded naked to the door and opened it a crack. "What is it?"

Merlin barged into our room, his face papery white.

I sat bolt upright, eyes wide, and pulled the covers up to hide my own nakedness.

"You'd better get dressed," Merlin said, a shake in his voice. "You need to come with me. Now."

Arthur didn't need telling twice. He pulled on the braccae and undershirt he'd discarded on the floor last night and slid his feet into his boots. As he reached for his sword belt, Merlin shook his head. "You won't need that."

"What is it?" I asked from the bed, the thudding of my heart loud in my ears. "What's happened?"

Merlin's anguished gaze met mine, but all he did was shake his head. Were those tears in his eyes?

Without a word, he hurried Arthur out into the Hall, and as the door banged closed behind them, I scrambled out of bed and grabbed my clothes from the top of the chest where I'd left them folded neatly the night before. As it was summer, all I had to do was pull on my knee-length linen tunic and sandals then run after the men.

The hall doors had just banged shut behind them, so I sprinted down the aisle and out into pale, early-morning sunshine. Two of the wall guards stood there, shifting uneasily from one foot to the other, their faces as pale as Merlin's, their eyes frightened. What was going on?

"This way." Merlin turned down one of the narrow alleys that ran between the closely packed buildings. Arthur followed, and I hurried after them. The two guards trailed behind me, their footsteps leaden.

We passed between the houses and reached the barns that bordered the horse pens. The scant remains of a thin mist hung in the air, not quite burned off by the early morning sun. On our left stood an empty shed, on our right a large midden, where the nearby householders threw their waste, and where dung from the animal sheds ended up. Steam and the smell of rotting refuse rose from it in the morning chill.

Sprawled across it lay a body, the limbs akimbo like those of a broken doll, head thrown so far back as to make the face invisible. The throat had been cut from ear to ear, and blood darkened the front of both tunic and undershirt. Already a swarm of flies buzzed around it, settling to lay their eggs.

I stopped dead. Those tasseled boots.

Arthur's face had blanched.

No. It couldn't be. I ran forward, scrabbling at the rotting vegetables and manure, but the body was high up toward the back and out of reach. My eyes fixed on that great gaping maw of a slash across a white throat.

One of the guards pulled me back. "No, milady. Don't." He choked on the words.

Merlin bowed his head.

Running footsteps sounded behind us. Cei slithered to a halt. "What is it? What's happened?" He, like Arthur, hadn't taken time to put a tunic on.

"It's Llacheu," Merlin said, turning anguished eyes to Cei.

His name. As Merlin said it, realization hit me so hard I staggered backwards against my guard, my hands to my mouth, nausea rising in a tidal wave. I had nothing to throw up but bile, bitter in my mouth as his name on Merlin's lips. The guard put his arms around me for support, but I shook him off.

"No." Cei shook his head. "It can't be. It isn't. No."

Bending over, I leaned against the barn wall and retched. No. This couldn't be true. I was in a nightmare. Not Llacheu. Not my beloved stepson. Not that vital, handsome young man, so kind, so loving, so generous, and so brave. Slaughtered like an animal and thrown onto the rubbish tip. This couldn't be.

"Get him down," Arthur said, his voice so quiet I hardly

heard him. "We need to take him to the Hall." He turned away, and for a moment leaned against the barn wall near me, his chest heaving.

I straightened up, spitting the taste of bile from my mouth.

He turned his head and our eyes met.

I'd not seen such anguish since the death of Rhiwallon. I reached out a hand, but he straightened, his face set in a hard mask, and I let my hand drop.

He cleared his throat. "I want him down from there. Now."

The two guards clambered up onto the top of the midden, their bodies obscuring my view. As though drawn by a powerful magnet, I couldn't tear my eyes away.

Merlin caught my shoulder, his fingers rough and firm. "Come away. Let them get him down. You shouldn't watch."

I resisted, anger welling. "Someone should watch. We owe him that, surely?"

"I will," Cei said. "I'll stay with Arthur. You shouldn't see this, Gwen. Go with Merlin." His blue eyes had filled with tears. "Go on."

Merlin clamped a strong arm around my shoulders and forcefully walked me back up the alley toward the Great Hall, my reluctant feet dragging in the dirt. A cockerel crowed on a rooftop, heralding a day Llacheu would never see. Voices came from up ahead. Normal voices on a day that would not be normal. A world that would never be normal again.

Outside the Hall, the fortress was coming to life, but somehow word must have got around, and people were standing about in groups, muttering together. So not normal after all. No, never normal. This was the day my heart broke.

The people stared as Merlin hurried me past them and into the Hall, his arm tight around my shoulders, holding me close. I kept my eyes down, afraid I'd trip and fall. As if that would have mattered. As if anything mattered now.

The doors closed behind us and the warm darkness that enfolded me somehow managed to feel comforting and homely, as though nothing bad had gone on outside its walls. As though nothing in here could be harmed. What a lie that was.

"Into your chamber," Merlin said, hurrying me across the reed-strewn floor. "Let them bring the body in and lay it out here in the Hall. You don't need to see that."

He pushed open the door and we went inside. It banged shut behind us, like a death knell.

The door to Archfedd's room swung open. Wearing just her long undershirt, she stood rubbing the sleep from her eyes. "What's all that banging about?"

Maia appeared behind her, similarly clad. "Milady?"

I shook my head, unable to speak.

Merlin went to them. "Your mother needs you, Archfedd. Get dressed. Maia, fetch hot spiced wine. For shock."

Archfedd grabbed Merlin's sleeve. "What is it? What's happened?" Her voice rose in panic. "Is it Father? Tell me."

"Not your father," Merlin said. "Llacheu. Maia, take her and get her dressed, then fetch that wine."

Archfedd's eyes went to my face. She must have read the truth in it. "What happened? How? An accident? What?" Her voice rose in fear.

"Murder," I said, surprised I could form the word. "Someone has murdered your brother."

From inside the Hall came the sound of men arriving. Carrying something. My hands went to my ears. I didn't want to listen. That wasn't my boy's body thumping onto the trestle table.

Archfedd's wide-eyed gaze went to the door. "What? Is he in *there*? Have they brought him *here*?" She made a start toward the door, but Merlin let go of me and grabbed her arm.

"No. Not yet. You can't see him like that."

"He's my brother!" Her voice rose in a wail. "He's my brother!" She crumpled against him, and he wrapped her in his arms as she burst into tears.

Over her head he looked at Maia, who'd just returned with the wine and set it on the table. "Take her. Leave the wine. Get the Princess back into her room and keep her there. I'll see to the Queen." He almost shoved Archfedd into Maia's capable hands, and Maia, holding her close, ushered her back to her room. The sound of her sobs rose to the sooty rafters.

As the door shut behind them, Merlin heaved an unsteady sigh.

We had only a moment's respite. The door into the Hall banged open and Arthur came in, his face waxy pale. He strode to the table where Excalibur lay in her tooled leather scabbard, picked it up and drew the sword.

The lamplight flickered over the sword's damascene blade, making it ripple like water, as he stood staring down at it for an eternity.

At last, he raised anguished eyes to mine. "I'll kill whoever did this with my own hands."

I nodded, my own heart breaking – for him, for me, for Llacheu, that glorious, handsome, brave young man, gone, extinguished, no more. "Someone needs to tell Ariana."

"Oh God," his voice cracked. "I'd forgotten her." His left hand went to his forehead, pressing against the skin. "My head aches. I-I can't…"

I went to him, but he waved me back with a frantic hand. "No. If you do that, I shall break." He shook his head. "And I must not. My son was murdered, and I must find the killer." He drew a deep breath, perhaps to steady himself. "When that killer lies dead, I will mourn. But not until then."

"And Ariana?"

"Let her sleep in peace a little longer. She mustn't see him like this. Let Bedwyr hide his… wound." His voice cracked with emotion and tears glistened at the corners of his eyes. He dashed them away on his sleeve.

I ached to take him in my arms. "Who-who could have done this?"

He shook his head, looking down as his fingers ran along the blade in his hand. "I don't know." He raised his eyes from the sword again. "But whoever it was won't get away. I've sent orders that no one is to be allowed out of the gates. We'll pen this bastard up inside our walls and I'll have my revenge on him if I die in the process."

I shivered. Was I the only one thinking back to the scene two days ago when Amhar had professed his hatred for his brother?

Chapter Seventeen

THEY LAID LLACHEU'S body out on one of the trestle tables in the Hall. Bedwyr and his apprentice healers stripped and cleaned the body – no such thing as preserving forensic evidence for us. Bedwyr stitched up the gash in Llacheu's throat and the apprentices dressed him again in clean clothes, ready for burial and for the fortress to pay their last respects. Dead bodies couldn't be kept hanging around long in summer.

Archfedd, Arthur and I went in first to see Bedwyr's work. That wasn't Llacheu lying there. What had made him who he was had gone, flown far away, his handsome face waxen from lack of blood, as were the still hands crossed on his chest.

Arthur stood in silence for a moment before bending to kiss his son's cold cheek, his face drained of expression. Like an automaton, I did the same, then Archfedd bent, her eyes red and puffy from crying, and pressed her lips to his skin.

I couldn't take my eyes from my stepson's face. Dark lashes brushed those pale cheeks, hiding eyes from which the light had fled. A scarf about his neck concealed his wound, and his hair had been washed clean and combed back from his smooth forehead with loving care. Was this how Arthur would look when he was dead? I swallowed the lump in my throat and bit my lip. I wouldn't think about that. I wouldn't.

Without a word, Arthur walked away from us and took his place on his throne, staring down the Hall toward the makeshift bier.

I took Archfedd's hand and ushered her back to the chamber where Maia waited. Then I went to the partly open door to watch, unable to tear myself away from the grim sight, as though hoping that perhaps it was all a mistake and in a moment, he'd sit up and laugh at us all.

A long stream of people filed through the Hall throughout the day, many arriving from the village and farms at the foot of the hill, some from further afield. Llacheu had been well loved from his childhood by all.

His mother, Tangwyn, came, of course, but without her husband and younger children. Grief-stricken and haggard, she made a tragic figure as she wailed over his body, tearing at her clothes and hair until her friends dragged her away, her screams audible for some time after she left.

I'd seen so much death in my time here, and yet this one could have been the first. I might not have given birth to him, but he felt as though he'd been my son, and it was with a mother's love I grieved him.

After a while Archfedd left Maia and came to stand by the door with me, her trembling body pressed up against me. One hand gripped mine, her eyes red and swollen from the crying she couldn't stem.

"I can't believe it," she whispered for the twentieth time. "I can't believe someone did this to him. To my brother."

"We'll find out who, don't you worry," I said, half afraid that I might be right.

She wiped her eyes on her sleeve. "But why *him*? What did he ever do to anger anyone?" She gave a big sniff. "He was so good and kind to everyone. He had no enemies."

The fear that she was wrong threatened to overwhelm me.

It was late in the day before Amhar, accompanied by Medraut, came to pay his respects. They filed in with some of their companions, all of them quiet and subdued for once. Perhaps the sight of someone as young as they were lying dead had come as a rude awakening. The young tend to see themselves as immortal.

By now I'd left an exhausted Archfedd in Maia's caring hands and gone to sit on my own throne beside Arthur, hoping my presence supported him. I had a good view as Amhar approached the makeshift bier with unsteady footsteps, his face nearly as pale as the corpse's. Medraut, more confident by far and with a hand on his friend's back, urged him forward.

Beside me, I sensed Arthur stiffening, and his fingers began to tap the arm of his throne. Could he be thinking the same thing as me? The terrible, unthinkable thing.

Amhar halted at the foot of the bier, staring at his brother's body, eyes round as saucers. What was going through his mind?

My eyes slid past him to Medraut's face. Unreadable – carefully schooled to be so, perhaps.

I wanted to berate myself for thinking my own son could have done this to his brother, but I couldn't. When last they'd been together in the Hall, the enmity between them had been tangible. Or rather, the enmity from Amhar for his brother. Horror that I, as his mother, could even consider he'd committed such a terrible crime – such a Biblical crime – ate into my heart and set it pounding, and my breath came fast and shallow.

I fought to control myself, terrified Arthur would hear, or read the thoughts standing in fiery letters in my mind.

Medraut gave Amhar an ungentle shove, and the two of them approached Llacheu's forever stilled face. In death he still possessed a share of the boyish beauty he'd always had, but with the departure of his soul, it had become nothing but a mask.

Medraut bent and kissed Llacheu's cold hands.

Amhar hesitated, guilt written across his face and in every movement he made. Conviction that he'd done this swept through me. Swiftly followed by a wave of my own guilt that I could think that of him. No. He couldn't have. Not Amhar.

Arthur stood.

I looked up at him, trembling with fear.

He pointed a finger at his son. "Honor your brother." His voice carried across the Hall where a dozen more people had crowded in by the doors and were waiting their turn to approach the body.

Amhar stared up at his father, his mouth hanging open, but he didn't speak.

"Kiss him," Medraut hissed, the words carrying in the silence.

"I can't," Amhar whispered, audible to all. "I can't do it."

Arthur seemed to grow in stature. "Then get out," he roared. "And don't darken my doors again."

For a moment, Amhar stood staring at his father, then he turned and bolted through the onlookers and out of the Hall, the doors banging shut behind him. With one measuring look at Arthur, Medraut bowed and hurried after him.

A heavy silence reigned.

Arthur sat down with a thud, nostrils flaring, brows lowered. "Continue."

The people who'd retreated to the doors, crept forward again, watchful, wary eyes on their lord.

WE BURIED LLACHEU the next day in the graveyard beside the tiny church at the bottom of the hill. Six warriors carried his bier and the priest performed a Christian ceremony in the fresh air for the benefit of his mother more than us. All the inhabitants of the fortress attended, and most of the farmers and villagers, from the youngest child to the oldest crone, making a crowd ten deep around the grave. And once the grave had been filled in, flowers from people's gardens and the hedgerows covered it in a mantle of color. A tribute to how highly he'd been regarded.

It was under cover of the funeral that Amhar fled. None of us noticed him missing until the evening, when Medraut, all innocent and puzzled, asked us if we'd seen him. We hadn't, and detective work by Merlin soon discovered that his horse had vanished as well.

"His flight declares his guilt," Cei said, as we stood together in the Hall, his usually affable face distorted in disgust. "He's run from fear of being apprehended. From fear of your rightful wrath."

Arthur's fists clenched. "I didn't want to believe it of him. I couldn't bring myself to. How can I even now?"

I put a wary hand on his arm.

Merlin met my gaze, his dark eyes troubled.

"I know it's hard to believe of your own son, but now it's proven," Cei said. "By his own actions, he's condemned. What will you do?"

I stared from one to the other of them in horror, remembering with reluctance how the renegade king of Dinas Brent, Melwas, had boasted of his climb to kingship over the bodies of his murdered brothers and how he'd gotten away with it. Fratricide was not unknown, so why was it so shocking that Amhar might have done the same to rid himself of a perceived rival? This was the Dark Ages, not twenty-first-century Britain. His jealousy of Llacheu had been brewing for years, and Arthur hadn't helped by singling out his oldest son, no matter what he said about having no favorites.

Arthur nodded, face set. "You're right. I am the High King and must be seen to uphold the law. No son of mine commits murder without retribution. But first, before I act, I need Merlin's wisdom." He turned to face his old friend.

Merlin shifted uncomfortably, probably not liking being put on the spot. "How can I help?"

Arthur frowned. "By using your Sight. Look, and tell me what you see. Find out for me if my son has committed this terrible crime. Did he kill his brother?"

Merlin hesitated, his tongue darting around his lips. "I have tried to look," he said, after a moment. "But my vision is clouded."

No wonder he looked shifty. This wasn't an answer liable to help in any way. And when men like my husband posed a question, they wanted an immediate and clear answer.

Cei moved a step closer, everything about him threatening. "Then tell us, Seer, what it is you *have* seen."

Merlin shook his head, shoulders sagging. "I cannot. Something clouds my Sight. The moment we found him, I tried to look. It's the best time to find a link. But nothing came to me but darkness. Don't think I haven't looked again. I have, but all I see is thick mist." He shook his head a second time as though to clear it. "I fear something is deliberately blocking me."

Or someone. Hadn't Morgana interfered with Merlin's gift before, to block it? Maybe she was doing the same thing right now. But why? What earthly reason could she have to prevent Merlin seeing who had killed Llacheu? Unless she had something to do with it herself. But why would anyone want to kill Arthur's baseborn son? Despite Amhar's jealousy, Llacheu had posed no threat to his position, and Cadwy, who might have done so out of a grudge, was long dead.

Arthur spun away and strode down the Hall on restless legs. "Then we must presume him guilty and act accordingly. He must be brought to justice."

Not my son.

What had we come to that Arthur was calling for something that might ultimately be a death warrant? My breath died in my throat, and my heart pounded so loud and so fast, surely those around me must have heard it. The world spun. The ground came up to meet me with a bang, and my cheek pressed into the dusty reeds. I shut my eyes to stop the incessant spinning.

"Gwen!"

"The queen. Give her air."

"Stand back."

Slowly the world ceased to roll beneath my body, and I managed to open my eyes to a steady view instead of a whirling vortex. My breath returned, and someone put their hands under my arms to hoist me into a sitting position. For a moment everything spun again before settling.

Arthur's face appeared in front of mine. "Gwen. Are you all right?"

I managed the smallest of nods, afraid to set off that spinning again, afraid I'd vomit in front of everyone.

"Can you stand?"

I held onto him while he helped me to my feet, unsure whether I might fall again. His arm went around my waist, strong and supportive, and I leaned closer to his body. "Don't assume it was Amhar. Please," I whispered.

His head whipped round, his face inches from mine. "I'm not assuming anything until it's proven. But as he's run, what am I supposed to think? That he's run because he's upset that the brother he resented has been killed? The brother he couldn't bring himself to show respect to even in death."

"That doesn't mean he did it," I said, aware of the desperation in my voice. "He could have run for any number of reasons. He could just be afraid you'd think it was him, after the fight they had. It doesn't mean he's guilty. You need to hear his side of it before you pass judgement. Please."

"And how are we supposed to do that with him fled?" Cei asked, anger in every word. He'd loved Llacheu like a son, particularly after the death of Rhiwallon. "He's run, and that's enough for me. As good as a written confession."

Oh God. Since when had gentle Cei become so judgmental? So narrow minded?

Arthur turned to Merlin. "Take Gwen into our chamber. She needs to lie down. Cei and I have things to discuss, and a pursuit to plan. It's clear *you'll* be of no assistance." His last sentence came out sharp with accusation.

Merlin put a strong arm around my shoulders, holding me close, but I didn't miss the angry look he shot at Arthur. In stony silence he escorted me through the door into my chamber. Someone closed it behind us, shutting out the Hall.

He sat me on one of the chairs by the table and poured a goblet of wine. "Here. Drink this. You've had a nasty shock."

He sat as well and filled a second goblet for himself, knocking it back in one go while I sipped mine. It was strong, unwatered Falernian.

"Why can't you see?" I asked, a question that had been nagging me since he'd said his vision was clouded. "What is it that's stopping you?"

He shrugged. "If I knew, then I could prevent it. I've tried, believe me, but I can't."

I bit my lip, unsure whether to broach my suggestion.

"What is it?" he asked.

"Do you think Morgana could be somehow behind it? Be blocking you in some way? She's the only person with the power to do that."

He looked me in the eye. "That's possible, I suppose. What makes you think she'd want to?"

"Because she has an agenda." Best not to mention my suspicions that her plans might involve his own daughter. "It suits her to prevent you finding out what it is. She's like an evil spider in the center of her web, spinning her silk to ensnare the unwary, writing the fates of others, and twisting history to suit herself." I shuddered. "I refuse to be considered amongst the unwary. I won't let her get the better of us." I seized his hand. "She means Arthur to kill our son in revenge for Llacheu's murder. In my old world, no son of Arthur is mentioned as following him after his death. We have to change that. Amhar *must* follow him as king."

"Put like that..." Merlin said, with a wry smile. "We can but try."

I nodded. "She needs to be stopped before she unleashes any more wickedness." Oh, how I'd like to be the one to do that. "Then you'll be able to use the Sight to see who really killed Llacheu, and if it's Amhar, he, and I, will have to accept his father's justice, but if it's not, then we can save him."

The conviction that I was meant to save Amhar, and with

him, Arthur, washed over me like a tidal wave. I could change history; I knew I could. This was why I was here. My purpose all along had been to save my son. All the doubts I'd felt about Amhar fell away, replaced with a rising confidence that he hadn't done this terrible thing, and I was going to prove it.

"As soon as Arthur and Cei set out after Amhar," I said. "Then we must head to Viroconium. Just you and me. We'll corner that old witch and force a confession out of her."

Merlin's brow furrowed.

I tightened my hold on his hand. "Amhar's my son. I *have* to save him. We need to get to Viroconium and find out what Morgana's done before Arthur finds Amhar and metes out his justice. It's the only way. I refuse to sit at home and twiddle my thumbs while my son's in danger."

He sighed. "Very well. We'll go together. But we'll take guards. We can't ride that far in safety if there's just the two of us. There could be brigands."

I nodded. "Llawfrodedd. I'd trust him anywhere. He should come."

The door from Archfedd's chamber swung open and she hurtled in. "If he's going, then I am too. You can't leave me behind. Amhar's my brother, and I know he's innocent. Llacheu was my brother, too. We need to find out who really did it. You have to let me come."

I looked into her determined face. She scowled. "And anyway, I refuse to stay here alone with Medraut."

No use telling her it was wrong to listen at doors.

Chapter Eighteen

FIRST THING IN the morning, Arthur, who'd not come to bed last night, Cei, and a force of forty men set off in pursuit of Amhar, leaving Gwalchmei in charge of Din Cadan. Arthur had asked Merlin first, but Merlin had declined, excusing himself on the grounds of being unable to make decisions with his Sight so clouded. Gwalchmei had stepped proudly into the breach.

I saw them off, my heart heavy and my nerves jangling with fear. With any luck, tracing Amhar would be like finding the proverbial needle in the haystack. He could have gone to ground anywhere and might very well no longer be in Dumnonia. At the back of my mind, despite my decision to believe him innocent, there was always that horrible, creeping fear that he might actually have been the perpetrator of this crime, and the suspicion that all Merlin and I'd be doing with our efforts was proving his guilt.

Occasionally, back in my old world, I'd seen on the news when a serial killer was at last apprehended, and the avid speculation as to whether his mother or wife or girlfriend had known of his guilt and kept quiet. Now I stood in their shoes, I understood all too well why they might have done. Would I keep quiet if we found Amhar to be guilty? The urge to protect your offspring is overwhelming, but Amhar's crime involved the young man I'd always seen as another son. How could I weigh my feelings for either of them and come up with a decision?

Arthur had been gone less than an hour, and I was busy packing my saddlebags, when the slight young girl who was maid to Llacheu's widow, Ariana, came running through the open door from the Hall. "Milady, you has to come quick," she gasped, her cheeks flushed red, probably with exertion and fear. "Mother Donella sent me to fetch you. Milady Ariana's took bad."

Oh God, no. She'd been carried down to the funeral yesterday on a bier, as Donella had refused to allow her to walk, and had sat sobbing quietly between her parents throughout, her pale face streaked with tears and her eyes swollen and red.

I ran with the girl, through the silent Hall and down the hill to Llacheu's house near the training ground. The door stood open, and when I ran inside, I found Anwyll, Ariana's father, standing by the cold embers in the firepit, his hands clasped in prayer. A wooden partition wall separated the living area from the bedchamber and from beyond it came what sounded like the cries of a wounded animal.

With a quick glance at Anwyll's stricken face, I pushed open the door and went into the chamber. Ariana, pretty little Ariana with the sweet, kind face, Ariana who'd waited so patiently for Llacheu to decide he loved her, lay back on her pillows, her pasty face shining with sweat and contorted with pain. Her undershirt had been pulled up to bunch on her swollen belly, and the bedclothes and her legs were dark with blood. Too much blood. An ocean of blood, like the blood that had drained from her husband's severed arteries.

Donella, her apron stained, bent over her on one side of the bed, and her mother, Adwen, knelt on the other, holding her hand. She was a woman a little older than me, her once dark hair liberally flecked with gray, and her body thickened by many births, all of which had been trouble free, unlike her oldest daughter's. Once she must have been as pretty as Ariana, but now her lined face sagged in fear as she sponged her daughter's sweaty brow.

"What happened?" I asked, even though I could see what was

153

going on.

Donella peered over her shoulder, her face drawn with worry. "She began in the night but din't tell anyone. Her girl found her like this not so long ago. The baby be a-comin'. There be nothin' I can do to stop it. Not now. 'Tis too late."

My eyes met Adwen's pale gray ones and read the terror written in them. This was too early. A baby born at six months could not live. Only a modern incubator in a Neonatal ICU could save it, and that lay fifteen hundred years away.

I hurried to kneel beside Adwen, putting my hand over hers where it held her daughter's. I had nothing to say, and neither did she. All we could do was pray for Ariana.

The baby came an hour later in a slither of amniotic fluid and blood. A boy. He never breathed, but lay, tiny and perfect but for that spark of life, in Donella's horny hands. Too small to have had any chance at all. Llacheu's son. Arthur's grandson.

Ariana lay back exhausted on her pillows, eyes closed, uninterested in the child she'd lost, as the lifeblood seeped out of her. None of us could do anything to staunch the flow. I'd heard of post-partum hemorrhages in my old world, and this must have been one. Only a total hysterectomy would have been able to save her, and that, like the ICU baby incubator, lay too far away in the future.

She died soon after her little son.

I trudged back to the Hall, leaving Donella and Adwen to lay Ariana out for burial beside her husband and Anwyll sitting alone by the cold embers of the fire with his head in his hands. My own head hung in despair, and tears streamed down my cheeks as I railed against the injustice of life. Maybe if Llacheu hadn't been so foully murdered, this poor girl might have been able to hang onto her baby long enough to have given him a fighting chance. Arthur's grandson. Not quite *my* grandson, but I felt as though that little mite they'd buried in her arms had been.

Merlin was waiting for me in the Hall, with Archfedd, Llawfrodedd and our saddlebags.

"We have to go," he said, a touch of gentleness in his voice for once.

I shook my head, swiping the tears away with my sleeve. "How can I? She's dead, Merlin. Dead. She *and* the baby. More deaths to lay at the door of a murderer who might well be my own son." The raging uncertainty in my heart seemed to vacillate from one conviction to the other too swiftly for roots to settle.

Archfedd bristled. "I refuse to believe my brother could be responsible for Llacheu's death," she snapped. "He doesn't have it in him."

Merlin's eyes met mine. I didn't want to consider whether I agreed with Archfedd or not. Too difficult. Something to be faced later.

Llawfrodedd studied his boots as though they were the most interesting things in the hall.

I looked away, unable to hold Merlin's troubled gaze. Perhaps he suspected that even if Amhar turned out to be guilty of these deaths, I might try to save him from whatever retribution Arthur had in mind. Well, wouldn't I?

"At least we'll be doing something," Archfedd said, touching my arm with gentle fingers. "We're none of us any use here. And Father might catch up with Amhar before we can reach Morgana in Viroconium. We have to try. We owe it to Amhar to believe him innocent. I don't believe he could have done it, but Father does."

Innocent until proven guilty. An all too modern concept. Not one Arthur would be likely to adhere to.

Llawfrodedd lifted anxious eyes to Archfedd's face, but stayed silent. Impossible to tell what he thought about the young man, so close to him in age, with whom he'd trained for so long. He might have had a better idea than any of us of what Amhar was capable. And wasn't all the training they'd done geared to one thing? Killing. Had we not made Amhar into the killer I feared he'd become?

But Archfedd was right. We had to leave and leave now. I

wiped my eyes on my sleeve and nodded. "Let's go, then."

Our horses were waiting ready-saddled outside the stables with our twenty armed escort warriors, and it was the work of only a few minutes to sling saddlebags over their quarters and mount up. In the bright, carefree sunshine of midsummer, with a girl and her baby lying dead behind us, we rode down the cobbled road and out of the gates of Din Cadan on our terrible quest.

Viroconium lay over a hundred and fifty miles to the north, along what remained of the old Roman roads, and on horseback, with necessity on our heels, we could manage fifty miles in a day if we pushed our horses hard and rode for long hours. But we and our horses were fit, and the grass at the sides of the graveled roads gave us the opportunity to canter, so to begin with we made rapid progress.

We didn't break our journey in any of the small towns or wayside inns we'd so often stayed at in the past. Instead, we camped under the stars, rising at first light and continuing on our way with no delays of any kind, riding until night fell.

Three days later, as evening drew in and our shadows stretched out long behind us, we reached our goal.

Gone were the days when Arthur's unpleasant and jealous older brother had ruled here. As we rode beneath the arched gateway of Viroconium, I couldn't help but reflect on how Arthur's relationship with Cadwy had now been repeated between his own two sons. Were the sons of kings destined to perpetual jealous conflict?

We rode straight to the Imperial Palace, that sprawling con-glomeration of classical Roman architecture with homespun British practicality strapped onto it. After we'd left Llawfrodedd in charge of our men as they attended to our horses in the stables, Merlin, Archfedd and I, accompanied by an aged servant, took the maze of corridors to the main courtyard.

At this late hour, torches already burned in iron brackets on every soot-stained wall, throwing circles of light across the flagstones of the colonnaded walkway and plunging the center of the large courtyard into impenetrable gloom.

We followed the servant's shuffling feet to the ornately carved double doors of the king's own apartments, where burly guards armed with spears and swords stood to attention on either side. They set their spears in a cross in front of the doors as we approached, their watchful eyes on us. No king is ever safe from an assassin's knife, as I knew all too well.

"The Queen of Dumnonia and Princess Archfedd to see the King," Merlin declared, and the servant confirmed his statement. The spears withdrew, and the guards saluted us, as the servant opened one of the doors and slipped inside.

A moment later he emerged and gestured to us to enter.

These were the rooms where King Uthyr Pendragon had lain dying twenty years ago. The rooms where Arthur had cleverly manipulated his father into insisting on our wedding, before Cadwy could engineer a putting aside of his wife so he could marry me, the Ring Maiden, himself. Something that would undoubtedly have happened but for Arthur's clever moves.

Not in love with Arthur at that time, I hadn't wanted any marriage, but the prospect of Cadwy as an alternative had driven me to it, and love had come later. A love so strong I'd remained here in the Dark Ages with Arthur when given the opportunity to return to my old world. And yet, if he got to our son first, and meted out his justice, how would I feel then? Was our love something that could stand that sort of test?

I didn't know, and the hollow emptiness in my stomach bore witness to that. A hollow emptiness of dread and fear, gnawed away at me all my waking hours and much of the sleepless nights I'd had on our journey.

Uthyr's outer chamber had changed very little. Underfoot lay the same black and white geometric mosaic, but the strewn furs had been banished. The faded fresco from Greek mythology still covered walls where every so often oil lamps sat in small niches, spreading their golden glow across the room.

Custennin sat at a solid oak desk in the best lit corner of the room. In front of this, two carved wooden bench seats stood, as piled with cushions as they'd once been, and between them the long low table where Cadwy had left poisoned wine for us to drink, so long ago.

In our boys' clothes, Archfedd and I bowed to our kinsman, and Merlin did the same, more deeply.

Custennin, who must by now have been in his late twenties, rose to his feet and came around the table to greet us. Not a handsome man, with thick lips too like his father's and a long, hooked nose, he was nevertheless clearly marked by the Pendragon genes. It being summer, and hot, he wore only a knee length tunic over bare brown legs and open sandals.

He held out his hands. "Aunt Gwen. Merlin. I bid you welcome, although it's a surprise to see you here without my uncle. Please. Sit." He gestured to the cushioned benches, and we all sat down, Archfedd and me on one, him and Merlin on the other.

"To what do I owe this pleasure?" he asked.

Now to the difficult part.

While I was struggling with what to say, Merlin took the lead. "We've come to see Morgana."

A frown flitted across Custennin's face, lowering his brows and giving him an unnerving look of his father. Thank goodness that was where any resemblance ended. "Then I have bad news for you," he said. "My aunt is not here, nor has she been for some weeks."

My stomach did a nervous flip and my shoulders sagged. All day, no, for the last three days, I'd been psyching myself up to face her, and now we were here, she wasn't.

"Do you know where she is?" Archfedd butted in. "We have urgent business with her."

"My daughter, the Princess Archfedd," I said in a hurry in case Custennin hadn't worked out who she was by our family resemblance.

Custennin shifted uncomfortably. "I believe she and her daughter are with her sister, my Aunt Morgawse, in Caer

Legeion."

I had the distinct impression he'd been glad to see the back of them. Wary distrust showed in his eyes, as if by wanting to see her, we'd allied ourselves with her faction.

His teeth caught in his lower lip. "At least, that is where she told me she was going."

My heart sank. Eighty miles due south. If only we'd known, we could have been there by now.

"Then that's where we must go," I said, with as much conviction as I could muster.

Chapter Nineteen

C USTENNIN FURNISHED US with overnight accommodation in the palace and politely pressed us to stay longer to recuperate after our headlong journey. We turned him down without revealing the reason we were searching for Morgana, and he didn't ask. By the look of wary concern on his face he'd guessed it was not for something good, but the fact that she was his aunt didn't seem to bother him. He had grown up with her, after all.

"I wish you well with that woman," he said to me as we stood in the dawn-lit stableyard with my men mounting up. "You will be careful when you find her, won't you?"

I met his gaze and nodded. Yes, he knew her well.

Despite the superficial facial resemblance to his father, he possessed nothing of Cadwy's innate churlishness nor his underlying malevolence. Yes, he probably plotted and spied on the other courts – most likely every king did the same. But he'd proved his reliability as an ally since Badon on many occasions, and if Arthur trusted him, then so did I. And the fact that he didn't care for his aunt helped a lot.

"We need to hurry," Merlin said. "I'm sorry, my lord, but speed is of the essence in this matter."

Custennin nodded, putting a steadying hand on my horse's reins as I mounted. "Godspeed to your mission, Gwen, whatever it is."

Our warriors, who'd maybe been expecting to sample the

delights of the city for a day or two, rode down the street behind us with glum faces and eyes red-rimmed from lack of sleep. Probably they'd all been out drinking last night. Llawfrodedd was the only man amongst them who looked like he'd had a good night's sleep.

Our road took us south through the lower-lying wetlands, with the mountains that would one day be considered Welsh on our right, and into the vast swathe of forest that covered central Britain. This was dangerous country rife with brigands, and I more than once found myself wishing we'd brought twice the number of warriors with us, something I didn't share with Merlin and Archfedd. Although Merlin was probably thinking the same.

Some time after midday, we approached the little, once Roman, town of Breguoin. This had been the scene of a bitter battle against Irish raiders and was where Llawfrodedd had spent his childhood as the son of a metal worker. It sat in open country on a rise above a small river, with dark forest fringing its fields to the east and hills to the west. Its tumbledown walls, and the houses within them that were a mix of patched-up Roman dwellings and newer wattle and daub, had seen no improvement since last I'd passed this way.

"Could we stop to eat here?" Archfedd asked me, as we drew near.

The day was warm, and we'd made good progress since leaving Viroconium, so I nodded, and we rode in at the northern gates between the low walls of the ruined towers and made our way down the main street toward the center. There was the little thatched church where I'd seen the raiding Irish warriors kill the village priest, there the small fields turned over to agriculture where once houses had crowded. Breguoin, like so many old Roman towns, had become a shadow of its former self, gradually dying in the failing light of Rome.

The people came out warily to greet us clutching weapons in their hands – hayforks, clubs, pokers. No force of armed warriors is ever a welcome sight, and we were no different. For all they knew we'd come to rob them.

I swung down from my saddle near the well in the little square – a shabby apology for a forum, but who cared? The Roman masters who'd built it were long gone, and, in their stead, small market stalls proliferated. "We come in peace," I called, my voice carrying to the people, arrested in their daily bartering and now huddled behind the stalls as though believing this action afforded them safety. "All we require is water for our horses."

Our skins of cider would do us – no way were any of us risking the water in this well, even if it suited our horses.

One of the older men pushed a young lad forward. He edged over to the well and set his hands on the winding mechanism. Keeping a wary eye on us, he began to wind the handle to bring up the bucket of water.

No one else moved, as though they suspected I'd lied, and it was all a ruse to lull them into a false sense of security. They continued to watch with ill-disguised suspicion from their inadequate positions of perceived safety. In the main street, a few more, drawn by curiosity, emerged from houses to edge their way closer to the square. All of them armed in some way.

Llawfrodedd slid down from his horse and came to stand beside me and survey our audience. "Who is the headman here?" He'd raised his voice to ring out loud and clear around the square.

No one stepped forward. He cleared his throat. "I seek Bredon the baker and his wife, Ailidh."

A mutter ran round the assembled, half-hidden people. I'd have been surprised indeed if any of them recognized the noble young warrior standing before them as being one and the same with the scrawny, under-nourished boy who'd left them seven years ago.

A door behind us banged open, and I turned my head. A tall, tonsured, gray-haired figure emerged from the thatched porch of the tiny church, brown-robed and leaning heavily on a long, knobbly staff.

Llawfrodedd turned to face him, a smile lighting his face.

"Is this the boy I see before me?" the priest asked, staring at Llawfrodedd out of kind eyes, his mouth widening in a smile to match Llawfrodedd's. "Returned as the man I dared to dream he could become?" He had a deep, melodious and well-educated voice.

All our warriors' heads turned in curiosity. A good few knew Llawfrodedd's story.

Tears formed in Llawfrodedd's honest gray eyes. "Father Aloysius." Three long strides and he dropped to his knees in front of the old man, pulling off his helmet in a hurry and bowing his head. "I am indeed the boy you set upon the road to a new life."

Father Aloysius put a bony hand on Llawfrodedd's sweat-dampened hair. "A blessing on you, my son, and all who ride with you. You come to seek your sister?"

Without rising, Llawfrodedd nodded. "I ride with the Queen of Dumnonia. I am her sworn warrior. We are on a vital mission, but she allowed us to stop here. For me. I need, after all these years, to know my sister is well."

Father Aloysius's eyes moved to take me in, standing there in my boy's clothes and armor, with my sweaty, red face, then flicked to Archfedd by my side, and disapproval clouded his face for a moment. Probably unused to seeing women in not just men's attire, but armor, as well. "You are most welcome here in Breguoin, my lady." He made a stiff bow, leaning more heavily on his staff.

I returned his bow. "Thank you, Father." And so did Arch-fedd.

Merlin, who never liked priests, had moved away to allow his horse to drink from the trough the boy was busy filling, a long, stone affair that could have doubled as a coffin, and our men were taking off their helmets. The fresh water slopped into the trough, splashing the flagstones at its feet as the sun beat down on the back of my neck. How refreshing it would be to dunk my head in that trough then let the water run down my hot back.

"I'll send someone for your sister," Father Aloysius said to

Llawfrodedd, taking his hands and pulling him to his feet.

He nodded to a lanky boy in tattered, long-outgrown clothes who'd been hovering nearby with his mouth hanging open. A few low words, and the boy galloped away down the main street toward the southern gateway.

"Ever feel as though you're an exhibit at a freak show?" Archfedd whispered, moving closer to me. "They're looking at us as though they've never seen a queen before."

I flashed a smile. "But they have indeed. And it was this one." I tapped my chest. "Your father fought a battle here, and it was up to me and the men I was leading to rescue the inhabitants before the Irish found them. We evacuated them to safety up there in the forest." I pointed. "There'll be men here – women as well – who'll remember me, I don't doubt. It's a long time ago, now. You were only a baby."

"I know." She smiled. "Llawfrodedd told me some of that a long time ago. This is *his* town." She glanced about herself. "Village, maybe. It's so small. His father died from burns he got while working for the blacksmith. Forging swords for Custennin's father." She leaned in closer. "For a long time, he's wanted to find the little sister he had to leave behind. She was only five, he told me, so he couldn't take her with him when he set off for Din Cadan. That priest," she nodded to Father Aloysius, "found her a family who had no daughter of their own, and sorely wanted one."

Until now, I'd quite forgotten he'd had the one surviving sister. She'd be about twelve.

A door in one of the houses down the street banged open, and a woman and a smaller figure, a girl, emerged onto the cobbles. For a moment the child stood staring toward the square before she burst into a headlong run. Her booted feet slapped on the road surface, her long mousy braids bounced behind her, and as she drew nearer, the look of joy on her face was enough to bring a lump to my throat.

Llawfrodedd hesitated only a brief moment then stepped

toward her. "Meleri!"

She hurled herself at him, her small arms clutching his body. Being a good foot taller than she was, he swung her off her feet and twirled her around, his own face suffused with so much joy, tears pricked my eyes.

Setting her down, he held her at arm's length, studying her. "My," he said after a moment, his voice breathless. "How you've grown, but I'd still have recognized you any day."

She had a look of her brother, with the same homely, but cheery face and kind eyes. She'd never have physical beauty, but the beauty of her soul shone out of her excited face.

The woman huffed up to us. Elderly and gray-haired, with the portly squishiness of a matron, a worried frown creased her brow.

"Mami," Meleri cried. "You were right. 'Tis my brother come back to me."

The woman looked Llawfrodedd up and down, a wary expression in her eyes. "My oh my, but she be right. 'Tis young Llawfrodedd come back to us all right." She took the girl's hand, squeezing it tight. "Come to see if your sister be doin' well, now you're a fine soldier, I see." Her voice prickled with defensive concern.

Meleri beamed up at her foster mother, the look of love in her eyes.

Llawfrodedd grinned as well. "Not just a soldier, Ailidh. I'm a warrior of the High King, and I'm escorting his Queen on a mission of much urgency. I have little time to pause here, but the Princess," he threw Archfedd a grateful gaze, "knew my longing to see my sister again, and she asked the Queen if we could stop here to water our horses and eat our midday meal."

The woman's frown lessened. Maybe at first, she'd suspected he'd arrived to take his sister back, and now she'd heard his reason for being here, she felt more confident. And all these armed warriors didn't look as though they'd be prepared to take a girl child along with them. A smile creased her wrinkled face.

"She does well, as you c'n see." She put an arm around the girl's narrow shoulders. "And she's been a boon to me with my sons grown and gone. A light for my old age."

"And Bredon?" Llawfrodedd asked, peering over her shoulder hopefully. "How does he?"

Mother and daughter's faces clouded. "My husband did die a twelve-month gone," Ailidh said, with a deep sigh. "A shortness of breath did take him. Weren't nothin' we could do. We sore miss him, the both of us."

Meleri's face puckered. "He were like a true father to me, Brother."

Time for me to intervene. I stepped up to Ailidh and held my hands out to her.

She bobbed a bow, and, rising, took them. Hers were rough and callused with work, the fingers ingrained with dirt from daily toil. "Milady."

I smiled. "May I offer my sympathies for your loss. I can see by the way your daughter looks at you that you've been a true mother to her. Have no fear – we are only passing through your town. No one will take your child from you." Just in case she was still worrying.

The girl looked up at her elderly foster-mother and smiled. The love between them shone like a beacon; she'd fallen on her feet there. I hoped Llawfrodedd would be satisfied now he'd seen her. It would have been too cruel to try and separate the two women.

Llawfrodedd nodded. "All I wanted was to see my sister again. And you, too, Ailidh. To thank you for your kindness to Meleri. I'm just sad I came too late to be able to thank good Bredon, too." He took a step toward her. "You have been the mother she could never have hoped for." He took her in his arms and held her close. "Thank you." The last words came out in a whisper against her ear that only I was close enough to hear.

When he released Ailidh, I saw her eyes shone wet with un-shed tears.

Things began to look up straightaway.

Once the townsfolk realized who we were and that Llaw-frodedd was one of them made good, they brought out all sorts of things: chairs to sit on, their best wine and cider that they'd been saving for a special occasion, fresh baked honey cakes, loaves of bread and a cauldron of soup from one house to share amongst us.

Stories were bandied about, made greater in the retelling, of how we'd ridden to their rescue and defeated the wicked Irish raiders. Oddly, their own part in this defeat, from the safety of the forest, had grown out of all proportion, but I made no comment.

Meleri sat close beside Llawfrodedd while he ate, her foster-mother watching with an indulgent smile on her lips, listening as he recounted stories of his life at the High King's court and all he'd seen to please his little sister. This would give them great standing with their fellow townspeople and be the stuff of tales to be told round hearth fires for years to come. The time when their own Llawfrodedd returned to his people as a great warrior in the company of Queen Guinevere, wife of King Arthur, their High King.

But all too soon we had to be on our way. Llawfrodedd embraced his sister with regret, and tears on her part, and her foster-mother with gratitude, then mounted up last of all of us. We departed with many backward glances as those kind people waved us off.

I couldn't help but notice Archfedd as she brought her horse up close beside her friend's. Her hand went out to cover his where he gripped the reins, his face set and sad. They would make such a good pairing. I'd speak to Arthur on our return, if all went well.

We pressed on another thirty miles that day and made camp as evening fell close beside the road in the ruins of an old farmstead. I posted sentries, and the men cooked a stew from dried meat, barley, onions and cider over a small fire. We scraped it up with the fresh bread the people of Breguoin had given us.

Unrolling my blankets, I spread them beside where Archfedd already lay curled up in hers, prepared for another sleepless night. The men were all doing the same, but for the ones on first watch. By the glowing embers of the fire, Merlin sat alone, shoulders hunched, wineskin in hand.

Abandoning my sleeping spot, I sat down beside him.

"Are we going the right way?" I asked.

He turned his head, his eyes catching the dying firelight. "I don't know."

"Can't you find where she is? With your Sight?"

He shook his head, his face miserable and exhausted. "She's hidden herself from me. It takes great power to do that, and will be tiring her, but nevertheless, she's done it." He sighed. "She must really want to remain hidden. I'm certain she's concealing something." He shook his head again. "Believe me, I've searched for her many times, but I'm like a blind man groping in the dark. All I see is mist. Every time."

I almost didn't dare to ask. "Still nothing of Amhar?"

Another shake of the head. "I keep on looking in the hopes her power will wane." He put his head in his hands. "I feel as though I've been castrated. My Sight is a part of me as much as my legs or hands, and she's stolen it. It's not just something I do – it has body. It's a physical part of me. Somehow, she's found the power to slice it away."

I chewed my lip, groping for words of comfort and finding none. Urgency pressed in all around me. We had to get his Sight back. We had to find out who killed Llacheu and save Amhar.

"Better get some sleep," Merlin said. "We've a long ride in the morning."

THE URGE FOR haste infected us all, and we were up the next morning before the sun. After a breakfast of the last of the bread given us by the people of Breguoin washed down with our own cider, we set off.

Caer Legeion, or to give it its full title, Caer Legeion gwar Uisc, had once been the site of a legionary fortress, one of only three in Britain. Now, with the legions long gone, it had fallen into a degree of the usual disrepair. The fortress had been abandoned years ago, and the stonework looted for new houses, the filling in of potholes in the roads and the constructing of field walls or reinforcing of the wharfs. What had once been the fort's vicus, the civilian settlement, had morphed into the town that now huddled on the western banks of a curve of the river Usk.

A muddy foreshore marked where the tide had gone out, leaving a flock of small fishing boats stranded, but with no sign of Theodoric's fleet being in port.

We'd crossed the river seven miles upstream by a wide, paved ford. With the late afternoon sun in our eyes, we passed through the haunted ruins of the fortress, where perhaps the sad shades of lost legionaries still stood sentry, and made our way to Theodoric's house, where Morgawse lived, and where we hoped to find Morgana.

As the house of a princess, it was the biggest building in the town and would have been easy to find even if I'd never been there before. Large and square, set around a courtyard as many Roman houses were, it sat just above the high-water mark on the river, with its own docks where Theodoric could tie up his flagship when he was in port and the tide was in. No ship was too large to sit for a while on mudflats, though, and his would be no different.

We halted in the street outside the porticoed door, and Merlin dismounted to rap on the silvered wood. Who knew what lay beyond?

Chapter Twenty

"**I**S SHE INSIDE?" I asked Merlin, as we stood in the paved street outside the house. And I didn't mean Morgawse.

Merlin shrugged, as non-committal as ever, his face drawn and tired, eyes shadowed. "I don't know. She must be harnessing some strong power, because she's able to hide not just herself and my daughter from me but Amhar as well. She has them all wrapped in a thick mist that clouds my vision every time I try to find them."

Bloody woman. But had he the foresight to have hidden himself from her as well? The thought that she might have no idea we were on her doorstep pleased me no end.

The door creaked open on hinges much in need of an oiling, and a wizened old face peeked out at us, eyes screwed up against the dying day's bright sunshine. "Yes?"

It had been years since I'd visited Theodoric or Morgawse, and I had no idea who this old crone could be, but I stepped forward with resolution, determined to get past Morgana's gatekeeper. "Queen Guinevere, wife of the High King, to see your lady," I announced with every bit of imperial dignity I possessed. "Now, let us inside immediately."

The old woman sucked her shrunken lips in over her gums. "I has me orders not to let no one in," she mumbled, her words made difficult to understand due to her total lack of teeth.

"Nonsense," Merlin said, putting his hand on the door and

pushing it wider open. "That order doesn't mean us. Your lady is my Queen's sister." He put his foot in the gap.

I glanced over my shoulder at my men. "Llawfrodedd, you come with us. The rest of you, take care of our horses. There are stables just up the street to the left, attached to this house." I caught Archfedd's hand. "You should come, too."

The old doorkeeper made a feeble attempt to push the door closed on Merlin's foot, but she wasn't about to win a contest of strength against him. He shoved it wide and stepped inside, and Archfedd and Llawfrodedd followed me as I joined him.

With a discontented huff, the old woman shut the door with a creak and a bang behind us, probably in case any others of our party tried to get in.

The house seemed much as I remembered. Mosaics covered the floor, and light filled the atrium from the opening in the roof above what had once been a pretty impluvium, but now had degenerated into an unkempt, weed-filled pool.

On the far side, double doors stood open onto a spacious courtyard filled with evening sunlight, the warm air redolent with the scent of the many aromatic herbs growing in beds beside the colonnaded walkway.

No one was in sight.

I turned to the old woman. "Take us to your mistress, please."

She sucked in her lips and saggy cheeks as though in a gurning competition. "I've told you already, I'm not s'posed to let no one in."

Merlin's eyes narrowed and he moved closer to me. "That doesn't sound like an order given by Morgawse," he said in a low aside, then turned to the old woman. "Who issued that order?"

Her faded eyes darted from side-to-side as though she might be contemplating flight. "The Princess." The words came out between almost clenched gums, fighting their way into the air, a strong hint of disapproval in them, or perhaps even of scorn.

Well, both Morgana and Morgawse were princesses, so that

didn't make the situation any clearer. Although it seemed unlikely this old retainer would feel scorn for her true mistress.

"Which one?" Merlin asked, his voice ominously stern, although I'd already guessed the answer.

She blinked up at him for a moment before answering. "Her *ladyship*, the Princess Morgana." More scorn heaped on with a trowel. Despite her toothlessness, she managed a creditable sneer. No love lost there.

Aha. She *had* come here. And it sounded, from her wish to let no one inside the house, as though she thought we might be following her. Or at least that *someone* was.

"Is anyone else here with her?" I asked, suddenly seized by the desperate hope that Amhar might have fled to his aunt. Not Morgana, of course, but Morgawse.

The old woman squirmed in her effort to make herself vanish into a crack in the floor.

Merlin loomed over her. "Well?"

It would have taken a far stronger person than this old woman to withstand the glare he gave her and his voice heavy with threat. She probably knew who he was, and that would only have added to her fear. Not to mention her possibly greater fear of Morgana, who the ordinary people suspected could turn them into toads. Talk about stuck between a rock and a hard place. I had to feel a little sorry for her.

"The Princess Nimuë be with her," the old woman muttered into her chest, cringing beneath Merlin's gaze.

He turned to me, his eyes alight with excitement. "My daughter."

He didn't need to say. It wasn't like I'd forgotten.

How long had it been since he'd seen her? A lifetime. She'd been a toddler when he'd woven his magic over her, a magic that had been at least some protection from her mother's wiles and had later served to protect me, as well. Every time we'd been to the Council of Kings since then, I'd been aware of his desperate longing to see his child, and every time he'd been disappointed.

And now, here he was, at last in the same house as her.

But as far as I was concerned, Nimuë held no importance. It was Morgana we needed. Morgana whose magic we had to halt. The only question was how.

"Take us to my sisters-in-law," I said to the old woman, at my most imperious. "Or feel the wrath of the High King on your head."

Most likely resigning herself to a miserable fate at the hands of one or other of these two practitioners of magic, or possibly the High King himself, the old woman hunched her bony shoulders and shuffled past us into the colonnaded walkway. She turned to the left, skirting the outside of the courtyard, where the strong stark shadows of early evening already crept across the flagstones.

Halfway down one side, she halted beside ornate double doors and peered up at me out of wary eyes. "This be Milady's chamber," she muttered. "You'll have to open that there door for yourselves. I'm away back to guard the front door in case more like you what won't take no for an answer turns up." And with that she shuffled off at a far greater speed than she'd previously exhibited.

I turned back to the doors. Each possessed a circular handle in the shape of a lion's head gripping a ring of metal between its teeth. Before Merlin could move, I reached out, took hold of one of the rings, turned it, and pushed that side open.

With a quick glance at Archfedd's nervous face, I stepped into the room beyond.

It was an antechamber of the same sort as Custennin had at Viroconium only on a less splendid scale. I'd been in it before, but many years ago, and a quick glance from side to side told me little had changed. In fact, little but its condition had changed since the Romans themselves had left. The faded fresco adorning the walls had patches of paintwork missing, and the mosaic underfoot had long ceased to be level as subsidence had given an undulating roll to the floor.

Windows placed high up in the walls cast bright light into the room, dust motes floating in the sunbeams.

The three women seated on chairs around a low table made a pretty enough picture. Each chair had a solid curved seat that owed more to Roman workmanship than British, with clawed feet and lion headed armrests, and the women all held sewing in their hands. If I hadn't known better, I'd have suspected them of having posed themselves for our benefit in this tableau of industry.

Two of them I knew, and the identity of the third I had no trouble guessing. Morgana and Morgawse, superficially as alike as sisters could be, with their long dark hair confined in braids, faced us in what looked like surprise. Beside them, the third member of their party and much the youngest, who'd had her back to us, twisted in her seat and stared, dark eyes flown open wide. Her father, Merlin's, eyes.

Morgana rose to her feet first, letting her sewing drop to the low tabletop, her gaze flicking between Merlin's face and mine. She couldn't have seen us coming.

"Good day, Guinevere," she said, with icy civility. "To what do we owe the pleasure of your company?" She must have been forty by now, and the liberal silvery strands streaking her dark hair gave me a smug feeling of superiority as, so far, I had none. But her lovely face showed no signs of ageing – at least not from this distance. I cherished no desire to get close enough to that scorpion for a better look.

Morgawse, who'd on and off been my friend for most of my time in this world, had no such reservations. She jumped up and ran to me, throwing her arms around me in a welcoming embrace. "Gwen! You've come to visit us! I'm so happy!" She planted a kiss on each of my cheeks and turned to Archfedd.

"And this must be Archfedd. You haven't changed at all. Bigger, of course, but still the same beautiful girl as before." She glanced at Llawfrodedd. "And is this handsome warrior your husband? You lucky girl." She chuckled in appreciation.

Archfedd colored hotly, and so did Llawfrodedd, but Morgawse sailed on, regardless, not waiting for an answer. "I've been telling my sister it's high time she saw Nimuë married. She's getting too old to be without a husband."

Nimuë, the object of this sentence, placed her own sewing on the table with careful precision and rose gracefully to her feet, a slight smile on her lips, and her eyes fixed on Merlin's face. Did she know who he was? I stared at the girl I'd last seen in a dream when she could only have been eight years old. Archfedd was pretty, but this girl was a beauty, like her mother.

Like Arthur's two sisters, she had her long dark hair confined in a single thick braid, pulled back from a face so perfectly formed it might have been taken from a Renaissance portrait by an Old Master. Long, thick lashes fringed her eyes, her nose was elegantly proportioned, and her lips formed a perfect pink bow, parted slightly to reveal even, white teeth.

But Morgana had never looked like this. Her beauty had been marred by the underlying current of coldness she possessed that this girl didn't have. I smiled at her and her own smile widened in return.

"Good day to you all," I said, remembering my manners. "As you might have guessed, we're not here by chance. We have a reason for our visit."

Merlin took a step forward. "It's Morgana we're here for."

Morgana raised her thin black brows. Did she pluck them? "What is your business with me? I'm sure I can't be of any interest to such powerful people as you."

If you're not innocent, it's hard to inject that notion into your speech. Her words came out stilted and guilty, her "poor little innocent me" wasted. Or was that just because I was biased and already convinced of her involvement?

Merlin's eyes flicked to his daughter then back to Morgana. Did we need to tell Nimuë who he was? No, she possessed a kind of magic of her own, so she must know. Surely.

His brows lowered. "You have been blocking my Sight. I'm

here to put a stop to it."

Morgana's cruel mouth curved in a smile. "Whatever makes you think I might do that?" she asked. "Firstly, that I would take the trouble to block your paltry party trick, and secondly that you might be able to stop me if I were?" She curled her upper lip in a scornful sneer that made me want to punch her on the nose. My fists balled in preparation, but I restrained myself. With difficulty.

Archfedd bristled as well. She, at least, had the benefit of never having met her aunt before, and had none of my preconceived ideas or fears. "You're stopping Merlin from seeing who killed Llacheu," she blurted out. "My father's searching for Amhar because he thinks he did it. We have to be certain he didn't. And find out who *did* do it. *And* stop my father punishing my brother. Merlin needs to be able to use his Sight. You're blocking it. I don't know why, but you *have* to stop."

"What?" Morgawse's single word hissed out on a gasp and her hand went to her mouth. "Llacheu is *dead*? Arthur thinks *Amhar* killed him? How? Why?"

I couldn't speak, couldn't tell her what had happened. Everything was still too raw. I didn't want to revisit the images locked away inside my head.

Llawfrodedd stepped into the breach. "Amhar and Llacheu argued – fought. Then, two days later, Llacheu was found with his throat cut, thrown onto a midden. Amhar fled during the funeral rites. The King has gone after him." He cast a glance at me. "The Queen needs to find out who really did this foul murder before the King finds Amhar and blames him for something he didn't do."

My stomach roiled as I lost the fight to keep those images hidden. I'd been trying so hard to keep what had brought us on this journey out of the forefront of my mind, but now it came rolling back like the waves on the beach as the tide comes in, only much faster.

"And you think *I* have had something to do with this?" Morgana said, the smile broadening as though she found the whole thing satisfying and possibly even funny. "That I'm stopping you from discovering the truth?" She laughed. "I'm flattered you think I have the power to do that." Her long lashes swept her cheeks as she lowered her eyes in fake humility. No way was she fooling me with this act.

Merlin seemed to grow larger, taking up more of the room. Morgana was a tall woman, but he towered over her as though she were tiny. The air around him vibrated, and the room darkened as if a heavy cloud had hidden the sun. "I know it is you," he said. "I see what you have done. I see what you keep hidden in your heart."

Nimuë, who'd been staring at Merlin the whole while, at last turned to her mother. "Mother? What does he mean?" Her eyes widened with fear, and her hand went out to touch her mother's skirts.

Morgana shook her daughter off like an irritating fly. "I think you *don't*," she said, with another laugh. "Your pathetic con-jurors' tricks are not enough to even *touch* my powers. You cannot know what's in my mind."

"You think?" Merlin spat, and I pulled Archfedd to my side, my arm going around her, as the room grew darker still and fear welled up inside me. Merlin's eyes flashed. "You think your women's magic is enough to lock horns with me and my powers? You think you can hide your secrets? From Merlin?"

Morgawse had fallen back a step, her hand clutching the back of one of the chairs as though for support, her face white with the same fear rising in me. Not Nimuë though. She got to her feet and stepped almost between her father and mother as though to keep them apart, her wide, anxious eyes going from one face to the other.

Llawfrodedd crossed himself then made the sign against the evil eye – hedging his bets. Archfedd's hand caught mine and held on tight, the warmth of her touch like a beacon in the descending darkness.

"I do not think," Morgana stormed, pushing her daughter to

one side. Her eyes flashed as much as Merlin's. "I know. You don't understand with what you interfere. This is the hand of fate, Merlin, writing the path of history. I am the hand that guides that fate, and you may not stay me." Her voice rose higher and louder as she got into her stride.

Merlin snorted in derision. "You're mad, woman. I thought you crazed before, but now I know it's true. You can't write history to suit yourself." His hand went to his sword hilt. "I'm here to make sure you don't."

I took another step back, and Archfedd came with me. I came up against the closed doors, the handle knobbly in my back. Nowhere further to flee to.

Nimuë held up her hand, palm toward Merlin, fingers splayed. "Father? What are you doing?"

His head swung around at the sound of her voice. "Nimuë?" All the pain of his years of lost love filled that one word: the longing, the anguish, the desperation. How wonderful it must be for him to hear her call him "father."

She took a wary step closer to her mother, her eyes fixed on his sword hand. "Do not make me choose sides. I am my mother's child."

Merlin released his hold on his sword hilt and held up his right hand, his fingers outstretched as though grabbing for something. "Out of the way, Nimuë. Your mother will answer my questions. Now."

Nimuë's anxious eyes darted between her parents' set faces. "What has she done?" But she stepped back a pace, perhaps reassured by his abandonment of his sword, perhaps from the knowledge that her mother had indeed done something wicked.

Merlin ignored her, his gaze fixed on her mother's face. "Who killed Llacheu?" he asked, his voice deep and commanding. "I know you know. Tell me, Morgana. Unbind my Sight that I might see the truth."

Morgana's hands flew to her throat as though an invisible grip had her in its hold and was strangling her. As though Merlin's hand, ten feet from her, might be doing just that. She gasped and choked, eyes wild, and her own hand came up to point at Merlin.

"No!" cried Nimuë, looking in desperation from Merlin to her mother and then back again. "Don't do this. Tell him, Mother. Tell him what he wants to know."

Merlin staggered back a step as though from a blow but held his ground.

Morgana went on choking.

"Stop it!" Nimuë cried, hovering between the two of them. "Don't hurt my mother!"

"What should I do?" Llawfrodedd shouted, his hand on his sword hilt. "Do you want me to kill her?"

Morgawse sat down hard in her chair, mouth hanging open but not a sound coming out, her hands gripping the arms, wise enough not to interfere. Unable even if she'd wanted to.

I shook my head wildly at Llawfrodedd. "No. We need to find out who killed Llacheu before she dies." Before she dies? Had I already made my mind up that she should? Did I agree with what Merlin was doing? With murder?

Merlin's clawed hand tightened, his fingers squeezing the life out of his one-time lover, his face contorted with something more than the effort – with pain, with grief, with self-disgust perhaps for what he was doing, maybe even with unrequited love. "Who killed Llacheu?" he cried. "You're behind this. I know. You *will* tell me, or you will die by my hand. Right now."

Morgana's face turned purple, and her eyes bulged. I'd never seen anyone strangled before and it wasn't nice. Eyes do bulge and the tongue protrudes from the mouth, and the sound of someone fighting for their last breath is a sound you'll never forget. How I hated that woman, how I'd longed for her demise, but this, this strangulation by magic, both terrified and disgusted me at the same time.

"Don't kill her," I cried. "Don't make yourself as bad as her."

He glanced over his shoulder. "She has to tell us, or Amhar will die. Do you want that? It's her or him. I have to make her tell us."

Nimuë's hand shot up so fast I barely saw her move. Merlin flew back across the room and hit the door beside me with a resounding thump. Morgana fell to the floor, her breath rasping into her lungs like a person in the throes of a severe asthma attack, her body curled in a fetal position.

Merlin struggled to his feet, gasping for breath himself. "Tell me, you bitch," he spat, his hand coming up to point at her again.

"No!" cried Nimuë, leaping in front of her mother. But Llaw-frodedd grabbed her and pulled her out of the way, pinning her arms to her sides.

Morgana lifted her head from the mosaic, her lips curled back in a furious snarl. "Medraut," she croaked. "Medraut did it." A hoarse laugh escaped her throat as she pushed herself up straighter. "And yes, I blocked you. And I've won. You're beaten. All of you. Arthur will kill his precious son. And Medraut will be his heir." Her laugh became a mad cackle of triumph.

Merlin was even faster than Nimuë. His fingers clicked. Morgana's head snapped back with an audible crack. Her body contorted, and she dropped to the mosaic floor once more, twitching, her lifeless eyes staring up at the ceiling in mute accusation.

Chapter Twenty-One

MORGANA'S BODY CEASED its twitching and lay still. For a long moment no one moved as the silence in the room stretched out like a piece of elastic about to break.

At last, Nimuë turned horror-stricken eyes on Merlin. "What have you done?" Her words hung in the air. She shook herself free of Llawfrodedd's hold, her mouth working but no further words emerging.

I dragged my eyes away from Morgana's body, and stared at Merlin as well.

He sagged against the carved doors, perhaps unable to believe he'd killed her. All color had drained from his face. His right hand hung by his side, the fingers slack, and his chin had fallen forward onto his chest, his hair flopping over his face.

Llawfrodedd regained his senses first. Two strides took him to Morgana's side. He dropped to his knees, his fingers searching her throat for a pulse.

He wouldn't find one. That crack had been her neck breaking.

After a minute's frowning concentration, he looked up and shook his head.

"Oh my God." Morgawse's voice rose barely above a hoarse whisper. "Close her eyes. I can't look at them." She hung onto the arms of her chair as though to a lifeline in a stormy sea.

Llawfrodedd pressed his hand against Morgana's frozen face,

holding her eyes shut. I well remembered how difficult it was to close the eyes of the dead. It's like they don't want to oblige – that they'd rather keep on staring at the life they've left behind.

"Mother?" Nimuë fell to her knees beside Llawfrodedd and caught hold of one of her mother's slack hands. "Mother?" A heartfelt plea that would never be answered. Tears rolled down her pale cheeks, making small stains of darkness where they fell on Morgana's clothing. Her slender body shook with sobs.

Archfedd let go of my hand, squaring her shoulders. "We have our answer," she said, her voice determined. "To save Amhar, we must leave. Now." She looked at Merlin. "She's dead. Your Sight is unbound. Use it and tell us where he is. Quickly."

I stared at her, taken aback by her cold indifference to Morgana's death when she didn't even have the excuse of knowing her of old like I did. This wasn't the daughter I knew.

She drew herself up taller and set her jaw. "She said Amhar would die. She said Father would kill him. Medraut did this, not Amhar. We have to get to my brother before Father does. We have to tell him it was Medraut."

Morgawse's eyes focused on my daughter, hard as pebbles. "You stupid girl. My sister was lying. She made that up to cause more trouble. Can't you see? This is what she wanted you to do. My son is no more guilty than Amhar is. She wanted to be rid of any rival to her own daughter. To *her*. That's Medraut as well as Llacheu and Amhar, and you and Reaghan too. She wanted you all gone."

Nimuë continued to sob over her mother's body, as though oblivious to the accusation that involved her, as though she couldn't be a part of it.

I turned to Merlin. "Look, then," I demanded, harsh and angry. "Look and see who did it. Then we'll know the truth."

"Wait." Llawfrodedd looked up. "What do you mean about Reaghan?"

Morgawse's face contorted. "My sister told me Cei's daughter has gone to join a religious house, pledging herself to God. That's one way of getting rid of any rivals, isn't it? And this is another. Setting the cousins at war against each other, and my brother against all of them."

Oh God. Morgana *had* been behind it all. She'd planned to get rid of everyone standing in the way of *her* child.

"I don't care about Reaghan," Archfedd cried, grabbing hold of Merlin by the shoulders. "I only care about my brother. Look, will you? Find him and tell us the truth."

Merlin lifted his head, and drew a deep, steadying breath. "I will search for Amhar first." He kept his voice low and flat, devoid of emotion. He sounded exhausted, spent, the shadows under his eyes like dark smudges on his gray skin.

"Yes, look," Archfedd said. "Hurry. We don't have much time."

He pushed himself away from the door, leaning one hand on it as if he might fall without support. "Give me a moment. I can't do this to order. Not like this."

Still kneeling on the floor, Llawfrodedd straightened Morgana's twisted limbs with gentle hands, lessening her look of a broken doll, making her more human. Beside her, Nimuë sat immobile, letting him do it, tears running down her cheeks in silent grief.

Morgawse pushed herself out of her chair onto legs that wobbled and dropped down beside her niece. Her arm went around the girl's shoulders, but she didn't speak. Her accusing eyes remained fixed on Merlin.

Still with one hand on the door, he closed his eyes.

I willed him to have the strength to do this. Our days of travel, the sleepless nights and his attempts to use the Sight had sapped his strength, and the perpetually youthful man I knew had gone, to be replaced by the old man standing before me.

Find my son.

Four pairs of eyes fixed on him, as Llawfrodedd slowly clambered to his feet. Only Nimuë seemed to pay him no attention, her shoulders shaking still.

My breath came fast, as though I'd been running. I tried to steady it, but the tension pressing in around us refused to let me. I'd hyperventilate if I wasn't careful. No paper bags to breathe into here in the Dark Ages.

Time ticked past, the only sound our own harsh breathing. Nimuë shot a glance at me, drawing her sleeve across her face to wipe the tears away, and I caught a momentary flash of cold fury in her eyes before she dropped a barrier between us. She wasn't as absorbed in her mother as we all thought.

Merlin's eyes snapped open, staring past us into an invisible distance, pupils huge. "I see a deep valley with a wide river running through it, and a high rock that rises above it." Almost, he sounded as though in a trance. "An old fortress stands where Ercing once was ruled from the Doward. They call it Caer Guorthegirn." He put a hand to his eyes. "The boy is there... but Arthur draws close, and danger threatens." He staggered, as though the effort had been too much for him, and I released my hold on Archfedd to catch him around the waist. He leaned heavily on me. "He is innocent... I... can see no more..."

"Merlin!" I found myself supporting most of his weight as he sagged against me, his eyes rolling up in his head. His body crumpled.

Morgawse let out an anguished cry. "Make him look for me." She abandoned Nimuë and scrambled to her feet. "Wake him up. He has to look. He has to prove my sister was lying when she accused Medraut. He has to."

Nimuë's body stiffened, but she kept her eyes down.

Llawfrodedd moved fast, grabbing Merlin under the arms as his head lolled to one side. Together, we lowered him to the ground. His eyes had closed, and his shallow breathing barely stirred his chest.

"We have to go," Archfedd cried, her hand on the door. "We have to get to Amhar before Father does."

Morgawse threw herself at Merlin, grabbing the front of his tunic and almost yanking him up off the floor. "Wake up! You have to look. You have to." His head flopped. She swung round to me. "It wasn't Medraut. My sister was lying. You have to believe me. She hated us and wanted us *all* to suffer. My son wouldn't have done that. He wouldn't. A mother knows these things."

Does she though? Hadn't I doubted Amhar and thought he might be capable of such a crime? Was I a terrible mother for thinking the worst of her child? And how could Morgawse be any more certain than I was?

I dragged her off Merlin, and he fell back to the mosaic floor, limp and unresponsive. "You're hurting him. Leave him alone. He's exhausted. Look what using the Sight has done to him."

But had it? I'd seen him use his powers before, and although they'd drained him, he'd never lost consciousness like this. Something else had happened here, something I didn't understand.

Llawfrodedd put his fingers to Merlin's jawline, feeling for a pulse. "He's alive, but his pulse is faint." He met Archfedd's anguished gaze. "But the Princess is right. We have to find Amhar before the King does. If Merlin's correct, we have little time." He turned to Morgawse, who I was still hanging on to. "Where was he describing? Where is this Caer Guorthegirn? Do you know? Tell us."

Morgawse, her jaw jutting in rebellion, shook her head. "Never. You're going to tell Arthur it was Medraut, and it wasn't."

I gave her an angry shake, desperate. "I believe you when you say it wasn't Medraut." Did I? "But we have to save my son. Tell us where to go. If you love your son, you'll know how I love mine. I have to save him."

Morgawse's eyes flitted from Merlin's recumbent form back to me, indecision written in them. "Swear you don't believe it was Medraut." She twisted herself free from my arms and seized my shoulders, her face inches from mine. "Swear to me you won't be giving Arthur another to blame instead of your son.

Swear it. Now."

I didn't hesitate. I had no choice but to nod, despite my doubts. "I swear. Tell us."

She turned her head to glare at Llawfrodedd and Archfedd. "I want your promises as well. I *know* my boy didn't do this."

"I swear," Llawfrodedd said. "Tell us where to go. We have no time."

She glared at Archfedd.

My daughter glanced at me and nodded. "I do too. Please. We have to go."

Morgawse licked her lips. "Some twenty miles north of here, beyond Blestium, the old fort Merlin saw in his vision sits on a hill above the River Guoy. It's lain in ruins since the people abandoned it after the usurper Guorthegirn died. It's said to be cursed, but a few peasants still cling on there with their flocks in summer."

"How do we get there?" Llawfrodedd asked.

Behind him, Nimuë turned her tear-stained face toward us, blotchy and red-eyed. She stared hard at Merlin.

"Up the Roman road to Blestium," Morgawse said, still hanging on tight to me. "Keep going northeast a mile or two, then, when the river bends away to the east, you'll see the hill the fortress sits on. You can't mistake it."

I prised myself free of her grip and bent over Merlin, my hand on his chest. He lay like the dead, face chalky white, but beneath my fingers his ribcage rose and fell. "What about Merlin? What do we do?"

Llawfrodedd gave him a shake. "Wake up. Merlin. Wake up." Nothing.

He slapped his face. Still nothing.

My skin prickled, and I turned my head to find Nimuë's stony gaze fixed on me, her head lowered, her dark brows meeting in a heavy frown. Was that triumph in her eyes, briefly glimpsed and swiftly hidden? I didn't have time to think.

"We'll have to leave him," Archfedd said. "If he won't wake

up, we'll have to leave him."

I shook my head, some deep instinct warning me not to do that, telling me Merlin shouldn't be left here with Morgawse and Nimuë. That danger threatened him. I swung my hand back and dealt him a ringing slap.

Still nothing.

I grabbed his tunic front much as Morgawse had done and shook him hard. "Wake up! We can't leave you! Wake up, damn you."

Nothing. If I hadn't felt that slight movement of his chest and Llawfrodedd hadn't reassured me that he'd found a pulse, I might have thought my friend already dead. What did I know about comas? Not a thing. Not even how to tell if someone was in one. And anyway, how could his magic – or Morgana's – have done that to him?

"We have to leave him," Archfedd said, tugging at my arm. "We have to go. Now."

Llawfrodedd turned to Morgawse. "Can you look after him?"

Morgawse pressed her lips together. "I can. But you must remember what you've sworn. My son is innocent. You cannot blame him for this in place of Amhar. Someone else killed Llacheu. Some other king's spy, most likely."

I nodded, every part of me screaming that we shouldn't abandon Merlin, but common sense telling me we had to. I bent over him again, hoping that somewhere inside his shut down mind he might hear me. "I'm coming back for you. Don't worry. I'll be back." I pressed my lips to his cool forehead. "Please wake up."

I turned away from him and so did Llawfrodedd. On an impulse, I reached out to Morgawse and covered her hand with mine. "Neither of our sons did this dreadful crime. I have to go, but I leave Merlin in your charge. When he wakes, tell him where we've gone. I'm entrusting him to you."

She nodded, tears sparkling in her eyes, but for whom, I had no idea, not being entirely sure whether she'd want to shed any for her sister.

From the floor, where she still knelt beside Morgana, Nimuë's baleful stare skewered me.

I bit my bottom lip. "I'm sorry, Nimuë. Sorry you've lost your mother." Only maybe I wasn't, not really.

She stared back, her face expressionless again.

"But you've gained your father, and he's far better. You'll see."

"Mother, come." Archfedd grabbed my arm. "We need to go, now."

Llawfrodedd flung the door open, and we staggered out into the shady walkway, warm and balmy as only a summer evening can be. How incongruous were the bees hovering on the flowering sage, the cooing of the doves on the tiled rooftops, the gentle sighing of a breeze. Behind us we left a life cut short, and even though she'd been a woman I'd hated for twenty years, I couldn't find it in me to be glad.

Chapter Twenty-Two

M Y MEN WERE not best pleased to have to saddle up their tired horses again when they should have been settling to their evening meal. However, I'd chosen them well, and despite a few moans and groans, they obeyed. Every one of them understood the urgency of our quest.

As soon as we were all mounted, I took the lead out of the stableyard and onto the street, heading back the way we'd come. My empty stomach twisted with fear at the needless extra miles we'd ridden, and the hours it had eaten out of our limited time. If only Merlin had been able to see Amhar was so close to Blestium, we could have saved ourselves a long journey. Well, two long journeys. If only Merlin's Sight hadn't been obscured by that bitch.

That dead bitch. How did I feel about that? Numb. Nothing. All I could think of was Amhar. Nothing else mattered.

I struggled to push thoughts of Merlin, and the fear that I shouldn't have left him, away, and tried to concentrate on what lay ahead, praying we'd reach the fortress of Caer Guorthegirn before Arthur did. And that Merlin had been right.

Archfedd and Llawfrodedd tucked themselves in behind me, as silent as I was, their knees touching. I looked back only once, taking in the line of tired warriors behind them, then fixed my gaze on the road ahead. The road that would lead us to Amhar.

The events of the last hour weighed heavily on my heart no

matter how much I tried not to think of them. The sound of Morgana's neck breaking echoed in my head, and its sudden jerk as it bent too far backwards replayed itself repeatedly like a film on a loop. And yet I couldn't find it in me to feel sorry for her. Not relief that she was gone, nor even disgust that Merlin had killed her. Just nothing, as though she didn't matter. Yet she'd been a living, breathing human being. And now she wasn't. Trying to shock myself like this didn't work either. The numbness continued.

I rubbed tired eyes as the sun sank toward the distant, purple hills ranged along the horizon to my left, ready to plunge the world into evening's twilight. My body ached with exhaustion from the miles we'd covered, but the strength of a mother desperate to defend her child still buzzed through me. I couldn't rest until I had him in my arms.

Enfys must have picked up on my mood because despite the lateness of the day and her own tiredness from having already made such a mammoth journey, her step quickened, and she tossed her head as though sensing the proximity of our prey.

The endless road stretched on ahead of us, as we snail-crawled our way along the rough grass to either side of its stony surface. The sun dipped below the horizon, its last hopeful rays shooting across the darkening landscape, and overhead the first stars popped out, one by one. Soon, they'd sprinkled the canopy of the sky with diamonds.

Llawfrodedd brought his horse up beside Enfys. "You look done in. Do we make camp for an hour or two to rest the horses?"

I shook my head. "Merlin warned us Arthur is close. We have to keep going and reach Amhar before he does. I'm not giving up now."

His kindly face, pale in the starlight, puckered in a frown. "How are you going to persuade the King to believe you? Have you considered that? We don't have Merlin to back us up."

I'd been thinking of nothing else. "He has to," I said. "I'm his wife and Merlin his adviser. He has to believe what we say." But my voice betrayed my lack of conviction. If only we had Merlin. What had been wrong with him? Why had he lost consciousness like that?

Llawfrodedd had the sense not to argue the point. His horse fell back until he was beside Archfedd again, and for a good while we rode in silence. Far away, an owl hooted, and another returned its call.

To either side of the road, forest pressed in a bowshot's length away, dark and forbidding, made darker by the onset of night. I tried not to think of the brigands who might be lurking there, nor the wolves or wild boar. Britain was a land abounding with dangers for the unwary who ventured out after dark.

Now night had fully fallen, our progress slowed for fear our horses would stumble on the uneven ground. I'd have given the order to ride on the road itself had I not known that could be worse for unshod hooves not designed for stony surfaces. Even the Romans had ridden their horses beside their roads not on them.

Only the thought that Arthur might have made camp some-where for the night and be no nearer to Amhar than we were comforted me a little.

We plodded on astride our tired horses into the endless night.

After what felt like forever but was probably no more than a couple of hours, we crossed the river in the same place we'd forded earlier that day, passing through the familiar tiny hamlet of roundhouses, dilapidated barns and pigpens like ghosts in the night. No one poked so much as a nose out to take a look at us – perhaps fearing our hoofbeats might be those of the ghosts of long-gone legions. They'd be snug in their beds with the covers pulled up over their heads.

Leaving the lower land behind, the road climbed as we head-ed further north, and our poor, hard-driven horses began to flag. At least the night air made the going easier for them, but sweat darkened their coats and foam had formed everywhere their saddlery rubbed them and between their hind legs – thick and white. We pushed them and ourselves as hard as we could, dismounting and walking as little as possible.

The itch of desperation drove me like the devil's hounds.

The moon rose at last and climbed high into the blue-black sky, its round white lantern face lighting our way. Our road gleaming in the soft light, we descended into the river valley again and turned eastward, heading for Blestium.

Llawfrodedd and Archfedd now rode by my side. We couldn't get our horses to go faster than a trot, and even that remained dangerous. But surely, my fevered brain kept saying, surely Arthur would be safely tucked up in his camp with his men, asleep, letting us catch him up as we rode through the night.

Those last seven miles to the little iron-smelting town of Blestium took forever, and already the sky had begun to lighten in the east when at last we spotted the first thatched houses. Our exhausted horses stumbled down the narrow main street as the first rays of the sun pierced the sky, promising yet another fine day.

"We can't go on like this. We need fresh horses," I said to Llawfrodedd. "For you and me if for no one else."

With the noise of our arrival, we had no need to wake the town with our demands. Doors opened and sleepy faces poked out. Curious expressions turned to fear. We must have looked a fearsome bunch, despite our small number – all of us fully armed, and with our dirty, exhausted faces.

"Fetch out your horses," Llawfrodedd shouted, standing in his stirrups. "Our journey is of the most urgent and the Queen has need of fresh mounts."

I slid down from Enfys's saddle, glad for the feel of sturdy cobbles under my feet. "And food," I called, as I hung onto her saddle horns in an effort to stay upright on my wobbly legs. Exhaustion threatened to overwhelm me. I couldn't let it.

One thing you could say about the people of the Dark Ages

was that they were well accustomed to obeying orders. None of them retreated inside and barred their doors. Instead, men shouted to their wives or servants and in a matter of minutes food appeared – just simple fare of bread and cheese and sweet cider, but better than any feast in a king's hall.

The headman of the town, a sturdy, red-faced fellow in just his undershirt and braccae, stepped forward and made a deep bow as I tore into my bread with ravenous hunger.

I took a gulp of the cider from the horn beaker someone had given me, the alcoholic sweetness revitalizing my exhausted body, and returned his bow. "We're looking for the army of the High King, my husband," I said, and wiped my mouth on my sleeve. "Have you seen him pass? He has a force of forty warriors with him. It's vital that we find him. We've ridden all night for this very reason."

The man must have been able to see the desperation in my eyes. He shifted as though uncomfortable, and his eyes slid to Llawfrodedd by my side, most likely more at ease with dealing with a man. He was going to have to rethink his behavior.

"Well?" I said, impatience gnawing at me. "Have you seen him pass through your town, or heard of anyone that's seen him?"

Llawfrodedd gave him a curt nod. "Go on. Tell the Queen what you know and hurry up about it."

I drained the beaker of cider and held it out for more.

The headman's gaze returned to my face, and he gave his scanty forelock a respectful tug, clearly resigning himself to having to speak to a woman. "Milady. Only yesterday an army like you describe were seen to the north, toward Caer Guorthegirn, by a farmer what come to town with two o' his fat lambs to sell."

Oh, God, no. He'd been here a day already. A full day ahead of us. My heart did a flip, and I had to reach out a hand to Llawfrodedd for support. "Which way were they going?" My voice came hoarse and edged with the terror rampaging through me.

The headman shrugged his burly shoulders, screwing up his face. "I couldn't rightly say, seeing as it weren't me what saw them. And that farmer went back home after he'd sold his lambs. So he ain't here to tell you what he saw." He had the grace to sound apologetic.

I swallowed down the last lump of bread, no longer hungry. "We have to get to the fortress of Caer Guorthegirn this morning. He might already be there." I looked imploringly at Llawfrodedd. "There's no time to waste."

"Only a few shepherds do live there now," the headman said, face puzzled. "That ain't no place for a king, Milady. Not nowadays. He won't ha' bothered to go up there, I don't doubt."

But Merlin had seen Amhar there.

I shook my head, determined. "Nevertheless, that's where we're headed." How hard it was to still the shaking in my voice.

Llawfrodedd turned back to the headman. "How many horses do you have?" His eyes scanned the crowd. "And we will need a guide to show us the way."

The man shook his head in further apology. "A guide, yes, I c'n do that. But we don't have no horses what'd suit you, Milord. This be a mining town, and the only horses here be for pullin' wagons an' plows. None as'd be fit for warriors like yourselves."

"I don't care," I said, panic rising in me. "Fetch any horses you have. If they're fresher than ours, we'll take them."

Quite a crowd had gathered by now, of people pulled early from their beds. In the chill, early-morning light, they huddled close together, muttering to one another in low voices, perhaps resentful that we wanted to take their only means of transport.

"Have no fear. You'll get your horses back," I said. "And be rewarded for your kindness. We'll return for our own mounts and expect you to have taken good care of them for they've given us their all, and more. Fetch out your beasts and let me see them."

I hadn't thought they'd have enough to horse all of us, but

they did. A motley collection of sturdy cobs and large ponies were fetched, and there in the little square we unsaddled our own horses in a hurry and saddled up these makeshift, workaday replacements.

A lanky young man leading a shaggy, flaxen-maned pony joined our new cavalry, his tow-colored hair hanging over his eyes like the overgrown forelock on his mount. He regarded his feet as the headman introduced him as our guide. "His own father do live up on that there hill with his sheep. He'll see you there right well."

I thanked the headman as the boy climbed onto his pony, his long, skinny legs dangling well below the animal's girth.

"Look after our horses well, and expect no work from them," Llawfrodedd warned the townspeople as we also mounted up. "These are your High King's finest warhorses, and he expects the best of care for every one of them."

Then, with the sun still low in the pale morning sky, we wheeled our cart nags around and trotted out of Blestium on the road north to Caer Guorthegirn, the silent, awkward boy at our head.

Our road followed the river, a wide and deceptively sluggish snake. On either side of it the high, forested hills rose to form the deep valley Merlin had described. We must be nearing the right place. Surely.

Our replacement horses weren't as eager as fresh, fit cavalry horses would have been, no doubt having worked hard the day before, but after the leaden hoofs of our own mounts they seemed lively and willing.

A bare half hour brought us to where the river curved away from the road and the high hill of Caer Guorthegirn rose on the northern bank. Smoke curled up from the top in twists of dark ribbon, but nowhere did we catch any sight of Arthur and his men. Might that mean he didn't know Amhar was there?

The boy silently indicated the way to go, kicking his pony into a canter with his bare heels. I urged my own horse into a lumbering canter, and her large ears twitched forward obligingly. But the steepness of the twisting, stony road where it ran between rocky outcrops defeated her. She fell back to trot then walk, her sides heaving. Horses that pulled wagons were not designed to gallop into battle, nor even up hills.

Llawfrodedd and Archfedd brought their sweating horses alongside mine, and she reached out a hand to clutch my sleeve. Her eyes were sooty smudges in a face pale beneath the tan. "I only pray we're here in time."

I nodded mutely in reply, unable to put into words how I felt; not wanting to even try.

Back in single file, we followed the boy's surefooted pony up a narrow track that might once have been much wider. As we approached the summit, rocky walls reared up above us, carved by nature out of the bare limestone. We passed through a narrow defile, and emerged into the wide, tussocky interior.

Small brown sheep galloped away as they spotted us, long tails flying. Fat lambs bounded after their mothers, bleating in panic.

In the center of the plateau a group of rough round huts clustered together, and it was from these that the smoke was rising into the clear blue sky. The men who'd been sitting around an outdoor hearth leapt to their feet in alarm. In moments they'd formed a defensive group on the edge of their camp, staring at us from weather-beaten, belligerent faces. Each man gripped a stout curved crook taller than he was, and had a hand resting on the long knife tucked in his belt. Not much to defend themselves with against armed warriors, but enough to do us damage.

Our guide cantered across the tussocky grass to join the men, one of whom must have been his father. He slid off his pony and edged closer, suddenly finding his voice as he muttered to the nearest man.

Hope soared in my heart at the lack of evidence of Arthur having been here.

I kicked my sturdy horse on and hauled her to a halt a bare

ten feet from the men. With shaking fingers, I undid the strap and pulled off my helmet, letting them see I was a woman. Llawfrod-edd and Archfedd brought their horses up on either side behind me, and I waved a hand to keep the rest of our men back. We didn't want to frighten these shepherds any more than they already had been.

Might they be sheltering Amhar here? Even an idiot could see no sign of Arthur or his men.

I sat straighter in my saddle. "I'm looking for my son," I said, letting my gaze run over the shepherds. "Prince Amhar of Dumnonia. Have you seen him?"

Chapter Twenty-Three

THE SHEPHERDS STARED up at me out of wary eyes. Above our heads a buzzard soared on a thermal, his mewling call plaintive and loud in the silence, and from further off came the bleating of the sheep. Several of the simple leather flaps that served for doors on the huts opened, and a few burly women in long, dirty tunics emerged to stand squarely to either side of the fire. As every one of them gripped gnarled cudgels, they looked, if anything, more dangerous than their menfolk.

I didn't care how threatening they looked. "Is my son here?" I raised my voice, even though the day was still with no wind to snatch my words away.

The men and women alike looked me up and down, wary curiosity in their gazes, no doubt taking in my long braid, my armor, and the helmet hanging in my hand. Low voiced and suspicious, they muttered between themselves for a minute, never taking their eyes from us.

One of them took a step forward, planting his crook butt-end on the ground by his wide-spread, booted feet. His long gray hair hung about his lined face in rat tails and his empty hand went up to rasp over the grizzled beard adorning his chin. "Who be *you*, then? A-comin' an-askin' of us poor ord'nary folk after a lost lordling."

I sensed rather than heard Llawfrodedd about to speak and held up a hand to silence him. I could do this for myself. I had to.

"I am the wife of your High King. His Queen. I am here to save my son and to beg your help."

Let him be here. Please, God, let him be here, hidden somewhere in one of these huts.

The man sucked his lips in for a moment, as though giving himself time to think. "What makes you think a king's son might have owt to do with the likes of us?" Deep distrust of strange armed warriors invading his home territory laced every word.

The men behind him muttered their agreement. "You tell her, Peibio."

"Tell her to clear off."

"We doan want nothin' to do with kings and queens."

"I have it on good advice that he is here with you," I said, squaring my shoulders in determination and fixing my gaze on the women. Some of them must be mothers, surely. They must understand a mother's love for her son.

I heaved a breath to steady my taut nerves. "I was sent here by one who possesses the Sight to find my son."

The women kept on regarding me out of cold, suspicion-filled eyes. Did they think I was lying?

I kept going, desperate to appeal to their dormant better natures. "I *must* find him before his father does, for the High King believes my son has committed a terrible crime." I scanned their coarse-featured, grubby faces, willing them to understand. "I *know* he didn't do it, and I must tell his father he's innocent before he finds him and punishes him… I have to find my son before his father does…" I faltered, at a loss for more words. My leaden weight sagged my shoulders and my imploring eyes fixed on the women's faces, waiting.

The men hadn't moved, but a low murmur of unrest ran between them as they continued to study us from beneath bushy, unkempt brows.

One of the women shouldered her way past the men to the front of the group, and they fell back to let her pass, eyeing her with respect. Tall and powerful, and probably a good ten years my junior, she had a strong face that had never been beautiful but always noble, like some mythical Amazon woman. "She do speak the truth," she said. "I saw her a-comin' in my dreamtime."

The leader took a hurried step back to give her prominence, bowing his head, a furtive look of something akin to awe in his eyes. This woman held a place of honor within her makeshift village.

Six feet from my horse, the woman halted, gazing up out of clear gray eyes. Eyes to be trusted. "I did see your man of magic send you here," she said. "And I must warn you to be quick, for you have gone an' left him in mortal danger." She stepped closer still, her hand moving to rest on my horse's mane. "Your son were here. Indeed he were, a-hidin' from his pa. A handsome princeling who'd done nothin' more than envy his brother. But he int here now. We couldn't keep him safe no longer. He had to run. Danger do threaten your boy even as we speak, same as your man o' magic. You must choose – your man o' magic or your boy."

What?

Not for a moment did I doubt what she'd said. The nagging fear that we'd abandoned Merlin when he needed us surged back to the surface, cheek-by-jowl with the terror for my son. Both of them in danger. Both of them at risk. Did she mean I could only save one? A terrible choice to make.

But Amhar was my son. My flesh and blood. *I'm sorry, Merlin.*

"Where is my son now?" I asked.

The woman's lovely eyes filled with compassion. "You must ride north an' follow the trail o' the High King's men. For he were here last night, a-lookin' for your boy. I seed him comin' and warned our princeling. He did flee before his father got here." She tightened her hold on my horse's mane. "You mus' ride fast, Milady the Queen, for I do see your son bein' bound in chains ifn' you doan find him quick."

If I hadn't been sitting on a horse, I'd have collapsed to the ground. As it was, I sagged forward over my horse's neck, gasping as the air thickened.

"When?" Archfedd asked, pushing her horse closer to mine, her voice sharp and commanding. "How long ago was my father here?"

"'Twas at sundown," the woman said. "I did tell your boy to ride north to the city of his kinsman. That he should ride as fast as he could. That time an' distance were what he did need above everythin'."

Did this simple countrywoman possess some hint of the power Merlin had? Of course she must, or how would she have seen us coming?

"Then we have to hurry," Archfedd said. "They won't have caught him up yet. We can still save him."

I forced myself back upright, drawing in deep, difficult breaths to steady my racing heart, a hollow feeling of doom already forming in my stomach. "Thank you for the help you gave my son," I said, the words echoing as though I were underwater. I made a small bow to the woman. "I shall not forget your kindness to my boy." I turned to my men. "Back to the road."

The feeling that fate was taking a hand here wouldn't leave me. Amhar was now fleeing north toward Viroconium, taking the road we'd so lately traveled, and he'd been right here, close to Blestium as we'd ridden past him, all unknowing. We might have been only hundreds of yards apart, yet hidden from one another as if by miles. Every move we'd made, we'd been six steps behind him, as though something, somewhere, didn't want us to find him. As though no matter how hard I tried, what lay ahead was something I couldn't change, and Morgana's hand still directed our lives from beyond the grave.

The roughness of the path back down the hill slowed us, but if we hurried, we'd risk a horse falling and taking a rider with him. I wanted to gallop, but all I could do was walk behind our guide.

At the road he pointed out a rough track heading west. "If'n you takes this path through the forest, it do meet the legion'ry road headin' north on t'other side of the hill. I've done my bit an' I'm goin' home, queen or no queen." A look of relief to be rid of us on his homely face, he turned his pony toward Blestium and kicked it into a shambling canter.

The narrow track, scarcely more than a dusty deer trod, led uphill through thickening forest, before at length descending toward the lower lying wetlands heading north.

In less than an hour we found the Viroconium road, but the sun was climbing higher in the sky, and urgency pressed down on me like some giant hand of fate. Using a switch cut from an elder bush, I urged my ungainly cob into a canter on the rough grass at the side of the road, and my men followed suit. We thundered north through scrubby lowland forest encroaching onto patchy heathlands. Herds of sheep grazed in the far distance, and the odd spooked pony or cow lumbered away from us.

If I'd had a fit horse used to marching, we'd have caught up with Arthur all the sooner, but none of us did. We had to make do with the heavy plow and wagon horses we'd been loaned. To give them their due, they did their best, but by the time we sighted Arthur's camp up ahead, sweat lathered their coats and they were nearly spent.

Llawfrodedd was first to spot the camp as we emerged from the forest edge into a wide valley sparsely sprinkled with farmsteads. "Ahead. Look."

I followed his pointing finger.

Sure enough, horses stood tethered to a picket line amongst farm buildings, and smoke rose from a few scattered campfires. Not much of a camp, but a camp, nevertheless.

I thumped my heels into my horse's ample sides, whipped her with the elder switch, and urged her into a canter. She lumbered across turf pocked with animal droppings, and Archfedd, Llawfrodedd and my men charged after me.

Arthur's men couldn't have missed our arrival. In a moment they were on their feet with their swords drawn, reaching for their shields. As I wrenched my poor horse to a skidding halt, they must have recognized me at last because they lowered their swords a little, although they lost nothing of their wary, defensive stance.

They'd set up their camp within a cluster of farm buildings – a couple of cattle sheds, some neat newly constructed hayricks, pigpens, stables and a long, low farmhouse, the thatched roof reaching almost to the ground.

The door of the farmhouse opened. Arthur and Cei stepped out. Cei closed it firmly behind him.

I slid off my horse, and raced to Arthur. "Don't kill him. Merlin used his Sight. It wasn't Amhar who killed Llacheu. It wasn't!" I grabbed hold of the front of his tunic and gave him a shake. "You have to believe me."

Arthur stood like a statue, looking down at me out of icy, anguished eyes.

I stopped shaking him.

Cei caught me by the shoulders and pulled me away.

Confused, I looked from one to the other of them. "We found Morgana and stopped her from blocking Merlin's Sight. He…" My voice trailed away at the memory of what Merlin had done to her. Arthur didn't need to know that… not yet. I gathered my shaky conviction. "He looked. He used his Sight and he *saw* it wasn't Amhar. He saw. He told us Amhar is innocent."

Why were they looking at me like that? Cei's grip on my shoulders burned like fire through my clothes.

Archfedd must have dismounted as well. Suddenly she was beside me, Llawfrodedd just behind her. "Where is he? Where's my brother?" She stared wide-eyed at her father as her voice rose.

"Hold her, Llawfrodedd," Cei said.

Archfedd rounded on him. "I don't need holding. Where's my brother?"

I shook Cei off. "Neither do I. Where is my son?"

In the pit of my stomach a horrible dread was forming, like a ball of cold stone, weighing me down. My legs had dissolved into jelly. How was I even standing?

I stared up into Arthur's gray-tinged face, his eyes ringed with shadows not put there just by exhaustion, and in them I read horror, disgust, despair.

"He ran," he said, the words emerging racked with pain from between rigid lips. "Tell me why he would run if he was innocent?"

Archfedd's eyes had gone so wide they looked as though they might start out of her head. "Because he knew you'd blame him," she cried, her voice rising. "Because you *did*! He thought you didn't love him and would blame him because of his fight with Llacheu."

"He ran," Arthur repeated. "What else was I to think?"

Shock had me in its relentless grip. "That he should have the benefit of the doubt. That you should hear *his* side of the story." How were the words coming out of my mouth? My heart pounded so hard and loud everyone must have been able to hear its thundering rhythm. It beat inside my head. My ears throbbed, and my body shook with it.

"Where's my brother?" Archfedd's demand came out on a broken sob. "What have you *done* to him?"

Cei made a grab for me again, but I shook him off. *"Where is my son?"* I spat out the words like bullets.

Arthur lifted a hand in my direction, but I stepped back, my own hands up to beat him off, not wanting to be touched. Not by him.

"He ran," he said again, as though this justified everything. "He ran because he was guilty. He did it, Gwen. He did it. He killed his brother like a thief in the night. He crept up behind him and opened his throat and dumped him on a midden like a dead dog."

"But he *didn't*," I spat. "He's innocent. Merlin *saw*. He *told* me Amhar was innocent." If only we had Merlin with us. Without him I was impotent and powerless, as though every argument I made were feeble. I rounded on Cei. "Where is he? Where's my son?"

Cei's blue eyes went to Arthur.

The conviction they'd done something terrible overcame me. I lunged for Cei, this time, hammering my fists on his broad, mail-covered chest. "You have to tell me." Tears ran down my cheeks. "What have you *done?*"

Arthur's strong hands grabbed me by my shoulders and pulled me around to face him. I kept on going, hitting him, now, as hard as I could with my balled fists. "You've done something to him. I know you have." Despite my determination to keep calm, I couldn't keep any semblance of control.

"No! Don't!" Cei shouted.

Still gripped in Arthur's hands, I craned my head around to see why Cei had shouted.

Archfedd had pushed open the farmhouse door and was standing in the oblong of darkness, staring inwards, frozen to the spot.

Cei ran to her, reaching her at the same time as Llawfrodedd. They snatched her away from the door and it banged shut behind them. Limp in their grip, her face blanched paper-white and her mouth hung open in a wordless scream.

I fought Arthur's grip. "What is it?" I had to make him let me go. In desperation, my knee came up and caught him in the groin. He doubled over and released his hold. I raced for the farmhouse door. Llawfrodedd and Cei were too busy hanging on to Archfedd to be able to stop me.

I flung the door wide, the bright summer sunshine streaming in across the beaten earth floor. Not much furniture. Just a long oak table in the center.

Amhar lay on the table. His head at an awkward angle. It had been severed from his body.

I screamed. The world spun and the ground came up and hit me hard. Merciful darkness descended.

Chapter Twenty-Four

S OMEONE WAS CARRYING me in their arms, the unsteady motion making my stomach lurch. My head lolled against a solid shoulder, and the familiar smell of sweat and leather and horses surrounded me. I tried to open my eyes, but the world spun, and I had to shut them again, drawing deep breaths to steady my pounding heart.

Even then, the dizziness continued, as though the whole world were rocking like a ship at sea. Nausea welled in my stomach, but I'd eaten nothing and all that came up was bile. I swallowed it and wished I hadn't. Sounds boomed as though I were underwater: voices, the whinny of a horse, a cockerel crowing, the crunch of heavy footsteps as they jarred through me.

Whoever was carrying me laid me down gently on a hard, lumpy surface. My groping fingers, desperate for something tangible to cling to, grasped the roughness of a blanket. I fisted my hands on the cloth, pulling it tight about me, as the world beneath me rolled as though the ship had met a storm.

"Drink this," someone's voice echoed close by. Whoever had spoken raised my head and shoulders and the coldness of a horn beaker touched my lips.

I tasted strong alcohol, gagged and spat, and it ran down my chin. "No." My voice came out thick and slurred as though my tongue refused to obey my thoughts. I turned my head away from the beaker, pressing my lips together.

Amhar. My boy. My beautiful boy.

The image of that lifeless body lying so awkward and broken on the farmhouse table flashed into the forefront of my mind. Every part of me convulsed in desperate denial.

A moaning noise began, like a wounded animal somewhere close.

It was me.

"Mami." An icy hand on mine. Wasn't it summer and this a sunny day?

I forced my eyes open a fraction. The frantic spinning lessened. The world came into blurry focus and stopped its mad gyrating. In place of the sky, the beams and thatch of an ancient, discolored roof hung over my head. The smell of straw and animal dung filled my nostrils. That cold hand clung onto mine.

A face I knew leaned over me.

Archfedd. My daughter. My child. My *only* child.

She was kneeling beside me just inside the wide doorway of a barn. If I looked to my left without even moving my eyes, sky came into view, blue and cloudless and achingly beautiful. On a day when nothing would ever be beautiful again.

I peered into her face. Tears had made runnels through the dirt on her cheeks. She met my searching gaze with red and puffy eyes.

"Archfedd." I'd meant to whisper, but it came out as a grating croak.

"Mami." She threw herself onto my chest, clinging to me, sobs racking her slender body.

For a moment I didn't know how to react. This wasn't just my grief, it was shared. And she was as racked by it as me. I released my hold on the blanket and put my arms around her, my hands on her back, her hair in my face. Her body sagged into mine, weighing me down, pressing me into the uneven barn floor.

I scanned my narrow view of this alien world.

Cei stood in the wide doorway of the barn, one hand on the

rough-hewn lintel, probably not for support but because in his awkwardness he needed somewhere to put his hand. He dropped his gaze to study his boots rather than meet mine; his face was as drawn and gray as Arthur's...

Arthur.

Desperation seized me. Where was he? I turned my head from side to side. No one. Only Cei. Bright sunshine streamed through the doorway, haloing Cei and bringing with it the sweet smell of fresh-cut hay and the earthier scents of the farmyard. The smell of life on a day when only death existed.

Under my stare, Cei released his hold on the lintel, shifting from foot to foot in self-conscious discomfort. He kept his head down, his gaze still fixed on his feet, and now clasped his hands before him, the fingers working, never still. Like Lady Macbeth trying to wash the black spot away from her hands in her nightmare.

"My boy," I whispered, at last. "What have you done to my boy?"

He didn't answer.

I closed my eyes. Flies droned. Outside, a horse whinnied. The sound of Archfedd's sobbing filled the warm air.

I couldn't lie here like this, with my boy dead in the farmhouse. I had to get up. Gently, I pushed Archfedd off me and sat up. The world stayed in focus. Archfedd sat back on her heels, tears coursing down her cheeks and her shoulders shaking. The time for sympathy for my daughter's loss would come later. I wasn't just a mother, I was a queen, and I had to deal with this myself.

Using the barn wall, I pushed myself to my feet and stood for a moment, sucking in deep breaths until my legs stopped feeling like wet spaghetti and a little strength returned. Then I lifted my head and fixed Cei with a stony stare.

He must have felt my gaze. How could he not have?

With reluctance, he raised his head and our eyes met. Cei, my dear friend and brother-in-law, who'd dandled Amhar on his knee as a baby, who'd given me a shoulder to cry on when I needed it, who'd been ever kind to me and to my children. And yet... he was part of this. He'd killed my boy. Him, Arthur, all their men. They all held joint responsibility for this, but Arthur held the most. My son's blood stained his hands.

"He didn't do it, Cei," I said, my voice flat. "He didn't do it. You killed the wrong man."

He licked his lips. "You believe that?"

I nodded, then wished I hadn't as the world spun alarmingly again. My empty stomach rumbled, but I didn't care. "Merlin told me."

Cei's honest face creased in a frown. "Where is he, then? Why isn't he with you?"

Merlin. Left behind. Lost. In danger. What had that wise woman at Caer Guorthegirn said? That I had to choose between my man of magic and my son. I'd chosen. And now perhaps I'd lost them both.

"We had to leave him in Caer Legeion with Morgawse," I said. "He... he took ill." I couldn't tell him yet that his sister lay dead by Merlin's hands. Even if he'd hated her, she remained his sister and a royal princess, and Merlin had killed her. He hadn't had to, but he'd done it, nevertheless. How easily had love turned to hate.

Cei's eyes pierced my soul. "Without Merlin, how can we know what you say is true?"

What? He thought I was *lying?* My indignation rose, before I remembered how I'd considered lying myself. How I'd thought I'd be prepared to say anything to save my child. I licked my lips. "Because it *is* true." Now I sounded as though I were justifying a lie. "Because Llawfrodedd and Archfedd were there when he said it. They can tell you it's true."

Cei shook his head. "No. Arthur was right. The boy wouldn't have run if he hadn't been guilty." His anguished blue eyes, that matched the sky outside, narrowed and grew cold. "You're going to have to face the truth. He *killed* Llacheu, Gwen. Not in combat. He could never have beaten him like that. No. He crept up behind him in the dark and slit his throat. Like a coward. And then he ran. As a coward would."

I stared at him. He didn't believe me. Despite what I'd said, he thought I was lying out of motherly love. He was party to the death of my son. The son he believed a murderer of the worst kind. The world swirled again for an instant, and I fought it back into focus. I mustn't faint. I mustn't. I had to see my son. My firstborn child. My baby.

I pushed myself off the wall. "Believe what you want. I *know* the truth, and it's you and Arthur who have committed the crime. Look after Archfedd." With determined steps, I shouldered my way past him and out into the hot, sunlit day.

In the farmyard, I stopped for a moment to get my bearings, blinking at the brightness. To the right lay the horselines I'd already seen, strung out between this barn and the next, the horses standing idly in the sunshine, back legs crooked and tails swishing at the irritating flies. To my left, a new horseline was being set up with Llawfrodedd in charge. He stopped and stared across at me, his jaw set, and his face pale with grief.

I turned away.

Opposite the barn lay the farmhouse, its weathered door firmly closed. No sign of Arthur.

In a lean-to beside the farmhouse huddled the farmer's family – a burly, balding man, his pregnant wife, five children from a snot-nosed toddler to a scrawny boy of eleven or twelve. Under my gaze, they looked away, all except that oldest boy, who met my stare for a moment, his eyes wide and frightened. Maybe they feared a man who'd execute his own son and would do the same to them if they put a foot wrong, even if he was their High King.

A man who'd executed his own son, possibly in front of them.

Dead. My son lay dead. How could I keep forgetting the finality of death? I'd never see him again, never talk to him, hold him close, tell him I loved him. Everything that had made him unique and mine had gone.

I took a hesitant step and nearly stumbled, heaved a breath, straightened, and walked toward the farmhouse, my heart thundering.

No one tried to prevent me, but every man stopped whatever they were doing, and every eye drilled into me. I drew myself up straighter. I was a queen, a warrior queen, and they wouldn't see me hesitate again.

The door had a rough wooden latch the farmer must have fashioned himself, worn smooth by age and greasy hands. With shaking fingers, I raised it. My hand, disembodied from the rest of me, pushed on the silvered wood, and the heavy door swung open on worn leather hinges. For a long moment, fear kept me motionless on the threshold.

Then I stepped through and the door swung closed behind me.

The long room that made the living area of the farmhouse stank of soot, rancid tallow and dog. Two tiny windows in the foot thick walls stood open to the left and right of the door.

I blinked as my eyes struggled to accustom themselves to the paucity of light, and my gaze went everywhere but to the table in the center, as though it and I were two like-poles on a pair of magnets.

A partition wall of split logs separated this living area from what would be a bedroom for the parents. Against one wall, the children's small beds lay tumbled as though someone had dragged their occupants from them in a hurry this morning. The hearth fire lay cold and untended, full of powdery ash.

There was only the table left. I forced my eyes to look.

Arthur stood at the foot of the table, staring at our son. A couple of smoking tallow candles burned at the other end. By Amhar's head. By *the head*.

Arthur didn't look toward me, and the gloom made it difficult to see his face.

Instead, I took in my son. *Mine.* My anger rose, curdling,

boiling, fomenting in my churning heart. Arthur had relinquished any right to claim Amhar as his own when he'd had him executed for a crime my boy hadn't committed. The hot hatred welled up so vividly, I feared it might come spilling out of my mouth, like vomit. I pressed my lips together to hold it in.

I'd seen dead bodies enough times, God knew. I'd seen Llacheu's body lying on that midden and kissed his lifeless corpse before his burial. And yet, this was worse. If Llacheu had been murdered, then so had Amhar, and his murderer stood before me. Needless deaths, both of them.

I took in every detail. I couldn't help myself. Now I was looking, really looking, I had to see everything, couldn't tear my eyes away. Now the magnets had opposite poles.

A dead body ceases to look alive. You'd think it would look asleep, but it doesn't. Something is lost, some vital spark that makes a sleeping person human. There's little of humanity about a corpse, still less one that's had its head severed. The person you loved is gone forever.

Someone had wrapped Amhar's neck tightly with a scarf. If I hadn't known, hadn't already seen, I might have thought his head still attached. But I had seen, and that scarf didn't manage to make his body look right, correct, like a body with a head still attached. And I *did* know. Under that innocuous scarf someone had cut through the living flesh and bone and killed my son.

Arthur. He'd told me once that if he condemned someone to death, he had to be the one to carry out the order. He'd done this.

I took a greedy step closer as though the sight of my son fascinated me, as though, perhaps, I was searching for some little, last-remaining shred of the boy I'd loved.

His pale, still face resembled Llacheu's, only younger, softer, more boyish. Bloodless lips, parchment-pale skin, thick dark lashes brushing cold cheeks, the shadow of downy stubble – like pieces of a person cobbled together by some Dark Age Franken-stein. Someone had swept his hair back from his face to reveal a touch of acne on his forehead. A boy's skin. Not a line or wrinkle marred it. Wiped clean of who he was by death.

I couldn't bring myself to kiss him. Not knowing how he'd died, how I'd seen him lying on this table in two pieces when Archfedd opened the door. I couldn't kiss a *head*. I couldn't.

My son. My beautiful son. Why couldn't I cry? I felt arid, like a desert, parched and dry. I longed to cry, to wail and sob like my daughter, but I couldn't.

Instead, I turned my head and looked down the table at my husband.

For a long minute, he kept his eyes on Amhar and didn't return my gaze. I kept on staring, waiting for him to give in. I had patience.

At last, he met my eyes.

"You killed my son," I said, my voice as icy as my heart.

He didn't speak. Just kept on looking at me, his face shadowy and distant.

"You killed him." Once again, the words shot out of me like bullets.

He pressed his lips together. "He was my son, too."

I shook my head. "Not now. He's not yours now. He's *mine*. *My* son. You murdered him. You took my son away from me."

"He killed Llacheu." Was that despair in his voice? For whom?

"No," I said. "He didn't."

Silence. I waited, not taking my eyes from his face, daring him to look away.

He shook his head like a horse bothered by a swarm of flies. "You're his mother. I forgive you. You don't want to believe what our son did. You don't want to believe him capable of murder."

I heard the anguish in his voice but didn't care. "*You* forgive *me*?"

How dare he? How bloody dare he?

He nodded. "I forgive you for refusing to believe he did this. I *understand* why you feel like that." He heaved a sigh. "I didn't want to believe it, either. They were both my sons. They're both dead. I've lost them both."

Inside me, a silent scream rose, and my hands covered my ears as though the sound of the scream were real. All I wanted to do was shut out Arthur's words. How could I not scream, when my husband, whom I'd loved more than life itself for nearly twenty years, had done this to our child? That he'd believed our son could commit so terrible a crime?

He fell back a step from the table as though he, too, heard the scream.

I lowered my hands and they turned to fists. "Fuck you." I spat the words at him. "I don't need your *forgiveness*. I need my son, and *you've* stolen him from me."

Why wasn't I getting through to him?

He came around the table, holding out his hands. "I need you, Gwen. We need each other." His voice cracked. "I need to mourn with you. We need to mourn together."

My turn to take a step back. "Well, I don't need you. Keep away from me. Don't even *try* to touch me."

He halted, six feet off, staring. His hands dropped to his sides.

The words came tumbling out of me. "You killed him for nothing. Nothing. He didn't do it. Merlin told me. You killed him for misguided revenge. He ran because he was afraid of you, because he knew you always loved Llacheu better." I was getting into my stride, my anger, hot like molten lava, spewing out of my mouth in a fountain of invective. "You talk of forgiveness? I can *never* forgive you for this. Never. You should have waited. You should have given him a chance to explain why he ran."

I didn't care about the pain and self-loathing in his eyes, nor how much he would have had to wrestle with his conscience before condemning his heir. I didn't care that tears streaked his cheeks for his lost sons. I didn't care that he was my husband and king and I'd given up everything for him. I didn't ask myself how hard it had been for him to do this. All I knew was that he'd killed my son.

He swiped away tears with his sleeve. "He committed the

most terrible crime, Gwen. The original crime from the Bible – a brother killing a brother. The law demanded his death, even though he was my son and heir. I had to do it. I had no choice. I am the High King and can never be above the law."

How could he say this? How could he? I wanted to hit him again. Not just hammer on his chest but punch his face, tear his hair, kick him, bite him if I had to. I wanted him to know how I felt, how I hated him, how I could never love him again.

Instead, I spoke four words into the pregnant space between us. "He didn't do it." And left.

Chapter Twenty-Five

OUTSIDE THE FARMHOUSE, the glaring sun, nearing its zenith, beat down on me without mercy. The door banged shut, and I halted, uncertainty flooding over me. I'd walked away from my son, left him lying there alone. Ought I to sit by his body, as we'd done for Llacheu? Could I even bring myself to do that? If I didn't look at him dead, could I hold him in my heart as he'd been alive, preserved forever in his golden boyhood?

I glanced around, finding every head bent to avoid my gaze, the men busy with their horses or their saddlery. Not looking. Embarrassed. No. Worse than that. Ashamed. Their shame washed over me in a sister wave to my uncertainty.

I sucked in my lips, pressing them between my teeth, fists balled by my sides. No. That wasn't *my* boy lying on that table, broken and still. What had made him my boy, my Amhar, had flown. And I didn't want to see his lifeless face, his still hands, his silent chest. I didn't want to touch his stiffening body, kiss his cold cheeks, smooth his soft hair.

But that was all wrong, because I *did*. I wanted him warm and alive and smiling at me about something he'd done or seen. I wanted him laughing with Archfedd or his friends. I wanted him back. Alive.

Never again.

All this time I'd been worrying about losing Arthur, and capricious fate had been saving this up for me like some spiteful trick. Smoothing Medraut's path to Camlann. Or was that Nimuë's path to power? I couldn't tell.

Cei stepped out of the barn and halted, the only one brave enough to look at me.

I squared my shoulders, set my jaw, and strode toward the barn, halting three feet in front of Cei. "Tell me everything." To my amazement my voice came out authoritative and cool, as though I hadn't just left my son lying dead on that table. I'd put away my grief and let cold determination take its place. For now.

Cei glanced back into the shadows of the barn. Llawfrodedd was sitting with Archfedd, holding her tight against his body, with one hand in her hair, and her tear-stained face pressed to his chest.

Cei's broad shoulders sagged. "Walk with me."

Luckily for him he didn't try to take my hand or put a supportive arm around my shoulders. If he had, I would've hit him or maybe something worse. My sword hung by my side, and I had my dagger tucked in my belt. I'd killed before and felt ready to kill again. Bugger that two wrongs didn't make a right – it would have taken very little to have had my sword tip at Cei's throat.

We walked through the horselines. None of the silent men looked up. Leaving them behind, we followed the dusty road for fifty yards or so, before he halted beside a solid Roman milestone. Maybe he felt he couldn't talk to me so close to where everything had happened. Maybe he felt guilty. He bloody well should.

"Well?" I said, still hanging on to my cold calm. "Tell me how *you* let this happen." Throwing the blame, at least in part, onto Cei seemed so obvious. I needed someone to blame so why not him? And he was not without guilt.

Cei's Adam's apple bobbed. His stubbly, gray-streaked ginger beard almost covered it. At some time this morning he'd taken off his mail shirt, but sweat beaded his brow and darkened his underarms. I still wore my mail shirt, and looking at him brought more sweat springing out on my body in sympathy. Too hot for the undershirt and woolen tunic I had on under my mail.

His gaze fell to where his fingers fiddled with the end of his thick leather belt. "I don't know where to start…"

"At the beginning," I snapped. The anger still boiling in me served to keep me calm and focused. If I didn't stay angry, I'd collapse and sob like Archfedd. I couldn't let myself do that. Not yet. "Tell me how you caught him."

Cei cleared his throat. "After we'd scoured the obvious places in Dumnonia, we… Arthur… thought Amhar might have fled to Morgawse in Caer Legeion. We went there first, but we didn't find him." Hot color rose to his cheeks. "We searched the house from top to bottom. She wasn't happy. Arthur didn't believe our sister when she said the boy had gone. And he'd been there all right – we found traces of him."

I bit my lip. "Was Morgana with her?"

He nodded, and bitterness tinged his voice. "She was, and her child. She had the look about her of a cat that had got the cream."

Not anymore, she didn't. But I didn't tell him that. She was his sister, after all. That could come later.

"Go on," I said, holding onto my sanity by mere shreds of self-control.

He shifted his weight and his hands clasped and unclasped, his leather belt forgotten.

I sucked in my lips to prevent myself from speaking my mind. He wouldn't like what he'd hear if I did. He was Amhar's uncle, but he'd tried to tell me my son was guilty. He *believed* Amhar had killed Llacheu. Didn't he? Or was he saying all this to support Arthur, the brother he loved? Would he do that? Back up Arthur at the cost of my son's life? Right now, I felt ready to believe anything of anybody.

I fixed my gaze on his contorting face, determined not to falter, but to find out the truth.

He bit his lower lip. "Morgana and Morgawse sent us off west, along the coast. Arthur said he didn't believe them. I didn't either, but we both thought it could well have been a double bluff, so we went anyway. Be just like Morgana to let us think she was lying when it was truth."

He had that right. The unwelcome image of Morgana's death flashed into my head. Of her head snapping back, of the loud crack as it broke, of her body twitching on the mosaic floor beside the table where her sewing lay, still with the warmth of her touch on it.

I mustn't think of her. She didn't matter. She'd gone. I had to convince myself of that. Although now, what did anything matter? I steeled myself. "If you were heading west, what made you come this way?"

Cei cleared his throat again and spat a gob of phlegm into the dust. "We rode west as far as we thought he might go, with him not knowing the land. Then we turned east again and picked up his tracks. They hadn't lied, after all. He'd ridden west and then doubled back into the valleys. He had no idea of how to travel without leaving a trail a mile wide. He was all too easy to follow once we'd found it."

How could we be discussing this as though nothing bad had happened? Why was I so numb? I screwed my hands up and dug my nails into their palms in the effort to feel something… anything, other than this cold acceptance of what he was telling me. As though all of this had happened to someone else, not to my son, not to me.

"Last night his trail led us to the hill of Caer Guorthegirn. He'd been hiding there with a bunch of shepherds who for some reason had taken him under their wing as a persecuted hero. He'd ridden in, a handsome boy on his exhausted horse, wearing armor and carrying a sword and spear, and they decided to protect him. A romantic hero, perhaps." He shook his head. "Or perhaps they seized upon him as their chance to cock-a-snook at their ruler? Who knows?"

Or perhaps their Seer had seen his innocence and his need for help.

I shook my head. "I went there. I was too late." Always too

late. Too far behind him. Never destined to be in time. I couldn't avoid the thought that fate had meant for me to arrive too late.

I'd thought I'd found my purpose in the Dark Ages – to save Amhar. I'd been wrong. I had no purpose. I could change nothing. I might as well have never come, or stayed. I'd made no difference at all.

If we'd not ridden to Viroconium or Caer Legeion, we'd have been in time. We'd have met Amhar before ever Arthur reached him. If Merlin had been able to see where Amhar was, we'd have been in time. If… if… if… But everything had been stacked against us. Fate had defeated us.

Cei grunted. "The boy had already left the old fort, riding north. He was heading toward Viroconium. Maybe he thought he'd get a hearing there. Maybe he thought Custennin would welcome him with open arms as his father used to be Arthur's enemy. Your boy never did have any sense."

"And you caught him here?"

He glanced around himself, shrugged, and nodded. "We did. His horse had gone lame. He had no other. He was walking, leading it, when our outriders caught up with him. They saw him hide in…" He stopped.

"Where?"

He licked his lips. "In the barn where we've left Archfedd with Llawfrodedd."

Someone had carried me into the very place where they'd captured Amhar. They'd surprised him in there with his lame horse, drawn their swords and taken him prisoner. How frightened had he been, knowing his father was on the way?

"When? How long ago?" I had to know. The question burning in my heart nagged me to ask the question. I needed to know by how much I'd been too late.

"They caught him a couple of hours after dawn."

I could have done it. We could have pushed on harder and been here in time. We could have, even on our heavy workhorses. "So, when Arthur arrived, you set up a kangaroo court? Here, in the middle of nowhere?"

His eyes widened at the unexpected word.

"A makeshift court."

He nodded.

"And whose idea was that?" Oh, the bitterness in my voice. Like I didn't know who'd been prosecutor, judge and jury. Then executioner.

"Arthur's."

As much as desperation had been driving me, it must also have been driving Arthur. I'd loved Llacheu like my own, or so I'd thought. But now, faced with my own son's death, I knew that wasn't true. I'd always loved Amhar that bit more. He was mine, and Llacheu never had been. I'd carried Amhar inside my body for nine months, nursed him, kissed him better when he fell, seen him grow into a handsome young man. A young man I'd loved.

How would it have been if Llacheu had belonged to me as well? Been really mine, not Arthur's bastard son. How if two sons of my body had fought, and one had killed the other? How would I have supported the one who'd killed his brother? That was how it had been for Arthur – how he'd *thought* it had been. Would I have wanted the killer dead? Or would I have been prepared to forgive – as old Olwyn had at the last forgiven her only surviving son, Melwas, for his cruelty and the murders of his brothers? Could I have done what she did? Or would I, like Arthur, have wanted him dead in revenge for his brother's death?

But Arthur had been constrained by the law. As High King, he saw himself as its upholder.

My mouth had gone paper dry. "Did Arthur not question him?" The words came out as a raspy whisper I could barely string together.

"He did."

"And didn't Amhar deny the accusation?"

Cei shifted uneasily. "No. He didn't."

What? He hadn't denied it? Had Merlin been wrong, after all, maybe guilty of telling me what I wanted to hear? My legs gave way, and I sat down hard in the scuffed dirt at the side of the road, my face in my hands.

With a thump, Cei sat down beside me. So close I could smell the sweat on him and feel the warmth radiating from his body. Despite the heat of the day, mine had gone icy cold.

My hands smelled of horses and dirt. I lowered them and stared at Cei. Tears glimmered in his kind blue eyes.

"He did it, Gwen." His voice was gentle. "He ran, and when we caught him, he didn't deny it."

I swallowed, conscious of tears brimming at last, determined not to let them fall. If I gave in to tears, I was lost, and I had to find out what had happened to my boy. I fisted my hands again, digging my nails into the soft flesh of my palms. "What did he say? His actual words when he was accused. I need to know. Tell me." This time my voice emerged fierce and angry.

Cei lifted his hand toward me but dropped it back again as I flinched away. If I accepted his sympathy, his kindness, then those tears would fall, and I couldn't let them.

He cleared his throat again, several times. "We caught up with the advance guard at the farm, and they brought Amhar out to us. They'd bound his hands and taken his armor and weapons. He didn't look as though he'd given them any trouble." He looked away from me into the distance, his eyes unfocused as though he saw the scene acted out before him as a replay.

"We all dismounted. Arthur walked up to him. Face to face. I thought he had it in his head to kill the boy right there, so I hurried after him." His voice wobbled. He'd loved Amhar like a son himself. But he'd loved Llacheu too. As had I. How difficult it must have been for him.

I fought to steady my breathing. "Go on."

"He-he asked him one question. "Did you do it?" And Amhar looked him in the eye and answered."

"What? What did he say?" I clenched my fists tighter still, if that were possible, but I couldn't still the shaking that racked my body.

"He said, "What matter if I did. You believe I did, so I must have. Who am I to argue with the High King?" And Arthur stepped back, drawing his sword.""

I caught my breath. Excalibur. The sword of Macsen Wledig. An emperor's sword. She hadn't been forged for this.

Cei swallowed. "He didn't deny it, Gwen."

I stared into his eyes, seizing on his words. "But he didn't admit it, either. Did he? That wasn't an *admission* you heard. It was Amhar saying his father always thinks he's right. It wasn't Amhar saying he did it. *It wasn't.*"

The tears in Cei's eyes overflowed and trickled down his dirty cheeks. "Arthur took it as one. He carried out the execution himself."

I looked away, fixing my gaze on my dusty boots, the hollow emptiness where my stomach had once been, enormous. "Merlin was right," I whispered. "He saw. He told us Amhar was innocent."

Cei gave a weary shake of his head. "And where is Merlin now?"

How bitter were his words.

He swiped the relentless flies away. "What happened to his Sight when it was needed? What's the use of a man of magic if every time you need him, he's not there, or can't see?"

I kept my eyes on my boots, fixed on the dust adhering to them, concentrating. "We had to leave him in Caer Legeion. At Morgawse's house."

"Why?"

Oh yes, why? I'd have to tell him. It would come out soon enough. And then what? He'd killed a member of Arthur's family. Would the same fate await him as had been dealt to our son? My hollowed-out body felt devoid of emotion, empty.

I licked dry lips. "He killed Morgana."

"What?" Cei's voice rose. "He killed her? Dead?" Disbelief radiated out of him.

"What other sort of killed is there but dead?" I asked, bleakness coloring my tone. If only there *were* another sort of killed than dead. If only.

"Why? What happened?"

This time when he put his hand out to me, I didn't flinch but turned toward him, determination in my heart. "I'll tell you exactly what happened."

So I did, in every detail, from our headlong ride on Morgana's trail to Viroconium then south to Caer Legeion, to regain Merlin's lost Sight, and our quest to follow Amhar and save him. All too late.

When I'd finished, we sat in silence, staring out across the sunbaked fields where the air shimmered and cattle stood idly under the shade of spreading oaks.

I wanted to cry, but I couldn't.

Chapter Twenty-Six

W E BURIED MY beautiful son in the early evening, with the great golden ball of the sun dipping down behind the Welsh mountains and sending shafts of bright, impossible light streaking across the land.

Arthur chose a spot twenty yards from the farm where an ancient barrow lay: a long mound half-obscured behind the barns and close to the western edge of the road. Bronze age, most likely. The trivial thought barged its way into my head as though it were the most important thing in the world. *Bronze age*. Who cared? I didn't. *Bronze age*. I had to stop myself thinking.

I couldn't. Who had been buried there in the distant past? A warrior, I hoped. Warriors in the plural, maybe. And now another would join them, unfledged in all but the smallest of skirmishes.

The grass-covered mound rose out of the flat land, cold and unwelcoming. Cold ground to receive a cold body. Half a dozen of our men had scrambled to the top and dug a hole down into the mound, the earth piled up beside it, a stark reminder of what we were about to do.

I couldn't stand with Arthur. He didn't ask me to, and I couldn't take those steps across the dusty ground to join him. He didn't even look at me. Instead, Archfedd and I huddled close together, off to one side, watching in silence as Arthur's men lowered the quickly made wooden pallet, on which they'd laid my son's shroud-wrapped body, into the hole. Just a white cocoon made somehow smaller by death, as though his flown soul had possessed physicality.

Whoever this mound had been created for all those centuries ago, surely he wouldn't mind sharing his resting place with my lost son, and if he did, he had no say.

Standing in stony silence, the tears I'd thought would fall earlier had dried to nothing.

Archfedd clutched my hand in her hot grasp, pressing her grief-filled body against mine. Beyond her, Llawfrodedd stood with his head hanging, the lines of shock deep etched in his young face. Did he *still* believe Amhar had been innocent? Did I, even? My mind a turmoil, I didn't know.

The whole thing was over quickly. Hurried, brushed under the metaphorical carpet, got out of the way. I didn't budge from my position as our warriors departed in somber dribs and drabs, and Llawfrodedd gently tried to shepherd Archfedd away. Instead, I watched the pallet bearers fill in the hole, shoveling the smothering earth bit by bit over my firstborn child, shutting off the light of day from his dead eyes.

At last, they heaped the final shovelfuls of earth onto the mound and stumbled down the slope to slink off without meeting my gaze. Alone, lost in my thoughts, I couldn't take my eyes from that cold dark earth. Six feet of it between Amhar's beautiful face and the reddened sky.

A small sound to my left. I turned my head. No. I wasn't alone.

Arthur hadn't moved either, but was staring at the grave mound, with Cei standing close, like an anxious sheepdog guarding his flock.

Hatred boiled up inside me. Had he *never* loved Amhar? Did he even now believe I'd lied to him after Amhar's birth and Amhar hadn't been his son? Every little thing that served to reinforce my suspicions welled up like lava from a volcano.

I was back, in an instant, on the fateful day when Arthur had slain Melwas, and with his dying breath, that wicked king had perhaps set in motion this tragedy.

Amhar, just two weeks old, slept in his crib, and only a few oil lamps lit our chamber. Arthur came in, late and angry, heavy with the burning knowledge that Melwas had claimed Amhar as his own child as he died, as a last, spiteful wound. I argued with him, fighting for my child. He said he believed me, but had he? For a while, back then, he'd thought he'd lost his son. And now he had, but by his own hand. No matter how much I assured him, how much I swore Melwas had never touched me, had he *ever* believed me? Did he even now think he'd executed Melwas's cuckoo in the nest?

The peasant girl Bretta's words came back to me, echoing down the years.

I curse you, Queen of Dumnonia, and I curse your husband and your son. You and yours shall know the loss I feel.

And, oh, hadn't she been right.

Archfedd, whom I'd thought gone with Llawfrodedd, came hurrying back. She tugged my hand. "Mother, you need to come back with me. I don't like it here. I don't want to look at it. I don't want you to."

I turned to her, almost puzzled at finding her here. What to do with her? My eyes fell on Llawfrodedd hovering at her elbow. "Take care of my daughter." I pulled my hand free and pushed her toward him. "Make sure she eats and rests."

"Mami." She reached out, but I retreated.

"No. I have other things to do. Go with Llawfrodedd. Please. He'll look after you." The time for me to comfort her was put off yet again. It would have to come later.

His arm went around her shoulders, supportive and strong. My heart ached. Who was there to support me now? No one. I had to stand alone.

I heaved a steadying breath and walked toward Arthur, peering at him through the soft, shadowy twilight.

He didn't turn his head.

Cei did, though. "Gwen."

Still, Arthur didn't move.

I halted six feet from them. Waiting.

Long minutes crawled past that could have been hours or days or weeks. I had no idea of time anymore. For me, all time had stopped.

At last, Arthur turned to face me.

I stared.

In his pale face his dark eyes sat in shadowed hollows. The dust of days on the road ran with streaks where his tears had fallen. Were falling still. His whole body, normally so strong and upright, sagged as though the world sat on his shoulders. It did. My world.

He drew in a shaky breath. "Gwen."

I regarded him in stony silence. I had no compassion for him. Let him suffer. Let him hurt as I was hurting. Let him never forgive himself for what he'd done. I never would.

His right hand came up as though he wanted to reach for me, before falling back under my cold scrutiny.

Cei cleared his throat. "I'll go. You need to talk."

I didn't watch him leave. His footsteps died away.

We stood in silence, looking at one another. Two wounded animals. No, I was the wounded one, and he the killer.

"I'm sorry," he said, at last. "I'm so sorry I had to do this. You don't know how sorry I am."

The colossal understatement served as a red rag to a bull. "You're *sorry*? You're telling me you're sorry for killing my son? For cutting him down as though he were a common criminal? Have you any idea how *inadequate* that is?" My voice rose with every word I spoke.

He put his hand up to rub his grubby forehead. "He *was* a criminal. That's why I had to do it. I'm the High King. My own son couldn't be seen to be above the law. No matter what he'd done."

"He didn't break the law." I was shouting now, as all my

careful self-control flew away like shreds of mist in the wind. "He didn't do anything wrong at all. You should have waited. You should have waited for *me*. I could have told you the truth."

His eyes flashed with anger. "And what truth would that be, then? Yours? That of a mother who refuses to believe wrong of her child? Your heart has deluded you. He was guilty of killing his brother – just as Cain killed Abel. He cursed himself by his actions just as Cain did. He could never have been my heir. He had to die. I couldn't let him live."

I stood my ground against this onslaught. "*Merlin* saw he was innocent! You should have waited. You *knew* Merlin couldn't use his Sight. You should have waited for him."

Arthur's fists clenched by his sides. "And where *is* Merlin? Not here. Not telling me himself that Amhar was innocent. No. Because it's a lie, Gwen, a fabrication of your imagination. You've convinced yourself it's true." He shook his head. "But you're wrong. He couldn't deny it when I faced him. He couldn't."

I took a step closer. "I know what he said," I spat, literally. "Cei told me everything. That wasn't a *confession* you heard. That was him giving up because he knew you wouldn't believe him. Because he knew he was guilty in your eyes already. It's *you* who've convinced yourself of his *guilt*. You're the one who's wrong. Not me."

He shook his head again as though he wanted to shake my words out of it. "No. He ran. He didn't deny it. He stood and watched me take my sword out, Gwen. He had time to deny it, but he didn't. God, don't you think I wanted him to? But he didn't. D'you know what he did instead? He went down on his knees in front of me, but not to beg for mercy. No, not that. He bent his head and bared his neck, ready for the killing blow. That's admission, Gwen. Admission."

A surge of nausea rose up in me, but I had nothing to throw up. I tasted bile and spat onto the dirt before I could speak. "You killed him yourself?" The words came out incredulous and laden with horror. Cei had told me, but I'd not wanted to believe it, not wanted to hear it put into words. "You used *Excalibur*, the sword *I* helped you find, the sword of Macsen Wledig, to *kill* our son?"

His expression told me everything.

My eyes went to where it hung on his belt, the ornate hilt suddenly tarnished, the blade stained black with my son's blood. Angry words fell out of my mouth. "That wasn't why we were sent to find it. Nimuë didn't intend you to use it this way. But this was what her mother wanted…"

I raised my eyes to Arthur's face, and saw inside his head for the first time, like a revelation.

He hadn't slept for days, and his skin was gaunt and gray with shadows like dark bruises around his eyes. Tears glistened on his long lashes and ran down his cheeks unheeded. His dark hair hung matted and unkempt to his shoulders. He looked what he was – a man who'd just had to execute his son and heir and broken his own heart with that killing blow.

I looked into the broken heart of the man I'd once loved but now hated.

His shining oldest son had been brutally murdered and thrown on a midden like a dead dog. He'd sworn revenge on whoever had done this, then every scrap of evidence had pointed to the jealous younger son who'd run like a frightened deer the moment he got the chance. The son who'd so recently forced a fight with his brother, and lost so humiliatingly. Why would he have thought anything else, but that Amhar was guilty?

Pain filled his eyes, a pain that would never leave him. A pain he deserved.

He'd ridden off in hot pursuit of Amhar, driving himself, his men and their horses into the ground. The exhausted faces in the farmyard had shown me that, as well as his. But his errant son had kept on running, running. And all that time, Arthur had been eaten up by the horror of what his boy had done. A horror he couldn't escape.

Cei's boy, Rhiwallon, had died a hero's death on the battle-field at Ebrauc, but neither of Arthur's sons had died well, with honor. His eyes told me I was wrong. He *had* loved Amhar just as he'd loved Llacheu. He still did. How hard must it have been to believe his child a murderer of the worst kind? A jealous, sneaking murderer. But he *had* believed it, and he'd known that as High King he could show no mercy for such a crime. Whoever had done it.

An impulse to go to him and take him in my arms swept over me, with a longing for everything to be better. I didn't move. I couldn't. Nothing would ever be better.

Morgana had named Medraut as the killer and I'd promised Morgawse that I didn't believe he'd done it. But now I didn't know. Morgana had wanted to clear the way for her own child, so getting rid of Amhar *and* Medraut would have suited her plan. A non-existent plan, now she was dead, of course. But could Medraut be the guilty one? Or at least have had some hand in what had happened?

Arthur's anguished eyes held mine. He'd had to kill the son he loved, and inside, it had killed something in him. And me.

That foolish urge to step forward and take him in my arms so we could grieve together welled up again in my aching heart. But only for an instant. How could I ever forgive him for this? How?

I turned away and walked back, dry eyed, toward the farm buildings to find Archfedd. I'd do my grieving with her, even if the tears wouldn't come.

Chapter Twenty-Seven

I DIDN'T SLEEP that night. Archfedd, who'd cried herself into exhaustion, slept curled in her blankets beside me, but I sat up, staring into the flames of the campfire where it occupied the center of the farmyard. Sleeplessness seemed to have infected many of the men as well. Those not on watch sat in huddled silence, or tossed and turned in their blankets, and no comforting sounds of snoring lulled my unquiet soul.

My mind refused to let me rest. In a constant whirl, my thoughts tumbled inside my head, twisting amongst each other, tangled and wild. Images of Amhar as a baby, a toddler, then a child, brushed shoulders with him as an angry teen, and then of him fighting Llacheu, punching and kicking as though the devil drove him.

Their fight replayed itself inside my head countless times, as though my brain were nagging me that I was missing something. Time and again, I saw Llacheu's body sprawled on the midden with the gaping gash in his throat grinning at me. I couldn't clear my head of that horrific image, side-by-side with the one of Amhar lying on the farmhouse table.

Dawn dawdled in coming. As soon as the sun poked its golden nose over the eastern horizon, exhausted men chucked wood on the embers of the fire, someone threw the ingredients for porridge together, and the farmer's family crept out of the barn where they'd spent the night.

Cei brought me a bowl of the porridge, but I waved him away, the smell of it making me nauseous, my head throbbing. I drank beaker after beaker of cool, clean water from the farmyard well, trying to wash away the parched aridity of my throat and failing.

Archfedd managed to eat a few mouthfuls of porridge. Llawfrodedd, ever attentive, stood over her and made sure she did. This morning she'd stopped crying, but despair had written itself across every part of her from her sad eyes and solemn mouth to her sagging shoulders. A girl of fifteen shouldn't look like that, shouldn't have experienced such horror.

Cei came to find me as the men were saddling up. I'd slipped away to stand behind the barn, my back pressed against the warm wood, and stare at the mound where my son lay forever sleeping. Two of the men had dragged a large rock up to the summit and were engaged in standing it upright on top of the grave.

"A memorial," Cei said, making me jump. "They unearthed it when they were digging and thought it a good grave marker. Maybe whoever built that barrow put it there on purpose to honor their dead. It's a stone of power. If you look closely, you'll see there are a few holes right through it, as though roots have burrowed into the solid rock."

Too small to see from where I stood. "On the Ridgeway, east of the Roman road, there's a stone like that," I said. "If you blow through it, the sound carries a long way. It's called The Blowing Stone. It's supposed to have powers."

He nodded. "This one's the same. I tested it when they asked me about setting it up. They're calling it Llygad Amhar – the Eye of Amhar."

A tiny memory jogged my fuddled brain. *That name.* Inside my head I heard my father's voice. "Here, under this road, lies a mound called Licat Amr, lost when the road was widened. According to Nennius, it was one of the *mirabilia* of Britain, along with a dog print in a rock near Snowdon. The print of Arthur's dog, Cabal."

I'd remembered the dog print story and when Amhar had scrounged a hound pup of his own, I'd suggested he call it Cabal. Until now the other story had escaped me.

I shook my head to clear it. Where were we when he'd said that? Had my mother been there as well, before she died? I saw her slender, jean-clad legs and her T-shirt with Greenpeace emblazoned across it and her "Save the Whales" badge pinned to her chest, but couldn't see her face. I heard her laughter as my brother raced away. Cars whizzed past on the road, but neither of my parents seemed to have noticed the danger to their offspring. My father had taken his tweed jacket off in the heat of the day, and I had a stone in my shoe.

I fought to clear the fog that wouldn't let me see past the pain under my heel. What was my father saying? To my mother, not me. I was too small for him to think me interested. And that stone hurt, but both of them ignored my whining.

"The story is," my father's voice boomed back down the centuries to me, "that King Arthur killed his own son here and buried him under the mound – the tump – and if anyone tried to measure it, then every day it would be a different length."

Realization dawned like the drenching of an icy shower. I'd stood here before in a long-ago life, by the grave of my own son, the story the only thing that remained of him by my time. Wait – the place had a funny name. I struggled to hear my father's words as my brother climbed onto a five-barred gate and bounced up and down.

There. His words carried down the years, further than he'd ever have believed. "Wormelow Tump – a name of Saxon origin. Who knew what was here and what it was called when perhaps this Pendragon prince died?" My father chuckled, unknowing that the Pendragon Prince buried there had been his own grandson. "Or if any of it's true."

I was back in the present with Cei looking at me out of sad, sympathetic eyes. "Please forgive him, Gwen. He had to do it. He's High King, and he couldn't be seen to be treating his own son as above the law."

I shook my head. "I don't want to talk about it. Have you told him about Merlin and Morgana?"

He nodded. "We're heading back that way today. I can't tell how he's going to treat it. I can't tell what he's thinking at all." He swallowed. "But I wouldn't like to be in Merlin's shoes."

I rounded on him. "*She* was behind all this. She blocked Merlin's Sight so he couldn't tell us Amhar was innocent. She said it was –" I ground to a halt. I'd promised Morgawse I wouldn't believe it could have been Medraut, wouldn't tell, even though now I thought it might have been. But maybe I was just desperate for it to have been him, to have someone other than Amhar to blame.

Sharper today than yesterday, Cei pounced. "What did she say? She told you someone else did it? Who? Tell me."

"Nothing. She said nothing important." Why was I protecting Morgawse and her son? Perhaps because I agreed with her on thinking Morgana had intended to sweep aside all other Pendragon heirs in favor of her own child. But that didn't make Medraut completely innocent. Not by a long way.

Cei gave me a disbelieving look but didn't press me. "I came to get you. We're ready to leave. We have to return your strange mounts to the good people of Blestium unless you want to ride them all the way home and leave our prized cavalry horses to pull their carts."

With one last long look at Amhar's grave, I went with Cei.

WE RETRIEVED OUR abandoned horses at Blestium, much to the relief of the inhabitants who'd looked after them like equine royalty from fear of retribution, and continued south to Caer Legeion. I kept away from Arthur and so did Archfedd, but he was still her father, and even though part of me felt glad she didn't want anything to do with him, common sense told me she shouldn't be encouraged. She rode close to Llawfrodedd all the way.

The day was drawing in as we clattered through the old legionary fortress between its roofless barracks and tumbledown walls and out into the town of Caer Legeion. Arthur called a halt outside Morgawse's house, and when he and Cei dismounted, so did I. If I'd failed at defending my son, I refused to fail in the defense of my friend. Archfedd went to dismount but I waved her to remain where she was. "Stay with Llawfrodedd. That's an order."

Cei hammered on the door. Down the street, a few doors opened and the curious peered out, alerted by the sound of so many hooves passing so late in the day and now the frantic hammering.

Nothing happened, so Cei banged again. He was just raising his gloved fist to knock a third time when the door creaked open the barest crack and the same wizened face we'd seen before peered out at us. "Wot d'you want?" she snapped, as though we were door-to-door salesmen come to sell her a new broom she didn't need.

"Open up in the name of the High King," Cei thundered, giving the door a good shove.

She sucked in her cheeks and spat onto the road close to Cei's feet. "Open up fer the High King again, is it?" she chuntered. "High Kings, queens, princesses, magic men. I doan hold wi' none o' them. You'd best come in, but doan go thinkin' I'm takin' you anywheres, because I ain't. Me legs is too tired."

Cei pushed the door wide open, sweeping her to one side, before she had the chance to tell us anything else about the way she felt.

Arthur stepped past him into the house's atrium, and I hurried in behind. The old woman stumped over to a stool beside the door and settled on it with a deep groan, sucking her flaccid lips as though she had a sweet in her mouth, or loose false teeth, neither of which could be true.

Arthur didn't need any guiding. He strode across the atrium into the courtyard and instead of taking the colonnaded walkway around the edge, marched diagonally straight to where Morgawse's rooms lay.

Cei and I hurried in his wake.

He didn't bother to knock on his sister's doors, but seized the lion-headed handles and threw both open wide. On an empty room.

For all of ten seconds he stood on the threshold gazing around, but the room had nowhere anyone could hide. With a sharp intake of breath, he crossed to the entrance to Morgawse's chamber and threw those doors open as well.

I didn't follow him this time, but stood waiting, half in the walkway, half inside Morgawse's rooms, acutely aware of what had happened here a bare forty-eight hours before. Viewed from the corner of my eye, the spot on the mosaic where Morgana's body had sprawled seemed to hold a shadow of her form, as though she'd not really gone. Easy to believe her malevolent spirit might linger on.

Where were they all?

Arthur turned on his heel and marched back out into the courtyard without a word. He halted near the central fountain, and bellowed. "In the name of the High King, show yourselves."

The servants, who might have been hiding or just reclusive, came edging out like wary mice from their holes. A good dozen of them, all as frightened as each other, not made any braver by the daunting sight of their High King in full armor and with a face like thunder, standing squarely on the low wall around the fountain so he looked a giant of a man.

"Who's in charge?" Arthur shouted.

A spare, middle-aged man with a tonsure of thin gray hair and a squint came forward, stopping at a distance as though afraid Arthur might hurt him. He might have been right.

"Where is your mistress?" Arthur asked, aiming his question

at the man but sweeping the rest of the servants with his gaze.

The man shifted uneasily. "My mistress in't here, Milord King." He rubbed his hands together then wiped them on his tunic. "She left yesterday, after…" His voice trailed off and he looked down at his bony, sandaled feet.

"After what?"

The poor man swallowed. "After we buried the Princess, her sister."

Hot weather, of course. No one would want to delay a burial. We hadn't with Amhar, after all, or Llacheu. A body in this heat would start to decay immediately after death, would stink, would bloat… No. I wouldn't think about that. My son should stay perfect, untouched, inviolate. But for his head…

"My sister?" Arthur's words hung heavily in the evening air.

"Yes, Milord." The man wrung his hands and sweat prickled out on his brow.

For a moment, Arthur's hand went to his head as though it ached, fingertips splayed on his forehead. He must have been exhausted. Maybe his head ached as badly as mine. "What about your mistress? Where did she go? And the Lady Nimuë?"

"And Merlin?" Cei put in. "Where's he gone?"

The poor servant looked as though he'd like the ground to open up and swallow him. "All gone," he said. "The Lady Nimuë took Milord Merlin with her, headin' west, I believe. He were sleepin'. I didn't go to look, but Dilic the kitchen boy did. He said they took the road toward Maridunum."

Carmarthen – Merlin's town. I'd asked him once if he'd been born there, and he'd laughed and told me no. It sounded as though he was going there now, and not willingly. What did the old stories say? That somehow, he'd fallen into the power of a woman called Nimuë and she'd locked him away forever in a crystal cave. But Nimuë was his daughter, and who would have expected her to turn out to be his nemesis? Not me. I'd been lulled into a false sense of security because she was his child and by how she'd helped us find Excalibur. I'd thought her on our side. But was she on anyone's but her own?

"I'll send men after them," Cei said.

Arthur nodded. "Have them brought back here." He surveyed the cringing servants. "But which way did the Princess Morgawse go?"

The man swallowed hard. "She told me she were going to see her son."

Din Cadan. She was going to Medraut.

Chapter Twenty-Eight

T HE SEARCH FOR Merlin and Nimuë proved fruitless. According to several witnesses Cei turned up, they'd left in a wagon with a single man in the front and Nimuë riding in the back, under cover, with the still sleeping or unconscious Merlin. Ten miles from Caer Legeion their trail vanished completely. Seen passing through one village, they'd never reached the next.

In case they'd turned off, Cei dispatched warriors to search a long way to either side of the road, almost taking apart any farm or barn they found, but to no avail. To all intents and purposes, the wagon, and its passengers, had vanished off the face of the Earth. Which made Arthur very angry.

"She was my sister," he railed at Cei, in the rooms we'd taken over in Morgawse's house.

"Mine too, worse luck," Cei muttered.

I watched them in silence, not wishing to intervene but thinking Merlin had done us all a favor and Arthur ought to be grateful, not furious.

"Don't think for one minute I mourn her death," Arthur snapped, as if he'd read my mind. "But she was murdered as much as Llacheu was. Merlin has to be punished."

"Haven't we done enough punishing?" Cei asked, looking up from where he was polishing his sword with an oily rag. "And don't you think it's caused enough anguish?"

Arthur rounded on him. "I'm the High King. I have to see

justice is done."

Cei snorted. "Right." He bent his head as though to indicate his participation in the conversation had ceased.

Arthur stormed out of the room into the courtyard, the door banging shut behind him.

I looked across at Cei. "Thanks."

He kept his head down. "Had to be said."

I leaned my elbows on the table and rested my chin in my hands. "I don't think anyone's going to be able to find Merlin or Nimuë."

That made him look up. "Oh? Why not?"

"Because she doesn't want anyone to find them. Take it from me. I know this." Just like in the legends.

Oh Merlin, where are you? What's she done to you? Was I the only one grieving his loss?

All the stories I knew about him said that Nimuë, as his protégé and the Lady of the Lake, had imprisoned him in a crystal cave, unable to help his king, before Arthur met his end. With Merlin gone, perhaps forever, Camlann must be just around the corner.

With the search for Merlin abandoned, Arthur declared we were heading back to Din Cadan.

We arrived home four days later, having ridden far enough north to be able to cross the Sabrina by a ford. We took the journey slowly, despite a change in the weather to a light drizzle, as all our horses were tired. The warm rain fell with no respite until we rode through the gates of Din Cadan, at which point it stopped altogether and the skies cleared as if by a miracle.

I left Enfys with a servant and marched straight up to the Great Hall. Without stopping, I strode up the central aisle past the glowing embers in the sunken hearth and into our chamber, banging the door shut behind me.

I had no intention of seeing Morgawse, and still less Medraut. And I didn't want Arthur intruding on my grief. This was mine, and now I was home, in the safety of my own domain, I could give in to it. I threw off my mail shirt and lay down on our big bed with my face pressed to the pillows and cried. All the unshed tears poured out of me, all the sorrow, the rage, the loss, as though the dam had at last been breached.

A long time later, or so it seemed but I couldn't be sure, Maia slipped quietly through the door from the chamber she shared with Archfedd and lit the lamps in their little niches.

I watched her through slitted eyes as my chamber sprang bit-by-bit into golden light.

She moved about the room like a wary ghost, tiptoeing from lamp to lamp and finally returning to the table where she lit two tallow candles. The room glowed with a warm homeliness that fell on the empty crib in the corner. Maia had long ago pushed it up against the wall out of the way, when no more babies had come after Archfedd.

Trying hard not to think of Amhar when he'd occupied that crib, I pushed myself upright on the bed.

She turned to face me, her plain face creased and blotchy with crying. She'd known Amhar from a newborn baby. "Oh, Milady," she whispered. "I'm that sorry for what's happened." Moisture glistened on her ruddy cheeks.

I dug my fingernails into the palms of my hands to prevent myself from joining her and crying some more. "Thank you, Maia." I swung my legs off the bed. "Do you know where my husband is?"

Her face darkened. "He be in the Hall," she answered, lower lip jutting. "Drinkin'."

Oh no. For a moment my heart sank, and then I remembered I didn't care any longer. Let him get drunk if he wanted to. Let him drink himself into oblivion. Maybe that was what I needed to do. Good idea. Why hadn't I thought of it before? "Can you fetch me some wine, please?"

She hurried off, but it wasn't her that brought it back. Archfedd came creeping in clutching a pitcher of wine and two goblets. "I said I'd bring them," she said as she sat down on the bed beside me. "Here." She passed me the goblets and filled them. Golden Falernian – only the best to mourn her brother.

I took a long pull of the wine, not even tasting it as it went down. The goblet drained, I held it out for more. Could you really drown your sorrows? I might try it and see if it helped. Arthur seemed to swear by it.

With a reluctant glance up at me, Archfedd refilled my goblet. "I've been in the Hall," she whispered, moving closer. "Father has named Medraut as his heir."

My goblet crashed to the floor, the wine soaking into the rug to be swallowed by the cracks between the flagstones. "What?" My voice came out a husky whisper. "He's done *what*?"

She bent and picked up the goblet, a mutinous scowl on her face. "Just what I said. Medraut is Father's heir now. Father announced it outside the Hall to everyone who was there – a big crowd. All come up to nose about."

The feeling of déjà vu swept over me. I might not have lived this moment before, but I'd read about it in so many books. How Arthur's heir was his sister's son, how this son rose against him by turning some of the warriors to his own faction. How they met at Camlann and Medraut was killed, and Arthur mortally wounded. That Arthur had lived on asleep in mystical Avalon waiting to return in Britain's hour of need. Only that last bit was all rubbish – I knew all too well that once you were dead, you stayed dead.

"How? Why?" I couldn't find any other words.

"He said he has to have an heir. He's going to train Medraut for kingship."

I would have swallowed but my mouth had gone paper dry. The pieces on the chessboard were gathering, the king was threatened, but I was the queen. I could move whichever way I wanted, and I could yet save the king and force a check, or if I were lucky, a checkmate. But where was Merlin when I needed him? He was the more devious player. He'd know what to do.

Archfedd gulped down her own wine like a seasoned alcoholic. "There's more."

What more could there be? A shiver of foreboding shook my body. What had I not predicted?

Archfedd squared her shoulders. "I'm to be betrothed to Medraut."

"What?" This time my single word shot out so loud we both jumped. "He can't marry you. You're cousins. Too closely related. You told him no, didn't you?"

Her stricken face gave me my answer. "Since when do we women get to agree about who we marry?"

So true. I'd had no choice myself in marrying Arthur, but I'd been lucky... or had I? If I'd truly been lucky would my son not still be alive? I put my hand over hers. "I'll speak to him."

A glimmer of hope flickered in her desperate eyes. "Can you? Will he listen?"

A good question. We weren't exactly on speaking terms. And even though we'd been married nearly twenty years, his outlook was still all Dark Age king. If I thought about it, I could even understand why he'd reacted this way and in part excuse him. Both his sons lay dead, leaving him with only a daughter. With me now unlikely to provide him with another son, he had two living nephews to choose between as his heir. Why would he choose Custennin, miles away and with a kingdom of his own, when he could mold the future king himself, here in his own stronghold? Of course he'd choose Medraut. And what more sensible thing to do to continue his own line than to marry his own daughter to his new heir.

I foresaw a nigh on impossible job of persuading him not to do this.

"I can try," I said, but without conviction. "At least I can try."

She gazed into my eyes in an abject plea. "I can't marry him, Mami. I love Llawfrodedd. It's him I want to marry, not that creep Medraut. It isn't that I don't love him, although I don't – it's that he makes my skin crawl." She shivered from head to toe. "I can't bear to think of him touching me – of having to share his bed – be *intimate*." No need to explain sex to her. A girl of her time had seen it enough amongst the animals surrounding her. She had no illusions about what would happen if Medraut married her.

I nodded. "I understand. I feel the same way about him. I don't want you to be married to him any more than you do. I promise you, I'll do my utmost to make your father change his mind."

Easier said than done.

With the men getting drunk in the hall, I asked Maia to bring Archfedd and me a tray of food to my room. We sat and picked at it with little enthusiasm while the noise from over the partition wall grew ever louder. I felt sick to my stomach and nothing on the tray appealed.

When we finally gave up the pretense of eating, Maia, a party to our plan by now, gathered up our plates. "Come along-a me now," she said, holding out a hand to my daughter. "We'll have to let yer ma sort this out by herself. We'd best be gone before yer pa gets in here."

With a final, pleading backward glance at me, Archfedd rose from the table and followed Maia into the room they shared. The door closed behind them, and I was alone with my thoughts.

I used the bucket in the corner and prepared for bed, brushing my teeth with the charcoal paste and mint leaves, and having as thorough a wash as possible in the cold water in my bowl. I'd have liked a bath, but it was too late now. Having blown out most of the oil lamps and one of the candles on the table, I slipped into our bed and waited to see what the night would bring.

It brought nothing.

I stayed awake as long as I could, but the exhaustion of so many nights of broken sleep finally caught up with me and my head nodded.

The next thing I knew, light was streaming in through the open windows. Light and the sound of a cockerel crowing his greeting to the day.

The space beside me in the bed was empty with no sign of it ever having been occupied.

For a moment, I lay wondering where Arthur could have got to before harsh reality came thundering back into my head, accompanied by the sound of a whole orchestra of snoring from over the wall. I sat up, pushed the covers back and set my feet in the wet patch on the rug left by the spilled wine. Oh yes, I had a job to do today.

A quick rummage in my clothes chest found me a light linen tunic that reached to mid-calf and a pair of sandals. I slipped these on and hurriedly fastened the sandals. Without even bothering to stop to brush my teeth, I opened the door into the Hall and stepped through.

Clearly a lot of our men had been drowning their sorrows last night and not gone home to their wives. They sprawled with their heads on tables or just lay curled in the dirty rushes on the floor. Good luck to them with that. Not a place I'd have even walked barefoot.

I scanned the room for Arthur, going from one snoring man to the next. Cei, Bedwyr and Gwalchmei lay slumped in unlovely drink-induced slumber, but I didn't wake them. No Arthur. And no Medraut, either. Where had they got to last night?

I pushed the double doors open and stepped out into the bright, early morning sunlight. All trace of the previous days' drizzle had evaporated, and the world sparkled afresh. How incongruous that seemed. I almost wanted rain to match my deep melancholy. No, that wasn't strong enough for the pain in my very soul, the hurt in every part of my body, the ache to have my son back home with me. But calling it melancholy would have to do for now. I had other things to sort out today.

People had already begun their daily work. Here in the Dark Ages, they began at sunrise whatever time of the year. Telltale steam rose from the long, low shape of the bathhouse. Might Arthur be in there? Might Medraut?

With determined steps I marched to the door of the men's

side and pushed it open. The bathhouse wasn't large. It boasted three stout wooden tubs on this side and two on the women's. Only one of the baths was occupied. Arthur lay with just his head above the water, his dark hair slicked to his head as though he'd been submerged.

Well, at least I hadn't barged in on some other man's ablutions.

He must have seen me straightaway, but he disappeared under the water again for ten long seconds before emerging and fixing his gaze on me.

For nine of those ten seconds, a terrible thought assailed me. Right now, while he was vulnerable, I could kill him. I could hold his head under the water until all the air had left his lungs. He'd killed my son. I could have my revenge.

Luckily for him, by the time his head came up I'd dismissed that thought to where it belonged. But I'd had it, and that frightened me.

"Gwen," he said, unsmiling.

"Arthur."

The water in his bath must have been very hot because the room was as full of steam as a modern sauna. Sweat trickled down between my shoulder blades and stood out on my forehead, despite my light clothing.

He sat up a bit straighter. "Have you come for a bath?"

I shook my head. "No."

Nothing would induce me to get in there with him, as I'd often done in the past. My whole body recoiled from the thought of touching him and a wave of unwelcome nausea almost made me gag.

"Then what?"

I compressed my lips. His cleanliness couldn't hide the gauntness of his face, nor the dark smudges around his eyes. He looked as exhausted and drained as I felt, and probably had slept as badly and eaten as little as me over the last two weeks.

"I'm here for Archfedd," I said.

"Ah." He sat up, his body glistening with water. My eyes went to the lumpy white scar on his shoulder where he'd taken that arrow at Badon. I'd loved him... then.

"She doesn't love Medraut."

He reached for his towel. "And how is that relevant?"

For crying out loud.

"Of course it's relevant. She can't marry a man she doesn't love."

He stood up, the water running down his naked body. Why, when I looked at him like this, did I still feel that treacherous stirring in my groin, that yearning to have him hold me and comfort me, to feel his hands on my body? I hated him, didn't I? For what he'd done.

He laughed, dispelling my lustful thoughts. "Why not? Don't all women do that? Didn't you?"

He had me there. I hadn't loved him when we'd married. That had come later. And he hadn't loved me. "But I didn't hate you," I said. "You didn't make my flesh crawl."

His eyebrows rose. "Do you hate me now? Is your flesh crawling right this moment? Is that how it is for you now our son is dead? After I executed him?" His voice held a challenge.

I refused to rise to the bait. "Archfedd can't stand Medraut. She's told me so a long time ago. You can't make her marry him."

He stepped out of the bath and wrapped the linen towel around his waist. "She'll come to love him."

How could anyone be so obtuse? "She won't," I snapped. "No more than I could have come to love Cadwy if I'd been forced to marry him instead of you. That's how she sees him. Like you and I saw Cadwy."

He shook his head. "It's not the same. You and I have no more sons. I have to have an heir, and the closest I have to that is Medraut. If he marries Archfedd, then their child, my grandson, will rule here after him. My line will not die out."

He had a fair point, but sacrificing Archfedd's happiness seemed to weigh little compared with his need for an heir. What to say? How to convince him? Already I could sense I had no ground to hold. This was the Dark Ages. Women's views on marriage didn't count.

He moved to the slatted bench at the side of the room where a pile of clean clothes lay. "If I were you," he said, "I'd go next door and take a bath yourself. It'll calm you down."

It took great self-control not to march over there and sock him one in the face.

Chapter Twenty-Nine

ARTHUR SET THE date for Medraut and Archfedd's marriage for three weeks' time. Nothing she, nor I, could do would change her father's mind. He had it fixed in his head that this would be the only way he'd see a descendant of his inherit his throne, and he clearly wanted to see a grandson born as soon as possible. As if my daughter were some sort of prize heifer. Unsurprising really, when I considered the way Arthur had been when I'd first met him and almost his first words had been "you have good child-bearing hips." Only now it wasn't funny.

Morgawse was ecstatic, of course, at both Medraut's rise to becoming Arthur's heir, and the imminent addition of Archfedd, whom she'd always liked, as her daughter-in-law.

"They're cousins," I protested to her, having given up with trying to dissuade Arthur from this match. "They're too closely related." We were walking together along the wall-walk, first thing in the morning.

Morgawse shook her head. "Nonsense. This often happens in royal families. They'll make a good match and concentrate the Pendragon bloodline."

"That's not what happens," I tried, but without much hope. The science of genetic inbreeding and all its problems would be lost on her. I changed tack. "Does he love her?"

Morgawse frowned, squinting a little into the low morning sun. "Love? What's that? You don't need to be in love to get married. If you're lucky, it comes later." She shrugged her slender shoulders. "I didn't love Theodoric when we married, but eventually I did."

"Eventually?" I raised my eyebrows at her.

She laughed. "Did *you* love Arthur when you married?"

With reluctance, I shook my head and forbore from pointing out that I hadn't been marrying a monster. Or he hadn't been one then, anyway. I wasn't so sure now.

"They'll get used to one another," she said airily. "Couples always do. She'll settle down to married life." A frown creased her brows again. "You've given her a bit too much freedom really. A princess should be learning sewing skills, not how to fight."

I snorted. "A princess needs to be able to defend herself." Perhaps against her husband. If only she were marrying Llawfrodedd, I could have rested easy. And their child would still have been Arthur's heir. I'd tried to get Arthur to name our daughter as his heir, but that had provoked an angry outburst I'd walked away from. Had he forgotten all the years I'd spent educating him about how capable women could be?

However, he'd spoken to Archfedd and Llawfrodedd and proved he wasn't so obtuse about feelings as I'd thought him.

"I'm well aware of your feelings for one another," he told them after he'd called them both to our chamber. "But they are childish feelings. Archfedd is a royal princess, and as such far above your station, Llawfrodedd. You could only ever have been friends and nothing more."

Llawfrodedd stood stiff and tall, chin up, more noble than many a royal prince. More noble than that sly Medraut, for certain. Archfedd hung her head, her cheeks tear-stained, but if I knew her, she was plotting.

Arthur's eyes flicked between them, probably searching for signs of rebellion. "As a princess, Archfedd cannot choose to marry where she wishes. She will be wed to her cousin without delay, and you two will not see one another again."

I'd had my fill with arguing with him, so held my tongue,

although I itched to interfere. To tell him once again that he shouldn't be doing this, and that whoever Archfedd married, her child would still be his grandchild and would be his heir.

"And you, Llawfrodedd, will leave within the week to join the garrison at Dinas Badan." The abandoned fort close to where the battle of Badon had been waged. A long way off. I hadn't realized Arthur had been considering making it a permanent garrison. Perhaps he'd only just decided.

Archfedd kept on studying her boots, and if Arthur had possessed the sense he was born with, he might have thought that suspicious in our daughter who was always so quick to protest. Her quiet acceptance of his decision had warning bells going off for me.

"Yes, Father." How meek and mild she sounded. And he was fooled.

"Yes, Milord King." Maybe Llawfrodedd was less devious being a boy. The memory of Drustans and Essylt and their illicit love affair jumped into my head. Would Archfedd and Llawfrodedd go the same way? If I'd been her, I would have, even if it risked death.

⫸⫷

As THE DAYS passed heading toward the wedding, I tried to keep an eye on Archfedd, but it proved difficult to do that all the time. Medraut came to visit her every day, and she sat demurely with him in our chamber, under the eagle eye of me, Maia and Coventina. Sometimes Morgawse came as well, flushed with pride that her son would one day be a king, as though she saw it as his right.

Archfedd answered when Medraut spoke to her, but kept her hands folded neatly in her lap, presumably in case he tried to take one, and her eyes on her untouched sewing. This was marked by big uneven stitches and blood spots. She was as poor a seamstress as I was.

The smallest part of me had to feel a little sorry for Medraut. He did seem to be going out of his way to play the gallant suitor, bringing her small gifts: a bracelet, a torque of gold with dragon finials like the one her father wore, perfume. She accepted each gift with polite coldness and set them to one side with the air of one who would never deign to look upon them again, then resumed her scrutiny of her terrible sewing.

Despite his arrogance, he seemed genuinely fond of her, or at least infatuated, and not just keen on this marriage to further his climb to power. She was a very pretty girl, after all. Perhaps his pursuit of her that she'd complained to me about had all been part of this. Perhaps in his own way, he really did love her. I didn't like him any better for it, but I begrudgingly allowed him a tiny morsel of compassion. Which only went to show how conniving he could be.

Morgawse did her best as well.

"Why don't you go for a stroll together along the wall-walk?" she tried, smiling sweetly at my daughter. "With Medraut, I mean. Just the two of you."

Archfedd gave her a look that would have frozen a blazing fire. "No thank you. It's too hot."

Morgawse possessed a firm determination not to give up, even in the face of such a setback, and tried again another day. "There's a lovely breeze blowing outside. What about a ride with Medraut across the grazing lands? You look as though you could do with some fresh air." Of course, this wouldn't have been on their own. An escort would have accompanied them.

"No thank you. I don't feel like riding." Archfedd's gaze returned to her folded hands and short-nibbled nails.

Medraut seemed bemused by her total lack of interest in him, perhaps convinced of his own attractiveness to women. I caught a look of hurt more than once in his eyes at her coldness, but couldn't bring myself to suggest she be kinder to him.

He approached me one day while I was taking my morning

stroll and fell in beside me as I walked. "Aunt Gwen, do you think you could find it in you to ask Archfedd to smile at me occasionally?" Nothing like getting to the point quickly.

I took a sideways glance at him. If I hadn't known the stories legend attached to him, I'd have thought him just another lovesick boy. However… beneath that seemingly open façade, a heart of stone beat, I was certain. He might think he loved Archfedd, might have convinced himself it was her he wanted and not his uncle's throne, might have half-convinced me he wasn't as bad as I'd thought, but deep-down, I knew better. "I can't make her do what she doesn't feel like doing," I said, uncaring about being blunt.

He frowned. "She's going to have to get used to being with me all the time. We'll be married by next week."

I halted and turned to face him, swiping away the loose tendrils of my hair blowing into my eyes. "She doesn't want to marry you. I can't make her want to. No one can."

He bit his lip, uncertain for once in his life. "When we're married, she'll come around. I know she will. She'll have to love me then."

Poor ignorant boy.

I sighed. "No one can make another person love them, Medraut. No matter how much you want her to, she has to come to it herself." I didn't add my certainty that she never would.

He frowned a little more, his brow puckering. "But she could at least *talk* to me. All I get is one-word answers and she won't even look me in the eye." He paused, maybe considering his words. "She won't even hold my hand. She hides hers away. And next week we have to… be together… as man and wife." Hot color surged up his neck to his cheeks.

How unlike Medraut to get embarrassed about anything. He had a well-earned reputation with women, and it wasn't a good one.

I sucked in my lips as I thought. "Medraut, she's young and she's her father's only surviving child. She needs delicate handling." If only I could smooth the way for her, get him to see that if he wanted to win her over, he had to be kind rather than demanding. "Make her your friend if you want her to care for you. Be kind to her, be gentle. Give her time."

"But I'm doing all that," he protested. "I bring her gifts and she just puts them aside as though I'd rolled them in dog shit first. I try to talk to her, and she behaves as if I'm some irritating fly she can't wait to swat."

"Kindness isn't just gifts. Kindness is understanding, allowing someone to be themselves, giving someone space when they need it. It's many things. If you could manage any of that, you'd have a better chance."

He rubbed his chin. "It wasn't my idea. The King suggested it, you know. In case you thought I was only after her to help pave my way to the throne. I don't need her. I'm already his heir. He *wants* me to marry her so my son and heir will be hers. And his heir as well."

My eyes widened at his candor. This also wasn't like him. Maybe love had softened him, if it really were love, that was.

"She's my daughter, Medraut, and I want her to be happy." I bit my lip. "I'll be honest with you as you've been honest with me. I was angry when she told me her father had agreed to the betrothal. I didn't want her to marry you. She's my little girl, still, even though she's nearly sixteen. I'm not used to girls getting married so young. They don't, where I come from, but I do understand it goes on here and is normal. It's hard for me to let her go, particularly as she doesn't seem to want it. I've asked Arthur to change his mind, but he won't. Now I'm asking you to treat her well and give her time. Don't expect... *everything* straight away. Don't force her. Please."

His eyes narrowed, the candor gone. "She's marrying me. She will be my wife in every way." His chin jutted determinedly. "And she *will* love me. I'll make sure of that."

Cold horror drenched me as I stared at his determined face. Oh God, he was going to rape her. How had I not seen this before? Was I stupid? She was my child. I couldn't let him do that. I had to do something. But what and how?

I had less than a week to save her. Less than a week to formulate a plan and put it into operation. My first thought, of poisoning Medraut, would solve everything, but the logistics of that seemed insurmountable. He ate in the Hall every night, of the same food as everyone else, and, when he visited us in my chamber, he ate and drank nothing, and even if he did, I couldn't get poison into only his goblet without being seen.

With regret, I had to dismiss that idea. The fact that I'd seriously considered it frightened me a little, but I soon got over it. I was a lioness defending my cub and I could be ruthless.

Taking Archfedd back to my old world also crossed my mind, but I had no idea if the doorway still existed, and if it did, and I took her through it, how would she cope? She'd be separated from Llawfrodedd by the yawning chasm of time, never to see him again. And if I wanted anything, it was to see her safely married to the young man she truly loved.

I racked my brain.

Abbot Jerome. Wasn't there something I'd once read about sanctuary being given to people in danger if they went to a church? If I took her there, might we be safe? Could Arthur and Medraut do anything to get her back? I went down the hill to the church in the village and gently probed the priest to see what he could tell me. I phrased it as though my question concerned some far-off problem, crossing my fingers that he wouldn't put two and two together and come up with five. But yes, if I could get her to the abbey, and into the church itself, she'd be safe. I dismissed his own church as far too close – the abbey would provide us with the protection of miles of marshland as well as sanctuary.

I put my plan into practice the next morning. No point in waiting. Leaving Arthur lying in bed and sleeping off his excesses of the night before, I dressed and tiptoed through to Archfedd's room. She and Maia shared a big bed, and both stirred when I came in.

Archfedd sat up. "What is it?"

I put my finger to my lips. "We're going for a ride. Get dressed. I need to talk to you away from the fortress. And make sure you bring your sword." A small lie, but I didn't want Maia getting into trouble for being complicit.

Five minutes later, we were down in the stables saddling our horses. As soon as they were ready, I pulled out the saddlebags I'd hidden under the heap of clean straw in the next-door stall. "Here, fasten this to your saddle."

She regarded me with widening eyes, but did as she was told, while I attached mine. We led our horses out, swung up into their saddles, then turned them downhill toward the gates.

A few people were already about, so I waved a casual hand at them and Archfedd followed suit. They all knew I liked to ride out whenever possible, and often in summer at first light. The guards had the gate wide open for us, and, as we started on the downhill road, the bang of the gates closing echoed behind us. An itch between my shoulder blades made me want to trot, but the hill path was too steep, and I had to control my impatience.

In my imagination, Arthur had already found me missing and gone to check on Archfedd. Any minute now he'd be shouting after us from the gates, having guessed my intention.

Nothing. We made it to the hillfoot without interruption.

"Now we have to hurry," I said to Archfedd. "Before they find us missing and work out what we've done."

"Where are we going?" she asked, glancing back over her shoulder as we trotted through the village. She didn't need to ask the reason why we were running.

"Sanctuary," I said. "Ynys Witrin and the abbey. You'll be safe there. No one can break the law of sanctuary."

Once out of the village we drove our horses hard. They were fit and well-rested and ate up the ten miles to the lake village, but then, so would the horses of any pursuer. A fit horse can do ten miles in under two hours, and it was still early when we rode into the cluster of barns and pens on the shore beside the village. Low mist shrouded the water beyond the little platform of squat thatched houses, the disembodied tips of distant stunted trees poking above its cottonwool whiteness. A skein of ducks rose in noisy flight, and the sound of a bittern booming echoed across the hidden reedbeds.

I'd been here a number of times with Arthur, but never with Archfedd. Her mouth hung open at the sight of the village perched out above the water on its platform of debris and rickety scaffolding. "We're going *there*?" she asked, as I dismounted.

A couple of coarsely-clad, shaggy-headed men emerged from the pigpens, pitchforks in hands, broad grins on their faces. "Milady the Queen, you're most welcome here." The taller of the two made a sweeping bow, and I saw with a start that it was Con, the little boy I'd met on the day I'd first found myself here nearly twenty years ago. He'd filled out now to the full proportions of a man grown and lost the softness of boyhood that had still hung about him when he'd helped Arthur and me retrieve Excalibur from its watery home on the island, seven years since.

"Con," I grinned back. "What're you doing here? I thought you lived on the island?"

He shook his head. "Not now I doesn't. I'm wed to Tybie, a lake village girl, so we do live here, along-a her family." He gestured at the pen full of chuntering pigs. "These be my pigs. I done well for meself what with the sheep the king sent me after I helped him."

I turned as Archfedd slid down from her saddle. "This is my daughter, Archfedd. We need to get across to the island as quickly as possible. Can you help us? Normally Nial takes us in his boat, but I don't see him today."

Con pulled a wry face. "'Tis early yet for old Nial. He ain't so snicky as he once were. He do like to stay in bed a while then take his time a-gettin' up. He be an old man, now, an' a bit bent an' stiff of a mornin'."

"Can you take us, then?" If I hadn't felt time pressing in on us, I'd have enquired more about Nial and perhaps asked to see him.

Con nodded. "We've finished doin' the pigs. I've a sow what's due to farrow, but she won't be a-doin' it today, I don't doubt. I've time to take you in me boat meself." His gaze ran over Archfedd's flushed face and open mouth, appreciation of her beauty in his honest eyes. "We'll have to go into the village to get me boat."

I looked at the off-puttingly narrow walkway that curved out across the murky water toward the village. It had never been my favorite thing, but I'd have to pretend bravery for Archfedd's sake. Her eyes had gone even rounder at the sight of it.

"Come on," I said, taking her hand. "We don't have time to waste. Let's go."

We retrieved our saddlebags, and Con's friend led our horses into one of the barns. They'd be safe there a while until Arthur found them.

I bestowed a determined stare on the walkway and took a deep breath. I could do it.

To my amazement, I strode across it as though I did it every day of my life, and Archfedd followed behind, with Con in the rear. I knew the way to go.

The houses clustered around a small central courtyard where nets were repaired and fish gutted, but only a few naked children played there now. Their mothers would be doing their household chores. I hurried past and down a narrow alley to the wooden jetty on the far side of the village's precarious island home. A dozen flat bottomed boats bobbed there on the current, attached only by tatty, reed-woven bow ropes.

"This be my boat," Con said, untying one of the ropes and pulling the boat round to the jetty, sideways on. "In you get, Miladies."

More bravery was required. Archfedd had never been in a boat, and I needed to show her it wasn't something to be afraid of. I stepped in first, feeling its unstable wobble. Gritting my teeth to ignore the movement, I took her hand and helped her in. Both of us sat down on the thwarts with shared relief, and she kept tight hold of my hand.

"I don't like this much," she whispered.

Con stepped onto the stern, feet wide-planted, his long pole in his hand, and pushed us off. We drifted out onto the misty lake and the current took us.

The boat being low in the water, we were below the height of the mist, swathed in its opaque white shroud, moisture settling on our clothing and in our hair. Maybe Con's head rose above it, but I couldn't tell. He stood like some colossus in front of us, his muscles rippling as he poled the boat along.

"Where is he taking us?" Archfedd whispered. "Isn't Ynys Witrin where Gwyn ap Nudd lives? Isn't it the doorway to Annwfn?"

I put an arm around her shoulders. "Old wives' tales. It's also where Reaghan has gone to be a religious and where the abbey is. It's always been associated with some sort of worship, but now it's Christian, so you're quite safe. I'm taking you to the abbot. He'll keep us safe."

The little boat glided silently on, skimming the water and making scarce a ripple across its mirrored surface. Silence pressed in from all sides, broken only by the splash of unseen waterbirds heading for safety in the thick reedbeds. Beneath the boat, braids of green weed trailed, like the tresses of some hidden water creature.

Archfedd, brave as she was, huddled close to me until at last Con's boat bumped the wooden landing stage of the monk's wharf and he leapt ashore with the mooring rope. Once he'd secured the boat fore and aft, he helped us out.

"No need to wait," I said. "We won't be going back."

Con's eyes shot into his shaggy fringe, but he didn't ask any questions. Instead, he tugged his forelock and after untying the ropes, hopped back into his boat.

For a moment our eyes met. "Look after our horses," I said. "Please." Then he was gone, swallowed up by the mist.

"If someone comes after us, they'll find the horses and know where we've gone," Archfedd said.

I nodded. "But we'll be safe at the abbey by then. Come on. Not far now."

We turned our backs on the wharf and the marshes, and set off inland.

Chapter Thirty

THE PATH FROM the monks' wharf to the abbey led at first through tall trees, keeping the high ridge of land that would one day be called Wearyall Hill on our left. Ahead of us rose the imposing bulk of the Tor itself, something I'd marked as an absolute last resort as it couldn't be relied upon to work.

The late summer morning warmed fast, dispelling the last shreds of mist. A bright sun beat down on us and made me wish I hadn't bothered with a cloak. Archfedd stopped and unfastened hers, so I did the same. We rolled them up and tucked them under our arms.

When we came to the rolling apple orchards, she stopped again. "Oh, my goodness, look at this place!"

For a moment I viewed it through her eyes. More apple trees than she could ever have seen ran away in every direction. Divested now of their pink and white blossoms, they sported countless small green fruits just waiting to ripen and be gathered to make into the monks' famous cider that we drank all year round.

She pointed at the Tor. "Is that the hill we can see from our walls? I never thought it would be this big up close."

Not the time to reveal all and admit to her how I'd ended up here, but maybe I was going to have to at some point, especially if I decided the only way to save her from Medraut was to take her back to my old world. Even though that would mean taking her away from Llawfrodedd as well as Medraut. *If* the door would even open… I'd cross that metaphorical bridge when I came to it.

We passed between the rows of trees, where the hundreds of island sheep had nibbled the grass short, and, as the trees thinned out, the abbey came into view. After the island's one village, this had been the first building I'd encountered when I'd arrived here, and the monks the first people. The first friendly people, at any rate, as the villagers had wanted nothing more than to hang me on the spot as a potential spy, especially Con's old grandmother.

The abbey buildings formed a compact square around a cobbled courtyard, with double gates facing the church at the far end, and storehouses, monks' dormitories and the abbot's accommodation and office down the other two sides. Small, stone-banked fields surrounded the low buildings, dotted with lay brothers working alongside monks who had their habits tucked up into their belts and scrawny hairy legs on show.

Heads turned, and men straightened their backs to peer in open curiosity as we approached the gates, but I ignored them. Taking Archfedd's hand, I hurried her into the oblong courtyard: empty and swept scrupulously clean. All the monks must be out at work at this time of the morning before the midday prayers of Sext began.

I didn't need any help – I knew my way to Abbot Jerome's office of old.

"This is the abbey?" Archfedd asked, staring around herself in wonder. "It's so big. I was thinking it'd be like the church in our village. How many monks are there? Were those all monks out in the fields?"

"Lay brothers, as well," I said, pulling her toward the left of the courtyard where a sizeable wooden door stood closed against us. "Now. Don't speak unless you're spoken to in here. Let me do the talking. I know the abbot well."

I knocked on the door.

For what felt like forever, nothing happened, and then the door creaked open halfway and a face I knew looked out at me, haloed by a cloud of unruly ginger hair.

"Gildas!" Relief at finding a friendly face swept over me. Years ago, after defeating his father at Dun Breattann, far to the north of the Wall, Arthur had brought the boy Gildas south as a hostage, and I'd engineered his placement in the abbey where he could follow his chosen vocation of learning. He and I had been friends ever since, although I'd not seen him for some time.

His too-wide mouth broke into a grin of delight revealing large, unevenly spaced yellow teeth, and he flung the door wide open. "Gwen!" He waved arms still gangly with persistent youth, despite the fact he must have been all of twenty-five by now. "Come inside, please. You're a long way from home. What can I do for you?" His gaze went to Archfedd. "This can't be your daughter? I thought she was a child, not a beautiful young woman." Even a monk isn't immune to a pretty girl.

Archfedd managed a wary smile.

I pulled her inside, and Gildas shut the door behind us, just that act making me feel a lot safer.

The big, square space of the abbot's office held only his substantial oak desk and a few ancient chairs. On the left-hand wall hung the same large plain cross I remembered, and an open document chest occupied the right. The shutters on the two small windows had been removed for the summer, and the morning sunshine danced over pens and papers where they lay scattered over the desk. Dust motes floated in the beams of light.

"Please. Sit." Gildas removed some rolls of parchment from the two chairs on this side of the desk and pulled them out for us.

We sat, and he edged his way back behind the desk and took his place in the abbot's ornate seat. He placed big, bony hands on the desktop in front of him. "To what do we owe the pleasure of your company?"

"We came to see Abbot Jerome," I said.

Gildas's freckled face fell. "I'm sorry to have to tell you he's unwell. That's why you find me here in his stead. He's been in his bed this past week with a chill that's gone to his chest. You know how bad summer colds can be for the elderly."

The elderly. Of course. When I'd first come here and met Jerome, he'd probably been at least forty, so must be over sixty now – old for this time period. A sobering thought. "I'm sorry to hear that," I said, my brain frantically trying to work out what to do. "Are you acting as his deputy?" Maybe Gildas could help us, or pass my request on to Jerome.

Gildas nodded, a satisfied smile on his face. "I've been working with him these past five years, and he's come to depend on me. He knows any decisions I make will reflect those he would make himself. I believe he's grooming me to become abbot myself one day."

Gone was the rebellious, too clever boy bullied by his classmates, and in his stead had arrived a confident, competent young man with an air about him of calm intelligence tempered with a certain lightness of spirit he'd not had before. I liked the changes in him.

"I would be most impressed if you were to become abbot here," I said. "I feel as though I've had a small hand in your success."

Archfedd glanced from him to me in open curiosity.

He grinned, showing me his teeth again. "You have indeed. Without you, I don't know where I'd be. Perhaps back in Alt Clut as a reluctant warrior, although my father's long dead now, or even just trudging behind a plough in the fields below Din Cadan. I owe you a great debt."

He'd played into my hands. "I'm here to call in that debt," I said, keeping my voice level. "I have need of sanctuary for me and my daughter."

His ginger eyebrows rose into his hairline, or they would have done if he'd had one, but his shaven tonsure was of the sort that started at his ears and encompassed the entire front of his head. "Sanctuary? Why? What from?"

I glanced at Archfedd, but she was watching him in silent fascination. She'd only ever met individual priests, and never an abbot before, not even a trainee one. "Do you hear news of Dumnonia here?"

The smile fell from Gildas's face. "We do. It comes to us via the lake village. We only receive what they can tell us, but I do know what happened to your sons. Bad news travels fast. I'm sorry for your loss."

I nodded. I'd had so little time to mourn my boys before being faced with Archfedd's dilemma it felt as though they'd been forced from my mind. I'd have to think about that later. "Their deaths have left my husband without a male heir," I said, steeling myself. "He's chosen his sister's son – Medraut. He's nearly twenty and unmarried. Arthur has decided Medraut should marry our daughter, to make a grandson of ours king one day."

Gildas, who himself came from a dynasty of kings, frowned in confusion. "Isn't that a good thing?" His gaze returned to Archfedd. "She looks old enough to wed. I don't see a problem there."

I took Archfedd's hand and squeezed it. "It's not her marrying that she and I object to. It's the choice of husband. You don't know Medraut. If you did, you'd understand. He wouldn't make her a good husband or Arthur a good heir."

Realization dawned on his rawboned face. "I think I begin to see. You've brought her here for the sanctuary of the church, have you not? To escape a marriage you do not favor."

I nodded.

He rubbed the gingery stubble on his chin. "Let me get this clear. You've taken a betrothed girl, a princess, away from her father and brought her here, to me... to us? To Abbot Jerome, hoping he... we... could help her?"

I nodded again.

Gildas sucked in his lips. "You've done a very dangerous thing."

"I know."

"Betrothed is as good as married in the eyes of the law."

"I know."

He sighed. "But you are right that I owe you much. However, I can't make a decision on this by myself. It's too big a thing. It could affect the whole abbey. I'll need to speak to the Abbot on his sickbed."

I opened my mouth to speak, but he held up his hand. "I understand this is urgent. If you will wait here, I'll do that now." He got to his feet, made a small bow, and left the room through the door that led into the living quarters of the monks.

Silence fell in the office. My heart thudded against my ribs. Would Jerome agree? And if he didn't, what would I do? Climb the Tor and look for the portal? Perhaps. Probably. I'd have to.

"How do you know him so well?" Archfedd asked, her voice scarcely above a whisper. "You talk to him like he's an old friend."

"He is," I said. "A very old friend. I've known him since he was a boy younger than you."

We waited quite some time, but it probably felt longer than it was. At last, the door opened and Gildas returned, his long, bony face solemn. He didn't return to his seat, but stood surveying us out of his pale, hooded eyes. "Father Abbot has agreed to offer sanctuary to both of you. He told me to take you to our church straightaway. He fears your husband will know that you've come here to hide."

I stood up, pushing my chair back across the flagstone floor with a loud scraping. "Come along, Archfedd. The abbot's right. We've no time to lose."

We followed Gildas, his robes flapping about his long legs as he walked, across the cobbled courtyard to the church at the far end. It was just a low, thatched building with a tiny tower on the top where a bell hung silent, and a rope dangling down by the plank door. A poor building, but probably one Christ himself would have approved of. Legend said he'd come here to Glastonbury as a boy, brought by Joseph of Arimathea. I liked to think that could be true, and that he would have liked what he'd seen.

Gildas pushed open the church door and we went inside, out of the bright summer sun and into a gloomy hall devoid of seating of any kind. Clearly monks either stood up or knelt on the flagstone floor for prayer. At the far end, a low altar, draped with a richly embroidered cloth, stood almost up against the white-washed walls, and behind it hung a huge wooden cross with the figure of Jesus carved as part of it, stark against the whiteness.

Gildas went up to the altar, and knelt, crossing himself and muttering a short prayer. Archfedd's fingers also sketched a cross, but I didn't move. If I'd ever believed in God, I didn't now, not after what had happened to my sons. What kind of cruel god would let that happen to two innocent young men?

Gildas rose and came back to us. "There's a small storage room at the back of the church. This way."

In the shadows to the left of the altar, he pushed open a low, narrow door that even I had to duck to get through. We found ourselves in a stuffy, windowless room barely seven feet square, with a low roof that sloped steeply to the back. Thick dust covered the floor, and in a corner, someone had stacked a pile of lumber and a few dry bundles of thatching reeds.

"I can't have two women in our church during our services," Gildas said, with a hint of apology. "By rights, we shouldn't have women here at all. But Father Jerome insisted you should be allowed to stay. Said you were an exception. So, when we're at prayer, which is every few hours during the day and night, you'll need to shut yourselves in here, I'm afraid. Father Jerome was adamant that this was to remain a place of worship free of women during prayer. We *are* monks, after all."

Archfedd wrinkled her nose. "It's not very clean."

He glanced at her. "I'll have one of the lay brothers come and clean it out for you and bring a couple of pallet beds and some blankets. And lamps. You'll be supplied with food from our kitchen, but you'll have to eat in here, alone. It's the best we can offer."

It would have to do. I turned toward him, plastering a grateful smile onto my face. "Thank you, Gildas. My daughter and I very much appreciate your help."

Archfedd remained suspiciously silent.

Chapter Thirty-One

W E DIDN'T HAVE long to wait before Arthur found our trail. Probably, when he'd discovered our absence, he would have thought at first that we'd gone for a normal, early morning ride. It would have taken half the day, and our lack of reappearance, for him to work out we'd run, but most likely only seconds to decide we'd have headed to Ynys Witrin.

He arrived halfway through the afternoon, accompanied only by Cei. At least he'd had the sense not to bring Medraut.

Two lay brothers had swept out the far-too-hot storage room and killed the family of mice nesting in the bundles of thatch, to my relief. Then they'd carried in two narrow pallet beds and a bundle of blankets, and found two rickety wooden stools for us.

To this unprepossessing collection they'd added a smelly leather bucket, for the "necessaries," as they called it. Lovely. We'd have to keep that delightful object in our tiny, unventilated room with us throughout every service, and the smell of it was already making me nauseous. Only the thought of having to put my nose closer to it as I bent over put me off throwing up.

By the time Arthur and Cei arrived, we'd already sat through Sext and Nones and our tiny chamber had taken on the strong stench of the bucket as though it never intended to relinquish it.

The door of the church stood open to let in light and some much needed fresh air. Archfedd and I were sitting together just inside, when Arthur and Cei appeared in the open gateway at the far end of the courtyard. Hoping they hadn't seen us, I yanked Archfedd back into the shadows and she clutched onto me, trembling.

We had a good view of them as they approached the abbot's office door. They were going to be surprised when they met Gildas in there and not Jerome. "It's all right," I whispered. "You're safe in here. Gildas won't let them take you back. He's my friend, not your father's. In fact, I'm sure he still nurtures a grudge against your father because he killed his brother."

"Like he killed my brother," Archfedd muttered, her brow lowering as she scowled. "He seems to make a habit of killing people's brothers."

"Gildas's brother merited having his head cut off," I said, then regretted it.

Archfedd's body stiffened. "Practice for what he did to Amhar."

I refrained from commenting. The door to Gildas's office opened, and Arthur and Cei went inside. What wouldn't I give to be a fly on the wall in there.

We waited in the shadows beside the door, the stools now tucked back against the wall out of the way. Could we trust Arthur to honor the law of sanctuary? He was High King, after all, and, as he'd said in justification for Amhar's execution, he had to be seen to be upholding the law. That thought went a long way to boosting my confidence as I stood peering out, clutching Archfedd's hand tight in mine.

At last, the door from Gildas's office opened again, and he came out with Cei and Arthur. They headed our way.

"Further back inside," I said to Archfedd, suddenly seized by the fear that if they could pull her outside, she'd lose the claim to sanctuary. We retreated toward the altar, still holding hands.

Gildas halted in the oblong of sunlight at the door, holding out his arms to either side to keep Arthur and Cei from entering. "This is far enough. You shouldn't enter." His voice held calm authority, and Arthur and Cei didn't try to push past but stood peering into the gloomy interior, their eyes probably blinded for a moment after the brightness of the day.

"It's all right, Gwen," Gildas called. "I've explained they have no right to touch either of you. That you've claimed sanctuary and they must uphold it. They have acknowledged your right to do so."

I glanced at Archfedd. Her scowl had deepened, giving her a distinct look of her father, and her lower lip jutted as it had as a child when she'd been fomenting rebellion.

"You wait here," I whispered. "Stay at the back where they can't reach you. Just in case."

She nodded her agreement, and I approached the doors.

Difficult to see the expressions on any of their faces with the sun behind them. I halted well out of reach and waited.

Arthur grunted in annoyance. "No need to stand here like some sort of sentinel," he said to Gildas. "We're not about to abuse your precious sanctuary. You can stand down."

Gildas hesitated a moment, then dropped his arms and moved to one side. I caught the guarded, resentful look in his eyes. He'd never forgotten the day when Arthur had rolled his brother's rotting head across the floor of Dun Breattann's hall, of that I was certain. An act likely to imprint itself forever on the mind of a sensitive eleven-year-old.

"Thank you," Arthur said, then turned his attention to me. "Maybe you'd like to tell me what you think you're doing here?"

"What Gildas said," I replied, keeping my voice level. "We're claiming sanctuary."

Arthur heaved a sigh. "I know *that*," he snapped. "But what from? Why on earth do you think you need it?"

Obtuse man. Had he not been listening to my arguments against the marriage he'd decided on all by himself without consulting either Archfedd or me? I folded my arms and glared at him. "Take a guess."

He glared back. "I'm not here to play games with you. I'm here to take you both home."

"Well, we're not coming unless you annul this betrothal between Archfedd and Medraut," I retorted, determined not to give an inch.

Arthur glanced at Cei as though for support, and Cei shrugged, encouragingly noncommittal. He'd never liked Medraut.

I shot him a hard stare, making sure he felt every degree of my disapproval that he was here supporting his brother.

Arthur's gaze returned to me. "That's not something I can do. It's already agreed with his mother and with him. It can't be annulled, and neither do I want to do so." His tone betrayed his rising annoyance.

Good.

"Well then," I said. "We're staying put."

Arthur took a step forward, one foot on the flagstones inside the door, and Gildas moved in front of him. "No. You need to stay outside."

For his pains, he got a look that would have had lesser men quaking like jelly on the floor. But not Gildas. He was made of sterner stuff. He glowered at Arthur. "Do I have to call the lay brothers?"

Arthur took back his foot. "Archfedd is a betrothed Princess. She's as bound by that as she would be if the marriage ceremony had already been carried out." He fixed me with a furious stare. "*You* can stay here as long as you want, but *she's* to come back with me."

The anger that had been bubbling below the surface in me erupted. "Do you think I'm stupid? No. She's not going anywhere. We're here in sanctuary to keep her safe. She doesn't love Medraut. In fact, she can't stand him, and neither can I." I was into my stride. "I've spoken to him. I asked him to be gentle with her and give her time, but he refused. If she marries him, he'll rape her on their wedding night. That's what it'll be, Arthur. Rape. And I've seen enough of that. I won't let it happen to my daughter."

Albina and Cloelia, raped by who knew how many of Cadwy's Saxon mercenaries and killed by their mother because she thought they'd have no life. Their hagridden faces, their bodies floating in the blood-stained waters of the bathhouse.

"That's ridiculous," Arthur snarled, as angry as I was. "Marriage can't be rape."

I had difficulty not rushing at him with my fists, but stood my ground. "Not true. Being married doesn't make a woman a man's property to do with as he wishes. If a wife doesn't want sex with her husband, and he forces her, then it's rape."

He shook his head. "Rubbish. Once she's his wife she'll do as she's told."

I was pleased to see he stopped short of "as you do," as he must have known it wasn't true and I'd refute it.

"She doesn't love him," I said. "And she never will. He revolts her. She loves another."

His brows lowered threateningly. "She doesn't need to love her husband. She needs to do as she's told and marry him and provide me with an heir."

Now I was really mad. "So, it's all about you getting an heir, is it?" I stormed. "Well, if you hadn't been so quick to jump to the conclusion that Amhar was guilty, then you'd still have one. Trust you to put that above anything else. Above your daughter's happiness. Above everything."

Cei's worried gaze flicked between the two of us as though he were watching a volley of tennis shots.

"Don't you dare bring that up again," Arthur snarled. "I did the right thing there. I didn't want to. You don't know how much it hurt to have to do that." He ran his fingers through his hair making it stand on end alarmingly. "I wanted him to be innocent. I wanted him to be my heir. But he couldn't be. Not after what he'd done."

I couldn't stop myself. "And now look how handily Medraut has presented himself to you and become your heir. Don't you think he might have been behind Amhar's behavior? Was he whispering to Amhar that you preferred Llacheu? Was he stoking our son's jealousy? For his own advancement? Don't you ever think that? Don't you?"

Arthur's hand went to his head. "I must have an heir, Gwen. Medraut is the only one who can follow me now." He looked up, real malice in his eyes. "*You're* unlikely ever to give me another son. You won't let me anywhere near you."

"And why d'you think that is? Give you a clue – you *killed* my son. My innocent son. Do you really think I want to sleep with a murderer? It's bad enough to have to share your bed. And now you want to hand over our daughter to a man who's going to rape her. You're not the man I married, not the Arthur I thought I knew. I never want you to touch me again."

He shut up. Maybe I'd got in enough blows. Cei shifted uncomfortably and took a step back into the sunlight. Gildas examined his sandaled feet.

I needed to finish this. "So just fuck off, why don't you, and find out how good having Medraut as your heir is really going to be. I don't see that working, do you? He's the one you should have executed. He's got a heart as black as a cesspit and a mind to match. See how you bloody well like that."

I spun on my heel and walked back to where Archfedd stood waiting by the altar. She caught my hand. "I never knew you had it in you," she whispered in something akin to awe, while keeping her eyes fixed on her father where he still stood framed in the doorway.

"You've not heard the last of this," Arthur shouted. "She *will* marry Medraut. But *you* can stay here forever as far as I care."

"I don't care," I shouted back, my dignity in shreds. "Just go fuck yourself. You're never having her."

Gildas abandoned his study of his feet and stepped forward, arms spread again. "I think you'd better leave," he said to Arthur, his tone calm but authoritative. He stood an inch or so taller than my husband and was big boned and solid now, much as his dead brother Hueil had been. Arthur retreated in front of him.

I turned back to Archfedd. "You're safe for now." I put my arms around her. "You can relax. He knows he can't come storming in here and take you."

She nodded, but her face had blanched. "But how long do we have to stay here for? The rest of my life? I don't think he'll give up. He *is* the High King, after all, and we've crossed him, and he doesn't like it."

I put my arm around her shoulders. "Let's not think about it for a while. He'll go back to Din Cadan, and tomorrow, you and I'll go and find that little chapel where Reaghan is learning to be a religious, and we'll see how she's getting on. That'll make you feel better."

Archfedd's face brightened. "I'd like that. I've really missed her."

I had some questions I needed to ask Reaghan.

Chapter Thirty-Two

I'D QUITE FAILED to consider how boring sanctuary would be. Twenty-four hours of doing nothing had both of us tearing our hair out by the next morning. With nothing to occupy us, all we could do was sit and twiddle our thumbs and talk to each other, or occasionally to Gildas. The other monks steered well clear of such strange creatures as women, even the lay brothers.

Luckily, Gildas came to us in the morning, after Prime, and told us he'd set a guard where he could spy on the monks' wharf. This man would warn us of the arrival of any boat from the lake village bearing a possible intruder.

So, after we'd eaten a spartan breakfast of bread, cheese and weak cider, we set off to find Reaghan's chapel, armed with Gildas's directions and wearing the sandals and rough homespun tunics he'd had the foresight to provide as disguises.

A blue sky arched over our heads, with just a light snaring of mist still clinging to the trees where the marshes began, and the walk was pleasant. After being cooped up in smelly sanctuary even for just a day, we both appreciated our regained freedom, and I for one had a skip in my step. On a beautiful day you can't stay miserable for long.

Our way led along the north side of Wearyall Hill, following the route of what would one day be the A361 and the A39. Sheep dotted the steep hillside to our left, and wet marshland crowded close on our right, with banks of reeds and small, stunted trees along the limits, one with a heron sitting looking prehistoric in its topmost branches. Open water glimmered in the distance, and further off the distant humps of the other marshland islands rose out of the thin mist like so many gigantic, beached whales.

A couple of gleaming swans rose into the air, the distinctive whump of their wingbeats so easy to distinguish from that of any other waterbird. They soared above our heads, elegant necks outstretched, and turned toward the abbey fishponds. A moorhen called, the sawing of unseen grasshoppers made music in the warm air, and a chiffchaff sang as we passed his gorse bush. If we'd been here for any other reason, I'd have found time to appreciate the beauty of the day.

After about a mile, a narrow track turned westward, to our right, heading out into the marshland, and in the distance a low hill rose above the reeds. Not convinced of the safety of this path, despite Gildas's reassurances before we left, I'd brought a stout staff with me. I went first, testing the ground ahead of us, but it was a path well walked by many feet, and although dank marsh crowded in on either side, someone had laid a fine log causeway and our feet stayed dry.

Bec Eriu was the name Gildas said the locals had given the tiny islet – little Ireland. An Irishwoman named Brigid had come over about twenty years since and spent two years establishing her chapel and a community of religious women before hightailing it back to Ireland. She'd left behind her hood, her rosary beads, her weaving tools and a hand bell, all of which he assured me we'd be shown if we asked. They seemed an odd selection of mementoes to leave for your followers. Surely she'd have needed to keep those things for herself?

Brigid must have been a woman of influence, though. The chapel, although small, appeared to have been well built, if only of wattle and daub. A substantial and well-maintained thatched roof rose steeply to an apex decorated with a small wooden cross at either end, as if to remind us we were visiting a religious house. It sat squarely on one end of a low ridge, just above the marshland, and around it clustered the usual array of more humble buildings – accommodation, no doubt for the acolytes, storage and a kitchen.

We'd arrived at Terce, it seemed, from the sound of chanting emanating from the open door of the chapel. Archfedd and I availed ourselves of the wooden bench standing against one of the barn walls, and settled comfortably in the sunshine.

A wave of nausea washed over me, and I took out one of the early ripened apples from the pocket in my shift and bit into it. Small and sweet, it reminded me of a Beauty of Bath. Perhaps it *was* a Beauty of Bath, or the ancestor of one. I'd filled my large pocket as we'd passed through the orchards, so I passed one to Archfedd.

We had a long wait. Whoever governed Brigid's little community now must be a stickler for prayer. But at last, movement caught my eye, and I turned my head in time to see half a dozen drably dressed women emerge from the tiny chapel, heads down, hands clasped in front of them. Despite the plain, homespun headdresses they wore, Reaghan, who took after her father in her height, proved easy to pick out.

Archfedd jumped to her feet, face alight with excitement. "Reaghan!"

Her cousin's head swung around, a matching smile on her face. The woman at the head of the line turned on her heel like a snake about to strike. "Sister Mary," she snapped, like the most ferocious of sergeant-majors. "Eyes down."

Reaghan dropped her gaze to her dirty bare feet.

I drew in an angry breath and stood up. I was the Queen, and no holy woman was going to get the better of me. I had twenty years of entitlement behind me, and didn't lack for confidence. "Stop," I said, as loudly as I could without shouting. "I need to speak with my niece."

The woman turned her harsh gaze on me. Whether by choice or by compulsion, she'd scraped her hair back so tightly from her face it had pulled her eyes almost slanted, and she looked as though she'd had a bad facelift. Her grubby headdress perched on top of her head as if remaining in place by willpower alone. Gray eyes, cold as the winter sea, regarded me in something akin to scorn, her thin lips forming a downward curving line under her hooked nose. Not a looker.

"Who are you and what do you want here?" she asked, as the five young women stood in line, heads down, waiting in an oppressed silence. Only Reaghan peeped at us sideways.

I drew myself up taller, conscious of Gildas's all too good disguise and that I didn't look like who I claimed to be. "I am your queen, and I need to speak with Reaghan."

The woman – mother superior, abbess, whatever – fixed me with a glacial stare. "This is not an order that welcomes visitors. Sister Mary is not free to talk with you."

I wasn't having any of that. "My *niece*," I said, glowering at the woman with all the regal presence I could muster, "is nothing but a novice." I was guessing here, based on the small amount of knowledge I had of modern nuns. "She's been with you a matter of weeks only. And I am your queen. You will do as I say."

The woman wavered. Uncertainty flickered in her mean, pebble eyes.

I pounced. "Take your other women away with you, and leave Reaghan here with us. We do not wish to be disturbed."

She didn't want to go, but with a resentful glare, she did, chivvying the remaining four young women in front of her before they showed signs of wanting to rebel as well. Reaghan stood where she'd been left, still studying her feet.

Archfedd threw me an impressed grin, and hurried to her cousin, catching her in her arms in a bear hug. "Reaghan, I've so missed you." She planted a kiss on each unresponsive cheek.

Reaghan lifted her head, a furtive, frightened look in her eyes. "Not here," she said. "She'll be listening. This way."

We followed her along the ridge for a good three hundred yards to where a low stone wall surrounded a well. She sat down on the wall, and we did too, one on either side of her.

"That woman's awful," Archfedd said. "What on earth are you staying here for?"

Reaghan pulled a wry face. "I can't go back to Din Cadan, that's why."

My ears pricked. "Why ever not?"

Hot color rose up her neck to her cheeks. "I can't say, but I have to stay here... where it's safe."

"Safe?" Alarm bells rang in my head.

"What d'you mean?" Archfedd asked. "Safe from *what*?"

Reaghan fidgeted in discomfort. Her fingers, the nails bitten to the quick, much like Archfedd's, pulled at the coarse threads of her habit. If that was the right name for the plain, calf-length sack she was wearing. It made mine and Archfedd's garments look like haute couture.

I took one of her hands in mine, and Archfedd grabbed the other. We had her sandwiched between us, unable to get away. An unclean smell hung about her, as though she hadn't been able to wash since she'd arrived here. "You can tell us anything," I said, as gently as possible. "No one will judge you or think you silly." I squeezed her hand. "We're here to help you, if you need it. Your mother is missing you very much."

Reaghan studied her toes and shook her head. "I *can't* tell you." Her words came out as a mutter into her chest.

The feeling there was more to this vocation than met the eye grew stronger. I let go of her hand and put my arm around her shoulders, pulling her against me. "Don't worry. I won't let anything bad happen. Just tell me what's wrong. I'm sure I'll be able to help you."

For answer she burst into tears, her shoulders shaking.

Archfedd met my gaze over her cousin's bent head, eyes wide with shock. She shuffled closer as well, and squeezed her arm around Reaghan's waist. "I'm here now," she cooed. "I'm with you to keep you safe. We're together again like we're meant to be. I can look after you now."

Even though it was really her who needed keeping safe. Ironic.

I tried to gather my thoughts. Reaghan had discovered her vocation very quickly while we'd been away at Caer Dore and Din Tagel. Very quickly. Too quickly, even. I'd been puzzled at the time, but had dismissed it as a whim of hers and tended to agree with Arthur that she'd be back as soon as the bad weather set in. What was I missing?

I tightened my hold around her shoulders. "Reaghan, whose idea was it that you should become a religious?"

She wiped her eyes on her bare arm. "M-mine... I think."

The memory of what we'd been told about her came back to me, from where it had been shut away after the events of the past weeks. "You were riding out a lot with Medraut and Amhar, weren't you? Did *they* bring you this way? Was it someone else's idea to come to Ynys Witrin, not yours?"

Archfedd met my gaze again, eyes wider still.

Reaghan sniffed. "I-I think Medraut said he wanted to come here..."

Why was I not surprised? Medraut was like his Aunt Morgana – a spider at the center of a web, but was it a web of his own spinning? Not that she'd be doing any more spinning of her own.

"Why did he want to come here?" Archfedd asked.

Reaghan looked up at her. "He said he was considering becoming a monk."

"What?" I had to scoff at that. Anyone less likely to become a monk would have been hard to find.

"I didn't believe him," Reaghan muttered, sounding annoyed. "I'm not stupid. I thought... I thought he *liked* me."

"Oh, Reaghan," I said with a sigh. "He's a slippery customer and if he wanted you to think that, it was for a reason. I'd better tell you why we're here."

I told her everything. The fight between Llacheu and Amhar, their deaths, which she hadn't known about, and which made her cry again, our frantic efforts to save Amhar, the loss of Merlin, and Arthur's adoption of Medraut as his heir and decision that

Archfedd should marry him.

When I'd finished, we all sat in silence for a while. A few flies buzzed, a skylark's bubbling call carried on the warm air, and the summer sun beat down on us as though nothing at all were wrong in the world.

At last, Archfedd broke the silence. "Mami, do you think Medraut could have encouraged Amhar to attack Llacheu? Is that what you're saying? Did he – did he have something to do with what happened to my brothers?"

Reaghan's eyes flashed. "Did Medraut kill Llacheu?'

I looked from one girl to the other, wishing I could be certain. "I don't know. His mother swore he didn't. You heard her, Archfedd. She made me say I believed her before she'd tell me where to look for Amhar. I think I *did* believe her then, just for a while, but now I'm not so sure." I paused. "I think he might have."

"But why did he bring Reaghan here?" Archfedd asked. "Did he want her to stay here?"

Reaghan wriggled in discomfort. "He frightened me," she said. "We came here, but he told Amhar to wait in the lake village – that he wanted to take me to the island by himself." She licked her lips. "Amhar always did what Medraut told him. I thought Medraut wanted me to himself. I thought he *liked* me." She clasped her reddened hands in her lap. "But when he got me here, he told me that if I didn't join the religious house of Bec Eriu, he'd kill my mother. He said no one would ever know he'd done it. He had a secret poison he'd give her, and it would look like her heart had given out. He said it would be easy, and he'd done it before, in the past, and no one had known it was him. He said Morgana had given the poison to him a long time ago and shown him how to use it."

Oh my God.

Archfedd frowned. "But why? What would he want you shut up here for?"

Reaghan shook her head. "I don't know, but I could see in his

283

eyes that he meant it. He frightened me. I didn't want him to kill my mother. I said I'd stay."

She looked me in the eye. "I think he *must* have killed Llacheu, whatever my aunt Morgawse believes. When he looked at me, I could see in his face that he has it in him to kill. I don't mean in battle – all men can do that. I mean deliberately and sneakily. Coming up behind someone with a knife, or slipping poison into their food or wine. I think he could. I think he did."

I had an answer to Archfedd's question, but I wasn't going to share it with them, despite the temptation. In forcing Reaghan into a religious house, he'd been getting rid of another possible Pendragon heir. Reaghan was right in her summing up of his character. He'd murdered Llacheu and set Amhar up to look like the culprit, and now he intended to mop up the surviving heir by marrying her. And there appeared to be very little any of us could do about it.

And then there were none, to paraphrase Agatha Christie.

Chapter Thirty-Three

W E TOOK REAGHAN back with us to the abbey. No way was I leaving her at Bec Eriu with that cold-hearted woman in charge, and she wasn't sorry to come. The little room where we slept became more cramped than ever when a third narrow pallet bed was moved in, but the girls both seemed happier at being together.

Something of their old camaraderie returned, and at nights when there were no services taking place, they lay and chattered together like the girls they'd both once been. Reaghan lost her downtrodden attitude, and Archfedd began finally to put the deaths of her brothers behind her. Never forgotten, but pushed gently to one side so she could pick up the threads of her life, such as it was within the confines of the abbey.

Arthur and Cei returned about a week later, and, thanks to Gildas's watchman, we had enough warning to ensconce ourselves inside the church, the two girls hiding from sight in our bedchamber.

"You're my wife," Arthur tried, possibly thinking to appeal to my sense of duty. Good luck to him on that one.

"I know that," I said, folding my arms and leaning on the doorpost. Gildas had come to oversee our meeting again, and Arthur was keeping his distance. "Tell me something new."

Intense irritation radiated out of him. "As my wife you are obliged to do as I say."

I shook my head. "In your dreams."

Was that amusement in Cei's blue eyes?

Arthur huffed. He didn't look so gaunt now, but his eyes betrayed his anger and frustration. "You can't stay here forever."

I gave him a sweet smile. "I think you'll find we can."

He departed in high dudgeon, if that was a word you could use to describe an incandescently angry man.

A few days after that, Medraut turned up, and again we had good warning.

He was a different basket of eels though, all smiles and gentle words. The girls stayed hidden again, but from the way his eyes roamed the interior of the church and lingered on their closed door, he had no trouble guessing where they were.

"Aunt Gwen," he wheedled, leaning on the same doorpost I'd leaned on myself, while Gildas watched him with eagle eyes and his hefty staff in his hand. I'd confided all our fears and suspicions in my friend, and he'd vowed to help.

"Please don't call me aunt," I said, cold as ice. "I don't wish to acknowledge any relationship with you."

He raised his eyebrows. "Then I shall call you Gwen."

"Only my friends can do that."

He grinned, reminding me all too much of Cadwy, only he was more devious and far cleverer than his uncle could ever have been. A much more dangerous opponent. "Then I shall count myself as one of your friends."

"By invitation only," I said. "And I don't recall inviting you."

He chuckled. "I relish your wit... Gwen. But enough of that. I'm here to collect my bride. The marriage is to be tomorrow. It's been delayed enough already, and she needs to return with me to Din Cadan to prepare herself."

"Well, you'll be disappointed then," I snapped. "Because she's not coming."

He threw back his head and laughed. "Oh, Gwen. Something you haven't realized, as yet. I *always* get what I want. I shall have your daughter and make her mine, and there's nothing you'll be able to do about it."

The itch to hit him welled up in me, my fists balling by my sides.

His eyes flicked down, and he shook his head, still laughing. "And don't think you could ever best me. If you even try to strike me, I'll be quicker, and I'll have you out of your sanctuary in a trice." He kept his voice low. No doubt he didn't want Gildas overhearing *that*.

I bristled internally and with careful deliberation unclenched my fists. Schooling my face into a sweet smile I looked him in the eye. "No doubt you could, as you have no respect for the law. A scoundrel who thinks nothing of creeping up behind an unarmed man in the dark to slit his throat would have no compunction about snatching someone from sanctuary. How lucky I am that you've come alone, and my dear friend Gildas is right here with his staff."

His eyes flashed in anger for a moment before he had himself under control again. "I've no idea what you're talking about. We know who killed my uncle's bastard – his brother. *Your* treacherous son. You're deluding yourself if you think I had anything to do with it."

But I could hear the lie in his voice and see it in his eyes. Why hadn't I realized before this? Could I have made Arthur believe me? Probably not. He'd have thought me trying to blame anyone but my guilt-tainted son.

I smiled back even more sweetly. "And you're deluding yourself if you think I'm going to believe your lies. We're protected here. Archfedd stays put. You'd better take yourself back to Din Cadan and pray my husband doesn't work out for himself who really killed his sons. Because even if you didn't wield the sword that killed Amhar, his death lies at your door."

Medraut leaned toward me, without moving his feet. His whisper hissed around the quiet church. "He won't. He has a mistaken idea of chivalry that'll keep him from the truth. You mark my words." He withdrew. "I'll leave you now to think about that. But I'll be back. And when I'm next here, I'll be taking your daughter home with me."

After he'd gone, the girls emerged, hot and sweaty from being incarcerated in that tiny, airless room, but I didn't reveal what he'd said. Instead, my heart hollow with fear, I brooded upon his words by myself, unable to decide what to do.

I'd known this was coming, well, I'd suspected it at any rate, for such a long time that now it seemed to be upon us, I couldn't quite believe it. Medraut was in the position the legends had given him, a position I'd never thought he could take. Arthur's heir. Merlin was missing in action, and I was stuck in Ynys Witrin, protecting my two girls. I couldn't get to Arthur to warn him about Medraut – and if I did he'd never have believed me. He'd have accused me of clutching at straws, of not wanting to blame Amhar. How cleverly I'd been played by fate.

We began to settle into our life at the abbey. From inside our storeroom chamber, we listened in on every service the monks held. Reaghan, possibly a little indoctrinated after her time at the chapel, knelt and joined in their prayers and chanting in a whisper so they wouldn't hear her. Archfedd and I lay on our beds waiting for the services to be over so we could get out of the stuffy heat and into the fresh air again.

The one thing that bothered me though, over and above the fear of being snatched from sanctuary, was the growing suspicion that after fifteen years, and at past forty, I was pregnant again. I'd been feeling sick on and off for weeks, but put it down to worry, and my lack of a period down to not having eaten and the tension I was undergoing. But at last, I could ignore it no longer. If I wasn't pregnant, then something weird was going on. However, as that was the least of my worries right now, I pushed it aside to think about later.

Knowing we were safe for the time being with the guard on the monks' wharf, we were able to help the monks and lay brothers in the abbey gardens, which kept us occupied during the days and made us tired enough to sleep well at night, despite the oppressive heat in the storeroom. Days passed, gradually turning into weeks, and in the fields the corn was almost ripe and ready to harvest. And to my surprise, no further visitations occurred.

Until the day Llawfrodedd arrived. We'd had warning that a boat had landed a warrior on the island, so were all inside the church when he came striding into the courtyard, his cloak over one arm and the dust of the road on his boots.

With a squeal of excitement, Archfedd abandoned caution and bolted across the cobbles to throw herself into his arms. Absence had definitely made her heart grow fonder.

Llawfrodedd wrapped his arms around her and swung her off her feet, his face alight with joy. Before he had time to put her down, she planted a kiss on his lips. "Llawfrodedd, I knew you'd come!"

He set her down and disentangled himself from her clutches, his face fiery red. "I-I'm sorry." He aimed this at me.

After so long cooped up in sanctuary, I couldn't have cared less if he'd kissed her himself. I grinned at him. "Don't apologize to me – give her a proper kiss. I've saved her for a reason, and that reason is you." Not quite true, but he wasn't to know that.

Archfedd blushed a similar shade of red.

I caught Reaghan's hand. "We'll give them a few minutes, shall we?"

Five minutes later we were all sitting on the grass under the shade of one of the larger apple trees in the orchard, well out of earshot of any of the monks and lay brothers working by the abbey. Archfedd had settled herself as close to Llawfrodedd as possible, and Reaghan and I sat opposite them.

"What are you doing here?" I asked our visitor. "And how did you even know where to find us?"

He had his arm around Archfedd's shoulders, and she was leaning against him. "I came back from Dinas Badan with a message for the king and found him gone," he said. "My commanding officer wanted more men for the garrison and decided I was the one who could persuade the king to allocate them." He cast a loving glance at my daughter. "I found Medraut in charge of Din Cadan and a good half of the army absent with the king."

News to us. "Where's he gone?" I asked, as chill fingers walked down my spine. "We've had no trouble with the Saxons for years now. Is it the Irish in the west? Or has he ridden north against the Picts? They've been quiet for a long time."

Llawfrodedd's face clouded with concern. "No. He's gone to Armorica."

"Armorica?" My voice rose in consternation. "Why's he gone there?"

"Where's Armorica?" Reaghan had clearly not been listening in the lessons she'd had from Merlin.

"Across the ocean to the south," the more conscientious Archfedd answered. "In Gaul. Hundreds of miles away. We have cousins there. Don't you remember the maps Mami drew? Of the world." The bit of the world they knew. I'd not wanted to shock them too much with a Mercator map.

Llawfrodedd gave a quick nod. "That's what I was told. The King of Cornouaille in Armorica, a man called Budic, requested the High King's help. I was told Arthur leapt at the chance. I don't know why. It's such a long way off."

I could fill them in on this. "Arthur's grandfather, Ambrosius the Elder, took his family to Armorica when the usurper Guorthegirn stole his kingdom. I think his wife, Archfedd's great-grandmother, was a sister of the then king. Her grandfather was born there. That must make this Budic a distant cousin."

"But why would Father go that far?" Archfedd persisted. "He's never crossed the ocean before. Has he?"

I shook my head. "The furthest he's been is north of the Wall, and that was years ago." A nasty nub of worry was forcing its way inside my head. Didn't the stories say that Arthur had gone to Gaul and left Medraut in charge while he was away? Didn't Medraut, Mordred in the stories I remembered, decide not to wait for his uncle to die naturally but to take over the kingdom in his absence? The horrible feeling that everything required for Camlann was sliding into place rocked me to the core.

Arthur was in Armorica, which was a part of Gaul. Medraut held the reins of power just as he'd always wanted. Merlin was missing, lost somewhere with Nimuë, the woman who the legends said locked him up forever in a crystal cave. And I was impotent and isolated on Ynys Witrin with Reaghan and Archfedd. How many queens had received the mortally wounded Arthur and taken him to the mystical land of Avalon in the legends? Three. We three perhaps, waiting here for his arrival.

"Llawfrodedd," I said, as a plan formulated in my head. "I want you to go back to Din Cadan and keep an eye on everything there. Report back to us every few days, if you can. I need to know what's happening there. Ride to the Lake Village and send Con with a message – he can be trusted."

"Why?" Archfedd pressed. "What's wrong? I can tell something is. You have to tell us."

I surveyed their anxious young faces, weighing up what I should reveal. Not the truth, that was for sure. No need to shock them with that. "I've had a premonition," I said, seizing upon something they might see as possible. "Medraut is going to try to seize the throne while Arthur is away. If he does, then there's going to be a huge battle. Not with the Saxons, but between Medraut and your father. It won't end well. We have to do everything we can to stop him."

I looked at Archfedd. "And to make his bid for the throne more legitimate, he needs you. We have to get you and Reaghan out of the way. Because he'll be back here to get you now Arthur's not there to keep him in line, and I don't think even Gildas will be able to stop him this time."

I pointed west. "There are other islands out there I can send you to. In disguise as servants so no one will even suspect you might be royal. We'll go back now and ask Gildas for help. You have to go straightaway. Medraut could be on his way even now. I'll stay here because it's not me he's after, and Llawfrodedd can send news as often as possible without causing suspicion."

"Have you forgiven Father?" Archfedd asked, a hint of hope in her voice. Perhaps she already had in her own way. The young are ever resilient.

Had I? Now Camlann loomed ever closer, I had to ask myself that question. I searched my heart. Did I care what happened to Arthur? Did I want to save him?

Yes. I didn't want him to die at Camlann, whatever he'd done. "Not quite," I said. "A little, but not quite."

Chapter Thirty-Four

B EFORE LLAWFRODEDD LEFT us, he saw Reaghan and Archfedd depart under escort with just two of the lay brothers, so as not to alert anyone to their importance. The lay brothers were going back to their own small village on one of the more distant and larger islands, and the two girls were to masquerade as serving girls they'd brought back with them. Needless to say, the men had been picked with care and warned, by me and Gildas in turn, and with Llawfrodedd standing by caressing his sword hilt, not to lay a finger on either girl on pain of death. And on no account to give them away should anyone come searching for them.

Archfedd had been hard to persuade to leave. "I want to stay with you, Mami," she implored. "I don't want to leave you where *he* could get you. It's not safe."

I shook my head. "I need to stay. I'm of no interest to Medraut. It's you he wants, and you I refuse to let him have. And I need to know what's happening, which I couldn't if I came with you." I hugged her tight. "You'll have each other. And these two good lay brothers will keep you safe."

The men tugged their forelocks in respect and nodded. Father and son, both possessed reassuringly gentle eyes and kind faces.

As soon as their party had set off, on foot and leaning on stout staffs, as befitted lay brothers and servant girls, Llawfrodedd took his leave of Gildas. I walked down to the monk's wharf with him on leaden feet, my mind a whirl with how fast things were moving.

We passed the guard on duty and found Con sitting on the jetty, bare feet dangling in the water, with a basket of sleek, silvery fish beside him.

He scrambled to his feet as he heard us coming and set down his rod. "Milady, how goes it?" Anxiety edged his voice. Did he have some inkling that things were afoot? Dangerous things that might well affect his life as well as mine.

I managed a smile. "Could be better, but don't worry yourself. Llawfrodedd and I have a plan." Not much of one, but I wasn't going to worry our young helper with that.

Llawfrodedd turned to face me. "Milady, please take care. I worry about you here alone. I think you should have gone with Archfedd and Reaghan."

I kept that smile fixed on my face. "No need to worry about me. Like I told Archfedd, I'm of no interest to Medraut. It's her he's after, and she's safe now. And if he does come here looking, he won't find her. You can be sure of that." I stepped up to him and gave him a hug.

For a moment he stiffened in surprise, as I'd never hugged him before. Then he lifted his arms and returned the embrace, a little self-consciously.

I patted his back. "Thank you, Llawfrodedd, for being a true friend when we needed one."

When we parted, his face had blossomed with color, but he looked gratified at the praise. With a quick, nervous glance back at me, he stepped into the little boat, and Con pushed off into the channel with his pole. The water lapped about the craft's shallow draft, and ripples arced away across the smooth surface of the water, shivering asunder the reflections of the blue sky and sleepy trees, just as this world was about to shatter.

Llawfrodedd, sitting on the thwarts in the bow of the boat, fixed anxious eyes on me as he lifted a hand in farewell before the marshy reedbeds swallowed him up and silence fell.

I stood for a while on the jetty as the ripples died away, gazing out at the reeds and the sun shimmering on the water as though nothing could be wrong with the day. Unbidden, my mind went back to another similar day, a long time ago, when I'd been here with Arthur. He'd sat on the edge of the jetty just like Con, beside old Nial, a friend from his boyhood, legs dangling, hair still wet from diving into the lake to find Excalibur. His words came back to me down the years. He'd said he sometimes wished he could stay like that forever, fishing in the sunshine.

I'd have had that day back a million times over if I could have.

UNFORTUNATELY, BEFORE LLAWFRODEDD had the chance to return with more news of what was afoot at Din Cadan, I received other visitors, and this time, not by boat. Years ago, when I'd first come to Ynys Witrin through that time portal, the abbot had sent me on horseback to Din Cadan, following a secret causeway through the marshes, presumably because there'd been too many of us to go by boat. Even though every time I'd been back since, I'd come by boat, I'd known that secret path still existed.

A scrawny village boy came running up from the fields shouting in panic at the top of his voice. "Soldiers! Soldiers!"

I was in the gardens outside the abbey weeding with a couple of women from the village, Bethan and Nyfain, when I heard his shouts. The fields, where harvest was heading to a close, were full of lay brothers, monks and villagers. Every one of them ceased their work and straightened, staring toward the running boy as a current of panic sizzled through their ranks.

The soldiers arrived hot on the boy's tail, emerging from the scrubby woodland that edged the monastic settlement in a body of glittering chainmail and helmets. Their mud-flecked horses were champing at their bits and tossing their heads at the still plentiful flies.

For one awful moment, the thought they might be Saxon raiders shot into my head. But no, Saxons would be on foot, so these had to be British warriors. Was it Arthur, come to find me? No. Not him. He was most likely still in Armorica. From behind Bethan and Nyfain I searched for the leader.

Medraut rode at the head, bare-headed and proud.

Ignoring the staring people, the column of riders approached the abbey. My two companions retreated toward the safety of the overhanging thatch, so I went with them, keeping my head bowed lest anyone saw my face, and wishing I had a hood to pull forward. I still wore the rough homespun of the other women. Surely no one would pick me out as a queen.

Medraut's gaze swept blindly over me as the riders, forty strong, clattered through the gates into the abbey courtyard and out of sight. Far too late for me to run for the sanctuary of the church. Thank God we'd got Archfedd away.

Bethan, a girl in her late teens with a very pregnant belly, let out a hiss of breath between her teeth. "I ain't never seen nothin' like them soldiers. All shiny bright like that. Can't mean nothin' good that they's forced some'un to show'em the way through they marshes."

Nyfain, older and a lot thinner, nodded. "She be right. No good'll come o' soldiers comin' to our abbey. They's arter somethin'." Her gaze went to me. "Might be you, I'm thinkin'." They all knew who I was.

I pulled a face. "I'm nothing now. It's my daughter that wicked man's after."

Bethan grinned, revealing crooked teeth. "Good thing your lass ain't here then, int it? You did right to get her gone. I'd do that for my babby in a flash." She put a supportive hand under her belly. "Does me good to git straightened up agin. Does my back in, weedin'."

I managed a smile, but, in my own belly, doubt gnawed at me. Medraut must have come here with the intention of snatching Archfedd from sanctuary and forcing her back to marry him. How angry would he be when he discovered his little bird had flown?

I didn't have long to wait.

Two warriors came striding out of the gates and headed for the garden where I still stood with my friends. Bran and Cyngal, the two young princes of Ebrauc who'd joined Medraut's faction, marched up to me and bowed. I'd clearly been more recognizable than I'd thought.

"Milady Guinevere," Bran, the older of the two said. "We're to escort you to the abbot's office."

No point in arguing. I handed the hoe I'd been using to Nyfain, shelving the idea of taking it with me to hit Medraut with. Not such a good idea while he was surrounded by his own supporters.

Bethan patted my arm, and I managed a smile for her. Then, girding up my metaphorical loins, I stepped past the two young men and marched, with more determination than I felt, up to the gates and into the horse-filled courtyard. Most of the men had remained mounted, and now they moved aside like the parting of the Red Sea to let me pass. Young faces, all of them. Arthur would have taken his most experienced warriors away with him.

My eyes went to the open church door visible between the horses, and for a moment it occurred to me that I could bolt for it. But a lot of men and horses stood between me and the doorway, and Bran and Cyngal were right behind me. They'd catch me in a few strides, and I'd lose my dignity being grappled to the ground. I shelved that idea as well and turned my head toward the abbot's office.

At the doors, I paused to draw a supporting breath, then pushed it open and walked in.

With Abbot Jerome getting no better and still confined to his bed, Gildas occupied the seat behind the desk, sitting upright and at attention, his clever eyes meeting mine as I entered. In front of the desk stood two men – Medraut beside Cinbelin, his short ginger friend from Alt Clut. They turned toward me as the door banged shut.

"Gwen," Medraut purred, as though he were here on a visit to take afternoon tea. "What a pleasure to see you again, and not hiding inside the church this time. How lucky am I. Do come in and sit down." He pulled out one of the two seats in front of the desk and stood holding its back. "Here. Sit here." Menace laced that simple invitation.

I could have stayed by the door, insisted I preferred to stand and looked an idiot, but I didn't. I played him at his own game. "Why, thank you." I smiled my sweetest smile and sat down, folding my hands in my lap, instinct telling me to cover up my ring.

Medraut took the second seat, and Cinbelin stood behind it, feet planted wide, arms folded across his broad chest, for all the world like a gingery canine guard. A pit bull, maybe.

Gildas cleared his throat. "I've just informed my Lord Medraut that the Princess Archfedd is no longer here and has not been for some time."

A slight frown slid across Medraut's ostensibly affable face before he had it under control and hidden. "It seems the bird has flown." That smile again, knowing and smug. "But I feel there will be alternatives on offer." He let his insolent gaze run over my body in a way that sent a shiver down my spine. "If I can't have the daughter, then I'll take the mother. For now."

I pressed my lips together.

He grinned in self-satisfaction, a man who knew he'd check-mated me. "The added bonus of having you instead of her will be the dragon ring you're wearing, and the belief that the man who holds you will be High King."

Gildas didn't rise to his feet, but he seemed to grow larger in his seat, like a bull frog inflating its body. "I have promised sanctuary to the Queen," he said. "You will not violate the law of sanctuary."

Medraut chuckled, and Cinbelin joined in, reminding me of Muttley in The Whacky Races. "I don't see her hiding in sanctuary right now." Medraut's upper lip curled in a sneer. "I see her here in your office. Sanctuary is your church, not here. She's coming with me."

My sword. If only I had it, I could defend myself from these two. They'd kill me if I attacked them, but surely death would be preferable to accompanying Medraut back to Din Cadan as his prisoner. But my sword was in my little chamber at the back of the church. It might as well have been on top of the Tor.

Medraut steepled his fingers. "I've even brought a horse with me especially. Mind you, as I'd hoped it would be Archfedd I'd be returning with, it's not your own horse. She's back at Din Cadan, you'll be pleased to hear. I'm sure you'll be happy to see her again."

"I'm not coming to Din Cadan with you," I said, the effort to remain calm enormous. "I live here now. And you have no right to take me back. I'm your Queen. It is you who must do as I say, and I say that you must leave Ynys Witrin immediately."

He laughed again. "Oh, Gwen, keep up, can't you? I didn't come here for Archfedd because I needed her to bolster my right to be her father's heir. I came here to get her because she crossed me. As did you. No one gets away with that." His callous eyes stared into mine. "But you encouraged her in her rebellion. You helped her flee. So, I'll take you instead. You're still beautiful. I could enjoy having you in my bed. I'm sure you know a lot more than she does about how to pleasure a man."

"You will not touch your Queen," Gildas said, his voice ringing out in the small room. "She is the wife of the High King and in my care. I forbid you to do this."

Medraut's head moved in a slight nod, and in an instant Cinbelin stepped around the table and set the tip of his sword against Gildas's throat, indenting the stubbly skin.

To do him credit, Gildas was undaunted. "This is my abbey, and you will leave. Now," he roared, like a lion defending his cubs. Did he see me that way? Was I his cub? Or was he the sacrificial bishop in this game of chess?

The sword tip pressed harder, and blood trickled down his throat into the neckline of his habit.

"If he speaks again, kill him," Medraut said.

Cinbelin, whom I'd previously thought a harmless young man, nodded, his eyes alight with excitement and blood lust. He looked as though he hoped Gildas would speak and enable him to make the killing blow.

"It's all right, Gildas," I said, my voice shaking a little despite my efforts to prevent it. "Don't speak. You mustn't die for me. You have much work to do and many books to write." *One book in particular.*

Medraut's look of satisfaction grew. How I wanted to smack it off his ugly face.

"Oh," he said, as he rose from his seat. "One more thing. How remiss of me to almost forget when it's one of the most important things about today. The reason why I came, really." He winked at me. Yes, winked.

I gripped the arms of my seat so hard my knuckles whitened, itching for the feel of my sword or dagger in my hand.

"My Aunt Morgana was kind enough to inform me some time ago that you are hiding the Sword of Destiny here in your abbey. Some time before she died at the hands of that fake magic man of my uncle's, she suggested I might need it."

He winked again as though making me complicit in this. "I had the good fortune to spend some time with my aunt in Viroconium. She made out she wanted to support me, but I saw through her. It was that brat of hers she wanted everything for. But luckily, my little cousin's vanished along with Merlin. Good riddance to both of them." He leaned forward in his seat. "And now I shall have my uncle's sword – the one he drew from the stone to prove he should be High King." He beamed around at us. "And I shall be High King myself."

Chapter Thirty-Five

O N MY ARRIVAL at Din Cadan, Coventina and I embraced in tears, once she got me inside her house. "What are you wearing?" she asked, staring at my homespun. "Where have you been? Cei told me nothing."

I quickly told her everything that had happened, and how Gildas and I had hidden the two girls where Medraut wouldn't be able to find them.

"My Reaghan? She's well? Medraut threatened *me* to make her stay there?" Her voice rose in anger, and her hand went to the dagger on her belt. "I'll kill the little bastard."

I hushed her. "Not so loud. He'll have men spying on us. And trying to kill him will only get you hurt, or worse, killed, and what help would that be to Reaghan? She's going to need her mother. No, we have to make a plan. Tell me what's happened here, and how Medraut managed to wheedle his way into this position of power."

We sat side-by-side on the edge of her bed, close enough that we could converse in a whisper. "A good many weeks ago, now," she confided, clasping my hands in hers, "a message came from Armorica, from the king there. I'd never heard of him, but his name is Budic. He's been having trouble with the Yellow Hair raiders the way we used to. Most likely they've been going there because they couldn't raid us after the Treaty of Badon." She squeezed my hands. "Budic heard how Arthur had dealt with them here, and being a cousin, begged him to come and help."

"But why did Arthur agree to go so far away?" I whispered back. "Armorica isn't part of Britain. He has no obligation to help them. And why did he leave that snake Medraut in charge like this?" If I'd been here instead of in hiding, could I have persuaded my husband to have taken Medraut with him and so averted this power grab?

Coventina shrugged. "I don't know. I didn't see the message. Cei said it was eloquent and praised Arthur as the mightiest of kings and pointed out their kinship. You know men. A bit of flattery gets you a long way with them. Maybe he went because of what Budic said about him? And because Budic reminded them of their blood tie."

Very possibly. Any man as powerful and successful as Arthur might at some point begin to believe the hype about himself. And I *had* told him he would be the most famous king ever, in a moment of rash weakness. With hindsight, perhaps not my best move.

"Well, for whatever reason, he's gone," I hissed. "Bloody idiot."

She nodded. "Didn't take long for Medraut to start imposing himself. Turns out he'd already won over a lot of the younger warriors – ones who would've followed Llacheu, if not Amhar. Ones who, if Llacheu *had* been here, would've remained loyal to Arthur and not given Medraut a second glance."

She shivered. "But young men like to follow other young men, and Arthur took all the older warriors – his friends – with him to Armorica. Left all the young ones behind. Bad move. They resented that – they wanted to see action. I've heard them talking in the Hall. They want action and enemies to fight, and plunder to grow rich on. Medraut's promising them that."

Her grip on my hands tightened so much it hurt. "Young warriors like that haven't got no sense. It's been more'n seven years now since Badon. The young men followin' Medraut haven't seen proper fightin'. All they've done is practice, practice,

practice. They're ripe'n'ready for a battle, all of them. And they don't care who with."

Oh my God. Worse than I could ever have imagined. Why had it never occurred to me that a big problem of prolonged peace would be a whole host of testosterone-fueled young men trained for war but with nothing to do but practice? Obvious, now I thought about it. This whole fortress must be a hotbed of male hormones all straining to get out. All these young warriors left in this melting pot were fomenting violence like a load of witches around a cauldron.

That brought Morgana to mind. Like me, she'd probably not even considered this. It would have saved her a lot of trouble if she had. Medraut and his cronies could have reached this point all by themselves with no help from her. Inevitable. And terrifying.

"He's stolen the Sword of Destiny," I said. "He thinks it gives him the right to declare himself High King."

"But Arthur has Excalibur," she whispered back. "He has the sword of Macsen Wledig."

I shook my head. "Arthur used that sword to execute our son. I don't know if his having it means anything now. He used it for something it wasn't meant for. It was Medraut who killed Llacheu. He told me so. Not in so many words, but he might as well have admitted it outright. Reaghan and Archfedd had already helped me work it out, though. Morgawse is a fool who doesn't know her own son. I knew mine, and that he hadn't done it. Medraut's utterly ruthless."

She put her arms around me and drew me close, the warmth of her body like a balm. "We'll think of something. I promise. We have to."

DIN CADAN'S HILLTOP fortress no longer felt like home. Instead, it had become a prison. Despite his threats to take me to his bed,

Medraut wisely refrained from even trying to do so, and having taken the royal chamber for himself, let me stay in Coventina's house beside the Hall. Maybe he felt that having seized the Sword of Destiny, he didn't really need me. No man likes to think it's because of a woman he's successful. Or maybe he was afraid I'd kill him while he slept. He was right. I would have.

The days dragged past all too slowly. In the fields below the fortress the farmers were laboring to bring in the last of the harvest while the weather held. No help from the warriors this year. If I'd suggested it, Medraut would have laughed in my face. I did my best to keep out of his way, in case he remembered his suggestion of taking me to his bed.

I barely saw him. Most of the time I spent with Coventina in her house, the two of us talking in low voices as we pretended to work at our spinning and sewing. Who knew what spies might be lurking on the other side of a wall?

I glimpsed Llawfrodedd from afar, but made no attempt to contact him. If he had something to impart, he'd find a way to get word to me, I was sure. Once or twice our gazes met across the fortress, but he quickly looked away. Wisely so.

Of course, he wasn't the only one amongst the warriors who didn't support Medraut, but if any of them had spoken out, they'd have suffered. One night as we lay tucked in her bed, Coventina told me something that had happened before I returned.

"D'you remember young Drem, Llacheu's best friend?" She had her mouth close to my ear and her voice rose scarcely above a breath.

"Yes."

"Him that had to get married on a sword point when his girl's father found out she were increasing."

I smiled, even though in the darkness Coventina couldn't have seen. "I remember that very well. They've got five children now, haven't they?"

"Just her now," my friend whispered. "Drem spoke out against Medraut not long after Arthur left. Said he were behaving like he were the king. That's all. Spoke a few words agin him and not even to his face, and Medraut took offense. Real bad. Didn't help none that he knew Drem had been Llacheu's friend."

I caught my breath. "What happened?"

"Trumped up charges against him of treason. Someone claimed they'd heard him threatening to kill Medraut and Arthur. Of course, threatening Medraut shouldn't have been punishable with death, and it was only words, after all, even if it were true. He had to say Drem'd threatened Arthur too, then he had an excuse for a public execution. Not been any more complaints since then. No one's bold enough to come out and say Medraut's behavin' more'n'more like a king."

"It's only a matter of time before he declares he is," I whispered.

Prophetic words. A week later, Coventina and I were summoned to outside the Hall, to find all the people of the fortress gathered there and Arthur's throne carried out to stand in the autumn sunshine. Medraut was standing in front of it, with Cinbelin, Bran and Cyngal lined up behind him, and behind them a phalanx of his warriors, armed to the teeth, presumably in case of dissent.

"Oh my God, what's he up to?" I hissed at Coventina as we were pushed to stand to one side of the throne, no doubt our presence being meant to lend legitimacy to his actions.

As soon as we were in position, Medraut took a step forward, holding up his hands like the winner of a boxing match. "My people," he cried, above the general hubbub of mutterings emanating from everyone but his warriors.

He nodded to his men, and their swords slid from their scabbards. The men pointed them at the crowd, who fell silent with begrudging glares.

Seeming satisfied, Medraut went on. "My people. My warriors. I come before you to present myself and take my rightful place. Your old king left me in charge in his absence, and told me to do my best to uphold his peace. I have fulfilled his wishes.

However, you see me before you with sad tidings. Your old king is dead. Behold your new king."

Disbelieving silence met this pronouncement.

For a moment the world rocked, and my heart slid down into my boots. Arthur was dead? How could he be? Wouldn't I have known, sensed, if he no longer existed? No. This couldn't be true. Medraut was lying to facilitate his snatching of the throne, the kingdom and perhaps even the High Kingship.

The crowd warily muttered together, but as soon as the swords were raised, fell silent.

Coventina gripped my hand in a vicelike hold. "He can't be dead," she whispered without moving her lips. "What about Cei? And all their men? He took half his army with him. Theodoric too. They went in his ships."

"It's a lie," I whispered back. "He's making it up. I know he is."

But was he? Did I have it all wrong and had Arthur died in Armorica, far from home at some Camlann of his own making? Would I never see him again? No. I refused to believe this lying bastard. Nothing that came out of his mouth was true.

Months had passed since Amhar's death, and I could finally recognize it for what it had been. A murder engineered by Medraut, helped in part by Morgana. She'd died for it, which had scuppered her plans for Nimuë, and I'd not been in time to save my son. Did I still blame Arthur? How much of it had truly been his fault, and how much of it was something he'd been forced into by his own upholding of the law? Because Morgana had known he'd do that.

I bit my lip. How would I feel if what Medraut was claiming were true, and I never saw Arthur's face again?

Tears formed in the corners of my eyes and trickled down my cheeks. The realization that I loved him, no matter what he'd done, cascaded over me. I always had, even when he'd killed my son. Love and hate were so entwined together. I could never forgive him for Amhar's death, but at last I could understand why he'd done it, and I could still love him, despite everything.

A great wave of longing for him, stronger than anything I'd felt before, almost bowled me over in a tsunami of emotion. Grief, love, passion, anger, anxiety, all mixed up together. He couldn't be dead. He just couldn't. We'd parted as enemies. I had to be able to tell him I still loved him. I had to.

Medraut was speaking again. "As his heir, it is my obligation to take his throne and crown."

Something glittered in his hands, catching the sunlight. A gold circlet. Arthur's gold circlet. Oh my God. He was going to crown himself with Arthur's crown. Suddenly I remembered Archfedd telling me on the beach at Din Tagel what she'd seen in her grandmother's scrying glass. Herself, wearing my crown. And yet, she wasn't here. Medraut would sit on that throne alone, the only one to wear a crown. Had we somehow changed what she'd seen in the scrying glass and made the world a little bit different? And if we'd done that, could we have made Arthur's future different as well?

Medraut raised the crown in both hands. "I am your new king," he announced, and set the crown amongst his dark curls. For a long moment, he stared around at the crowd, as if daring any one of them to step forward and protest. They didn't. With a self-satisfied smile, he sat down on Arthur's throne, resting his hands on the arms.

Cinbelin threw back his head. "Long live the king," he bellowed.

The cheer that rose toward the sky came mostly from the armed warriors. It pleased me to see the crowd of ordinary people mutter under their breath as they glowered at the man sitting on Arthur's throne.

Chapter Thirty-Six

"**A**RTHUR ISN'T DEAD, I'm certain of it," I said to Coventina when we were at last back in her house and out of earshot of anyone who might report our words to Medraut.

She nodded. "And if he's not, Cei's not either. I refuse to believe either of them can be dead." She kept her voice low and scowled at the door we'd made sure to close behind us as though it had sprouted ears.

Were we both clinging to this as a forlorn hope? I wouldn't think about it. We had to work on the belief that it was all a lie, that what I knew of the legends was true.

I paced up and down next to the fire where a cauldron of stew sat simmering in the hot ashes. With the door shut, the atmosphere inside the hut had grown warm and smoky. "If Arthur's not dead, then we have to warn him what's happening here. He'll be returning from Armorica before too long. He'll want to do that before autumn storms might make crossing the Channel difficult. We have to let him know what Medraut's done."

My heart flipped over. What the hell was I planning on doing? Luring Arthur to his Camlann? It felt like it. But Camlann was no longer something to be avoided. Instead, it loomed as something inevitable to be met head on and overcome.

Coventina gave the stew a stir as Keelia, her maid, wasn't with us. "But how? What can we do that Medraut won't find out about?"

I halted beside her. "I'd gladly go to warn Arthur if I could, but if I go missing, he's bound to notice and guess what I've done. Likewise, you can't go. And anyway, you couldn't ride that far. Not with your health problems."

Coventina straightened, her jaw set in rebellion. "I'd ride to the Wall and back if it meant saving Cei. I wouldn't mind the pain."

I nodded. "I know you would, but Medraut would notice you were gone, just like he would me. We have to send someone he won't miss." I paused, knuckling my forehead as though I could beat a solution to our problem out. It worked. "I know. Llawfrodedd. He's been keeping out of Medraut's way like us, so if he goes missing, no one's likely to say anything. They might even think he's gone back to his post at Dinas Badan. We'll send him."

"But where to? He won't know where to go."

I sat down at the table by the wall. "Do you know where Arthur took ship for Armorica?"

Her brow furrowed. "I-I'm not sure. Let me think. They rode off south, I know that, to meet up with Theodoric and his fleet. Cei said Theo's ships had been patrolling the south coast. I think he said they were heading for somewhere near Caer Durnac. Somewhere called... Clavinium, I think..." Her voice wavered with uncertainty.

I seized on her words. "South of Caer Durnac there's an old Roman port on a wide river estuary. That must be Clavinium. A bit silted up, now, but deep enough for ships the size of Theodoric's. Theo could still get his ships in close enough to take on men and horses. If they left that way, which I think they must have, then they'll be returning by the same route, surely. Far enough away from the Saxon landholdings in the east."

Caer Durnac was modern Dorchester, so the port south of there had to be Weymouth, or somewhere near it, where in my old world a huge car ferry daily took passengers to Brittany – our Armorica. "That has to be it," I hissed in excitement. "And it's not far. We'll send Llawfrodedd to wait for them there. To catch them and warn them the moment they land. He'll have to go as soon as possible."

But how were we to attract his attention without alerting anyone else?

We waited for nightfall, and sent for Kala, Keelia's oldest daughter, who was married to Seisyll, one of Llacheu's old friends. She came creeping in as though she'd taken on the persona of a cartoon spy. "You'll have to move naturally," I told her, cross at her obvious subterfuge. "If anyone sees you creeping about like that, they'll know you're up to no good."

"But I am up to no good," she whispered. "And I feel like everyone do know."

Keelia, who was at work in the kitchen, snorted. "Everyone'll know if you act like that, you idiot of a girl."

Kala sniffed and hung her head.

I patted her shoulder. "Don't worry. We're not angry. You're just going to have to pretend everything is normal. Take a wander down to see your brother in the barracks, and get him to give this note to Llawfrodedd. Don't let anyone see you when you pass it to him. Laugh a bit as though he's told you a joke. Look natural." I managed an encouraging smile. "You can do it."

Keelia picked up a pile of shirts. "Here, you can take him these. Clean ones. That'll be your excuse for going. Tuck the note under the top one, but mind and tell him 'tis there. And not to tell no one."

Kala gave us a doubtful look. "I'm a-scared I'll go an' do it wrong."

"Nothin' to it," Coventina said with a brisk firmness. "None of us can go because it'd be too obvious. You can, because no one'll notice you. You're just a servant girl. Your mother can't go because she happens to be *my* servant. But you can, to see your brother. You'll be fine."

Poor Kala. She didn't possess much in the way of brains, and we were expecting a lot of her. Maybe we shouldn't have, but who else did we have to send? We shooed her out of the door with the clean washing, and settled down to wait. The stew was ready, but somehow my appetite had dwindled to nothing, and anyway, my nausea had returned, reminding me of the new life growing in my belly. Neither Coventina nor Keelia showed any inclination to eat either, even though they didn't have the same excuse as me.

At last, when I'd decided Kala must have given herself away and been caught with her message and was at present languishing in the noisome lockup, a timid knock came at our door, and Keelia let her back in. Another figure loomed behind her in the dark, tall and decidedly male.

Llawfrodedd slipped inside the house and Keelia closed the door.

I looked at Coventina. "I think Keelia and Kala should leave now. So if anyone asks them they can deny all knowledge of what we're doing."

She nodded. "Off you both go. And thank you for your help. Both of you."

Kala couldn't wait to be out of the house, but her mother left with marked reluctance. "I don't mind being part o' this," she said to her mistress. "I want to help save Milord Cei and the king if I can."

Coventina gently urged her through the door. "No, Keelia. I don't want to involve you in any more of this if I can help it. You've done enough, and you've got your own family to think of. Now go."

With the servants gone, we turned to Llawfrodedd.

"Is it true?" he blurted out, far too loudly for my liking. "Is the king dead?"

I shook my head, my finger to my lips. "It's not true. I can't be sure, I know, but I'm certain Medraut is lying. Think about it. Did you see any messengers arriving today? Or yesterday? I didn't."

Coventina caught her breath. "Of course. No messenger means no message. Why didn't I think of that?"

"Why didn't everyone?" Llawfrodedd added.

"Because no one dares to cross my nephew, so they don't even think about it," I said. "They're all too scared to think for themselves."

Coventina nodded. "You're right. They didn't even question what he said. And he's got all the young warriors eating out of his hand, the slimy bastard. They all think the sun do shine out of his shitty backside."

My eyes widened. I'd rarely heard Coventina use language like that.

She grinned, a twinkle of satisfaction in her eyes.

I turned back to our visitor. "Arthur took all the experienced warriors with him – except you, Llawfrodedd, because you were at Dinas Badan. Thank goodness you were there."

Color rose to the young man's cheeks. "The King gave me a future here, when all I had were the clothes on my back, and they were rags not worth mentioning. He put me with the other boys, the sons of warriors, and taught me how to fight. And now I want to fight for him." He put his hand to his heart. "I'm ready to die for him if he asks me to."

I caught his hand. "Good. We don't need you to die, but we want you to do something for us and him."

"Anything, Milady. Anything."

"Can you get out of the fortress tomorrow do you think? Is there a chance you can? On horseback?"

He rubbed his chin. "I don't know. Medraut's got his own guards who're all loyal to him on the gates. They'd see me approaching and might stop me. Since he brought you and the Sword of Destiny back from Ynys Witrin, things've got a lot tighter at the gates. It's like he doesn't trust any of us. Not even the ones who've sworn allegiance to him."

Like any bad leader.

"What about if you went over the wall at night?" Coventina asked. "You could take a horse from the village. They have a few down there. Horses for wagons and work – and there are some half-trained warhorses as well, that we don't have room for up here. They've all been backed. Might be best to take one of them. Less likely to be missed. Better than drawing attention to yourself by trying to leave in daylight by the main gates."

I nodded. "She's right. Can you go now?"

His turn to nod. "Where'm I going?"

We told him everything we knew, including that we felt certain it was Medraut who'd killed Llacheu.

When we'd finished, he rubbed his hand across his eyes. "You have it right there. That bastard wants to catch our king unawares, then he really will be dead."

Was that how it had happened in the legends? Had Medraut surprised Arthur's army and slaughtered them? Was I changing history here? Maybe that was why I'd fallen back in time – for this very moment. Or maybe whatever I did the outcome would be the same and I was pissing in the wind.

Llawfrodedd squared his shoulders. "I'll go now. The sooner the better, as it'll give me a whole night's head start should they notice me gone and come after me. But I doubt they will – I'm unimportant to them." He glanced at Coventina. "Clavinium's not much more than thirty miles south of here, and the road's good. But I won't be able to go flat out in the dark. If I leave now, and only have a half-trained colt, I should be there by morning. I'll find somewhere out of the way to hide myself, and I'll wait for the ships to come up the river."

Oh, how I wished I could go with him. But it felt essential that Medraut shouldn't know we'd warned Arthur what was happening. Two could play at this game, and if my plan worked, it could be Medraut walking into a trap.

"I'll come with you to the wall," I said. "If anyone gets suspicious, I'll make it look like I'm the one they saw. They'll not guess you'll have just gone over."

"Is that a good idea?" Coventina asked, her hand going to her mouth.

"If I can't go myself, then I can at least see Llawfrodedd safely on his way," I retorted. It irked me to be stuck at Din Cadan, forever waiting and doing nothing.

Coventina bit her lip. "You will be careful, won't you?"

I hugged her tight, then wrapped her darkest cloak about my shoulders and drew the hood up. Then Llawfrodedd, already hidden by his own dark cloak, and I slipped out of the door and into the cool night air.

Overhead, stars spangled the blue-black canopy of the sky, but no unfriendly moon shone down on us. Thank goodness. We both knew our way about the fortress too well to make a noise, and we slipped on silent, boot-clad feet between the close-packed houses and barns until we came to the practice grounds. Nothing. No one. But up on the walls there'd be guards posted, and we'd need to avoid them.

We crept closer, keeping to the shadows, and I spotted the silhouettes of guards fifty yards apart along the wall. Night watch was never a good posting, and they'd already be fed up and bored, and possibly a little drunk as Medraut had been breaking out the fortress's ample alcohol supply for all his men. Nothing ever happened in the night, and they'd be at their least attentive. Some of them might even be taking a nap.

Llawfrodedd climbed the wooden steps set into the grassy bank, and I followed him, keeping an eye on the men to either side of us, each a bare twenty-five yards distant. I'd peered over this bit of our fortifications many times. A solid stone wall with a wooden, crenellated palisade on top, on the far side it dropped a good fifteen feet. If Llawfrodedd could hang by his hands he'd make the drop less dangerous, but at the foot, the ground dropped away steeply into a wide ditch. Four concentric ditches and banks surrounded Din Cadan, dug long before the Romans came. They'd be hard work to negotiate on his way down the hill.

Neither of the guards were looking our way. The one on the right was leaning against the palisade as though nodding off, and the one on the left was looking toward the next guard along, to his own left.

"Now," I whispered to Llawfrodedd.

He slipped across the wall-walk like a ghost and shimmied over the wall in a matter of seconds. His hands gripped the wooden crenellation for a moment, before he let go and disappeared from sight. I strained my ears to listen. A thump, but neither lazy guard reacted. Standing at the top of the steps, my eyes level with their feet, I cocked my head and listened harder, but heard nothing else. Hopefully he hadn't broken his leg on landing and would be halfway down the hill by now. Hopefully...

I waited five more minutes, then slid down the steps and crept back across the practice grounds and between the houses, my heart pounding in overtime. I slid inside Coventina's door to be enfolded in her tight embrace.

"Thank the gods you're back," she gasped into my left ear. "I was picturing all manner of awful things happening. Did he get away safely?"

I nodded. She might be relieved, but I doubted very much she could be as relieved as I was to be back safely.

Time to eat that stew.

Chapter Thirty-Seven

THE WAITING AND not knowing felt interminable. And on top of that Coventina and I had to pretend we'd believed Medraut and were mourning our husbands. Not that it was difficult to look strained and sad – I'd have had a much harder job mustering up a smile than I did a scowl.

Every night when we went to bed, both of us hoped that by the morning Arthur would have arrived to defeat Medraut, and all this would be over. But every morning we awoke to no change in our circumstances. For ten long days.

On the morning of the eleventh day, after yet another broken night's sleep, sounds of chaos disturbed me. I sat up, shivering in the early morning chill. A moment later, Coventina opened bleary eyes and peered up at me. "What is it? What's going on?"

"I don't know." I pushed the covers back and scrambled out of bed. "But I'm going to find out." I pulled on my long tunic over my undershirt, slipped my feet into my fur-lined boots and snatched up my cloak.

Coventina struggled out of the other side of the bed, wincing as her damaged nerve endings kicked in with their malicious contribution. "I'm coming with you."

I pursed my lips, itching to find out what was happening but constrained to wait for my friend. "Can you manage?"

For answer, she pulled her own tunic over her head and grabbed her boots. "If you can, I can. It's both our husbands in danger."

I waited, fidgeting with impatience.

She struggled into her boots and stood up, swaying slightly, one hand on the wall for support. "I'm all right." She gritted her teeth as she gathered up her cloak. "Come on."

I pushed open the door into the living quarters of her house. No sign of Keelia, which was odd as she was usually here before we got up, laying the fire and getting the porridge cooking. But the fire lay cold and lifeless, and a smell of stale, damp soot hung in the cold air.

Drawing my cloak tight about me, I pushed the door open a crack, and we peered warily out. The side of the Hall, with its low-hanging thatch, took up one side of the courtyard, with houses and barns crammed cheek-by-jowl around most of the rest to make a rough square. Some of the other women who lived here were peeking out of their homes with equal wariness, as puzzled and curious as we were.

The next door along swung open, and old Cottia emerged, leaning heavily on a stick. She'd been Arthur's nurse when he was a small child. I'd met her on the day I arrived here, when I'd been a confused girl convinced I'd found myself in some weird re-enactment. Lately, she'd shrunk in on herself with old age, like a wilted flower, just the bent and twisted husk of the old Cottia remaining. Thin as a rake, her pouchy skin hung off her bones. But she still possessed all her faculties.

She tottered over to me, a look of smug satisfaction plastered onto a face so wrinkled she'd have made a Shar Pei dog jealous. "My boy be here. I knowed he weren't dead."

"Arthur! And Cei!" Coventina gasped, then clapped her hand over her mouth as though she feared someone would hear.

"Are you sure?" I asked Cottia. "How do you know?"

She peered at me out of her milky eyes. "Milady Gwen, 'tis you. I might be old, but I'se not stupid." She put a gnarled claw on my sleeve. "My granddaughter's husband did come by ten minutes ago to tell me the news. Had a grin across his face a mile wide. He don't hold with no *usurpers*." She shook her wispy white head. "An' I don't, neither."

An impulse to hug her swept over me, but I restrained myself. How many of the warriors still here felt the way her granddaughter's husband did? And how many would stay loyal to Medraut?

"I'm going to look at the Hall and stables," I said to Coventina. "You stay here with Cottia. Two of us will be more noticeable than one. I won't be long."

Before she could protest, I hurried across the cobbles to the entrance. Keeping well out of sight, with my back pressed up against the Hall's side wall, I craned my neck around the corner and peered out.

Down by the stables, men were rushing back and forth in a frenzy of activity carrying armor, weapons and saddlery. No sign of Medraut. Would they stay loyal to him with their true lord back? They weren't the men who'd grown up with Arthur and fought by his side in the battles leading up to Badon. They were young, and they wanted the same booty and plunder and glory their elders had been given. I cherished no illusions. If they thought Medraut likely to provide that, they'd support him. But as so far all he'd given them were promises, maybe their ties of loyalty to him wouldn't be that strong.

Added to this was the fact that young men tend to flock to the banners of other young men and shun those they perceive as their elders. And Medraut was young, whereas Arthur, although only in his early forties, was old in comparison.

Speak of the devil. Medraut stepped through the open Hall doors, fully decked out in his shining, well-oiled chainmail, a fancy plumed helmet on his head with the straps left dangling loose in cocksure confidence. A splendid sight indeed. He halted, hands on hips, and surveyed the chaos of preparation before him. A grim smile curled his fleshy lips.

I pressed myself further back, keeping in the shelter of the Hall's heavy overhang of thatch, lest anyone should turn my way, but determined to keep watching.

Cinbelin swaggered out to stand beside his friend, his helmet swinging by its straps from one hand, and a moment later Bran of Ebrauc joined them. They stood there like three young lions, basking in their youth and strength as they soaked up the pale morning sunlight. But where was Bran's younger brother, Cyngal?

It seemed Medraut had noticed his absence as well. "Where's your brother?" he barked, frowning at his follower. "He should be here with us, preparing for our victory."

Bran scowled, and I strained to hear his muttered words. "He's angry because you told us the King was dead, when he's not. He refuses to take up arms against him. Says he's not fighting the king who saved our city from the Yellow Hairs when he came to the aid of our great-grandfather." The sneer in his voice sounded forced, and he kept his gaze on his booted feet. Embarrassed, maybe? About his brother's refusal to fight, or about his own decision to do so?

Medraut snorted his disgust. "I'll deal with *him* on our return when we've beaten that old has-been. I'll put my uncle's head on a spike by the gates. Your brother'll regret not backing the winning side – maybe I'll put *his* head there as well. And *don't* call my uncle king. He's not any longer. *I* am." He patted the hilt of the sword in his scabbard. "Don't forget. It's me who has the Sword of Destiny on my hip, not him."

Cinbelin laughed, the sound harsh. "Anyone who doesn't fight with us'll feel the sharp edges of our swords when we're victorious and Din Cadan and Dumnonia are yours, Milord King. What punishment do you have in mind for that cowardly dog who calls himself my brother?" He spoke with a relish that made my blood run cold.

Medraut chuckled. A menacing sound that boded ill for Cyngal.

A red-faced warrior burst through the crowd down by the stables, pounding up the steep hill from the gates, and I had to duck back further in case he saw me. "Milord Medraut," he called, gasping for breath. "King Arthur's army have massed in battle formation on the plain a mile to the west, this side of the River Cam."

Without warning, Medraut swung a gloved fist and knocked the man sprawling into the dirt. "How many times do I need to tell you all? He's no longer king. I am."

The man, blood trickling from his nose, scrabbled away crab-like, scuffing up the dirt.

I ignored them. The River *Cam*. Arthur was beside the Cam, waiting for Medraut. *Cam... Camlann... the bank of the River Cam?* Not Camboglanna on Hadrian's Wall, but lurking under my nose here in Somerset, biding its time just outside our home, a bare stone's throw from us and Ynys Witrin – mythical Avalon.

I had no idea if Cam was still the name of the river in my old world, but I did remember the village of Queen Camel being close to South Cadbury. My father had driven through it with my brother Artie and me quarreling in the back seat, and it had stuck in my head because I'd liked the name. This *had* to be Camlann. It could be nothing else. Whatever I did, the chess pieces were slotting into place with alarming regularity, but so far, the queen, hemmed in by the warriors of the enemy, had no power at all to protect the king.

Medraut turned away from the frightened messenger, and his thick upper lip curled in scorn. "My uncle lines his old soldiers up to face my young ones, does he? Fool." He glared around at his friends as if defying them to gainsay him. "But someone must have warned him we were waiting for him. When this is over, I'll get to the bottom of that. Have no fear; whoever did it will pay." He fixed Bran with an accusing glare. "Come on. To horse. We've a battle to win and an ex-king to kill."

He strode off in the direction of the stables, Cinbelin and Bran dragged in his wake by the tide of his going.

I watched them for a moment, my mind churning. What should I do? I couldn't just wait here and do nothing, resigning myself to the role of helpless spectator. I didn't have it in me.

On frightened feet, I scurried back to Coventina and Cottia. The old woman had sunk down onto the rickety stool outside our front door, and her middle-aged, widowed daughter had come out with a horn beaker of something to revive her.

"Arthur's less than a mile away," I said, unable to keep the heady mix of excitement and fear out of my voice. "He's drawn up his army on the plain to the west, as though he's waiting for Medraut to come out. It looks like Medraut's obliging him. The bastard sounds full of confidence that his green, untried warriors can beat Arthur's experienced ones."

Coventina's face brightened. "My Cei'll be there, too."

Cottia handed the empty beaker back to her daughter. "My boys, both o' them." Her faded eyes shone with a reflection of the anticipation I felt.

"How big was the army Arthur took to Armorica?" I asked Coventina. "Do you know?"

She frowned. "More'n a hundred and fifty. Maybe two hundred? P'raps more. Don't forget he had to get them all on Theodoric's ships. I wasn't countin' them out. But he took his best warriors, so even if Medraut has more, which I'd wager he don't, our men're better."

"True," Cottia mumbled, sucking the few teeth she had left. "An experienced warrior'll beat any green boy. Hands down."

I hoped so. I really did. Because if Arthur only had a hundred and fifty men with him, Medraut would definitely have more. Providing the full garrison of Din Cadan turned out on his side, which was debatable given Cyngal's unwillingness to fight. He couldn't be the only warrior not wanting to take up arms against the High King, although he might be the only one brave enough to say so.

"We need to see what's happening," I said. "I'm putting my braccae on and finding a sword and going to help." My own weapons had been left behind at the abbey. They'd been in the storehouse with all my other things, and Medraut, wisely perhaps, had not returned them to me with my clothes. I'd just have to find another. Not that difficult.

Coventina bit her lip. "I wish I knew how to fight."

"That's not your calling," I said. "You should go to the walls once Medraut's left. You'll get a good view."

From her seat, Cottia nodded. "I'll be goin' there m'self if 'tis the last thing I does." She patted her daughter's hand. "My girls'll get me there to cheer on my boys."

"Now, Mother," the daughter said, frowning. "I'll do my best, but I can't promise anythin'. You come inside now, and get some breakfast – there'll not be a battle startin' afore you can eat yer fill." She raised her eyes to mine. "And if you're plannin' on joinin' the fight, you should get some food inside o'you, an' all."

I looked at Coventina. "I couldn't eat a thing."

She nodded. "Me neither. I feel sick."

Not as sick as me. I put my hand protectively on my belly for a moment. No. I couldn't think about this baby now. No more could I think about Amhar and Llacheu, both Medraut's victims already. I had to think only of Arthur and Archfedd and how to save them.

We hurried back inside the house, and I found my boy's clothes and chainmail and put them on in a hurry, buckling my empty sword belt around my waist over my mail shirt. Medraut had given *that* back to me, along with my shield and helmet, laughing as he did so. Clearly, he hadn't thought I'd find the opportunity to use them. How wrong he'd been.

When I was ready, Coventina, who'd been waiting by the cold remains of the fire, pushed a beaker into my hands. "Drink this," she said. "It'll give you strength."

I downed it in one, a streak of fire blazing its way to my stomach. Then I coughed as the afterburn hit. "Good stuff," I choked at her, and we both laughed, albeit a little nervously. Not the time to confide in her about my pregnancy or she'd never let me go.

Outside in the courtyard again, I returned to the entrance and peered out with caution. Medraut had joined his men by the stables and was already mounted up, his muscular bulk an impressive sight on his big warhorse. Even as I watched, he turned the horse downhill, and his young men – our stolen, renegade men – fell in behind him.

As the last rider joined the column heading for the gate, a shadow moved in the dark stable entrance. Morgawse, her hands clasped to her heart. She made a lonely figure, watching her son ride to what I hoped would be his certain death. I couldn't spare the time to think of her.

Medraut was already riding through the gates, his men behind him.

Now that I felt differently about Arthur, it was good to have someone else to aim my fury at. If thoughts could have come true, Medraut would already be lying dead behind his horse, never mind heading out to die on the battlefield. Manipulative bastard. Everything he'd done had been leading to this. Morgana might have had a slightly different objective, but she'd played into Medraut's clever hands with the help she'd given him.

Only she'd lost. While she lay dead, he was still here, like Banquo's ghost at the feast, a constant, unwanted presence.

He'd casually slaughtered Llacheu after the fight between my sons, knowing full well that everyone would think Amhar had murdered his brother. And knowing how it would affect Arthur's relationship with me, he'd stood back and let Arthur assume Amhar's guilt. Probably he'd even suggested to Amhar that his father believed it was him and he should run.

He'd driven a wedge between me and my husband as thick as a redwood tree, and I'd let him. Because of Medraut and how he'd manipulated Amhar, I'd hated Arthur, shunned him, ill-wished him. Maybe that was why he'd gone to Armorica – to put more distance between himself and me. Maybe because of that, I'd made it possible for Medraut to seize power. And on top of everything, I'd run off with Arthur's precious daughter, because that slimeball Medraut wanted her for his wife.

Inside my head a nagging voice kept telling me I should have seen this coming, that I was stupid to have missed his hand in this. Like an idiot, I'd believed Morgawse when she'd told me he couldn't have done it. I hadn't seen she was a mother like me, who couldn't believe a son of hers capable of committing such a callous crime. I'd been so taken up in half believing Amhar had done it, I'd missed that Medraut had been the guilty one.

God, I *was* stupid.

The tail end of Medraut's force – how many of them were there? – disappeared down the track to the gate, the morning sun reflecting off their bright armor. Riding out to the fate of Camlann.

A sword. I had to have a sword.

I ran across the summit of the hill, careless now of anyone seeing me. No one who could do anything to stop me remained.

Morgawse's head turned as I raced past, her mouth hanging open.

The armory stood on its own beside the training ground. I shoved the wooden latch across and wrenched open the door.

Darkness.

Blinking, I stepped inside. A good array of weapons, but all I needed was a sword and dagger and maybe a spear. Easily found. I slipped the sword and dagger into the empty sheaths hanging on my belt, feeling better by the moment. No longer naked and vulnerable.

Without bothering to shut the doors, I raced to the ramparts and galloped up the steps to the wall-walk. No guards remained. Careless of my breath rasping in my chest, I hurtled around the perimeter, booted feet thumping on the wood, toward the now closed gates that overlooked the western plain and the River Cam.

Medraut's army had reached flat ground and was heading west, like a deadly glittering snake, kicking up a cloud of dust as they jog-trotted toward their foe. Shading my eyes, I peered beyond them. Further off, more armor glittered bravely in the sun, and weapons flashed. Warriors, waiting in a line, spread out ready for battle. A banner rippled in the breeze. A black bear reared up against a white background.

"Arthur." His name came out on an exhaled breath, like a prayer.

But what was my plan? Not to stay here, that was for sure.

I almost tumbled down the steps beside the gates and charged up the steep hill toward the Hall. Morgawse had moved up from the stables to stand by the doors, her face white and drawn. She grabbed my arm and yanked me to a halt. "What're you doing?"

I shook her off. "Stopping your bloody son's rebellion," I snarled back at her.

She fell back a step as though I'd hit her. I left her and ran inside. Empty, but for young Cyngal sitting at one of the tables, head down and nursing a goblet in his clasped hands.

I skidded to a halt in front of him. "Cyngal. Your brother's ridden out in rebellion against the High King. Are you going to sit here drinking and let him commit treason? Your true King has his men lined up out there on the plain, and he needs our help. Will you join with me?"

Cyngal raised his head. A handsome boy, he had a head of shaggy brown hair the long hot summer had streaked with highlights and a wispy beard. "What makes you think I'm on his side? Just because I won't take up arms against Arthur, doesn't mean I want to join him. Why should I take *any* side in this?"

I glared at him. "Because my husband *would*. He's always ready to support any British king against our enemies and right now *he* needs *your* support. He came to Ebrauc's aid fourteen years ago, the moment he was asked. He fought by the side of your father, Dyfnwal. It was *Arthur's* army that saved Ebrauc from the Saxons. Saved the lives of you, your brother and all your family. Will you stand by and let Medraut steal my husband's kingdom?"

Cyngal sighed and rubbed eyes bloodshot from too many nights spent drinking our Falernian with his so-called friends.

"Medraut will kill me if I join you. And what difference will one man make? Or one woman."

I banged my fist on the table in front of him. "He's going to kill you anyway for not supporting him, if you sit back and let him win and he rides back in here as the lawful king. He's a man with no moral conscience, and he'll swat you like a fly for not supporting him. And by doing nothing, you're helping him. You're not the only one who's refused to fight. There are other warriors here who haven't ridden out with Medraut this morning. Help me gather them, and we'll join Arthur. You owe it to him. You wouldn't even be alive if he hadn't come to Ebrauc's aid. You think the Saxons would have let any member of Coel's royal family live if they'd captured Ebrauc? They'd have raped your mother over and over and skewered you and your brother on spears for fun."

Cyngal looked up at me out of his hungover, red-rimmed hazel eyes. "You really believe we can make a difference, don't you?"

"Yes," I said. "I do. Are you with me? Are you joining the winning side?"

I sensed the balance shift. I had him. He was mine.

His eyes brightened, his spine visibly straightened, and he pushed back the bench seat with a clatter and rose to his feet. "Very well. We'll do it. If I'm going to die, then I'll die on the right side. Let's assemble what men we can. I've a mind to see Medraut brought to his knees. I don't much like him, even though Bran seems to think he shits solid gold. Come on. We can't ride into this only half-prepared."

I held up my hand and he smacked his into it. A Dark Age high five. "Let's go."

Chapter Thirty-Eight

T HE THIRTY MEN we collected didn't look like much. Most of them were older and semi-retired from fighting due to injury: a bunch of graybeards that included Goff the smith, and a few boys scarcely old enough to shave, led by a woman. But thirty was better than nothing. And they'd come out willingly and bravely to my call, hauling rusty, long-unused mail shirts over their heads and buckling on swords found in dusty corners. A few younger men too, as disgruntled with Medraut as Cyngal.

Watched by the silent women of the fortress who'd come crowding to their doors with children clutched to their sides and babies at their breasts, we mounted up outside the stables, shouldering our spears. Coventina hobbled down to see us off, and stood nervously clutching her cloak to her, running her eyes over our motley ranks.

"Take care," she said, putting one hand on my leather-clad knee. "This isn't just *observing* you're planning to do, so you can put it in that book of yours. This is a real battle you're getting yourself into. Against men who probably won't even notice you're a woman. And even if they do, they won't care."

I covered her hand with my gloved one. "I do know that. But I can't just sit up here and watch it happen. Not when I have men who need leading." I bent so only she could hear. "I feel responsible. I saw this coming a long time ago, and yet I let it happen. I owe it to Arthur to try to help him and his men." We locked eyes.

"But if I don't come back, tell my daughter I love her."

Straightening up, I swallowed the lump that had formed in my throat on my last words. I refused to consider that I might be killed, or I'd be running back into Coventina's house and hiding under the bed. I was a warrior queen, and the time to prove it had come. This was what Merlin had brought me here to do, surely.

I turned Enfys away from my friend and kicked her forward to the front of my men. Truly *my* men this time. I didn't look back at Coventina and the other women. I couldn't. With my heart beating hard in my throat and threatening to leap out at any moment, I led my little troop down the worn track to the gates.

A single warrior remained there on duty – one-armed Curig who couldn't fight. The rest were with me. He'd offered to come, but he was right-handed, and it was that arm he'd lost.

"You serve me better here," I'd said. "Should Medraut attempt to retreat, you can lock the gates against him."

Standing on the tower above the gates, he saluted as we approached. A proud old soldier, with a heart as brave as a lion.

Two women swung the gates open, and we clattered through.

"Kill the little shit," Curig shouted down. "I want to see his head up here on a spike and his body left out for foxes to eat."

I twisted in my saddle to give him a thumbs up.

The steepness of the road forced us to keep our horses to a walk as we descended toward the plain, but as soon as the last horse reached the hill's foot, I let Enfys, buzzing with energy as if she knew what lay ahead, break into a canter.

On the plain, Medraut's army had come to a halt, weapons and armor glittering in the autumn sunlight. His warriors' heads turned to stare as I swung my small force sharply south away from them, our galloping hooves eating up the hard ground.

Arthur had chosen his battlefield well and stationed his army where a ridge rose above lower lying land that in winter was good for nothing. We'd had a long dry summer and autumn, and hungry cattle were grazing in the hollow, where the grass grew lusher than elsewhere. At the sight of our horses approaching, they raised their heads for a moment before returning to their meal. Not much would budge them from their food.

Medraut couldn't have missed us, but we were moving fast and out of bowshot. And what could he have done, other than divide his troops and send men after us? Too late now, anyway. We were almost at Arthur's lines, their spear tips turned to point at us.

I hauled on my reins to slow Enfys to a trot, and held up my hand in a gesture of peace. Couldn't they see who we were? But then, the men riding out to meet them under Medraut's command were their fellows as well.

"Arthur!" I shouted, and yanked off my helmet to let the men see my face. "I bring reinforcements!"

From his position in the frontline of his forces alongside Theodoric, he turned his head to stare. Across the lines of horsemen, our eyes met, and his widened in what had to be shock.

"We're here to join you," I shouted, as acknowledgment rumbled through the waiting ranks of his warriors.

He spun Taran and cantered along the front line, yanking her to a halt beside me.

Our eyes locked. He'd lost the drawn look of exhaustion he'd had when I'd last seen him. His dark eyes blazed with a heady mix of battle lust, pure excitement, and long-brewed anger. Perhaps his time in Armorica had helped heal his damaged soul.

"Gwen."

Just one word, but laden with meaning. I reached out a hand to touch his mail-clad arm, emotion almost choking me. "I couldn't stand by and see you die." I gestured at the men gathered behind me. "These men remain loyal to you and refused to fight on Medraut's side. I know we're not many, but we make up for it with our loyal hearts."

A hint of a smile flitted across his handsome, bearded face. "Thank you. And thank you for sending Llawfrodedd. He told me everything." He waved his hand at his warriors. "We found horses for Theodoric and some of his sailors. The rest are on the south coast, awaiting new orders." He leaned in close. "If we lose, then you're to gallop south with whoever survives, and take ship to my cousin Budic in Armorica. He will take you in. Do you understand? Take Archfedd with you. And Coventina and Reaghan if you can."

I nodded, buoyed up by seeing him again, drinking in everything about him. "But you won't lose. I know you won't. Medraut's the one who'll die today. Believe me." I spoke with confidence, but deep in my heart I couldn't be sure of my scanty knowledge. Might I have changed history so much that this wouldn't be the Camlann I'd been fearing for so long? Might it have a totally different outcome? Not necessarily better.

Arthur's eyes glittered with pent up menace. "I made a grave mistake in elevating that young man so high. No, don't tell me. I already know. Llawfrodedd held nothing back." He pulled off his glove and took my hand in his, fixing me with a gaze penetrating enough to see past the skin and flesh and bone, deep into my soul. "We both know what he did, how he manipulated our son, and through him, us." He shook his head. "I was a fool. I let him come between us. He got what he and Morgana wanted and drove us apart. Can you ever forgive me, Gwen?"

For a moment I didn't know what to say. Arthur had killed my son. No matter how he'd been manipulated into doing so, he'd still chosen to do it, even if it was through a misguided sense of upholding the law. Not my law, his. But this was Camlann, and he might be riding out to die, and he was my husband, and whatever he'd done, I did still love him so much it hurt.

The thought that I might never see him alive again exploded in my heart.

"I never stopped loving you," I said, my grip on his hand tightening. "For a long time, I thought I had. I thought my love for you had turned to hate because of what you did. It might have done for a while. Forgiving you will be difficult, but I can't hate you anymore." I looked into his dark eyes, at the flecks of gold that caught the light, the eyes of the young man I'd first fallen in love with so long ago, and given up everything for. "Why do you think I'm here? Don't you *know* how much I love you? More than life itself. So much it hurts, like a constant ache inside my heart."

He didn't smile, but his eyes burned into mine like the hot embers in a fire. He leaned forward in his saddle and put one hand around my waist to pull me closer. His touch branded my skin even through the chainmail. For a moment, I hesitated. Always within me there'd be Amhar, deep down in my heart, but I couldn't fight the way I felt about his father.

I could resist no longer. The longing for what I'd feared never to feel again took me in its grasp. His lips met mine, warm and alive and demanding. My lips parted, and the kiss deepened. My body melted into his as his hand pulled me closer, and that old familiar tingling ran through me. The ache in my heart dissolved as a yearning I'd not felt for months took hold of me.

He released me, and I straightened in my saddle, more than a little breathless and flustered that he could still do this to me when I'd thought until a short time ago that I hated him and never wanted him to touch me again. Love and hate are two strange, interchangeable things, capable of living side-by-side in our hearts.

I stared into his eyes. Should I tell him? Now? Would it give him something to live for if he thought he might be getting another son?

"I love you, Gwen," he said, gathering Taran's reins.

My hand shot out. "Wait."

He held her in tight check, fidgeting under his grip.

"I'm with child," I said, before I could think better of it. "That day on the headland at Din Tagel three months ago." I bit my lip. "Don't die. Please don't die. I need you." I put one hand on my belly. "Your unborn son needs you."

His eyes widened for a moment before a delighted smile lit his face. "After the battle," he said, and spun Taran away from Enfys. Without a backward glance, he spurred her back to the center of the frontline to rejoin Theodoric.

I stared after him, for a moment only aware of my heart pounding to the rhythm of his horse's hooves. A rising wind soughed in the trees along the edge of the River Cam, and in their topmost branches a colony of rooks cawed, raucous and angry. I put my helmet back on and did up the strap one-handed.

"Gwen." A voice I knew. "Good to have you back with us." Cei brought his horse up beside mine.

I turned to greet him. The same as ever: big, good-natured, kind, but not smiling.

He held out his hand and I took it, his huge paw enveloping my much smaller one. "And you've brought warriors to help us, too," Cei said. "Our warrior queen."

He stood in his stirrups to address my men. "This way. Line up here. Spears at the ready." Then he turned to me. "I can't have you in the front line, even if you want to be. You'll have to be at the back. No arguments." Lucky he didn't know I was pregnant, then.

I knew better than to cavil, and anyway, no time remained to object. I spun Enfys in a creditable pirouette on her haunches and took her to the back of the rows of warriors, acutely aware of my heart's galloping beat and the breathlessness tightening my chest. Look well if I had a heart attack and died before the battle even began.

Oh God, the battle. Camlann. I was lining up to fight at *Camlann*. For a moment, I was back in Eigr's stuffy, dark hut, staring into her scrying glass at a battlefield littered with broken banners and the humps of dead horses. The little river ran red with blood, and scarlet even stained the clouds.

I shook the unwelcome vision from my head before it could show me Arthur... dying.

Overhead, the bright autumn sun climbed higher in a sky devoid of red but dotted with incongruous, picture-book-perfect white clouds. From their roost in the riverbank trees, the colony of rooks set up a cacophony of screeching cries, and high above us, half a dozen buzzards soared on thermals, no doubt attracted by the glitter of our armor and the knowledge that where there were soldiers, there'd soon be carrion for them to feed on.

Enfys swished her tail and tossed her head at the swarming flies as the day warmed up. Standing in my stirrups, I peered between the ranks of warriors. Medraut had drawn up his army on the flat land between us and the high hill of Din Cadan. It spread out in a long line facing us, spears pointing skyward in a forest of death. Briton facing Briton, just as the legends said.

As far as I could tell, he had more men than we did, although Arthur had augmented the expeditionary force he'd taken to Armorica with Theodoric's sailors and now added the ones I'd brought. Ranged on Medraut's side were mostly the easily swayed, green young men he'd spent all this summer wining, dining and winning to his cause with promises of war and booty to be seized. But our men were the more experienced, and surely that must more than make up for the vigor of youth in the opposing force. I hoped...

The men in Arthur's ranks had fought at Badon, and before that, against the Picts in the far north and in the Saxon Wars that had led to the accomplishment of the peace of Badon. Medraut, like most of his followers, had been too young to take part. Training at home, or a few excursions against Irish raiders, ought to be no match for experience in battle. Only there were more of them than there were of us... and they were younger...

I could just make out Arthur at the front, beside the huge shape of Theodoric, more at home on the deck of a ship and too big for the horse they'd found him. How must *he* feel to be facing his own son in battle? His loyalty to Arthur must run strong, or he wouldn't be here at all. The ties of friendship and a brother-hood forged in battle.

Perhaps he thought Arthur's aim was to capture Medraut and chastise him. But if Amhar's supposed crime had merited death, then, even more so, Medraut's did as well. Not only was he the true murderer of Llacheu, but he'd committed treason against not just his own king, but the High King of Britain.

I wouldn't have liked to have been in his boots.

What was I thinking? That cocksure young man would have no doubts in his head that he'd emerge from this the winner, or he wouldn't have led his men out to meet Arthur. He'd be hightailing it in the opposite direction with a few stalwarts and leaving the rest to face the consequences of their actions. But he wasn't. He was here.

The two armies could only have been three hundred yards apart, at most. Nowhere near close enough to see the whites of each other's eyes, but close.

Now, as I strained to see between the ranks of silent warriors, Arthur urged his horse forward maybe twenty yards. Close enough for him to shout to our opponents, but out of range of any clever dick amongst Medraut's ranks who might think to take him out beforehand with a well-aimed arrow. Any bowman firing over that distance couldn't be sure what he'd hit, if anything.

"Lay down your arms!" Arthur's voice echoed across the plain, deep and commanding. "Lay down your arms, and submit to the judgement of your High King. Your *appointed* High King."

Medraut stood at the front of his men, the solid shape of Cinbelin beside him. As I watched, he too urged his horse forward, but not so far as Arthur had done, perhaps afraid one of our archers might be a better shot than his. The sort of trick he'd play, and one I'd not shy away from myself. How easily Camlann could be averted, and the legend changed by a sniper with a rifle. If only.

Clearly both leaders had the measure of each other.

"Walk away, old man," Medraut bellowed back. "While you're still alive. Your time is done, and Din Cadan and Dumnonia belong to me, now." He paused, probably for breath. "You can keep your Ring Maiden. What would I need her for, when I have the Sword of Destiny?"

With an overly theatrical flourish, he whipped out the sword Arthur had long ago pulled from the stone in the forum at

Viroconium and brandished it above his head. Probably it had played a big part in winning the young warriors over to his side. Arthur's men had always been a superstitious lot, and the young were as bad, or worse, than the older ones. Medraut was more than clever enough to have used this sword to his advantage.

Medraut's warriors set up a rousing cheer, and a rumble of disquiet rustled through the ranks of Arthur's army. They must all have known by now that Medraut had the sword, but seeing it probably hammered it home. Most of them were of an age to have been present when their king drew it from the stone.

Arthur wisely didn't let them ruminate on that for long. With the air of a conjuror pulling a rabbit out of his hat, he drew Excalibur, an altogether more splendid weapon, from its sheath and raised it solemnly above his own head.

The damascene blade glimmered in the sunlight, flashing and reflecting the light in arcs that shot across the battlefield. As if by magic, the cheers of Medraut's men died to nothing, as the sword drew every gaze.

"What is that plain warrior's weapon when compared with Excalibur, the sword of the Emperor, Macsen Wledig?" Arthur shouted into the silence. "A sword that lay waiting, hidden where none could find it, for the chosen heir to take it up. I put aside the sword you bear, because its time and usefulness was over. *This* is the sword of kingship. The sword that makes me High King and will defeat you today."

Movement whispered between Medraut's men, who'd no doubt been swayed by Arthur's words. Every man here, on both sides, had seen Excalibur on Arthur's hip enough times, and they all knew the story of how he'd come by it, augmented a little in each telling, often by me. Not for nothing did I know the stories of the Lady of the Lake, and I'd seen no reason not to repeat them. They'd not been disbelieved. Now everyone believed a mysterious arm had risen from the waters of the lake and handed Arthur the sword he'd had to dive for. I had past experience at recreating legends.

"And I already *have* the Ring Maiden," Arthur shouted, after a pause to let his words sink in. "She's here, with me, and she has the ring." He threw a glance over his shoulder at his warriors, a complicit grin on his face, then turned to face Medraut again. "Your last chance to surrender, nephew. The last chance your men will have to live. What do you say?"

Silence fell. Might Medraut be considering surrender? Might he turn tail and run? The better choice. No chance. If he did, he'd never command the respect of any man again, and this was a proud young man we were facing, one who wouldn't want to lose face and who thought he had a better than good chance of winning. No, a man who believed he was facing men who were past it and that he *would* win.

"Fucking little bastard," one of the warriors nearest to me muttered to his neighbor.

The neighbor nodded. "I'd like to nail his balls to the door of the Great Hall and stick his head on a spike by the gates."

"And chuck the rest of him in for the pigs to eat."

They shifted their grips on their throwing spears and exchanged macabre grins.

"Just let me at him," the first one said. "I'll show him who's old."

Medraut swung his horse around and urged it back to the ranks, where he spun it again to face us. Still with his sword in his hand, he stood in his stirrups. His voice carried across the battlefield. "Sound the charge!"

Battle horns rang out from within his ranks, long and strident.

Arthur's shout rose above the distant braying. "Sound our horns. Ready to charge."

I tightened my grip on Enfys's reins, knowing she'd try to join in. In front of me, the horses' backs lowered as the powerhouses of their quarters bunched beneath them.

"For Dumnonia!" the cry rang out.

Like coiled springs released, they leapt forward from standstill into gallop. I fought for control, spinning Enfys in a circle while trying to keep my eyes on the backs of the charging warriors.

Spears lanced through the air. Dull thuds sounded as they sank into wooden shields, the metal tips bending as they did so, forcing men to throw down their suddenly unwieldy only protection. A hundred and fifty yards from where I struggled with Enfys, the two armies came together with a crash that rose to the sky in a cacophony of raucous, tearing sound.

Chaos.

A battle is never ordered no matter how the two sides start. Wood splintered, swords rang, hooves trampled in the dirt, horses squealed. The dust of a long hot summer rose in a cloud about the fighting men. Choking, it stuck to sweaty bodies, got up noses and into eyes. Men fell underfoot and were trampled. Swords slashed and blood spurted. The buzzards swooped lower, the smell of blood luring them ever closer.

Impossible to keep track of our men. Impossible to keep Arthur in my sights.

Any man fighting for his life is an ugly thing. There's nothing noble about the hacking of swords, the spouting blood, the spraying of brains, the cries of the wounded and dying. Still less when the men fighting are old friends: fathers against sons and nephews; sons against fathers and uncles.

Arthur had trained most of the men now fighting against him. He'd sparred with them on the practice grounds, laughed with them, congratulated them on learning a new tactic. They were *all* his men and yet Medraut had turned them with easy offers of booty and glory. How fickle is a man, how treacherous and greedy, how out only for his own advancement.

Camlann, being fought on the plain below Din Cadan on the edge of the tiny River Cam, where one day the quiet village of Queen Camel would lie, was a battle that should never have been fought. A battle I'd known was coming but hadn't been able to avert.

Men on both sides fell dying to the blood-soaked ground. Horses, impaled on the throwing spears, collapsed into the churned-up dust in the charnel house of battle. Their riders, if they were lucky, struggled up to fight on foot, dark with blood spatter, caked with dirt.

But where was Arthur?

Still fighting to control Enfys, who had a death wish, I scanned the battle in desperation, snippets of it ingraining themselves onto my retinas. A single riderless horse, its chestnut shoulder soaked with blood, cantered out of the mêlée, heading home toward Din Cadan. A man on foot staggered backward with a spear stuck through his belly from front to back. A sword swipe sent a head spinning through the air. Blood fountained like a geyser all over the rider who'd struck the blow, darkening his horse's coat. The rooks rose screeching from their treetops then settled again, beady eyes fixed on the churning mass of men. And above the battlefield, the hungry buzzards circled ever lower, patient and attentive.

I had to help. The conviction that all this was my fault and I owed it to Arthur washed over me. I couldn't watch while my loved ones died. This was Camlann where my husband was destined to be mortally wounded. Perhaps it was up to me to save him. Madness coursed through me, the same madness of battle that men must feel, with no care or thought for my own safety.

I took my reins in one hand and drew my sword, a weapon heavier to hold than the one I was used to. I was a warrior queen. I could do this.

Gripping the sword until my knuckles whitened, I turned Enfys toward the fray and gave my horse her head.

Chapter Thirty-Nine

"GET OUT!" CEI bellowed, wild with a mix of anger and battle lust. "You're a danger to others. Get back!"

He'd appeared out of the seething mass of fighting men as if from nowhere, his face contorted with rage, sword raised ready to swing, and eyes wide with shock as he saw my face.

"I have to help," I shouted back above the din of battle. From behind, a young warrior lunged for Cei, and, instinct kicking in, I slashed at the warrior's sword arm. My blade cut into flesh, grating on bone. Blood spurted.

Cei twisted in his saddle, his own sword slicing through the air. The young man's weapon dropped from his inert right hand as his severed head went flying. For a few long seconds, his body remained upright, before it toppled from the saddle to land on the ground with a thud.

All around me, men fought up close and hand-to-hand, yet for that moment, I was isolated in a cocooning bubble as though none of them could see me. I was on the outside looking in, on the edge of the battle yet not a part of it. Excluded.

Ignoring Cei, who was already exchanging hammer blows with another young warrior, I searched the seething mass of men for Arthur. He'd been so easy to spot when he'd had Llamrei with her gleaming white coat, but Taran was different. Every man rode a bay it seemed, and all of them were sprayed with blood.

Another warrior went for me. His shield hand gripping his

reins, he barged his horse toward Enfys. Mad eyes stood out from his head, wild with bloodlust. Lumps of gray matter and blood splattered his youthful face.

I stared, the brief second of warning stretching out like a piece of elastic.

Was this a boy I'd seen grow to manhood at Din Cadan? A boy whose *mother* I might know?

In slow motion, he swung his sword, and I raised my shield to block the blow. The impact shivered up my arm to jar my shoulder. Time sped up and he struck again. This time my sword met his. I didn't have his strength, but I had all the skills I needed.

Our swords clashed again and then again. Every blow jarred my joints in wrist, elbow and shoulder. As if from far away, I viewed the fight dispassionately. How long could I keep this up before he killed me? The mêlée receded into a noisy blur. Only this warrior and I existed, exchanging blow after blow, each of us intent on killing the other.

The muscles in my out-of-practice sword arm ached. This strange sword was too heavy for me. Any minute now he'd get the better of me and I'd be dead. Would I care? Sweat ran freely down my back and stood out on my forehead, trickling into my eyes and mouth, salty on my tongue. My shield shivered from another blow. My opponent had youth and strength on his side, and I was a mere woman, but I'd be dying as a warrior queen. How odd that I didn't care, how odd that my soul felt calm.

Without warning, the young warrior's chest blossomed into an exotic red flower, the shaft of its stamen thrusting from between his ribs. His eyes flew wide in shock. His sword arm fell, and his mouth hung open as though his jaw had dislocated. Cei released his hold on the spear he'd run him through with, and the young man tumbled sideways from his horse.

Eyes rolling wildly, the horse kicked out as the dead man's foot twisted and snagged in his stirrup, catching the young warrior in the head and sending his helmet flying. Terrified by the unexpected heavy weight dangling from its saddle, the horse bolted away from the mass of fighting men, the body bouncing across the uneven ground behind it.

I dragged my eyes away from the sight and back to Cei, as purpose rose its head again. "Where's that *shit* Medraut? I've a score to settle with him."

As if for answer, from out of the crush a rider emerged, heading toward Din Cadan. The plume on his helmet blew out behind him; I'd have known that helmet anywhere. Alongside him galloped two other warriors. Fleeing the battle like the cowards they were. My heart leapt. Arthur must be winning.

To my left, the battle eddied away from me, but I had no eyes for it.

Only a dozen or so strides behind the fleeing riders, a lone horseman followed. He crouched over his own mount's neck, a black bear rampant across his white shield and Excalibur gripped in his right hand. Without a glance to either side to see whether he had backup, he charged after Medraut. His voice rose above the sounds of battle. "Come back here, you coward!"

Medraut didn't slow, but one of his followers, short and sturdy Cinbelin, hauled his horse into a handbrake turn, raising a spear he must have snatched from somewhere. He didn't throw it, but lowered it like the lance it wasn't and kicked his horse into a gallop heading straight for Arthur.

The momentum of Arthur's gallop carried him headlong into the unavoidable impact. They hit one another with a resounding crash, Cinbelin's spear splintering Arthur's shield.

On the edge of the battle, heads turned.

"Do something!" I screamed at Cei.

Arthur reeled in the saddle from the blow but didn't fall. Half of his shield fell away in shattered fragments. His sword arm swung Excalibur in a deadly arc. Cinbelin, despite his sturdy, muscular build and his youth, was no match for the man who'd bested Melwas and Cadwy in hand-to-hand combat.

Ahead, Medraut and his companion wrenched their horses to a halt to stare back at Arthur and Cinbelin. For a moment that seemed to stretch out forever, they didn't move. Then Medraut's legs swung out. His heels thumped into his horse's sides. I had no need of the Sight to work out *his* thoughts. He'd seen a way to turn the tide of battle.

"No!" I shouted.

Cei's horse leapt forward. Enfys went with her. I drummed my heels against her flanks as her hooves ate up the open ground between me and Arthur.

"Stay back!" Cei shouted at me. "Don't get in the way."

Ahead of us, so far away and out of reach, Excalibur sliced the air and Cinbelin's head shot back as blood fountained from his throat. His horse took off with him still on board, held firm by the horns of his saddle, his body jerking back and forth with every stride and his almost-severed head lolling like a broken puppet's, blood spraying everywhere.

A horse breasted mine and the rider reached out and grabbed my reins beside the bit, yanking Enfys to the right. I swung my sword and the rider ducked.

"It's me, milady," Llawfrodedd shouted. "I've got orders to keep you safe."

"Let go!" I screamed at him, as he dragged Enfys to the right, away from where Arthur had already turned to face Medraut's charge. "I have to help Arthur."

His eyes met mine. "He told me to keep you safe."

"Let me go!" Furious, I tugged at my reins but to no avail. Llawfrodedd had them tight and was slowing both horses down.

Arthur. Medraut. My head turned sharply to look where I couldn't go.

Arthur had thrown aside the remnants of his broken shield. Excalibur glittered in the autumn air, pale sunlight shimmering across the bloodied blade.

Medraut was galloping toward him, unholy glee lighting up his hated face. Had he thought the battle over and done with and his men defeated? He must see this as a God-given opportunity to reverse his defeat. His legs hammered his horse's sides.

Arthur urged Taran toward his nemesis. Cei wasn't far behind.

As Medraut passed a fallen horse, his right hand reached out and grabbed the skyward-pointing shaft of a spear, just as he'd been taught in our practice ground, preparing for this day. He jerked it free and swung it up, the point leveling at Arthur all in one swift movement.

They were so close, I had only a moment to see what he intended.

Medraut wasn't aiming the spear at Arthur.

It took Taran full in the chest, driven deep into her heart by the momentum of both horses' speed. Arthur's sword arm swung, Excalibur flashed, but as he struck what should have been a killing blow at the now weaponless Medraut, Taran crumpled under him. Her legs buckled as her heart stopped, and her head went down. Arthur vanished as she crashed head-over-heels and skidded along the bone-hard ground.

Paralyzed with shock, all I could do was stare in horror.

Medraut, who'd badly overshot his foe, was turning his horse to ride back to the hump of Taran's body.

Get up, Arthur. Get up and fight him.

I found my voice. "Let me go!"

Llawfrodedd, too, had been paralyzed by what he'd just seen. His hand slipped off my reins.

Nothing moved by Taran's body.

Medraut's other companion, who must be Bran, thundered past Taran and Medraut to meet Cei's headlong charge.

Medraut hauled his horse to a skidding halt close to Taran and flung himself off, the Sword of Destiny flashing in his hands.

Where was Arthur? My heart pounded painfully in my chest as I gathered my reins and turned Enfys's head toward them. Had the fall killed him?

I threw a desperate glance at Llawfrodedd. "We have to help him!"

Llawfrodedd's honest eyes regarded me in anguish. "He said I was to keep you safe…"

"I don't care," I gasped. My eyes fixed on the spear attached to his saddle. "He didn't know *this* would happen. Give me that spear."

Something moved on the far side of Taran. A sword flashed.

"I'm your Queen. I order you to give it to me now!" I bellowed.

Out of the corner of my eye, I saw Medraut swing his sword. Desperation flooded through me ripping a gaping hole in my stomach.

Llawfrodedd unhooked his spear.

Don't let me be too late.

I snatched the spear out of his hand and dug my heels into Enfys's sides. She needed no second bidding but leapt into a gallop. Without hesitation, I levelled the spear just as Medraut and Cinbelin had. Like them, I'd practiced this enough with the targets on Din Cadan's training ground.

Ahead of me, swords flashed. To my right, Cei fought Bran of Ebrauc. I fixed my gaze on Medraut's figure.

Taran had fallen forward on top of Arthur, pinning him to the ground, yet somehow, he was managing to fight off Medraut. Light reflected off Excalibur's blade as Arthur fought to keep Medraut at bay and prevent the killing blow he must so much want to make.

From the battleground, riders were heading our way, their hooves drumming on the hard ground.

I didn't look but kept my eyes on Medraut. Aiming.

Arthur's sword arm came up to parry blow after blow. Sparks flew, Excalibur against the sword in the stone. I hammered my heels against Enfys's side. Were the other riders our men or Medraut's? I had no idea. I didn't care.

The riders swallowed up Cei and Bran.

Time stood still. Enfys's hooves drummed the ground.

The tip of my spear wavered. I had to fight to hold it steady.

Medraut was still frantically trying to disarm Arthur and

strike the killing blow. Despite being pinned down, Arthur fought back with gusto. Excalibur rang against its predecessor.

Medraut had his back to me. He didn't see or hear me coming.

My spear took him in the middle of his back, the momentum wrenching it from my grip and carrying me past Taran's inert body. With both hands back on my reins, I hauled with all my strength.

Enfys skidded to a halt. I pulled her round.

Somehow, without me noticing, the whole battle seemed to have shifted to center on the fallen king. The riders had already dismounted and surrounded Taran's body. Were they Medraut's men? I drew my sword. I'd kill every one of them for Arthur if I had to.

No one was fighting.

Weapons hung loose and forgotten in the hands of the men surrounding Arthur. The sound of their labored breathing filled the air as a deathly quiet settled over the battlefield.

The autumn sun, past its zenith now and cooling as the clouds in the west thickened, hung smiling over the battlefield of Camlann in defiance of the carnage. The humps of dead or dying horses lay scattered like small islands in the trampled, blood-soaked grass. Men lay spreadeagled between them, moaning softly or silent and distorted in death. The patient buzzards dropped from the sky to perch on horses' flanks and tear and rip, without discrimination, at any flesh, be it living or dead.

Amongst the dead and dying, exhausted men stumbled. Only they didn't look like men. They wore armor and carried swords, but the blood and brains that soaked them robbed them of any humanity. And there were not many of them left.

Who lay here dead? I couldn't tell. Whose faces would I see? None that I could recognize. Sprawled, they were no longer human, but toys discarded on the rubbish heap of death, limbs akimbo, severed, broken, incomplete. If anyone chased away the buzzards with their savage ripping beaks, they swooped down on another corpse too far away to reach.

Medraut's men lay dead or dying, or had fled. The men surrounding Arthur were our men. I kicked Enfys into a trot, and shouldered my way between them.

Sliding to the ground onto unsteady legs, I let her reins drop from my slack fingers.

A huddle of men stood around Arthur's dead horse. I stumbled the last few yards, my stomach twisting in horror.

Arthur lay pinned by his left leg beneath the horse, eyes closed, his face a mask of dirt and blood. Someone had taken off his helmet, but in his right hand he clutched Excalibur still.

Was I too late? Was he dead?

Bedwyr kneeled by his shoulder, his fingers exploring a gaping wound on his king's arm, the chainmail torn and buckled.

"Oh my God." I dropped to my knees as well, ripping off my helmet. "No no no. Arthur. Arthur!" My voice rose in panicked beseeching of who knew what deity or power. I reached for his left hand.

His fingers squeezed mine.

"Arthur!"

His eyes flickered open, unfocused for a moment and bloodshot. I bent over him, cradling his head, my fingers touching his face. "My darling. My love." I looked up at the other men, searching in desperation for faces I knew. Llawfrodedd's appeared.

Bedwyr wrapped a bandage around the wound in Arthur's arm, over the broken mail and his tunic.

"Cei." Arthur's voice came out as a mumble, incoherent and faint.

Cei stumbled forward from amongst the men and fell onto his knees by my side. He'd thrown his helmet off, and his graying red hair stuck wetly to his head.

"Cei." A faint grin spread over Arthur's face.

Cei's bloody hand covered mine and Arthur's. "We beat the bastard. He's dead." His anxious blue eyes met mine. "Gwen killed him."

Arthur gave a tiny nod. "I saw." He coughed and winced, and blood trickled from the corner of his mouth. "The bastard didn't see that one coming." A little chuckle escaped his lips.

Bedwyr slipped his fingers under Arthur's jaw to feel for his pulse. "We need to get you out of here."

Arthur's eyes closed for a moment.

I nodded, frantic with fear. "Yes. Get this horse off him. Now."

For answer, Bedwyr frowned at Taran's inert body, resting on Arthur's leg. "We're going to need some help."

"Is Medraut really dead?" I asked, fearful that he might be lurking, despite the spear right through him, ready to finish Arthur off, just the way villains in horror movies are never truly dead when you think they are. "Did I *really* kill him?"

Bedwyr nodded and jerked his head. "Over there."

I looked where he pointed. A spear stood upright like a flag-pole, protruding from a corpse's chest. Had *I* done that? Had I finally killed him? Should I have done it long ago and avoided this terrible day? If only I had.

"That was you, was it?" Bedwyr said, wrapping another bandage around Arthur's free right leg where a gash had sliced through his leather braccae. "I need to stop this bleeding." He turned to the waiting men. "Get hold of the horse's legs, and pull when I say."

Taran must have died almost instantly. Not much blood marred her shining coat. I wouldn't look at her beautiful, dead face.

The men set their backs to it and heaved on her legs.

Arthur groaned, and I clutched his hand tighter. "It's going to be all right. We have to move your horse." I looked up. "You're hurting him. Be careful. Do you have poppy juice?"

Bedwyr nodded. "I do, but it'll suppress his breathing too much, and I don't want to risk that. He'll have to put up with the pain."

A huge figure pushed its way between the crowding warriors, helmetless and with his blonde hair dark with blood but recognizable anywhere. Theodoric, seemingly unhurt. Had he seen his dead son lying on the plain? He could share our grief. Everyone's sons were dead now. The flower of Arthur's army.

"Here. Let me." He put his brawny shoulder to Taran's body and heaved the weight off Arthur as the other men tugged her clear of him by her legs. Bedwyr put his hands under Arthur's arms and dragged him out from under. Theodoric relaxed his hold and the horse's body slumped back into place.

Arthur's eyes rolled up into his head as he went limp in Bedwyr's arms. A little more blood trickled from the corner of his mouth, and my heart did a frightened flip. Internal injuries?

I looked at his leg. It lay at an awkward angle and blood soaked the leg of his braccae below the knee.

"It's broken," Bedwyr said without even touching the leg. "Badly."

Even I could see that. "What can you do?" I asked, grabbing his arm.

He shook his head. "I'm sorry. Not much when a leg's broken like that." He put his hand on the left side of Arthur's chest, pressing with gentle fingers. "His ribs are broken, too. The horse rolled right over him and crushed him. That blood around his mouth shows me he has blood pressing on his lungs. I've seen an injury like this before. It's not survivable."

"What? You haven't even looked. How can you know?"

He shook his head. "There's nothing I can do for a chest injury like this."

Panic seized me. "But you haven't even bloody well looked at it."

"I don't need to – the blood tells me how he's been injured, and I can feel the ribs moving. And this break on his leg is bleeding. Infection will get in and I'll have no way of stopping it."

An icy hand closed around my heart. "No," I said. "That can't be. He can't *die* from broken ribs and a broken leg. He *can't*."

Bedwyr sucked in his lips. "Many die from lesser injuries than these."

I shook my head. "No. They don't. Not where I come from." I wouldn't let him die. I couldn't. I had to do something. But what? I stared about myself in panic for a few moments, desperately trying to order my thoughts.

There was only one thing left that I could try.

But before I did anything, I had to look at his broken leg. I had to sort it out or he could lose it. I'd seen enough hospital soap operas to know that losing circulation with a bad break like this could cost the patient his leg. Years ago, I'd done an extensive first aid course with the library, but nothing had prepared me for this.

I grabbed Bedwyr's hand. "Cut his braccae open and let me see the leg."

He gave me an odd look.

"Now," I said. "Or I'll do it. And someone get his boot off."

Theodoric eased the boot off. Arthur made no response, but at least his chest still rose and fell, albeit scarcely, as he breathed. I could see why Bedwyr had hesitated with the poppy syrup.

Bedwyr didn't need telling twice. There on the battlefield, with the dead all around us and the buzzards settling on the bodies, he slit Arthur's braccae from hip to heel. He'd been right in his assumption. The ends of bone stuck out of the flesh of Arthur's lower leg, and his thigh was twisted as though that were broken as well. The flesh was already coloring with angry bruising.

Wasn't that a bad thing too? Weren't there a lot of blood vessels in the thigh? I'd worry about that later. I had other more pressing injuries to cope with.

"We have to straighten his leg," I said. "Get the bones back into position."

Bedwyr's eyes widened. "Why? We can't save him."

"Yes, we can," I retorted. "You watch me." I'd seen this done on TV a good few times – why not try it myself? What had I got to lose? Bedwyr said he was going to die anyway. "You hold his hips still."

With Bedwyr steadying his torso, and a circle of anxious faces watching, I took hold of Arthur's foot, and pulled. Not hard enough. I needed more power. I tried again, terrified I was hurting him, but his eyes remained closed. The tip of the bone moved. I pulled harder still. It slid back inside the jaggedly torn flesh. At least his braccae had kept the visible dirt out.

"Splints," I shouted at my audience. "Fetch me some of those spear shafts. I have to make sure the bones don't shift again when we move him." I glared up at Bedwyr. "Send someone for a wagon and a stretcher to lay him on. Something solid that won't move. We should jolt him as little as possible. And blankets. Lots of blankets. And send someone to the Lake Village for a guide who can show us the track through the marshes. I'm taking the wagon to Ynys Witrin."

"To the abbey?" Cei asked. "Do they have a good healer at Ynys Witrin?"

I nodded, determination giving me strength. "An excellent one." *If only.*

Chapter Forty

ON THE PLAIN below Din Cadan, surrounded by a sea of death, I knelt beside my semi-conscious husband and tried to steady my nerves with a few deep breaths.

I'd told him he couldn't die. He couldn't. He had to live.

I raised my eyes and fixed them on Cei, where he sat by Arthur's head. His face had gone as ashy pale as his brother's. With deliberate determination, I blocked out all but his strained face, the crowd around us melting into blurred obscurity.

Cei returned my gaze, his blue eyes brim full of pain.

My fingers touched Arthur's cheek. Clammy with icy perspiration.

Keep breathing. Don't die.

After an eternity, someone brought the spear shafts I'd asked for. My hands shook too much to take them.

Bedwyr saw. Without being asked, he tore Arthur's leather braccae into strips and bound the spears to his mangled leg with steady, practiced fingers.

Embarrassed at my own inadequacy, I clasped my hands together in an effort to still their trembling, my heart thundering in overtime as I prayed we were doing the right thing.

Bedwyr had me put pressure on the gaping wound in Arthur's shin, from which the bones had protruded, while he fixed a dressing over it. By the time we'd done all that, a wagon from the village was trundling across the plain toward us, drawn by two sturdy cobs.

The driver's horses, more used to agricultural tasks, balked at the stink of charnel house, and he couldn't force them any closer than thirty yards. As they ground to a wary halt, eyes rolling and nostrils flared, a woman leapt down from the back and raced across the short grass. Her hair flew loose behind her, and her eyes stretched wide with mad emotion.

"Where is he?" she screamed as she ran. "What have you done with my son?"

Theodoric, solid as an oak, caught Morgawse in his arms and held her tight. She battered at his body like the madwoman she looked, legs and arms flailing, mouth wide in breathless screams of animal fear.

"Where's my boy? Where is he?" Her cries rent the sky and sent the buzzards flapping away in alarm.

I shut out Theodoric's answer. I couldn't speak to her, or I'd have to tell her how glad I was I'd killed him. That I'd done it, and I wished I'd done it sooner. But he didn't matter. Nothing did but Arthur. He was all I had left.

Her screams morphed into a banshee wailing, high and piteous and wild. She'd found his body. Beyond her, other women and girls poured down from the fortress to find their menfolk – alive or dead. Like hopeful ants they streamed down onto the plain alongside our craftsmen, laborers and servants.

Bedwyr caught Llawfrodedd by the arm. "Go and fetch the stretcher. Take someone with you. Quickly."

"I'll go," Cei said, getting to his feet. He had the look of a man who needed something tangible to do.

The stretcher turned out to be a narrow wooden door. Llawfrodedd and Cei set it on the ground beside Arthur, then, with Bedwyr's help, they lifted him onto it as gently as they could, while I kept a close eye on his leg. If the bones moved again, they could cut off the circulation to his foot. His head lolled to one side, a trickle of frightening blood running from the corner of his mouth, and one hand hung off the edge.

I lifted his hand and rested it across his stomach, careful not to touch his chest and broken ribs lest I made them worse. *He couldn't die. He couldn't. But God, he looked dead already.*

Now he was on the stretcher my racing heartrate began to settle and common sense took over. "Tie him down. I don't want him to be able to move and do further damage."

Under my instructions, they tied him across the waist and legs. Then, with gentle care, they carried the pallet to our makeshift ambulance and slid it onto the wagon bed, trying hard not to jolt him.

With reverence, Llawfrodedd placed Excalibur and Arthur's helmet beside him, and we covered him in blankets. My old first aid training came creeping back – I needed to keep him warm in case of shock. Shock after something like this could kill all by itself.

I climbed in beside him and looked at his pale and clammy face and the purple bruises shadowing his eyelids. Bloody bandages bound his leg and arm, and the rise and fall of his chest seemed scarcely perceptible. Could we do this? Could we get him there in time? We had to.

I swallowed down my fear. "Now, let's get him to Ynys Witrin," I said to Bedwyr, with a lot more confidence than I felt.

By Medraut's body, Theodoric had gone down on his knees beside his wailing wife, her keening cry still tearing the air. I'd blocked it out but now the sound came hurtling back into my head, loud and insistent. Someone needed to shut her up.

Cei climbed into the wagon beside me. "I'm coming with you."

I met his eyes. "What about Coventina? She'll be anxious for your safety. And this..." I waved a hand at the chaos of the battlefield.

He shook his head. "Theodoric can take care of this. And someone will tell her I'm alive. Arthur's my brother. I'm coming." He beckoned to a group of still mounted warriors. "This way. We'll need an armed escort."

His gaze returned to me. "I have to be with him… if he…" The words remained unsaid as his voice trailed off.

I stared into his anguished blue eyes. Had it been worth it? With all these men lying dead, had any of it really been worth it? What did we have to show for this? A kingdom riven in two. A generation of warriors dead. A dying king.

"I'll come with you, as well," Llawfrodedd said, and leapt up onto the seat beside the driver.

Bedwyr scrambled into the back of the wagon with me and Cei. "You're not going anywhere without me."

I didn't argue. It felt right to have them all with us. At the end…

The driver clicked to his horses and cracked his whip. They moved off with their precious load. Our warriors fell in as a silent, subdued escort.

The wagon shook too much. Never before had the ground felt more uneven and bumpy. The old wooden door serving as Arthur's stretcher rattled and shook. I had to hold his head still with my hands on either side of his face, my fingers touching the soft hair of his too-long beard and the cold, clammy dampness of his skin. He didn't stir, but remained unconscious and hopefully oblivious to the pain.

Time ticked past. Every minute lasted forever. I could have ridden to the Lake Village in less than two hours, but this wagon moved slower than a snail. If I'd had a watch, I'd have been checking it constantly. I moved my fingers to Arthur's throat to feel for his pulse, terrified of finding it gone. Was it thready and faint, or was I just no good at finding it?

"Why is it taking so long?" I asked Cei, sitting pressed up against Arthur's side to prevent his body moving. "Are we even going the right way?"

He put a reassuring hand on mine. Blood darkened his nails and stained his skin. Not his own blood. "We'll be at the marshes soon, but we can't start into them without a guide. It's too dangerous. I've sent a rider on ahead. We're going to have to wait for him."

That did nothing to make me feel better.

We must have been three miles from the Lake Village when our guide arrived, riding fast with the man Bedwyr had sent to find him.

A guide I knew. Con's long legs dangled down below his horse's girth as he rode bareback on a small, hairy garron, his thatch of hair standing up around his head in spiky curls.

The wagon had ground to a halt, so I got to my feet, shaky with lack of sleep and food, and with the relentless fear that we'd be too late to save Arthur.

"Milady." Con bowed as best he could from his pony's back, his eyes going to the blanket-swathed body in the bed of the wagon. "What is it you wants me to do?"

"Quickly," I said, one hand on the back of the wagon seat for support. "The king is wounded. There's no time to lose. Lead us through the marshes. His life depends on you."

Without a word, he set his jaw in determination and trotted his pony to the front of our horses, waving us to follow. Our heavy wagon trundled behind him down the faint and narrow track into the marshes, our escort bringing up the rear.

If only we wouldn't get stuck in the mud. If only the track remained wide enough for a wagon. These thoughts jumbled around in my head as I sat beside Arthur, my hand holding his lifeless one, my fingers on the thready pulse beneath his jaw.

His leg and chest weren't the only things I had to worry about. Blood had soaked through the bandages Bedwyr had put around his arm and right leg. Blood matted his dark hair from a cut on the side of his face, and his sweaty skin had a more deathly pallor by the minute. I didn't dare move him in case I jolted his leg bones out of place again and cut off his circulation. *Oh God, couldn't this wagon go any faster?*

The silent, oppressive marshes closed in around us. Patches of water shone between stunted trees and bushes, and a heron flew in stately splendor over our heads. Underfoot, the ground grew wetter, the horses' hooves squelching and kicking up clods of mud. But we'd had a dry summer and autumn, and it wasn't as wet as it could have been. I hoped. The wagon rumbled on.

Amongst the trees a thin mist began to form. Shreds of it clung like chiffon in skeletal branches or hugged pools of dark water, shrouding the banks of mysterious reedbeds where marsh birds raised their strange, ghostly voices.

Arthur lay still and unmoving on his makeshift stretcher. Was he losing blood somewhere? Bleeding internally from the crashing fall? I had no way of knowing if he had internal injuries and nothing I could do if he had.

A horse can only walk at three or four miles an hour, and it took all of three hours to reach the island of Ynys Witrin. The last bit through the marshes seemed to take forever, with the mist thickening fast as evening drew on, and Con telling us we couldn't hurry, or we'd risk getting lost and sinking into the soft ground. Once or twice, he stopped us altogether while he sounded out the ground, and I sat tapping my fingers on the boards of the wagon in frustration.

At last, the tinny clanging of a bell rang out ahead. A bell I knew all too well. The bell calling the monks to another of their interminable prayers. My heart rose, and within minutes, the cart was jolting up onto higher ground and out of the scrubby undergrowth, the mist thinning as we left the marshes behind. The reedbeds fell away, and in front of us opened the vista of the stubble fields around the abbey, still dotted with sun-bleached stooks of wheat and barley.

The driver turned his horses toward the abbey buildings.

I leaned forward and caught his arm. "No. Not there. The Tor."

"What?" Bedwyr blurted out. "Why not the abbey? I thought we were going there for their healer?"

Cei stared, and Llawfrodedd twisted in the driving seat to look over his shoulder at me.

"What d'you mean?" Cei asked.

"I mean 'no'," I said. "That's *not* where we're going."

Bedwyr touched my arm. "But I thought you said...?"

"*I* never said the abbey. *You* said that. I didn't say we were going there. You just *assumed* we were."

"But why the Tor?" Bedwyr asked, looking at me as though I were mad. Maybe I was.

The abbey bell stopped ringing.

Cei nodded. "Yes, why the Tor?"

Llawfrodedd remained silent, staring.

The driver peered over his shoulder as well. "Make yer minds up or his lordship'll be dead."

"It's the only way to save him," I said. "Believe me when I tell you, I know what I'm doing." I nodded to the driver. "I'm the Queen, and it's me you'll obey. Take us to the Tor. As far up it as you can get."

The driver turned to face the front and clicked at his horses again. Heads down into their harness, they took the strain and moved off.

Cei and Bedwyr exchanged worried glances. Perhaps they thought I wanted to pray to the old gods. To Gwynn ap Nudd for intervention. Let them think that if they wanted. That might well be all I'd get to do.

The wagon rumbled past the abbey. No monks in the fields to see us pass as they must all be at prayer. Vespers, probably, or even Compline. I knew a lot more than I wanted to about abbey prayers.

The path curved through woodland. As we emerged from its sheltering gloom, I caught my breath.

Two lonely figures stood at the start of the narrow path up the Tor. Archfedd and Reaghan, hand in hand. How had they even known to be here? I'd ask that later. The pawns had been turned into queens and we were assembled to greet our king. No matter that neither were queens now – I felt sure they both would be one day, even if I never saw that day.

The mud-splattered wagon halted beside them.

They darted to the back and Cei jumped out to take his daughter in his arms.

Archfedd pushed past them. "Father?" Her gaze fell on Arthur, and her hand went to her mouth.

"It's not as bad as it looks," I said, ignoring Bedwyr's sharp intake of breath at my judicious lie. "He's *not* going to die. I won't let him." I caught her hand. "Medraut's dead, though. You're safe. *I* killed him, and I very much enjoyed doing it."

Archfedd's eyes widened but she made no comment. We'd gone beyond that between us.

I glanced at Reaghan and Cei, then back to Archfedd. "We have to get Arthur up to the summit of the Tor. You need to come. All of you."

Archfedd's eyes went wide with shock. "Is he…?"

Had she not been listening? "No, of course he's not dead. Pull yourself together. You're stronger than this. Get Reaghan."

"Doan ask me to take my horses up there. Thass as far as I can get ee," the driver said, tugging his sparse gray forelock as his lower lip jutted in rebellion. "My horses ain't fit fer pullin' up a hill like thissun. 'Twud be dang'rous in a wagon."

I hadn't expected anything else. Hence the board.

I slithered down from the wagon and nodded to the men who'd ridden with us. "Dismount. Tie your horses to the wagon. You four men take a corner each. We're going up the hill. The rest of you can come too and take it in turns carrying him. Hurry. We've wasted enough time already. You too, Con."

They did as they were told, and we started up the long drag, the least steep access to a very steep hill. Carrying their precious load as though made of glass, they all too slowly followed the path up toward the distant summit where the circle of standing stones stood stark against the paling evening sky. As we walked, the sinking sun cast our lengthening shadows across the grass in front of us.

I wanted to shout at them to hurry, but they were being careful, and I couldn't sacrifice that for speed however much I longed to. I wanted to check he was still alive, but I couldn't spare the time to stop. He lay still, like the dead, but sweat still beaded his skin. *He must be alive. He must.*

I walked behind the stretcher party, the better to reassure myself they weren't bumping Arthur too much. Archfedd held tight to my hand, and Reaghan walked behind at her father's side in frightened silence.

Like the wagon ride, this walk up the Tor took forever. Impatience racked my soul. *Would we be too late? Would my idea work? Was I as mad as Bedwyr thought?*

At last, though, with the sun nearing the western horizon, we made it to the top. "Put him down inside the stone circle," I said, at my most authoritative, still barely clinging on to reason.

Exchanging nervous glances, the men lowered the wooden stretcher to grass short nibbled by the island sheep, no respecters of holy places, and liberally speckled with their droppings.

"Now what?" Bedwyr asked, the worried frown on his face fixed in position.

Arthur stirred, and his eyes opened. "Bedwyr." Very faint. "Come here."

Bedwyr and I dropped to our knees beside him, the grass prickly and dry. "Yes?" Bedwyr took Arthur's hand.

Arthur shifted his head and his fingertips touched Excalibur where it lay by his side. "Take my sword." A little more blood trickled from his mouth. *Where was he bleeding from?*

Bedwyr's eyes widened at the request. I could have told him what was coming next. The legend yet again. Could I *never* escape it?

"Take my sword," Arthur repeated, his voice gaining strength. "Throw it into the lake. Con will show you where." His eyes flicked to Con, who'd moved back to allow us space.

"Milord," Con muttered, sketching a clumsy bow.

"But it's the sword of Macsen Wledig," Bedwyr protested. "I can't throw it in a lake."

A sad smile flitted over Arthur's face. "I used it badly, Bedwyr, my friend." He paused and drew a painful breath, brow furrowing. "I used it to kill my innocent son." He coughed and more blood bubbled. "I can't blame Medraut for that... he didn't *make* me do it." A tear trickled down his cheek. "But he made me think Amhar killed Llacheu. He knew I'd execute the killer." He paused again, struggling for breath. "But I was wrong."

I looked at Bedwyr. "You have to throw it away. It's fated. You have to do it for Arthur."

Arthur gave a small nod. "It's tainted." He coughed up a little more blood. "I'm dying. Cast it back from whence it came, so no one can touch it again. Ever. It brings ill luck."

I bit my lip. *No, you're not dying. Not if I have my way.*

"You need to go now, Bedwyr," I said, urgency pressing in, and terror that what I so wanted to happen wouldn't. "Go with him, Con. Show him where we found the sword. That's an order." I looked at Cei. "You have to go back down the hill, all of you, and don't return until morning." My gaze moved on to Archfedd. "You too. All of you."

Bedwyr and Cei looked uncertain. Their looks said they thought me mad. Our warriors hung back, eyes worried, hands resting on the pommels of their swords.

Arthur lifted his hand toward Llawfrodedd.

I nodded to him, and the young man stepped forward and went down on his knee before his king.

Arthur licked his lips. "Marry my daughter, Llawfrodedd. Rule with her as king and queen of Dumnonia. Cei will help you." He had to pause to regain his breath. "I always thought he'd make the better king." His sad eyes moved past Llawfrodedd to Archfedd. "My little Chick will make a fine queen."

Llawfrodedd bowed his head. "My Lord."

Archfedd choked back a sob. "Father."

He held out his hand and she came to him, kneeling by the stretcher, her tears falling on his hands.

"Kiss me goodbye," he said, his voice weakening. "You won't see me again alive."

She bent and kissed each cheek. "Goodbye, Father. I love you." With Llawfrodedd's help she struggled to her feet, the tears falling freely. He put his arm around her and held her close. I had no worries about them. She'd wear the crown she'd seen on her head in her grandmother's scrying glass and wear it well. My crown.

"Now go," I said to them all. "Go and don't look back."

They went.

I waited, sitting quietly by Arthur's side. When they'd vanished from sight, I turned back to him. His eyes had closed again. "I won't let you die," I whispered. "I won't. I've brought you here for a reason."

Exhausted from the effort of talking, he didn't respond. For a moment, terror clutched at me, and I had to check his chest still rose and fell. It did.

Was I mad? Here we were, already within the circle of ancient standing stones, and nothing was happening. Had I brought my dying husband all the way up here for nothing? Just to sit here alone with me while death crept up on him with the departure of the day?

In the west, the sun had almost vanished below the horizon, its last shafts of light arcing across the land in piercing spears of brightness as night settled over the marshes. What did I have to do? How could I make this work like it had before? I stared around in frustration, but the dark stones remained just stones.

The last rays of light died, and darkness fell, wrapping us in her gentle mantle.

Silence, like a blanket muting the world.

Bereft, I lay down on the grass, curled against Arthur, and closed my eyes. "I love you," I muttered. "I love you, and I won't let you die. I love you. I love you. You can't die. You can't." Like a mantra, I kept repeating the words. They burned themselves inside my head, they stood in letters of fire inside my eyelids, they hung almost touchable in the cool night air. And as I muttered the words, my fingers found the ring on my finger and turned it.

A gentle rumble broke the silence, like a distant explosion, and beyond it a single piercing note rent the air. The ground beneath me shook, and I hung on tight to Arthur, anchoring myself to his stretcher's solidity, my face pressed against his side.

The shaking stopped. I opened my eyes. Gray stone walls rose around me, and an archway opened onto dim gray sky.

Chapter Forty-One

FOR A FEW long moments, I lay motionless on the cold flagstones, not daring to believe it had worked. My chest heaved as though the air I had to fight to force in was too thick to inhale, and the sound in my ears of my heartbeat's frantic pounding lessened.

My breathing steadied. I'd done it. We were here. Both of us.

Or were we?

What if all I'd done was take us forward to the first time a tower had stood on the top of the Tor? What if we were somewhere like the fifteenth or sixteenth century? Or some other time without the medical skill to help Arthur?

I levered myself into a sitting position and twitched back the blankets still covering Arthur. The old door had come with us. He still lay strapped to it, the spear shafts holding his broken leg firm. Fresh blood had seeped through the dressings on his wounds, and his eyes remained closed. I touched my fingers to his face where cold sweat beaded on deathly pale skin. Was he not meant to have traveled with me? Might I have done something terrible in bringing him through the portal?

"Good heavens," said a woman's voice. In English.

I turned my head toward the arched doorway. She stood outlined against the evening sky, a small backpack hooked over one shoulder, a wooly hat on her head and walking boots on her feet. An expensive Nikon camera hung around her neck. Not sixteenth century then.

"What's going on here?" She stepped toward us, curiosity and compassion on a lined, middle-aged face, devoid of makeup. "Are you all right?"

Did I look it?

I shook my head, groping for words and surprised when they came out in English as well. "My husband's hurt. I need an ambulance." My voice cracked and tears welled in my eyes. Tears of overwhelming relief. An urge to jump up and hug that woman to my chest came over me. I didn't. She was looking wary enough as it was, and it might have sent my savior running for safety.

The woman came closer, getting out her phone, and squatted on her haunches on the other side of Arthur. "He doesn't look too good. But where did you come from? I was in here only a moment ago, and you weren't here then." Almost accusatory. How dared I manifest myself without her knowing it. She drew in a breath. "However did you get here?" The phone leapt into bright life, and her stubby fingers tapped out 999.

Two more people, similarly attired, appeared in the archway. "Moira? What's this? What's going on?"

Moira looked up at her friends. "No idea." She shook her head at them for silence as someone must have answered her call. "Ambulance." She had an air about her of quiet self-assurance that filled me with confidence.

The two other people, both women, came closer as Moira stepped into the archway, turning away as she spoke to emergency services.

"Oh, my dear," one of them said, bending down to me and putting a gentle hand on my shoulder. "Whatever's happened to you? What can we do?"

"Glastonbury Tor," Moira said. "The very top. Straightaway. The man's in a bad way. Unconscious. Broken leg, I'd say, but he looks like he has other injuries as well." She turned her head and took a harder look at Arthur. "Barely breathing."

At Moira's friend's touch and kind words, my reserves of bravery disintegrated to nothing, and the tears that had been collecting coursed down my cheeks. "Tell them to hurry," I managed. "Please."

Moira's friend put her arms around me and pulled me into a smothering hug against her ample bosom. "There, there. Don't cry. Help's coming. What's your name, my dear?"

"G-gwen," I managed in between the sobs now convulsing my body. I'd been brave for long enough. How wonderful to delegate all responsibility and let myself cry. I didn't hold back but let the sobs rack my body in their wonderful abandon.

When I'd been able to cry at last for Amhar, I'd been given so short a time and it hadn't been enough. I'd had to put it all aside for later when I'd had to fight to save Archfedd. Neither of us had been able to mourn as we'd needed to, and neither had Arthur. Then Camlann had come, and I'd had to become a brave leader. Never again would I be that.

Moira's friend, who told me her name was Sandra, kept her arms around me, comforting me as best she could and patting my back with her gentle hands. "Are you hurt, Gwen?" she asked after a while. "How did this happen? Did someone do this to you and… your husband? I'm sorry. I'm just assuming he's your husband."

All I could do was shake my head and keep on crying.

The ambulance arrived very quickly. Of course, the hospital wasn't far. Two paramedics and a couple of policemen climbed up the path to the summit with a proper, modern stretcher and examined Arthur, putting an oxygen mask over his face, wrapping him in a foil blanket, and getting a line for an IV drip into his hand.

"Who put this splint on?" One of the paramedics, a balding, kind-faced older man, asked me, as he and his colleague replaced it with an inflatable one.

"I did," I hiccupped, my sobs having died down at last. "I knew I had to straighten out the bones to restore circulation to his foot."

He raised his eyebrows at me. "You did *that*?"

I nodded. They exchanged glances that might have been impressed. I didn't care. All I wanted was for them to get Arthur to a hospital. Quickly.

Maneuvering the bulky stretcher down the hill proved awkward, but they did it. At last, I found myself sitting wrapped in a red blanket in the back of their ambulance with the younger of the paramedics checking the drip and listening to Arthur's chest with his stethoscope.

He gave me a thumbs up, his face telling me not to worry, they had it all under control. Probably the face he used all the time for relatives of the injured. I didn't trust that face.

The back doors closed, and the older man climbed into the front. "It's going to be noisy, I'm afraid," he called back. The siren came on. Arthur didn't stir.

The young paramedic adjusted the oxygen mask. "Can you tell me your names and how old your husband is?"

Now he was asking. For a moment I couldn't think what to say, before inspiration came. "King," I said. "I'm Gwen and he's Arthur. He's forty-two." That was it. We'd have to be Mr. and Mrs. King.

He grinned at me. "Very appropriate for Glastonbury."

I managed a watery smile. Little did he know how right he was.

In the front, the radio crackled as the driver called ahead to let the hospital know we were coming. I glanced forward to see traffic moving out of our way as the driver zipped his vehicle between stationary cars. The paramedic kept working on Arthur, his eyes darting forward from time to time toward the driver.

I prayed in terrified silence, unsure if there'd be anyone listening. To God, to the gods of the Dark Age world. To Gwyn ap Nudd himself. *Let us not have taken too long to get here. Let there be no hidden complications. Let him live. Please, let him live.*

We seemed to take forever to arrive at the hospital. The local one must have been too small. At last, our ambulance drew up outside a porticoed entrance and the paramedics swung the doors open. A doctor stood waiting for us.

In a trance, I didn't hear their words. The noises and smells of the surrounding town battered on my eardrums: the stink of exhaust fumes, the smell of tarmac, the honking of horns, the distant roar of engines and the shouts of voices.

I followed the paramedics as they wheeled the stretcher into a room filled with men and women in scrubs and masks, who crowded round to shift Arthur onto a bed. Someone told me to wait outside. I protested but was ushered out. Alone, afraid, I stood with my nose pressed to the doors, my hands splayed against the glass, muttering my prayer over and over again.

The two policemen, who'd followed the ambulance in their car, approached with something akin to diffidence, notebooks in hand. "Mrs. King. Can you give us some details of how this happened?"

I snapped back into their world. I'd have to talk to them. This was what happened in the twenty-first century. And it was going to be tricky.

Without shifting my gaze from what was going on around Arthur's bed, I nodded. "I'm not moving. You'll have to talk to me here."

The older of the two opened his notebook. "Can you tell us how your husband came by his injuries?"

I couldn't very well say in battle. A partial truth would have to do. "Something fell on him." Inside the treatment room they were cutting off his clothes. One of them had fetched bolt cutters for his mail shirt.

The policeman scratched his head. "What was it fell on him?"

In for a penny. "His horse." The mail shirt was cast aside. They were attaching monitors to his bruise-mottled chest. A green line blipped across a screen. I pressed my hands harder against the glass in the door, willing him to fight. Why couldn't these policemen leave me alone? Did they possess no compassion or understanding?

The first policeman frowned, and his colleague pulled a disbelieving face. "On top of Glastonbury Tor? How did you get a horse up there, and where had it gone when you were found? We didn't see any horse up there."

"It didn't happen there," I said, aware that despite my efforts to be evasive, I was digging myself in deeper with every answer. The doctors were working on Arthur's chest just as I'd seen doctors do in the hospital soap I used to watch, in another life. A drain. They were draining blood from his chest to help him breathe. I had no idea what that was called.

"Well, if it didn't happen there, how did he end up on top of the Tor tied to an old door? And with what looked like a pair of broken spears splinting his leg. Did someone do this to him?"

"I don't remember," I snapped, deciding amnesia was the easiest option. "Can you please leave me alone? That's my husband in there. I don't want to talk right now. Just go away, can't you?" I let my voice rise in frustration, and they both stepped back, suddenly wary, as though I might be dangerous.

The first policeman shrugged. "Don't go thinking we've finished with you, though," he said, managing to sound threatening. "We'll have questions for your husband when he wakes up, as well. If your stories don't tally, we'll be taking steps."

With a final suspicious glare, they departed.

I waited. A nurse came out and ignored me. Another went in. I could see the doctors talking but not hear what they said. At last, one of them came out. "Mrs. King?"

I nodded. How weird to be called Mrs. anything.

"Your husband has crush injuries. We're taking him up to theatre now. We did a portable X-ray, but he needs a scan. He'll have to have pins inserted in his leg – both upper and lower. His broken ribs should heal by themselves, and we've dealt with his haemothorax – we'll leave the drain in for a day or two. And he has a concussion. The surgeons will deal with his other wounds at the same time. We've stopped the bleeding, but they need stitching." He paused, brow furrowed. "If I didn't know better, I'd say they were sword wounds." His eyes narrowed. "And he was wearing an empty scabbard. Is this a reenactment gone wrong?"

A feeling of déjà view swept over me. Hadn't I thought I'd landed in a historical reenactment when I'd first fallen back in time? The circularity of the world amazed me.

I shook my head. "I don't know." Best to stick with ignorance before things became even more complicated. "Is he going to be all right?"

He gave me an encouraging smile. "Don't worry. We can deal with all of this. I'll have one of my nurses take you to the relatives' room near the operating theater where you can wait." He beckoned a passing nurse. "He'll be a while in theater, so Robin will find you something to eat and drink."

The nurse, a dumpy girl in blue scrubs with her ginger hair in a tight French plait, smiled at me out of friendly blue eyes as the doctor turned away. "I can do better than that," she said. "I can find you some clean clothes as well. And how would you like a shower?" She wrinkled her freckled snub nose and touched my bloody sleeve. "I bet you'll be glad to get out of these. Were you at a fancy-dress party?"

She had it right. I would be very glad of clean clothes. She took me to a bathroom near the relatives' room and gave me a set of scrubs like her own, and a pair of rubber clogs. "I'll put a pack of sandwiches and a can of drink on the table in the relatives' room for you when you come out. It's up there, on the left. And I'll come and tell you when your husband's out of theater and you can go and see him. Don't worry. The surgeon operating is the best in the business. You couldn't have come to a better hospital."

The shower had shampoo and soap supplied, and I spent longer in there than I'd intended, luxuriating in the feel of the hot water on my skin and how clean I felt afterwards. I braided my wet hair and put on the scrubs and shoes, and found a plastic bin bag to stuff all my dirty clothes into. Then, carrying the bag, I proceeded to the relatives' room.

I peered through the small square glass window in the door, the wariness of my old life not having left me, hoping for it to be empty. It wasn't. Long floor to ceiling windows took up the far wall, the blinds open on the bright lights of the town sparkling in the darkness. A man stood by the window, staring out. Tall and thin and wearing jeans and a black T-shirt, his untidy, short brown hair stood up around his head as though he'd been running his fingers through it in desperation. Maybe he had someone to worry about in one of the other operating theaters. Like me.

Taking a deep breath, I put my hand on the door, then paused. Something vaguely familiar hung about the man's stance. Nonsense. I couldn't possibly know him. How long had I been gone? There wouldn't be anyone here I knew.

I pushed open the door and went inside. The man didn't move. He must have heard me, but he didn't budge an inch. Just kept on staring out of the window. As I sat down on one of the many fake-leather, pastel-upholstered armchairs lining the room, I had a brief glimpse of his reflection, distorted in the glass.

The thought resurfaced. Did I know him? I narrowed my eyes and studied his rear view.

The man turned around.

My mouth fell open. I'd have known him anywhere, even in jeans and with short spiky hair.

Merlin.

The shock would have knocked me over if I'd been standing up. I couldn't find a thing to say, but sat staring at him, unable to close my gaping mouth.

He smiled. "Good evening, Gwen." Perfect English too. Not even the smallest hint of any accent.

"What on earth are *you* doing here?" I managed, at last.

"Waiting for you."

"For me?" I kept on staring, my brain a blank, struggling to process that the man I'd last seen lying unconscious on the floor of Morgawse's house, fifteen hundred years ago, was standing here, in jeans and a black Motorhead T-shirt, and smiling at me as though he'd just popped in for a cup of tea on a Sunday afternoon.

What I really needed was a stiff whisky, and I didn't even *like* whisky.

"How *can* you be here?" I finally managed to stutter out. "Am I *hallucinating*? Did you follow us through the doorway on the Tor?" Of course, I'd seen him before in my world as a child, although then he'd been wearing clothes that had made me christen him "the Fancy-Dress-Man." Not jeans.

He shook his head. "I'm afraid I had to get here by the slightly slower route. You and Arthur took the quick one, but I couldn't."

That totally lost me. I blinked at him; a rabbit mesmerized in the headlights.

He crossed the room to stand in front of me. "It's taken me a while, but I'm here now."

I put out a hand and touched his leg. How weird to see him in jeans. Skinny jeans as well. A hole in one knee. And trainers on his feet. I couldn't get my head around him wearing clothes like this.

Yes. He was real. The suspicion that he was a figment of my imagination hadn't wanted to go away.

He sat down next to me. Was that *aftershave* I could smell? This short-haired, fragrant, jean-clad man was *not* the Merlin I knew.

"Where's *my* Merlin?" I asked, without thinking. "What have you done with him?"

He took one of my hands. "Your Merlin has had hundreds of years to get used to living in your world. That's what. You made me wait a long time before you and Arthur finally turned up. When you told me your time was fifteen hundred years in the future, I had no idea how long it would take me to get there."

"You *knew* I'd be coming?"

He nodded. "Of course. I now have all the same privileges

you had back in my old world. I live *here* now. *This* is my present. I found out what happened to you both after Camlann – the popular story of how three queens had taken Arthur to Avalon and that he was sleeping still, waiting to come to Britain's aid in her hour of need. You think I believed that?"

He laughed. "However, the truth of it was that both of you had just vanished off the face of the earth. Your people came back the next morning and both of you had gone. Everyone assumed you'd gone to Annwfn. I had to do a bit of guesswork, of course, as to what had really happened, but don't forget, I have the Sight. Comes in very useful for doing the National Lottery."

"But how? Where did you come from? You weren't there when we needed you. You were lost. We searched but we couldn't find you. Nimuë took you." I shook my head. His hand was warm enough, his body felt real under my touch – I dismissed the continuing worry that he might be a figment of my fevered imagination.

He tapped his nose, looking smug. He hadn't lost any of his annoying traits. "Took me rather a long time to escape the prison Nimuë locked me up for killing her mother, but I did it. Made it out in time for the Renaissance. Very interesting time period. Had to keep a low profile for quite a while in case I ended up being burned as a witch."

"You mean you've been living… been alive… for all the time since we lost you back in the Dark Ages?" I paused, scrabbling for understanding. "How did you do that? Are you… are you really what they said? The son of a demon?"

"Don't call them the Dark Ages," he said, side-stepping my second question. "Not a nice name. I believe the preferred title now is the Late Antiquity or the Early Medieval Period. Did they feel dark to you? Wonderful time, and I'd go back if I could." He wrinkled his nose. "They smelled a lot better than this world does, for a start."

"Late Antiquity then," I said. "Stop being pedantic and tell me the truth. How can you still be alive fifteen hundred years after everyone else?"

He squeezed my hand. "When I got out of Nimuë's prison, it was a bit of a shock to find history had passed me by, I can tell you. I'd missed a lot. And the only person who could tell me what I'd missed was her. She was still about, and she'd calmed down a bit by then, so we had a bit of a father-daughter chat, and she told me all about Camlann."

Camlann. Fifteen hundred years before today, probably eight or nine hundred years before Merlin woke up. Everyone involved in it long gone, except for us. All of them just dry bones or dust: Cei, Archfedd, Reaghan, Coventina, Llawfrodedd. All swept away by the tide of time. I swallowed down a lump as tears welled. I had to find out the truth. "But you're like me. You're human. No one can live forever like you have. No one."

He tapped his nose again. "Why have magic and not use it? And I had a reason to survive. I knew you'd be returning. Nimuë told me all about what happened with Medraut. That he turned out just as you and I had always feared. She seemed quite pleased about it. Didn't take much for me to work out where you'd gone. All I had to do after that was wait and listen out for you. Breaking through the portal together like that created enormous waves. I came straight here. You drew me like a magnet."

I stared at him. "You really *are* my Merlin?"

He frowned. "Did you doubt it? Could there be two like me? Of course I'm your Merlin."

I threw my arms around him. "Oh Merlin. I couldn't stop any of it without you. Arthur executed Amhar for a crime I was too blind to see Medraut had committed. Arthur and I fell out, and Camlann happened even though I thought I could stop it. Everything came out like the legends." God, how wonderful to be able to tell someone the truth, to load on him the weight of responsibility that had been crushing me.

He hugged me close, one gentle hand soothing my hair. "I know. I know all the legends now. I haven't spent the last five hundred years in idleness, you know."

I couldn't help a chuckle. "You look a bit weird in modern clothes."

He extricated himself from my arms. "But you did what you were meant to do. You brought Arthur here to where he wouldn't have to die. You brought him to Avalon."

I stared. "You mean *this* is Avalon? The present day, here? My world?"

He grinned. "I think it must be. I think you've made it into Avalon."

The truth stared me in the face. "So, Avalon's *never* been some magical world of fairies at all? It's today. It's now. This is where Arthur was always meant to come to. In all the legends, when they said he didn't die – they were right. Because he didn't. He's here, with us, in the present." My brow furrowed with the enormity of the realization.

But now I paused to think about it, how cool was that? I'd been born and brought up in Avalon, just never known it.

Merlin nodded. "So you see, he *did* need you. All the way through, he needed you for everything. And I was right when I told you I saw you with him to the end, if there was one. Because there wasn't one back then, was there? Whatever end there's going to be will be here. For both of you."

I frowned, then laughed, a bit of a mad laugh. "But how's he going to take to living here? To not being a king? And where are we going to live? I don't even have a house. Nor a job. Nathan'll have the house I used to have a share in. I can hardly take Arthur there. And I'm certain he wouldn't like our towns."

Merlin's mobile mouth widened in a grin worthy of the bloody Cheshire Cat, looking as though he had the answer to everything. "You remember I told you my skills came in handy for the National Lottery? Well, I've been planning for your return a long while now. For meeting Arthur again. And you. I've invested my somewhat substantial winnings in property. I think you're going to like it."

The door of the waiting room swung open, and a doctor

wearing scrubs like mine came in. He smiled. "Mrs. King? Your husband's just come out of theater. Thanks to your prompt action with those rather unorthodox splints, we've been able to save his leg. He's somewhat the worse for wear, but he's going to be fine. You can go and see him when he comes out of the recovery room."

Chapter Forty-Two

M Y FRESHLY MADE coffee in my hand, I step out of the kitchen onto the flagstone patio where Cabal still lies in the sun, long tail twitching in some dream. He's nearly five now, middle-aged for a Wolfhound, so he's inclined to taking siestas. I set my coffee mug on the table and shade my eyes to peer down the slope towards the river. Twenty yards from the patio the garden ends and the hay meadow begins, the grass standing tall already, even though it's only May. Beyond, drooping willows mark the twisting watercourse.

Even from here I can hear the music of the rushing water and the wind that makes the branches whisper together like naughty schoolgirls. And birdsong, sweet and melodious and joyful. The sound of springtime.

If I turn my head to the right, I'll see our horses grazing in the meadow, tails swishing against the flies the warm weather has brought out. And beyond them, our sheep graze in the fields that climb toward the mountain's foot. Then purple heather, rocky outcrops and golden gorse dot the moorland under a powder blue sky.

The smell of the casserole in the Aga curls out of the open kitchen door behind me, and Cabal lifts his shaggy head and sniffs. I bend and caress him, my fingers rubbing his silken ears. Cabal. A name to remind me of a long gone world. We named him for the dog my lost son Amhar once had.

Many memories abound here. We live our lives enmeshed in memories of the past. We surround ourselves with hope for the future. The future comes out of the kitchen onto the patio behind me. Four and a half years old, sturdily built with a head of darkly curling hair, a little clone of his lost brothers. He's wearing dungarees over an Arran sweater and has his Wellington boots on the wrong feet.

"Con." I sweep him off his feet and hold him close, our cheeks touching. I breathe him in. The child who will never be a warrior.

He giggles and plants a kiss on my nose. "Mami, put me down."

He calls me mami just as Archfedd did, and every time he does my heartstrings pull. The daughter I left behind. Thanks to Merlin, I know what happened to her. He had it from Nimuë, who made it her business to keep a watch on the surviving members of her family from afar. I've never asked him how he persuaded her to part with the information. Perhaps I don't want to know. But she was his daughter, so maybe she told him willingly.

Archfedd did marry Llawfrodedd, and they ruled Dumnonia together with great success. She wore my crown, just as she'd seen in her grandmother's scrying glass. And Arthur's peace, forged at Badon, survived for many years. They had sons, and grandsons, and greatgrandsons, but the Saxons came, of course, as I'd always known they would, and Dumnonia was lost at last. Perhaps out there in the wide outside world they have descendants, *my* descendants too. I'll probably never know.

I set Con back on his feet, and he runs to fetch his little fishing rod from where it leans against the wall. Arthur made it for him from a willow wand and thin string just last week. "Here, this is how I learned to fish with old Nial," he said, as Con watched him work. "You'll be able to fish just like I did. So long ago." I didn't miss the wistful look in his eye as he spoke.

Con jumps up and down. "Can we go fishin' with Dadi? Both

of us?"

I glance at the chickens where they're edging toward the patio with a look of nonchalance about them, then back through the open kitchen door. "We'd better close the door, or those pesky buckbucks'll be in there again." I pull the door shut, and Cabal lumbers to his feet and gives Con's cheek a friendly lick. Con squeals and wipes the slobber off on the sleeve of his handknitted jersey.

I take Con's small, grubby hand in mine, and we negotiate the half dozen slate steps down onto the lawn. Where the lawn ends, we follow the narrow path Arthur's mown through the hay meadow, Cabal trotting at our heels.

Our river, just a big stream really, meanders through our property, heading west toward the not-too-distant sea, sometimes quiet and moody, sometimes exuberant and wild. Full of fish, though, if you have the patience to sit and catch them.

Arthur is sitting on the log he's put there as a seat, his back against the trunk of the shady tree and his fishing line trailing in the water. His favorite fishing spot. A quiet pool sits dark and inviting on a bend in the river. He gets up as we approach, warned by Con's joyful shouts, and sets his rod in its support. It's a fancy carbon fiber one, and he's very proud of it.

Con runs to him and he sweeps the little boy off his feet just as I did, laughing with our son. He's learning to be a proper father, his relationship with Con quite different to the one he had with our two lost boys. He has time to play with him, to read him bedtime stories, to sit him on his knee and tell him tales of magic and long-ago battles. Of a world our boy will never see.

"I see you've brought your rod," he says, popping Con down on the log seat and smiling at me over his curly head. "Let's put some bait on the hook for you." He offers Con the container of wriggling maggots, and Con picks one out.

"This one." He puts it in his father's palm. "*He'll* catch me a big fish."

Arthur puts the maggot on a hook for Con and shows him

how to drop the line in the water. Con settles himself on his father's seat, a look of concentration on his small face. How like his brothers he is. How like both of them.

Arthur limps to stand beside me. A few gray strands silver his hair now, and the short beard that frames his jaw is grizzled, but he's lost none of his whipcord strength and musculature. His arm goes around my waist, and he kisses me on the lips. "Thanks for bringing him down."

I smile, the love I have for him warm and satisfying, and move closer, my hand on his back. From his seat, Con giggles with delight. "I'm catchin' a fish for my supper."

We settle on the short grass beside our little boy. This close to the river, we can't leave him by himself. I constantly worry about him, my last chick in the nest. My only surviving chick. I lean my head on Arthur's shoulder, content and happy in the warmth of the sun and think about my children.

The silence stretches out, tranquil and companionable.

"Do you remember the day I found Excalibur?" Arthur asks.

I nod.

"Afterwards, I sat with Nial on the monks' wharf and said I never wanted to fight another battle."

That day is as clear in my head as if it happened yesterday. I remember the peaceful waters of the marshes, clear of all but the last shreds of mist. I see again the heron as he takes off and the bobbing waterfowl as they rush to hide in the tall reedbeds. Arthur sits on the wooden jetty beside old Nial with the newly discovered Excalibur lying on the rough wood by his side.

And I remember how much I feared that sword heralded Camlann's imminent arrival.

All gone now. All done with. Only peace remaining.

He smiles at me, one hand touching my cheek. "And now I have that wish."

"Are you happy?" I ask.

His dark eyes, flecked with gold, regard me solemnly. His hair, cut short now, curls about his face just like his son's. He's not lost his boyishness, though. "Yes, I'm happy. All I ever wanted for my Britain was peace. I got it, so everything I did had a purpose. Archfedd and Llawfrodedd reaped the reward of that." He pauses, brow furrowed. "I can't say this world, so much bigger than the one I knew, has it now, but it's not my responsibility any longer. This Britain doesn't need me." He glances at Con. "He does, though."

I lean in for a kiss. "And so do I."

We sit together, his arm around me, for a long time while Con thinks he's fishing.

At last, footsteps sound on the path above. Merlin jumps down the little bank to join us. He's wearing shorts. Yes. Shorts. And his legs are already bronzed. He's taken to twenty-first century life as though born to it.

Arthur grins at his old friend. "Have you brought your rod?"

Merlin shakes his head. "Not today. But I've got news for you." His eyes glitter with excitement. He lives in a cottage half a mile away, walking distance across our fields. We have no other neighbors to disturb us. We own all the land in this little valley, and, with only one road in and out, we can keep the world at bay. Merlin couldn't have picked a better spot for us to live, with his lottery winnings.

"What news?" I ask, more interested than Arthur as this is my old world and even after five years still new to him. He's not quite a part of it like Merlin and I are. Coming the quick way has its disadvantages.

"Have a guess," Merlin says, plonking himself down on the grass.

I frown. I don't like guessing games.

"What is it?" I ask. "Tell us."

Arthur lies back on the grass, his hands behind his head, as handsome as the day I met him. He snorts a laugh. "You might as well tell her. She won't even try guessing. She never does."

Merlin clears his throat. "They've found your book."

That makes Arthur sit up. "They've found her *book*?"

The Book of Guinevere. I'd forgotten all about it, and if I'd recalled, I'd have assumed it lost long ago and never to be found.

A self-satisfied smile spreads across Merlin's face. "Yes, Gwen's book. An old recluse died, here in Wales. Not far from here, in fact. He had no direct heirs, so a distant relation came to sort through his papers. They found the book amongst them."

My book. It's been in someone's house all this time. In the house of some old man. Was it there while I was growing up? Before I was born? While Merlin slept under Nimuë's spell? Such are the vagaries of time travel.

"Who was he and how did he get it?" I ask. "What happened to it after I left Din Cadan? Did Archfedd keep it safe?" She must have. My heart does little leaps of excitement I can't control.

"When?" Arthur asks, as interested by this as me.

Merlin shrugs. "A while since, I think, but I don't know for sure. It's just made the national papers. I can only tell you what I've read. No one seems to know how the old man came to have it in his possession. The papers are saying it had been passed down through his family for generations. They've interviewed the heir, a very distant cousin of some sort, and specialists are looking at the book right now."

I stare at Merlin. "But how can his ancestors have got hold of it? Didn't Archfedd keep it?" A thought pings in my head. "Might that old man have been descended from my daughter?"

Merlin shrugs. "We'll probably never know. He probably wouldn't have known himself."

I glance at little Con, but he's still concentrating on the important job of fishing. He's a determined child and focuses on everything he wants to do. At the moment that's catching a fish. In everything he does, he reminds me of Llacheu and Amhar, and sometimes of Archfedd too. A lump forms in my throat when I remember my lost children. So far away, but never forgotten.

I gather my addled wits. "Think what that means." I lay my hand on Arthur's. "Everyone will know you aren't just a legend. They'll know you really existed. You'll be history at last and not a story."

Merlin grins. "They're suggesting it's a hoax, of course, like the Hitler Diaries. That some clever scholar forged the book and planted it. That maybe the recluse himself forged it."

I grin back, wanting to laugh out loud. "Well, we know that's not true, don't we?"

Arthur does laugh. "You know what? I don't care whether people nowadays think I'm real or not. It doesn't matter. *I* know I'm real. You and Merlin and Con know I'm real. I don't care if no one else believes it. A load of scholars analyzing my story. *Our* story. I almost wish it hadn't been discovered."

I nod. "When I started writing the book, I had no idea we'd be here to see it found. I just wanted to leave a record – in the hope my father would have come across it, perhaps. He didn't, of course, but I wish it had been him. Maybe if he had, history would have been different, and I wouldn't have gone up the Tor on that morning to scatter his ashes. I don't know."

Merlin shakes his head. "No, that couldn't have been changed. You had to go up there and I had to take you back to fulfill your destiny, and for Arthur to fulfill his. It was a fixed point that could never be changed. Every road we trod was leading here, today. To this. You couldn't change anything, no matter how hard you tried."

Arthur lies back down again. "Do we care? We're here, the sun's shining and fish are biting. Do I want to think about anything else?"

I gaze at the face I was destined to love, at his dark eyes flecked with gold, at his smile, the scars on his cheek and in his hairline. This is the man I *will* grow old with. The thing I longed for will happen. I saved him.

"Dadi!" shouts Con. "I've got a fishy!"

And sure enough, a fish is dancing on his hook.

THE END

Author's Note for the *Guinevere* series

I've been fascinated with all things Arthurian since my parents took me to see Disney's *Sword in the Stone* at the cinema when I must have been about five or six. Since then, I've spent a lot of time researching every aspect, from the medieval romances to current thinking about whether he ever existed, via deep and enjoyable research into what Britain would have been like back then. One thing I don't do, though, is read Arthurian novels by other writers.

In about 1998, my husband, Patrick, and I went on a visit to Glastonbury Tor. We parked around the back and walked across the field toward the steep path to the summit. Patrick had his camera loaded with infrared film (this was before he went digital). We stopped, and he set it up on a tripod to take four photos of the Tor on motordrive. Then we climbed to the top for more photos.

When he developed the negatives that evening, he spotted that although the first and fourth photos were quite normal, in the second, the ruined tower on the top was fading and in the third it had vanished altogether. A mystery. Perhaps he'd captured on film a view back in time to before the tower was built? We'd seen nothing odd with the naked eye, but infrared film is very sensitive. But… what might have happened had we been inside the tower when it vanished? Would we have been transported back in time? The germ of my idea for *Guinevere* was born, although destined not to come to fruition for another twenty years.

I've had great fun working out a believable (if you ignore the time travel and touches of magic which it's difficult to write an Arthurian story without) timeline, setting, and storyline for the sort of man I think Arthur could have been. Before I even started, I worked out a thorough background history for the period up to his birth, so that my characters had an in-depth and authentic sounding world to inhabit.

I've used real places for every location – places that if you want to, you can go and see. With Gwen being from the twenty-first century, she's also handily been able to change the Dark Age names into the placenames she knows, to make it easier for the reader to understand the geography of the Dark Ages. And on my website, there are some excellent maps drawn by my son for each book.

Arthur's stronghold is Din Cadan, modern name South Cadbury Castle, an Iron Age hillfort in Somerset, long rumored to have been his Camelot. Of course, he never had a castle by the name of Camelot – that's a name more closely associated with Roman Camulodunum (Colchester in the East of England) and would never have been Arthurian as it's too far east.

Excavations of South Cadbury by Leslie Alcock in the 1960s turned up evidence that it had indeed been refortified at exactly the right time for a powerful warlord to have used it as his stronghold. And as it's very big, he would have needed a large force of men to man the run of the walls, so he must have been one of the most powerful men in Britain. Why not Arthur? Or the man Arthur is based on.

I've walked up there many times, usually with no one else to be seen but my husband, our dog and me. From the summit of the largely tree covered hill you have a view across the flat lands of the Somerset levels, once marshes but now drained, to the distant hump of Glastonbury Tor with the finger of its ruined tower pointing skywards. A view I like to think Gwen saw every day.

My Din Tagel, modern Tintagel, has been associated with the birth of Arthur for a long time, but was until relatively recently thought to have only been a religious site. Now it's known it was the fortress of another warlord and the center for importation from the Mediterranean. So maybe Arthur was indeed born there.

I've been to visit the Tristan Stone near Castle Dore (Caer Dore in my books) and read the inscription Gwen composes for Drustans after he dies. It was great fun to have her "making history" in this way, as she does when she causes Merlin to create the sword in the stone in the forum of Viroconium.

I find it a great help to have visited the places I write about. In fact, I've been to most of the locations in these books, and I've often stood where Arthur and Gwen would have stood, visualizing the landscape as it was in their time.

For example, in book five, The Quest for Excalibur, Arthur fights the famous Battle of Badon, and I've placed that close to the site I favor – Liddington Castle, near where the old Roman Road, the Ermine Way, crosses the ancient Ridgeway track. I've visited the old hillfort, just grassy banks now, many times, as it's close to where I live. Not a frequently visited tourist attraction, an ancient, mysterious atmosphere clings to the old earthworks.

It was great fun to work out where I thought Nennius's battles should take place. The decision to use his list (he wrote it in The Historia Brittonum in about 830, so a long time after the late fifth century) was an easy one to make. Whether they were genuine or not, they are traditionally associated with Arthur, and I felt I owed it to those who love Arthurian literature to use them. And doing so gave me a good framework to compose the books around, as at least one battle needed including in each book.

I made a couple of more innovative decisions that shied away from popular opinion in placing the Battle of the City of the Legion in York rather than Chester or Caerleon, as I felt this better suited a conflict against the Saxons. The other one was putting the Battle of the River Tribuit (Tryfrwyd) on the Loddon at Twyford near the River Thames. I felt the Saxons could have easily brought their ships upriver to attack local settlements. We've taken our own boat along the Thames, although it's changed a lot since the Dark Ages!

Having a woman narrating the story in the first person did pose a few problems as the book centers around a warrior society, but I did manage to find several different ways to include Gwen in the battles without her becoming an actual combatant most of the time. I particularly wanted to show that although this was a martial society, and the British were the victors in the main, the battles and violence were terrible things, and even the winners suffered greatly. I couldn't see how anyone could participate in vicious hand-to-hand combat without being psychologically affected. Hence Arthur's PTSD after Rhiwallon's death in book four.

One place I didn't visit for my research was Dumbarton Rock (Dun Breattann, King Caw of Alt Clut's stronghold). This is because I have a morbid fear of heights and looking at this on Google Maps was enough for me. I also don't like Tintagel for the same reason. But I did visit Hadrian's Wall and Vindolanda, where I set a large part of book three.

I've had a very good reaction to the historical settings and accuracy of the books, with one person memorably saying he wondered if I'd actually fallen back in time at some point myself. I haven't, but I wouldn't tell you if I had. I have, however, done a vast amount of research into all manner of things in my efforts to make my readers feel as immersed in Dark Age life as possible. I've gone down interesting rabbit holes of investigation in my search for such things as medical treatments, Dark Age diapers/nappies, toilet facilities, food, underwear, contraception, weaponry, pastimes and saddlery to name but a few.

The fun of having a main character who is from the future is manifold. She views the world around her through the same eyes as the reader, turning up her nose at anything she finds disgusting, from brushing her teeth with powdered charcoal to the prevailing attitude of men to women. Everything she sees is new to her so can be remarked upon, whereas had my Gwen been a girl of the fifth century she would have had no need to do so. Gwen's fascination with the history of the period enabled me to explain things in more detail.

She can also be innovative – she introduces stirrups for comfort when riding, a little too early for when they truly arrived, but who cares in a work of fiction. She also teaches Merlin and her boys to play chess several hundred years before it came to Britain, although she regrets playing with a man with the Sight who might be able to predict her next move.

Many of the characters I've used come from real legends and "historical" sources. The kings all do, although they were not all quite as contemporary with Arthur as I've implied. I've used a little artistic license, and I hope you, the reader, won't mind too much. For the most part, I've chosen the names associated with Arthur from the earliest legends. Melwas from book two should really have been ruling from Glastonbury Tor, but as I'd used that for a slightly different role, I placed him at Brent Knoll, aka the Isle of Frogs, on the Somerset coast, and found that worked well. He becomes Meleagaunt in later romance and his early legend involves him kidnapping Gwen. In the legend, she's rescued by the abbot of Glastonbury – Gildas! But my Gildas is too young to do that, so I had Jerome fill his boots.

Gwalchmei and Bedwyr feature in all six books in minor roles, but Merlin takes center stage a lot of the time, although in reality he probably wasn't contemporary with Arthur. I like to think Arthur would have had an advisor of some kind, so why not call him Merlin? I wanted to limit his magic as much as possible in an effort not to let the books transform into a total fantasy, but this rather got away from me in the final book as I tried to follow the legends. Merlin, Morgana, Eigr and Nimuë all possess the Sight, and some further powers that I like to keep as mysterious as possible.

Both Amhar and Llacheu are named in legends as sons of Arthur. Llacheu is actually killed by Cei, but as my Cei is such a lovely chap I couldn't have that happen, and his death at Medraut's hands fits far better into my overall plan. I always knew Arthur would have to kill Amhar himself to fulfill the legend mentioned in Nennius's Mirabilia – that at Licat Amhar, at Wormelow Tump, lies the tomb of Amhar, whose father, Arthur the Soldier, killed him. I just didn't know how I was going to get there until I began writing book six.

I wanted a daughter for Gwen, and in my research found a single mention of a Llawfrodedd who was married to an Archfedd who was a daughter of King Arthur. Perfect. With that destiny in mind, I introduced Llawfrodedd early on and gave him a humble beginning and worthy personality, linking him to Archfedd in friendship during their childhood. It felt right that Archfedd, who would have made a far better king than her brother, would end up ruling Dumnonia with Llawfrodedd.

I wrote book one in early 2018 and once it was written came upon an online writer's forum called Critique Circle. It was a fortuitous discovery. Writers can post one chapter a week in public queues or as much as they like in private queues. At first, I posted in the public queue but for a long time now I've only been in my private queues with a small and select group of my friends making editing suggestions about my work.

Without Critique Circle and my wonderful friends on there from all around the world, I would never have reached the point of publication. I've learned so much from them and it's all been a joy. I feel as though I have a lot of penfriends all with the same hobby/job as I have. I've even met up with some of them and have done FaceTime or Zoom with others. It's a friendly, helpful community I'd recommend to any budding writer.

So I'd like to thank the following CC members – Rellrod, Dorothea, Qbragg, Harpalycus, Ml2872, Alcasada, Attaree, Oznana, Kevinc, Michelleg5, Bibliophyl, Martyleo, Casey, Jeff65, Shayward, Tonimorgan, Cesanchez, Jeffmoore, Aventurist, Emrthe2, Nerissamcc, Fitzfan60, Trevose, Pauly, Trisham, Magnusholm, Artemisrn, Fantasist, Toadbears, Mistymarti, Lauraholt, Mariannefr, Stacesween, Fran, Bjensenjr, Montavon, and Oznana.

I'd also like to thank my wonderful editor, Amelia, for all the help and advice she's given me, and Dragonblade Publishing for choosing me as the winner of their Write Stuff Competition in 2021 with *The Dragon Ring*, and setting me on this wonderful path of publication. Thank you Kathryn.

About the Author

After a varied life that's included working with horses where Downton Abbey is filmed, riding racehorses, running her own riding school, owning a sheep farm and running a holiday business in France, Fil now lives on a widebeam canal boat on the Kennet and Avon Canal in Southern England.

She has a long-suffering husband, a rescue dog from Romania called Bella, a cat she found as a kitten abandoned in a gorse bush, five children and six grandchildren.

She once saw a ghost in a churchyard, and when she lived in Wales there was a panther living near her farm that ate some of her sheep. In England there are no indigenous big cats.

She has Asperger's Syndrome and her obsessions include horses and King Arthur. Her historical romantic fiction and children's fantasy adventures centre around Arthurian legends, and her pony stories about her other love. She speaks fluent French after living there for ten years, and in her spare time looks after her allotment, makes clothes and dolls for her granddaughters, embroiders and knits. In between visiting the settings for her books.

Social Media links:
Website – filreid.com
Facebook – facebook.com/Fil-Reid-Author-101905545548054
Twitter – @FJReidauthor